PRAISE FOR *THE BRIAR BOOK OF THE DEAD*

'Slatter nestles stories within stories, immersing readers in a richly imagined world, and leading them on a journey full of unexpected twists and turns. This is an expertly woven tale of intrigue, magic, family, and righting old wrongs.'
A.C. Wise, author of *Wendy, Darling*

'Slatter writes witches like none other, and her newest is a darkling feast, jewelled and blood-stained, rich with secrets and seething with unbearable power.'
Cassandra Khaw, author of *The Salt Grows Heavy*

'Dark, witchy, and downright delicious, The Briar Book of The Dead *is the perfect read for shorter days and longer nights.'*
Ally Wilkes, author of *All the White Spaces*

'Angela Slatter hits it out of the park again. With gorgeous prose and a heart-breaking story about family, magic, and the weight of the past, this is a darkly fantastic masterpiece that shouldn't be missed.'
Gwendolyn Kiste, Lambda Literary and Bram Stoker Award-winning author of *Reluctant Immortals* and *The Rust Maidens*

'This is a ghost story like no other, weaving past, present and future, life, death and the in-between. Angela Slatter is at her very best in this masterful blend of folkloric storytelling, family conflict and dark horror. That the shadowy pathway is illuminated here and there by a flickering candle of kindness makes The Briar Book of the Dead *even stronger.'*
Juliet Marillier, author of the Sevenwaters and Blackthorn & Grim series

THE
BRIAR
BOOK
OF THE
DEAD

Also from A.G. Slatter and Titan Books

ALL THE MURMURING BONES
THE PATH OF THORNS

THE
BRIAR
BOOK
OF THE
DEAD

A.G. SLATTER

TITAN BOOKS

The Briar Book of the Dead
Print edition ISBN: 9781803364544
E-book edition ISBN: 9781803364551

Published by Titan Books
A division of Titan Publishing Group Ltd.
144 Southwark Street, London SE1 0UP
www.titanbooks.com

First edition: February 2024
10 9 8 7 6 5 4 3 2

A CIP catalogue record for this title is available from the British Library.

Printed and bound by CPI Group (UK) Ltd, Croydon, CR0 4YY.

*To Lulu, the wickedest little Irish Terrier, common farm dog,
snatch-pastry, faithful companion, so sorely missed,
the once and forever best dog.*

1

My great-aunt takes the knife to my wrist.

Maud means well.

I catch glimpses of my cousins and grandmother behind her, four figures not too close, but jostling for a peek. Hoping to catch the moment when what's meant to happen *does*. All of us equally anxious – gods know the others proved themselves well before this. At eight, I'm a very late bloomer.

Around us, the stone circle, the sacred place, deep in the woods. If it's going to happen, it will – must! – happen here. Above, bright blue sky, summer-solstice warm. Beneath me, the cool smoothness of the sandstone altar. Birds singing somewhere, the murmurings of my cousins, the jingling of Maud's silver chatelaine at her waist, our grandmother Gisela calling her sister's name.

However: nothing.

Still.

My forearm's littered with cuts, mostly shallow, all red. I feel no pain and I'm urging Great-Aunt Maud on because I share her belief that if I just surrender enough blood to pay the red price, my magic will – finally – manifest. That I will be like my family. That I'll belong.

And she slashes again – a little frenzied by frustration – and I think she's done it because I'm getting dizzy. The menhirs are beginning to spin, I'm light as a feather, lifting up, flying, and at last – at last! – I'm a witch.

Except Gisela isn't calling anymore; she's yelling and doesn't sound relieved. Sounds panicked. 'Too deep, Maud! She's bleeding too much!'

And after that I don't remember a thing about the days that followed, nothing except the cold and miserable disappointment of knowing I'd failed yet again.

* * *

The autumn sun on my face is gentle, shining red through my eyelids, and the scar on my wrist feels like thick silk under my fingertips.

Such a deep cut, no less noticeable than it was eleven years ago. Malice was absent from the act – or mostly – although vexation at my lack of 'development' ran high. Maud had been trying, I believe, to shock something out of me. Or into me. To awaken the magic that should have been lying just beneath my skin, or deep in my bones, or growing at the roots of my light-brown hair – but was clearly missing from any part of me.

It serves as a reminder of my basic flaw, that ridge of healed flesh; hastily pulled together with cousin Eira's neat stitches even though she was only a year older than me – because everything's a learning experience – but her magic wasn't quite good enough to leave no cicatrice. Every morning, my family take their fine silver knives and make small cuts in arms and hands and thighs, release a little blood, offering the red price, the crimson tithe for any magic they might do during the day.

A ritual from which I'm forever excluded.

Out past the hedge-fence that surrounds the Briar House, Silverton bustles at its usual afternoon pace, the particular sort of babble a town of almost two thousand souls makes. People going about their days, working hard, preparing for what comes next. For life. For tomorrow night. Not me, though. Not at this very moment, no.

I think about Great-Aunt Maud's little office with its shelves filled with account books, banking records, rules and regulations and procedures, letters patent of the guilds, applications and permissions for various activities, records of censure and acclamation, maps, schedules for civic maintenance, rolls of citizens and their businesses and what they owe to the Briars, lists of those who wish to access the communal stores in the tithe-barns, and what others have contributed to them. Neat as a pin with everything in an ordered fashion, notebooks and pens aligned perfectly on the large blotter, two stained-glass desk lamps perfectly positioned at each corner for symmetry. And her leather-bound grimoire in green and gold lying on the carved wooden lectern in one corner – admittedly with a covering of dust because I've not been near it since she died. I do my best to keep it as Maud did.

A perfect little office for a steward.

The little office that's been mine for the past six months, give or take, and has been suffocating me in the days and weeks leading up to tomorrow night. Which is why I took the opportunity – when the banker's clerk had delivered a message that Mr Aberwyn was unwell and could we reschedule? – to sneak outside and hide in this corner of the garden. And to contemplate my major failing, wondering if it will lead to A Terrible Thing.

It was lovely and quiet for all of ten minutes before an avian screech came from above and almost immediately after a screech from Grandmamma Gisela. From the clarity of the sound, she could only have been standing on the front veranda.

'Ellie Briar, where are you?'

I stay very still and quiet. Gisela may well be a witch – *the* witch – but she doesn't know everything and can't see through hedges or walls, nor can she sense the presence of those who might be staying out of sight for reasons of their own.

'It's no use hiding, Ellie Briar.' She mutters, 'I know where you live.'

Indeed.

Still, I keep my mouth shut. Eventually, there's the clip of footsteps and a door closing. My fingers seek the scar again. Forcing my muscles to soften, relax, I lean back on the bench. Another five minutes, I think, calculating how far I can push it. Ten. Fifteen at the most.

* * *

'The letters,' begins Grandmamma Gisela, but I've heard this all before and am staring out the library window.

The owl is large, with a tawny lace pattern for camouflage, limned with gold; the feathers appear delicate as spider webs. My grandfather, on one of the rare occasions when he told me anything interesting, said they have no oil on their plumage; this makes their flight silent, much to the detriment of mice and rabbits and even runty lambs. This one, early roused, sits in the yew tree that's grown up too close to the house. Round eyes wide in a blankly pretty face. It notices me at the open window, shivers, chest puffing, doing a discontented little dance on the branch. Doesn't take off, however, merely calms its feathers, gives me a haughty stare. It had best hope Nia's not around with her hunting bow.

'The letters,' repeats Grandmamma Gisela loudly from her desk, 'are very *important*. They keep the ecclesiastical wolf from the door. After I'm gone, make sure they continue.'

'Uh huh.' Behind me is a room lined with books (far more interesting than those in the steward's office next door), and in it the grandmother I adore – she who raised me – but I'm staring out the tall broad window because she's talking about matters I don't want to discuss.

'Ellie, are you paying attention?' A sharp tone, something I seldom hear because – unlike some in this house – mostly I am biddable, mostly obedient. Mostly because I feel a need to make up for what I lack.

'Not really, no.' An honest answer which makes Gisela laugh. The heavy polished ebony chair scrapes on the floor – almost a throne, with roses and apples carved across its arched top – then her steps pad light and sure as she crosses to me.

'My mother,' says Gisela fondly, 'insisted on politeness to the owls because they might be more than they seemed. She didn't hold with shifters – rash creatures, most like to get themselves and others killed – and you never knew with whom you were dealing until they revealed themselves. Owls, she said, were wiser than most, though they are knowledge thieves. Mind your manners around them until you know if they are feathered both inside and out.'

Proper witches, Gisela's always said, don't take other shapes – although I've read of some who *do* – and shifters are our cousins at best, generally with no inherent ability to cast spells. They're too close to the beasts they turn into, inclined to either fight or flight, nothing in between. As a result, they are most commonly caught.

And yet still closer to true witches than I.

The owl gives us one final flickering glance – strangely irritable – then unfurls its wings and takes off with a great displacement of air and evergreen leaves. I feel a quick tug of envy, though I can't say precisely why: its freedom? That it might take another form? I press the ache down, shove it under my other jealousies, all the things I know to be foolish and pointless, and watch the bird's flight. Over our front garden, over the high hedge-fence, then the market square busy with customers, stallholders and shopkeepers clustering around the fountain and its bronze sculpture of the Three Brothers Bear. Over the roofs of the shops (butchers and bakers and candlestick makers), businesses like solicitors and coffin-makers, fabric merchants and carpenters, tiny modistes, perfumiers and jewellers, and the church, the townhall, the bank, the papermill and one of the flourmills, the smithy and the tearooms and coffeehouses. The big houses of grey stone and black wood and thick shining glass, the smaller ones and smaller still until they become tiny cottages out at the edges before Silverton bleeds into fields and the forest that hides the stone circle. The owl, no more than a speck now, continues on towards the deepest part of the mountains where the river begins. I wish my resentments onto its back, that they'll be taken far away, dropped into a ravine, lost somewhere I'll never find them again.

My grandmother nudges my shoulder with her own, nods downward. A small, neat figure darts from Prothero's in Butchers Byway around a corner and into Eldin's Bakery. Beres Baines in a bright pink dress, wicker basket hanging heavy, filled with treats. *Not* for the festival, I suspect, but to tempt an appetite that's fled.

My stomach swoops. Once more I'll try; once more before I admit defeat and speak to Audra. Ask for help.

Gisela pulls the windows to, not completely closed, the pigeon's egg ruby ring glinting on her wedding finger – no promise to a husband, but to her family and home. The symbol of the Briar Witch. There's a fire in the grate but Grandmamma has begun feeling the cold more and more. A sign that time is marching on her, when we'd have it otherwise. We must prepare, she keeps saying, for a passing of the old and a herald of the new; we insist she'll be with us for many years. It's also the reason I've come to hate these conversations, these preparations for when she's no longer here. Gisela wishes to make me consider things I cannot change. And in truth, the loss of Great-Aunt Maud is still too fresh.

'I trust you'll listen to me now it's gone, lovely distraction though it was?' Gisela asks mildly.

I smile. 'Of course, Grandmamma. The letters.'

Except whenever Gisela mentions the letters I feel adrift and uncertain; the clicking of the grandfather clock in one corner doesn't help, feels like a reminder. *Tempus fugit.*

'Heed me, Ellie Briar. No matter what else Maud forgot or ignored, she *always* sent the letters.'

For all the good such diligence did her.

Gisela purses her lips as if reading my thoughts, then gestures to the sofa. It could fit four comfortably and is set in the middle of a colourful silk rug that's been worn by too many feet; until there are actual holes in it a replacement is

15

considered an unnecessary expense. As if we are paupers. We sit, and I nod, show her I'm taking it seriously, just as I do every time she mentions Maud and the missives. She doesn't mention other things about her sister, however.

'Have you been practising?' Unconsciously, she plucks at her long, thin fingers. A small silver vial of unguent hangs from the chatelaine at my waist (once Maud's, but unlike her I wear it to the side, tuck it into my pocket so the jingling doesn't give me away), and I take her hand; the ointment helps with the arthritic chill. Blood warms beneath her papery skin as I massage. She smiles. 'Thank you, sweeting. But: have you?'

'Of course. Maud had me write the last few. *She* trusted me.'

The letters are a twice-yearly annoyance. Reports to the Archbishop of Lodellan, written in the script (or an excellent approximation thereof) of Father Tobias, the last god-hound to grace Silverton with his presence. He was also, by the by, my grandfather and Gisela's paramour for quite some time. Such reports assure said exalted princes of the church that the Briars are behaving themselves. 'Never fear, Grandmamma, I'm well-trained and careful with my calendar. I may not be a witch, but I am a clever little steward. I'll not fail in this, nor in any other task you set me.' I sound sulky. I *am* sulky.

She's beautiful still as she smiles, with silver hair and violet-blue eyes, cheekbones sharp and high, lips with no sign of wrinkling or subsidence of the teeth behind them. Though none of us are by any means ordinary-looking, only Audra can truly hold a candle to her.

'I nag, my dear, because this single task is the one to keep us safe. You are sensible, if stubborn, and your cousin will need you, when the time comes, Ellie. Audra has talent for many things, but administration is *not* one of them. She can be hot-headed as you well know and a little autocratic' – *a little!* – 'but I'm teaching her to lead. Audra's had her wild times, but she's settled now. However, it will be you who keeps the wheels of Silverton spinning. People need to know her power is here for their protection, but you'll be the one who makes their lives bearable.' She clears her throat, corrects: 'You *already* do so. You've stepped into Maud's shoes admirably.'

When the time comes, we cousins (Nia and Eira and I) will bend to Audra's will as those before us bent to Grandmamma's, and so on back to when Gilly Briar was the very first Briar Witch. When the time comes, I will toil away with no more acknowledgement from Audra than Gisela gave Maud in her lifetime; in death, Gisela's praise of her sister is effusive. I'm the steward and I'll serve with nary a glimmer of glory. Perhaps it wouldn't be so bad if Audra wasn't already so favoured…

I love her and know bitterness is foolish when I could never have been the Briar Witch anyway – not without any kind of eldritch power. I'm good with brewing potions, making medicaments, my powders can calm fevers, cure headaches and coughs, speed up recovery, even drag the sick from the doors of death. Yet no matter my intent or how closely I adhere to a spell-ritual, I can't make any sort of enchantment work, cannot perform miracles of any stripe, either good or ill, small or large.

There's not a scintilla of magic in my bones.

Gisela changes tack: 'Did you hear, Ellie? Edgar's tale this morning?'

The tinker – or 'gentleman-merchant' as he prefers – had recounted it as he laid out his wares on our kitchen table, fine and strange things from far-off places. Gisela adores histories of ill-fortune visited upon the godly: a fire in an abbey that hoarded its profits and let peasants starve; a cathedral collapse while a grand prelate delivered a fire-and-brimstone mass; a bishop's palace overrun by rats and locusts ('There's one of our kind behind that, you mark me!'). Best of all, some crashing catastrophe such as the one Edgar shared.

The Monastery of Saint Ogg's-of-the-Way (far from us, close to the tiny hamlet of Jago's Rise) would allow nothing female within its walls, neither human nor animal. The hens and nannies and geese, the sows, cows, ewes and mares were all penned outside the compound and attended to by three laymen from the nearby village so the holy brothers would not be tainted by contact. When word came of a fearsome group of bandits bearing down upon the area, the villagers presented themselves at the monastery gates, seeking sanctuary. Men and boys were admitted; women and girls were left outside to await inevitable violation and death that accompanied such events – because compassion could not be allowed to bend the rules.

However, something unforeseen happened: the rogues and ruffians had other ideas, perhaps because, to a man, they were women. Retribution was their intent – the abbot was notorious for giving absolution to murderers, rapists and men who denied their own children – and these women came with fire. As the monastery burned with each and every heartless monk, each and every traitorous man and boy inside, the leader of the troupe made an offer to those who'd been left to fend for themselves: *Join us*.

And if we do not? asked one of the newly widowed.

The robber-in-charge shrugged. *Then do not. Go your own way; if you must marry again, be more particular in your choices.*

The raiding party, Edgar reported, was much augmented that day.

We'd all laughed heartily and Audra had described the loss of priestly life as a good start.

'Yes, Grandmamma, I heard it as well as you did. Have you forgotten I sat by your side? Does your memory slip from you so soon?' I ask archly and she slaps my wrist.

'My point, facetious child, is that you never know what the future brings, and what looks like certain death from one angle may well be salvation from another.' She gives an exasperated huff.

'Edgar also said that there were whispers of *other* bandits setting up camps in the forests not so far to *our* north,' I point out. 'I'd suggest sending—'

'I'll discuss reconnaissance with Nia.' She raises a finger. 'Now, the letters…'

I roll my eyes.

'Ellie Briar, you're the only one I'll trust with this task. I have raised you all to be mindful of your duty to your family, to the Briar Witch, and to the town. Promise me you'll stand by your cousin and support her in all things.'

I should simply answer *Yes*, but instead I choose to be a brat: 'As long as I am able.' And she who's known my voice longer than my own mother did hears that I feel obligation hung around my neck like a noose.

Gisela lowers her lids until only slivers of violet-blue show. 'And what might make you *unable*?'

'Death,' I say defiantly. Confess: 'Love. Marriage.'

'Ellie…' Gisela's expression is pained; her head drops back, the silver hair falling over her shoulders. I count the beats before she gives me the full strength of her glare. This is a performance I've seen many times (not always directed at me) and I'm keen to its nuances. 'Ellie, that boy—'

'He's the one I want,' I declare, then with less certainty, 'and he wants me.'

'Does he?' she demands. 'Do his eyes rest only on you? Or are you too busy mooning over him to notice that he watches others? Are you drinking in his face, Ellie Briar, when he's drinking in another's?'

I go cold all over and hate her. Years of adoration and loyalty swept away in seconds as I feel I'll never love my grandmother again, before remorse rushes in and makes me despise myself more than I ever have her. There's a pricking in my mind, a questioning that my desire for Dai Carabhille could have made me loathe the one to whom I owe everything. I push the thought aside.

Gisela says more gently, 'He's a boy, Ellie, and not fit to marry a Briar.'

'Dai *will* marry me when the time's right.' I say this with more conviction than I feel.

Gisela, with her witch's sense, knows it. She knows, too, that I've been enamoured of him since first I laid eyes on him, when we were both small and I would follow him at a distance, too shy to do otherwise. That I've loved him so intensely it's like a pulse in my veins. Yet I still have no certainty that he'll be mine. My bottom lip begins to tremble, and I look away.

Grandmamma hooks two fingers under my chin and makes me

meet her gaze. 'Ellie Briar, Dai Carabhille is all well and good. Fine men are few and far between. He may well be one in years to come, but he's definitely not *now* – and I have my doubts about his future prospects, my darling.' She pauses as she always does when she's about to say something hurtful. 'I'll not trust our safety to some blow-in boy even when – especially when – you've got your nethers all in a tizz for him. And certainly not for some boy who's not yet done with others.' She shakes her head. 'Mark me, my girl: you need a partner who supports you in what you do, doesn't take your attention from your duties – like Eira's Sally. We Briars must choose our mates carefully, it's how we survive.'

And I want to hurt her in return, so my tone's as mean when I say, 'And did you? With Grandfather Tobias?'

The barb strikes home. She clenches her hands into fists in her lap. I shouldn't have said that. My grandfather's actions scarred us all.

When Gisela next speaks, her voice is rough though even. 'If you need a lesson in choices, child, then let my example be your warning.'

'I'm sorry,' I say quietly.

'You're nineteen, Ellie Briar, old enough to make bad decisions as well as good. And old enough to bear the consequences – but do not let those consequences affect your family.'

I bite at the inside of my mouth; the grip of teeth on tender flesh helps me focus. I swallow and say what I could have said in the first place to avoid all of this: 'I will stand by Audra no matter what.'

'Good girl.' Grandmamma nods. 'We need a little discontentment in life, Ellie, for how else would we recognise joy but by contrast? Remember to put the family first, Ellie, in

21

all things, even ahead of your heart.' She pulls me into a hug, speaking against my hair, tawny as hers once was; she smells like old roses. 'We are so few these days, my girl. I've not schemed and kept us safe all these years for the Briars to go up in flames through carelessness.'

She holds me a moment longer before pushing me gently away. 'The last report was sent just before… before. The next letter is due for despatch in a few weeks, yes?' I nod. 'Edgar will collect it on his return journey.'

'Yes, Grandmamma.'

'Tomorrow is your first Balefire Eve – yes, yes, as you well know. Remember: it must go smoothly.' She's silent for a moment, letting me chew on the comment. 'Make sure your cousins are doing their parts' – utterly unnecessary, as if any one of us would shirk this duty, as if the others have not done *their* parts for years, but she's giving me busywork so I don't fret, or no more than is reasonable – 'And don't forget the lanterns. We'd never live it down.'

'Yes, Grandmamma.'

'And, Ellie?'

'Yes, Grandmamma?'

'Someone will come for you. The one you need.' She gives me a serious look. 'I don't ask you to forgo the pleasure of a husband, I don't ask you to be as your great-aunt was – as she chose to be. All I ask is that you wait and are wise.'

When I nod she smiles and rises. Remaining on the couch, I stare at the three items above the mantlepiece: a black obsidian mirror, a woodcut, and a framed document. The mirror is meant for scrying but no one's got the knack of that anymore. The woodcut shows a couple, she sitting, he standing behind her chair (the same chair that's at Gisela's desk even now). There are drawings of them, too, in some of the books on the shelves, but I'm partial to this carving because of its fineness; their features are clear, as are their expressions. Gilly and Sandor Briar started here – or rather, they fled here, found a place to call home, a foundation, and we remain three hundred or so years later. The wood's tinted so I can tell that Gilly had blue eyes and golden-brown hair turning to silver at the temples, her mouth in an obstinate set; Sandor's mid-brown hair is mostly greying, but his eyes remain a light green, his expression sweet. I wonder if I'd be a disappointment to them. The document, the dispensation with its purple script and a gold and purple seal, is our guarantee of safety.

Shaking my head, I stand to leave. Gisela giggles as I close the door behind me. It's not directed at me. My grandmother's still thinking about St Ogg's; it will keep her amused for days. I'll seek out my cousins soon, but first there's another visit I must make.

2

'How are you, Deirdre?' I speak softly so as not to startle her; she gives no sign of having heard.

All I can see is the back of her head, the dirty blonde, dishevelled hair she's neither washed nor brushed since she gave birth seven days ago. She's not washed herself either even though her mother's tried to talk her into it. Beres Baines's daughter faces the bedroom wall. Before, this was a pretty space in tones of lavender and blue, the floor polished, the dresser and 'robe of honey-wood, the bedlinen of finest cambric. Now the curtains are closed, the only light is from a dim lamp; there are the smells of old blood and dried excrement, stale body odour and fresh vomit. Deirdre's not keeping down the small amount of food Beres feeds her. I suspect she eats just to get her mother to leave, then brings it up again into the chamber pot beneath her bed, not too fussy how much gets in and how much misses either. Deirdre Baines was one of the prettiest girls in Silverton before all this (a dead ringer, so it's said, for her Aunt Seren, who ran away). Today, like many days prior, she's a broken doll.

None of this is a surprise, really. Even before she began to swell, before anyone realised what was happening to Beres

Baines's only child, she'd become monosyllabic and morose until at last she stopped speaking at all. The baby's not yet been buried; he's in the mortuary attached to Eira's infirmary even though A'Lees' Coffin-makers have begun their work on a tiny death-bed. Beres didn't want the wee thing in the house, not with Deirdre so fragile, so she'd swaddled the boy and handed him to me. Just until her daughter can be persuaded to name him, then there'll be a funeral. We do not consign our dead to the earth without a name; in such a state they are not whole, they are lost, they wander. Not ghosts, no, for Silverton has no ghosts – but nameless newborns become something else… and it's only a matter of time before Deirdre's stillborn son changes.

I delivered the child – the other Briars were all occupied elsewhere and it's not as if I've not done it a hundred times; the birth was uncomplicated, timely, easy even. Except the child was dead.

Gingerly, I sit on the edge of the mattress and put a hand on Deirdre's shoulder, which has grown thin, the bones more pronounced as if trying to escape her skin. She trembles, the movement going through her like a ripple on a pond. We were at school together; she was always happy, laughing. Hard to believe now. I've checked on her every day and kept Gisela informed of progress or the lack thereof. Last night I barely slept for worrying what I might find this morning – there's no real change, which somehow feels worse.

'Deirdre. Deirdre, you need to talk to me. Please.' There's a long, frozen moment broken only when she turns, a slow rolling from her side to her back, and I'm reminded of a dead fish sinking into the depths; belly up, then down, then up, then down, a terrible spiral that can end only one way. I've known her all my life. She's a little younger than me, fatherless, and no one would have cared that her own child was thus. The face I see bears little resemblance to the girl who's sung at weddings and celebrations, been her seamstress mother's apprentice, always chattering. This girl looks like she's being devoured from the inside out, her eyes pale grey stones weighing her down.

My words dry up; I force them out. 'Deirdre, I know it hurts.'

She gives me a glance that I can only interpret as scornful. *How can you know, Ellie Briar?*

'I—' There's the urge to shake her, but I remind myself she's in pain. 'Deirdre, you need to name the little boy.'

My hand trembles as I brush hair from her brow, slick with sweat. She doesn't shake me off, nor does she lean into my palm either. It's like she's impervious to the world. Deirdre doesn't want to live. She doesn't care about herself, anything, anyone. I suspect the only satisfaction she can find is in pointing her pain outward. 'Deirdre. I *do* know loss. But I also know that if you don't give your son a name you'll never find any peace, either in this world or the next or the one after that.'

Nor will the rest of us.

She stares, lips quivering, fingers grasping at each other and pick-pick-picking at the already-torn skin; blood's dried in the cuticles, over the knuckles and in the webbing between thumb and forefinger. I touch her cheek, shivering at the chill. 'Deirdre, what's your boy's name?'

But she doesn't answer, just turns to the wall again and will not speak. I want to shake her, slap her, pull out the black part of her heart that will selfishly leave a little child wandering forever. But I don't. I pat her shoulder and rise, leave the foetid-smelling bedchamber, and step into the sitting room where her mother anxiously awaits.

I'm almost blinded here – curtains are open to let the afternoon sun in. Beres is a small woman with the same dark-blonde hair as her daughter and red-rimmed eyes. Her hands, like Deirdre's, have been tortured and tormented, scratched crimson, though hers are meticulously clean and held firmly in the lap of her pristine white apron; she wouldn't want to bleed on the fabrics with which she works. She's sitting on a loveseat embroidered with roses and jasmine, and the entire room is filled with floral patterns, like a wild garden. Through the window behind her is a carefully tended vegetable patch and beyond that the river, running sluggish now as the cold weather approaches. Beres looks up hopefully, but that hope quickly crumbles at my expression. I'm keenly aware that she has no other family in a place where such a thing means a great deal; parents and husband long dead, her sister disappeared many years ago. Family means comfort and protection, the difference between feeling wanted – *needed* – and being excluded. Not always, of course.

'I'm sorry.' I sit across from her, smoothing my sage-green skirts and tucking my booted feet neatly beneath them. 'Could you guess at the father? Even if he's married, perhaps we could ask him privately? A mother's naming is better, but a father's will do.'

Beres shakes her head, not with disapproval but despair. 'She won't say. Probably one of those tinker lads who come and go with Edgar, and I didn't notice.'

She could be right. Edgar's had some handsome apprentices in tow; I've even been tempted but the idea of Dai has always crowded them out. Besides, I doubt I've ever seen the same tinker lad twice. No one cares that Deirdre's got herself pregnant, nor that

27

the father's nowhere to be seen, but they'll care if her baby goes without a name. They'll care if a melyne comes upon us as a result.

'Beres, I'll send Audra. I've no other choice. Heart's ease is all we can try now,' I say and Beres nods resignedly. 'I'm sorry,' I say again and I truly am.

'You've done your best, the Briars always do.' She gives a fractured smile. 'She's all I've got.'

'See if you can get her to come out tomorrow night.' It's a foolish suggestion. 'She's always loved to dance on Balefire Eve. If she won't, then come yourself, Beres, at least for a little while. You need a break. We can give her a sleeping draught…'

But Beres is shaking her head.

* * *

I maintain my composure as the door closes, as I walk down the stairs, out the garden gate of the Baines' cottage. I even make it through the market square and the four or five brief conversations I have with townsfolk who have questions about Balefire Eve. Silly questions, really; a little insulting in fact. Checking to see if I've remembered the most basic things, as if I wasn't trained by Maud Briar. As if I'm an idiot. I force myself to smile and answer politely, remind myself that they're as nervous as am I about this first festival without my great-aunt. I have so much to prove, and I know they're trying to judge whether I'm up to the task. It's made even more difficult when I already feel like a failure because of Deirdre.

It's only when I'm free of the press of bodies, ducking down a narrow alley between two blocks of shops, that the tears win out and I press myself into the shadows, a wall of stone at my back. No matter how hard I try, sometimes my potions and powders and words and *care* have no effect. In this very moment, it doesn't matter how many times I've helped. Without magic, I can't fix anything *bigger*. More important.

When I'm spent, empty but feeling no better, I continue on my way. Stepping onto a wider thoroughfare, I hear a voice, clear and melodic. Familiar. Coming from the schoolyard a little further along Adalind's Row, and not unexpected.

'Is everyone comfortable?' Audra's on one of the carven benches in the middle of the small playground, the school mistress, Rowella Bisbee, standing a little way off, always an observer at such times. My cousin comes once or twice a week to tell tales, as she does with all four of the schools in Silverton. Classes should still be in progress, but of course all things grind to a halt when Audra appears. In a semi-circle before her, a crowd of children, faces avid with anticipation. I lean against a tree just outside the fence, draw no attention. 'Hmmmm.' My cousin taps a finger to her lips, as if pondering – she'll already have chosen her story but, as she says, the performance is part of the pleasure.

'Something brief, I think – I do have pressing duties, after all – something sharp and clever to keep you focused.' Audra lifts her hands as if about to conduct a symphony. 'So: The Tale of the Girl and the Mage.'

An intake of breath from her audience. I smile in spite of everything, let myself be carried along by the enchantment of her tone, her words, her invention. Admiring how effortlessly she makes the children feel they're blessed to get part of her attention.

'Audra's had her wild times,' Gisela had said by way of understatement. What my cousin had were several years of disappearing for a day or two each week, with friends Gisela wouldn't let in the house. Maud hissing what if Audra got herself pregnant and Gisela shrugging, saying what did it matter when we needed new blood, new witches? What were they going to do, she and Maud, dried-up old women – and with the rest of us showing no signs of reproducing, what did it matter where the seed came from? And Gisela was right: while Audra sowed her drunk and disorderly rebellions, all those friends fell away to be replaced by better society as she prepared to be the next Briar Witch. No pregnancies, though. Now, here she is, telling stories to children.

'Once upon a time, there was a girl who was sold by her parents to a mage. They didn't consider themselves bad parents – do they ever? – but they had six other mouths to feed and the price of the oldest child would keep the family afloat for a good year or more. After that, surely their fortunes would have turned around – and if not, there were always other offspring to sell. Oh, no. Such a thing would *never* happen here!

'But, back to the once-upon-a-time girl.

'The mage, who was awful and satisfied to be so – they say monsters don't know they're monsters but that is, quite frankly, frogshit. That mage put our girl in a chamber at the top of a tower and there was nothing in it except ash. Not piles as such, because ash doesn't lie that way, it's too light and fragile, it builds in tentative layers, and in the usual way of things flies at the slightest provocation. Now, though the window was open and shutterless and there was plenty of opportunity for this ash to take wing – it never left, merely made the air thick with grey-black shards of things-that-no-longer-were. The mage told the once-upon-a-time girl that if she could make a rope of it, she might escape the tower. Why did he say such a thing? Mages are a strange breed.

'And then he left, safe in the knowledge that she was a stupid village girl and she'd still be there in the morning, or the afternoon, or the day after, or whenever he decided to return and put her to his purpose.

'But *this* girl was different.

'She'd learned things from a wood-wife who lived out in the forest. Whenever she'd been sent to gather sticks and twigs for the fire, berries and mushrooms for the table, that girl would visit the tumbledown cottage and talk to the old woman. She'd mastered tricks her mother didn't know – although let's be honest, the lessons our mothers teach never really sink in until years later, when we're older and find her pain growing in the very soil of our being. But that's by the by and a different story altogether. It meant, however, that the once-upon-a-time girl knew what to do.

'She pulled three dark hairs from her head and curled them on the windowsill. Then she gathered a small, shivering covey of ashes and balanced them on the strands. Next, she cut her palm with the little knife (unsuspected by the mage) she always carried deep in the pockets of her skirt or the side of her boot and sprinkled the crimson droplets over the accumulation.

'She whispered to it, the little pile, secret words to make the components dance and twist and entwine. The other ashes joined in, and soon enough she had a length of dark red rope. Our clever girl tied it tightly to a hook in the wall by the window (for there are always such things in towers), hitched her skirts and tucked them into her belt, then clambered over the sill.

'Yet before she went, she cut off a piece of this newly forged cord and coaxed it into a noose, which she hung from the wooden

31

ceiling beam. She whispered to it a wish – compelling, a spell in and of itself – that the mage would find it irresistible.'

There's a collective gasp from her audience, a mix of delight and shock, some horror. Rowella Bisbee – a Silverton girl and graduate of Mater Hardgrace's Academy in Whitebarrow – had been as rapt as her charges. Now, lips pursed, she seems to break from a trance, and thanks my cousin, no doubt hoping no nightmares will visit her pupils. There's nothing can be done about Audra's visits, and Rowella's not silly enough to complain; her tuition fees were paid by the Briars on the understanding that she'd return home for a few years at least, to teach and live in the neat yellow cottage in the schoolgrounds. She knows which side her bread's buttered on. With a word of thanks, she gathers up her charges and shepherds them back into the small building to resume their studies.

I push away from the tree, grinning as Audra exits the school gate. 'Now, did that really seem appropriate for your audience?'

Audra startles – I'm good at not being seen though on occasion I wish it weren't so – then laughs. She wraps me into a hug, warmth radiating through her lilac woollen frock even on this cool day. Then she examines my face. 'A regular little shock never hurts, Ellie. Lessons to remember.'

'Wait until they wake screaming and tell their parents about your amusements, cousin.'

'Pish.' Her eyes are sapphire blue, hair pure gold, skin porcelain, lips as red as blood. She looks like a doll, perfectly beautiful. Eyes narrowing, she runs a gentle finger across my cheeks, perhaps noticing the remaining dampness. 'Whatever is it, cousin, to cause you tears?'

'Deirdre Baines. I can't help her. A week since the baby came; she won't rouse, she won't name him. Won't speak at all. She *must* name him. There's only one thing left to try.' I swallow. 'Will you give her heart's ease?'

It's a rare power (not a spell to learn or skill to acquire), to be able to make burdens feel lighter. It won't remove them, the effect generally isn't permanent, but the pain *will* be bearable for a while at least. They'll be able to do the things they must – like naming dead babies. We use it reluctantly for it means changing an integral part of a person's nature, for however long it sticks. And it doesn't give a chance to work through grief, to mourn properly and learn from it – merely postpones it. Some few, it takes to like a weed and remains forever; others find it's a temporary solution only, all their sadness rushing back in later, as overwhelming as a flash flood. Some do not survive. Of all the Briars, Audra is the only one with heart's ease.

Audra knows I would not ask lightly. She does not question me further, merely nods. She hooks a curl back behind my ear and smiles sadly. 'I'll go this evening.'

'Thank you.'

'And, Ellie? It wasn't your fault. The child would have died no matter who'd delivered the baby.'

I wish I could feel as certain as she sounds.

33

3

Audra and I part, and I continue on my way through busy thoroughfares. Saddlers Street, Leatherworks Lane, Butchers Road, Gilly's Byway, Dorothea's Lane, Holda's Alley, Smithy's Court, Romelia's Road, and the like.

We live far from anywhere, anything, everything. A town that began as a village. A town that was dying when Gilly Briar arrived, or so the stories say, and she brought it back to life. Somewhere that attracted those who valued their privacy, liked mountain air, were sometimes running from other places and found Silverton is as good a spot as any to settle down. For those who sought a little less church oversight, an isolated town far from where the god-hounds held sway was ideal. We Briars must, ostensibly, answer to the princes of the church, but our past few years have been relatively untroubled.

I pass by the large church – smallish cathedral really – built of stone quarried from nearby. It hasn't really kept pace with the population. It hasn't really had to. There are no great basilicas here, no chapter houses, no seminaries; there's only the priest's empty house beside it. No cardinals or archbishops reign there in the magnificent purple-hued robes of silk and brocade their

God commands them to wear. It's meant to set them above we dull sparrows; Grandmamma says it makes them easier to find by whichever divine is taken by the mood to strike. The folk here (hardy and obstinate) know they owe their survival to the Briars, not to the god-hounds or their deity. Not to something the existence of which there's no proof – unlike the power of the Briar Witch.

The sound of rushing water grows louder as the crowds bleed away.

The Carabhilles' papermill is a broad, long, wooden building about ten minutes' walk from the centre of town. The shopfront's an elegant hunter-green and gold room with glass-topped display cases and shelving. Through a narrow door is the workshop, filled with tubs and presses, frames, machines for beating wooden fibres into pulp, racks for hanging, guillotines to cut things to size, and that peculiar damp smell. The family have a large home in one of the finer areas, but two apprentices live above the mill. It's similar to the three flourmills upstream, having its own waterwheel dipping into the river beside it.

The Carabhilles are bookbinders as well. You'll find leaves of different thicknesses and textures and colours, envelopes and scrolls, journals and account books, invitations, calling cards, screens, handheld fans, and pretty boxes for storing trinkets and love letters. Originally from the cathedral-city of Lodellan, an ancestor apparently found the quality of the water in Silverton produced astonishingly good paper and moved his family to the mountainous middle of nowhere; their products are traded far and wide. In fact, *Carabhille's Birth of the Book*, though several centuries old, remains one of those tomes still sought after by collectors, creators and libraries (there are two copies in Gisela's library). They also stock exquisite hand-carved pens, some made locally, others imported by other merchants, and even rarer ones brought in by Edgar.

They also make lanterns, lovely things, light as a soul, carefully fashioned in hues of red and yellow and orange, perfect for Balefire Eve. Folded into shapes like boats and bells, some are towers, some balloons; all have a recessed well for tiny, short-lived candles to sit. Sending me to collect our annual order is Gisela's idea of a sop to my hurt, a chance to see the object of my desire.

I almost knock, then remind myself this is a place of business. My palms are sweaty. I push open the door, feel my face begin to burn with a blush.

There's no sign of Dai however, only his younger brother Hari, who's nice enough but pallid in comparison. Dai's black hair and blue-blue eyes are faded to muddy brown and grey in Hari, the imposing height not nearly so impressive in the younger sibling, and the muscles not as pronounced beneath the shirt. Unfair – Hari is handsome and even I will admit that he's the cleverer of the two, sharper. But what appeals to me about Dai isn't rational or intellectual; I'm clear-eyed enough to know that my *brain* does not engage when I see him. And there's nothing about Hari to make a shy girl give him small gifts for no reason at all, as if laying offerings at the foot of a deity.

Hari, pen in hand, looks up when the bell over the door tinkles, and gives a smile. He's polite and prompt, whereas Dai would take his time acknowledging me, grinning slowly, finishing whatever task he was doing. Hari straightens and turns to a shelf behind him, retrieves a neatly wrapped bundle, its string knotted into a carry-handle.

'Hello, Ellie,' he says. 'Dai said you'd be looking for your lanterns.'

Instinctively I know he's not here and the disappointment flows over me. That he didn't wait for me to stop by, just left the parcel with his brother. I swallow down an idiot's question – *So, he's not here then?* – and fumble in my skirt pockets for the black velvet purse that was Maud's for the silver bits we owe. Usually, we pay on invoice, but not for this – not for a sacred service; for this there may be no debt owing. My fingers graze Hari's palm as I hand the pieces over.

'Thank you.' My tone's a little flat.

'No trouble at all. Is everything ready for tomorrow? Anything I can do to help?'

I shake my head, manage a smile. 'No, but thank you. It's all under control.'

'Well, then, good luck, Ellie, with your first Balefire.' I know he says it to be kind, to make conversation, but it feels as if he's like everyone else: expecting me to fail. His face goes red so there must be something in my expression that's unfriendly.

'Thank you.'

'Well, then. Bye, Ellie. We'll see you tomorrow night.'

I nod, repeat *thank you*, and wonder how much more careful people might be around me if I had any magic at all. If I were someone to fear.

* * *

Discontented, swinging the parcel, I go in search of Nia, my least favourite cousin.

Down the sloping path and onto the common, which is a hive of activity. A wide expanse, roughly circular, bounded by the lake on one side, trees on the other – pine, oak, yew, blackthorn, alder, hawthorn and cedar. No holly, however. The early Briars made sure those were winnowed out for they dilute a witch's power, weaken us (not *me*, obviously), and there's not much point in tending something that can be used against us.

Nia's bright red hair picks her out, in the middle of the green, hands on hips, standing head and shoulders above most of the army of husky young men and women she's bossing around. Members of the various trade guilds and several of the uniformed vigilants who answer to her in her capacity as marshal. They're arranging trestle tables where food will be laid out and served, and where a variety of innkeepers will set up barrels of ale and wine, whiskey and mead. Others are digging firepits for oxen and boar to roast. Yet others – and these are the most important from my point of view – are setting a thick pole into the ground. Not far away lie mounds of kindling and Nia's latest creation, stretched out as if exhausted. She's done this task since she was ten and every year it's a success; beautiful.

But this is the first time I'm the one at the helm. The first time without Maud, even though I've assisted her almost since I could walk. A failure tomorrow night will tell everyone that I'm not even fit to do *this* despite my Briar name. I'm the one with most at stake, yet I can tell I'm nowhere near as anxious as Nia. Perhaps because she's used to success and here I am, just waiting to mess things up. That and the resentment.

Her face sours when she spots me. She doesn't even try to hide the irritation. I don't let it intimidate me, just stride steadily towards her.

All these months since I took over from Maud as steward have been filled with an increased tension between Nia and I. Of all the cousins, she's most frequently taken the chance to remind me that I'm not like the rest of them. As we grew, Audra and Eira fell away from the habit – and Audra even took to defending me – but Nia's never really stopped no matter how many spankings were administered by Gisela. We're not tiny anymore.

'Good afternoon,' I call.

'What do you want?'

'Merely to see if there is anything you need.' If I say *Gisela told me to check up on you* there'll be an outbreak of temper and I'd rather not have that today. Nia huffs. I jerk my chin at the sculpture lying not far from us. 'She's glorious, Nia. As ever. Thank you.'

And she is, there's no denying that. Nia's expression softens; she might have been less fussy this year if she were less proud of her skills. But even making my life difficult isn't sufficient incentive to make her ruin her *art*. She nods, an abrupt movement. 'I don't need anything.'

'Then I'll see you at dinner.' I turn on my heel and head back towards town and the Briar House.

Gisela has always insisted my cousins love me, even after it became clear I wasn't like them, but our differences remain an abyss between us. Grandmamma has always said that my lack of power was not a bad thing. That one day I would find my place. Grandmamma has always said that my calling would make itself known at the right time. What she meant, I've come to realise, is that I would settle in to being Audra's right hand. I *am* an able administrator and organiser; I've a fine eye for seeing what is required, a sharp mind for analysing how things should be done;

I'm very good at seeing the bigger picture and all its working parts. A perfect steward as long as no magic is required. *If we were at war, Ellie, I would want you by my side: no one would starve in my ranks, there would always be the required weapons and others for just-in-case, horses would be fed and fierce and trained to do their duty, and my soldiers as well, all due to Ellie.* In a war – a Witches' War like the one Audra's mother used to tell tales of – I'd be a general. But we are not at war and I am, instead, a glorified secretary. So, what Gisela actually meant was that I would accept my fate.

Perhaps it wouldn't bother me quite so much if another area of my life were fulfilled.

* * *

In the kitchen of the Briar House the air is rich with the smell of spices and wine and sugar about to burn. In the large oven are trays of Balefire biscuits, seconds from flaring from gold to brown to black. No sign of anyone; not Mistress Reynard who cooks for us, nor Gisela, nor my cousin Eira, who's in charge of this festival delicacy and therefore freed of her physick mantle for the day. Swiftly I remove the trays and slide them onto the plain pine table, leaving them to cool; new scald marks to join the old. No one's in the pantry or laundry room. It's an otherwise comfortable kitchen in blue and white hues, copper pots suspended from the ceiling, a sideboard to hold crockery and glassware.

The door to the cellar is ajar however. A glow's emanating from somewhere down there. I call 'Eira?' but there's no reply.

The cellar's extensive, even bigger than the house that rises above it, a series of rooms for varied purposes, some open, others locked and their keys kept elsewhere. It's cooler here. My footsteps are soft on the stone floor. Up ahead, near where the last of summer's peaches are preserved and a legion of dried meats are suspended from a beam, comes a series of noises: gasps and whimpers, someone in pain. I rush forward, thinking Eira must have fallen and hurt herself – there's no other reason why she'd have left the kitchen unattended.

Except I'm wrong about that. I find her in a far corner, or rather I find *them*. Beneath the hanging lantern, Eira's eyes are closed in bliss, her breath hard and fast, with a tiny cry on exhalation; she sits on a barrel that contains flour or wine, I'm not quite sure which but that's hardly relevant anyway. She leans against the stone wall, hands clutching spasmodically at the air; legs apart, knees lifted, yet her long scarlet skirts are modestly covering her. From beneath the hem I can see a pair of delicate tooled leather slippers peeking out, and a pink skirt pulled tight under a pert backside, its frills frothing like petals.

'Eira!'

My voice seems overly loud and it strikes me that I shouldn't have said anything. Should have just let them have this moment. There are two squeals, one after the other like an echo, and Sally Eldin scrambles out from under my cousin's dress, wiping her full lips and grinning madly.

'Honestly, Ellie, can't a girl get some privacy?' Eira complains, sitting up, making herself decent. Her face is flushed, jewelled with perspiration, and her reddish-blonde hair pulls the light from the lantern so it seems she's wearing a halo. Unlike her sister Nia, Eira isn't anywhere near as antagonistic towards me.

'Stop showing off. You don't need light; Sally knows how pretty you are, otherwise she'd never be doing that,' I say and Sally goes off into peals of laughter that sound like a church bell gone mad. 'You left the biscuits in the oven. What if they'd burned?'

'Oh!' Eira makes a sound of irritation then recalls what it would have meant; that any tiny ill-fortune would take on larger proportions at this time of year. 'I'm sorry, Ellie. I got – distracted.'

My cousin grumbles but rises and brushes down her skirts. She gives Sally a smacking kiss, is rewarded with a big dumb smile. Sally has fine eyes, but everything else is unremarkable about her rather plain face; she's sweet and kind and makes my cousin laugh. She and Eira will marry, soon enough, and I'm happy for them. Grandmamma raises no objections to Sally; she's female, after all, and in Gisela's view, less likely to be traitorous. But they won't live in the Briar House; too many secrets there. Sally's parents (the most prosperous of our bakers) gave her a neat cottage with bluebells growing all around it. I'm fairly sure Mr Eldin didn't intend for her to share it with my cousin, but he's long dead and Mrs Eldin doesn't mind as long as there's someone to look after her in her dotage and provide grandchildren. Any number of townsmen will oblige, and they'll have babies filling every nook and cranny of the little home, which will be welcome – we could do with some new blood to swell the Briar ranks.

Someone at least, I think gloomily, *will get what they want.*

Their contentment makes me ache, just for a moment. 'Please, Eira, make sure everything is well for tomorrow. And I left the lanterns in the kitchen too, we mustn't forget those. Sally, it's almost dinner time – your ma will be waiting.'

And off Sally goes without a word, just another smile for Eira.

'Don't forget to check your gown is ready, Ellie,' says my

42

cousin, as if to regain some control. 'And we must do something about your hair.'

* * *

My tasks done, I take refuge in Maud's – my – office. I think about tomorrow night and my hands start to shake, so I clasp them tightly in my lap, stare at the lectern in the corner. At this very moment it's merely a blur as I fight for calm. It's the same cedarwood as the desk, and after a while it comes into focus: carved with vines and blossoms, and the heads of horned hind-girls peeking out of the foliage that climbs the plinth.

I imagine Maud's voice, while she still had it: *Calm down, Ellie Briar. Calm down. Panic will get you nowhere.*

The steward has always kept the town ticking along. If Gisela and Maud hadn't believed I was suited they'd never have trained me; though there are fewer of us than in the past – the loss of an entire generation didn't help – we're not so few that Gisela was obliged to give me the steward's chatelaine, the symbol of office. She could have given it to Nia, appointed some trustworthy non-Briar as marshal.

But we've been apprenticing since we were so very young; childhoods not exactly cut short but a little circumscribed by responsibility. I, learning to count taxes at the age of nine; Eira up to her elbows in blood in the infirmary at age ten; Nia hunting the forest and bringing back the corpse of a buck before she'd reached twelve; Audra making decisions in the courts on people's fates, settling disputes and negotiating sentences for crimes ever since she was eleven. Serving the town before ourselves. Apprenticing to become the steward, physicker, marshal and Briar Witch respectively.

Gisela didn't have to give me the chatelaine, yet she *did*, to Nia's great resentment.

The Briar Witch makes the decisions, is our figurehead, our protector. The steward is her support, her right hand, her facilitator – and the physicker (attending to public health) and marshal (security and our environment, wild and built) report to her. Briar Witch and steward are intertwined and the prosperity of Silverton as well.

The rug in this little room is new – newer and thicker than the one in the library because Maud was in charge of the purse strings and wasn't above spending some of the family fortune to make her space more comfortable. Briars don't have personal coin; only the steward can access the bank account and keep track of outgoings and income, the rest must ask for pin money.

Calmer, I open the bottom right-hand drawer, pick up the thick creamy envelope, slide out the parchment. Scan the words, the handwriting that's both mine, and not – a fine forgery, even if I do say so myself. I run my fingers over the signature – again, a fine forgery – then slip the letter back where it belongs. I know I can do *this* part of the job. That I won't let my family down in this regard at the very least.

There are many versions of how the Briars came to be in Silverton, and I've read all of them – when you're the one child who can't *do* magic, you spend a lot of time with books while your cousins are being taught enchantments. Initially, it was because I thought that somewhere there must be a spell, *the* spell, that would make me into a witch. In the end, I kept reading because I liked it. I liked gathering knowledge, knowing more than anyone else. That was the power I *could* have. There are a lot of tales, yes, but these are the two I like best.

Once there were, and there were not, three brothers: The Brothers Bear.

And while they'd begun as bears – truly and actually ursine – there'd been a... well, an unfortunate incident with a forest crone. As a result the brown, black and honey bears were transformed into humans. Not the worst sort – because they'd never been the bad sort of bears – but as freshly made men they had new needs, or rather the same needs but in different form.

Food: raw fish was less and less interesting so they mastered fire to cook what they hunted. The brown-haired brother discovered the joys of warm berries and crispy pastry and set about baking (and consuming) as many pies as was humanly possible.

Clothing: not because there was cause for shame but because nudity in a mountain winter would not end well. The black-haired brother taught himself to skin and cure pelts, to turn flax into fabric, and to sew and cobble it all together into outfits and boots that kept the cold at bay.

Shelter: caves and hollows no longer appealed, so they built wooden huts – terrible rickety things, like as not to collapse under the weight of the first snows, but gradually bigger and better, sturdier and warmer. The blond brother kept building, building, building until he'd constructed a large village.

The Three Brothers Bear found wives among mountain folk and high-pasture farmers. They had children and filled all those houses. The village prospered until it didn't. Until illness came and the sturdy bear strain grew thin in the blood and the folk got weak and fewer.

And then one day, a witch came by...

Or perhaps, according to one of the drier accounts, it happened like this:

In the years behind our years, the sorceress Gilly Briar wandered the Earth.

She was the first of her kind – not the first witch, of course not, but the first of the Briars – and carried the most powerful of magics in her skin and etched on her bones, and the greatest of grimoires, The Bitterwood Bible, *in her rucksack. Wherever Gilly Briar went, she healed the sick, punished the wicked, protected the weak, helped the hurt; she made rivers change their course, raised and levelled mountains, caused barren fields to bloom and set unholy high places afire.*

But like so many, Gilly Briar was hunted by the god-hounds, chased from pillar to post. Tired and weary beyond measure, she came at last to a mountain village, fallen on hard times and liable for extinction if something wasn't done. With her magic and spells from her great grimoire, Gilly made the crops grow once again, and the population too, and soon enough the folk begged her to lead them and care for them. The town attracted those as didn't care that a witch lived there – and anyone who did moved away or was moved on gently or otherwise as required.

Gilly's daughters were witches too (though none so great as she) and they have guarded Silverton ever since in an unbroken line, kept it safe from brigands and murderers, god-hounds and ghosts, plagues and natural disasters, and any tragedy as you might care to imagine.

This second story is old and told well before the plague that took my mother and aunts, depriving Gisela of her daughters and a generation of Briars to keep Silverton in hand. Leaving her and her sister with just us four children, barely out of infancy. And Hebe, Audra's mother, who was left little more than a child herself after… After.

I think that in between the two stories, between the Brothers Bear and Gilly's grandiose "history", there is a truth. A dying town revived by a woman and her husband – her dear Sandor who receives no mention in that second tale – who'd been running for some time. Had Silverton been in a better state, the descendants of the Three Brothers Bear less desperate and more proud, its folk might not have been so welcoming. But they had nothing to lose, did they? Not really. And Gilly, footsore and exhausted, found a safe place and did everything she could to keep it thus for *her* descendants.

Those first Briars knew enough of history and human nature that in order to make oneself at home, to make others forget you didn't begin there, you adopt their habits, their beliefs and rituals. Follow them devotedly. Adapt them. One thing that ran from the old town to the new was the Balefire Eve, to mark the coming of wintertide and ask whatever gods might reign to let the town survive the cold season and all its terrors. The Briars just made one adjustment.

4

I can't stop my palms from sweating.

In the mirror I'm all green eyes and black lashes, and every bead of perspiration on my face stands out. The nervousness and nausea are threatening to break free. Last night's sleep was fleeting, the noises of a settling house, of nocturnal things on the roof, even of my family's breathing in other rooms, all louder than they should have been. The rollcall of items to check running through my mind like a waterwheel, splashing thud after thud.

And today spent rushing from one end of the town to the other, making sure people and places were ready, foodstuffs and beverages, decorations and tables, plans on plans on plans. Over and over and over until Gisela sent me off to get dressed, shouting there was no way I could control everything – even though she's spent years telling me that's what the steward must do – and even Maud herself couldn't have found something I'd missed.

The red dress our great-aunt always wore on Balefire Eve has been taken in and restyled (by Beres before… everything) so I don't look like a child playing dress-up; Maud was taller and broader in the shoulder. Audra, already pristine and prepared, did my hair and make-up because my own hands shook too much. She's laced up the gown, tight enough so it's almost difficult to breathe; I look like a ruby hourglass. Audra's in gold that's still not as bright as her hair, glowing beside me so beautifully that I know it doesn't matter how lovely I'll ever look – I'll never be as glorious as my cousin. Yet tonight, I don't quite care. I am the best of myself.

'Ellie, you look like a priestess – a goddess even.' And her tone is so gentle, so filled with love that I forgive her everything – her beauty, her grace, her cleverness and kindness, her magical abilities and those times when she loses her temper – all the things she can't help. Audra takes my hand and leads me from my room, keeps hold of me as we go along the corridor, down the staircase, into the foyer where the others wait, impatiently. Gisela's dress is a shimmering amethyst, shot with silver; Eira in deepest blue; and Nia in vivid emerald. My family smile up at me and I don't care if it's just reflected glory from Audra – tonight, some of the magic is *mine*.

We set off along the silent streets – I lead, the others following two by two – there's no one but the Briars about, wrapped in silks and velvets, elaborate gems at throats and ears, fingers and wrists (except Audra, who wears only the simple necklace that was her mother's, a large black tourmaline pendant). Torches line the path we must tread, a circuit around the town, and finally along the river to where it widens into a lake beside the common where Silverton's folk wait, dressed in their finest, quiet, solemn. Each holding a colourful paper lantern. Though the trestle tables groan beneath the weight of the feast (including Eira's irresistible, unburned sugar biscuits), though there are gallons of alcohol awaiting them, no one is indulging. Even though the population's been gathering since the dusk turned a gentle mauve, loitering for hours until just before midnight strikes from the townhall clocktower, just before we arrive, no one is bored or impatient – or not showing it at least. Even children are somber and silent.

I keep my gaze straight ahead, concentrating, coiled in upon myself, trying to draw up the power I do not have.

We light the candles in our lanterns; once we Briars have set ours to float on the water's surface, the gentle current pulling them to where lake becomes river once more, the rest of those gathered follow suit. An armada of brightly glowing beacons. Fire, paper and water; whatever their end, a breeze of whispered wishes propels them to a place where the blackness of the lake and night are indistinguishable.

Only when we finally step into the centre of the green, when my family hang back, when the crowd arrays itself around us, do I allow myself to look at what Nia has wrought – the symbol upon which so much of my success or failure rests.

The piles of brush and twigs, trunks and lightwood from yesterday have been turned into one enormous mound around the tall pole in the ground. Hanging from that is the tree-wife. The wood-witch. Shaped to suggest a woman with her arms outstretched, head thrown back, ecstatic. Constructed only from branches and logs already fallen, limbs already dead and discarded, of oak and pine, cypress and cedar, with fragrant herbs twined around her head to look like flowing locks.

Nia created her, but she's *mine*. My first tree-wife. My first Balefire Eve.

I'd give anything to have this moment stretch forever because it too is *mine*.

All too soon, Nia stands beside me.

Opening my mouth, the words flow forth, a call and response that's been our song for hundreds of years; this ceremony that we took and made ours. Adding the wood-witch to the Brothers Bear's wintertide ritual just for *us*. To keep the Briars safe.

'Who has made her?' I ask.

'I have, Nia out of Susannah out of Gisela,' replies my cousin proudly. *She's* done this before, many times.

'How have you made her?'

'As best I can, with love and care, devotion and loyalty.'

'Do you give her freely?'

Only a small hesitation, as there is every year because relinquishing such a glorious thing is hard; relinquishing it to *me* is harder still. 'I do.'

'Will she burn?'

'She will burn for all of us.'

And under our breaths so no one else can hear, we intone, 'She will burn so we do not.'

For this night is about more than keeping Silverton safe through the frozen months; it is about keeping the Briars from the flames when so many of our sisters have become cinders. We have the dispensation, yes; we have distance; but we'll leave nothing to chance. We'll not become complacent. This is a version of "throwing magic", as one might with pain or ill-fortune, sending it to someone else. We throw a fiery fate onto the wood-witch, give her to the pyre once a year in the hope it will keep the rest of us whole.

At my nod Nia moves closer to the balefire construct. Maud used to do this part. Maud, tall and thin, same high cheekbones as Gisela but thinner lips, more furrows across the forehead, hair proper white, grey-green eyes, standing like a pitiless goddess. It's the steward's task, but one I can't do so Nia does it for me. The cut she's made on her palm to pay the red price gleams darkly.

My cousin raises her arms to mirror the tree-wife, spreads her fingers as wide as they'll go and a flicker begins, comes from within her very skin, turns her hands pearlescent. The glow intensifies. I cannot see her face, but her lips will be moving, whispering an apology to the child of sticks and tinder who'll be so bright, so brilliant, so briefly. Nia leans forward and touches the kindling.

Everything ignites, the silver-white turning swiftly to an orange-gold-red tinged with blue breaths.

The voracious hues tear upwards and soon the tree-wife's torso, arms, head, twig-fingers are ablaze; the movement of the flames makes it seem as though she's swaying, dancing against the sky. Nia steps backwards until she bumps into me and I steady her; she stiffens at the touch. There are tears on her cheeks. Someone wraps my shoulders: Audra is smiling, dazzling as the moon. Grandmamma and Eira join in and we are one for a moment, united by blood, by history, by love. I breathe a sigh of relief, feel my tension drain.

Gisela says, 'You've done so well, Ellie!' and the others echo her. Pride burns inside me, blazing like the wood-witch.

Behind us, shouts go up – laughter, chatter and singing. Children race to the food tables, parents hot on their heels. The pop of kegs and bottles opening, the glug of pouring, of toasts being made. Once they've eaten their fill, little ones will be sent to bed and adults will drift off in pairs. In nine months, there will be new babes; perhaps some hasty marriages before, some less hasty ones after, perhaps none at all.

Across the fire I spy a familiar shape, well over six feet, broad-shouldered and deep-chested, black hair curling at his collar, a square jaw, dark stubble no amount of shaving can remove, brows emphatic as crow's wings and unfairly long lashes around deep blue eyes. For such a large man he doesn't ever seem clumsy or lumbering, he's graceful as a wolf. The cut of Dai's grin is sharp. I lift my chin defiantly. He's watching me and I don't care if it's the glamour of my position or appearance, or just the intoxication that fills everyone on Balefire Eve. I don't care because Dai Carabhille is looking back at me after all the years I've stared at him. Finally.

I feel everything that we – the Briars – are run through me: the strength of earth and fire, air and water. Or I imagine I'm filled by the things I cannot know for they have no more affinity for me than I have for them… except on this strange night it seems I'm allowed a hint of them, a whisper. Or perhaps it's simply that my yearning for them is stronger than ever. What I do know is that the light from the torches catches my eyes, the gems in my carefully coiffed braids and curls, and the gloss on my lips. This night, I *am* a priestess, powerful despite my lack of magic.

This night I *will* have at least one of the things I've wanted for so long.

Soon we'll begin to move, do the slow dance of lovers-to-be, around the circle, not being obvious, nor appearing too anxious. We'll stop to talk to people on the way, allowing the anticipation to grow, to build (after all these years, what's another hour or so?), as we dance and sway and dip, shifting closer and closer through groups of families and friends, acquaintances. Couples less patient than we wolf down food and disappear, not caring who sees. Idly I wonder if, when I unbutton his shirt, the medallion I gave him will be underneath; if he's been wearing it this whole time, close to his heart.

From above comes the great creak and snap of the wood-witch – always expected but never less than shocking. All eyes fasten on her in awe and sadness as the fire at last has its way: she folds, she crumbles, tumbles, all her limbs broken. Nia's excellent work has ensured that she plummets safely straight down, and *whumps* into the bed of cinders and soot, sending sprays of sparks upwards, which glare for a moment, then die against the velvet of the sky.

A collective sigh is released from those gathered, a mourning that's brief but no less real. The chatter starts again soon. I look for Dai, searching the sea of faces and forms, yet the one I seek is no longer there. I frown, turn and turn and turn, only to hear a keening. The thudding of boots beating on the path from town to green.

Beres Baines, no longer her neat self, comes tearing into the circle, makes a beeline for me. She grabs at my arms, shrieks, 'I can't find her, I can't find Deirdre.'

5

I should have stayed with Deirdre.

I should have sat while Audra ministered the heart's ease. Should have held her hand, grounded her while magic was sent through her body, heart and mind. Should have slept on the floor beside the bed, alert to any change in her breathing, to sobs in the night. Should have done so many things, but the Balefire called and I wouldn't ignore it. Couldn't. Was anxious for whatever it might offer me, was too concerned with that. And, perhaps, just a little irritated with Deirdre's intransigence; something I'll have to live with, depending on how matters fall.

The vigilants at the north and south watchtowers didn't see her, but she didn't have to pass by either of those. There are no walls around our town, another condition laid down by the church, because what horrors might come of witches with a stronghold? Any road, armies no longer march by this way, and when bandits last tried to raid us a century ago Gisela's mother and aunts were in their prime. That day, the populace was armed to defend their home, to back up the small company of vigilants, but Romelia and her sisters made short work of the robbers and their leader. Men were turned into balls of fire, or drowned on the spot in sudden waterspouts, or found themselves buried alive when the ground opened beneath them, or suffocated when the air where they stood was unexpectedly sucked away. A hefty crimson tithe paid that day by the Briars, but memories are long around here, and fear is a seed that grows with time. A worthwhile investment, a tale that's grown into a cautionary legend.

No walls, so Deirdre could walk out into the woods from almost anywhere, unseen. Some of the search parties have taken dogs, but they'd still not found a scent when Nia and I (oh, what a pairing!) left. Deirdre might have taken to the river or even rubbed citrus on her shoes to confuse the smell. If she was thinking that deeply.

It's deathly cold, as if winter decided the perfect time to make her presence known was the moment Beres's cry pierced the night. Festival finery was swiftly replaced by thick coats, sweaters, trousers, stout blackthorn batons and sturdy boots, but we're still shivering as we search the high ground behind the town. The places where the air is a little thinner, the woods thicker. Sometimes we stray near to the border between us and the Darklands. As we tramp along the path lit by Nia's silver lantern, I imagine movement in the darkness beyond, that misty shapes, red eyes, things that cannot get at us watch nonetheless – but they're not there. I'm being paranoid. My fingers close around the baton hanging at my waist, and I'm glad that Nia's bow is slung on her back with a full quiver. When we veer away from the invisible boundary line, I relax, and switch the rolled-up lightweight stretcher from one shoulder to the other.

We've been out here for hours, examining every hidey hole, every shed and lean-to, every hollowed tree, ditch, crack, crevice, anywhere someone might conceal themselves willingly or otherwise. Up here, the earth is riven by geological shifts, fissures and waterfalls that pour into pools, eventually to tumble into the winter-slow river.

No sign, however, of one sad and broken girl. How far could she get, in her state, in this cold? She may not even have come this way. May have taken a different route. It's possible one of the other search parties has already located her, alive if not entirely well.

And this night, which seemed so full of promise, is now heavy with dread, yet strangely empty.

'She'll be found,' says my cousin, which is not the same as *She'll be alright*. I don't reply, and she insists, 'Ellie, someone *will* find her.'

How bad it must be if *Nia* is trying to comfort *me*? 'But in what state? And even if she's found, what then?'

'Ellie—'

'You know the risk with heart's ease. If it didn't take. If she wasn't strong enough. If it simply twisted everything out of true.'

'Audra knows what she's doing, Ellie.' A rebuke: a proper *witch* knows what she's doing. 'She'd have made a judgment, done her best. It's all we can do.'

'What if it just widened the cracks in Deirdre?'

It's Nia's turn for silence.

I'm less worried about Audra's magic having gone awry than my decision to wait. Seven days. Was it too long? Did I let her suffer needlessly? Let her mind sour, expecting her to recover? Gisela had counselled patience, that sometimes these matters fix themselves. But the choice was mine and mine alone. As is the fault.

Abruptly, my cousin stops and I almost bump into her. The path's been steadily rising and we're both puffing, breath making angry shapes. There's a pond in front of us, fed by a small cataract to the left, dropping off a cliff to our right. Nia holds her lantern higher; the circle of light pushes out and spreads across the rippling black water, to the opposite side of the pool. She shakes her head.

'Honestly, Ellie, I don't think she could have made it this—'

I touch her arm.

'Over there.'

She follows the direction of my shaking finger.

Washed up against the incline of the far bank, at the limit of the light, is a white, white thing, unmoving.

Nia waits on terra firma as I wade in, mostly naked, the icy liquid soaking and settling into my linen corset and knickers, darkening the white fabric, making it heavy, heavy. The water's freezing and ever deeper until the mud and waterweed slip away beneath me and I'm swimming, teeth chattering so hard I fear they'll chip. By the time I reach my goal I'm made of ice and lumbering, a frost giant slipping and sliding on the slick mud, falling onto the white, white thing lying half-in, half-out of the pond. My face presses into Deirdre's wet hair; no matter how long she's spent submerged the smell clings to her, all those days of being unwashed, all the sweat, the sadness, the old blood and untapped milk. The vomit. Coming from her very pores and follicles, as if she'll never be rid of what she'd become before she died. Her eyes are open, glassy.

A length of rope's looped around her neck, skin torn red by the coarse fibres. A branch, one end rotted, is in the knot. In an act of purest hope, I feel for a pulse in spite of everything. Nothing.

Nothing.

Gently, I touch her head and the skull moves beneath my fingers like broken eggs in a sack. I look at the waterfall; there are rocks at its base. Above, where the water throws itself off the cliff, there's a tree close to the ledge. The selfish thought enters my mind that at least she didn't float down to the lake beside the common, didn't drift ashore as the wood-wife burned. I'd like to sit and weep but what use would that be? I tug Deirdre into the water, floating her along behind me, her hair like weeds beneath the surface.

Nia's unrolled the stretcher and helps me heave the body onto it. I wrap my shirt around Deirdre's poor head so the journey won't disarrange her features any further – and so Beres won't see it, then remove my damp underclothes, secure them under Deirdre's body. She's in no condition to complain. I dry myself off as well as I can with my sweater, trying to coax warmth into my blue-marbled skin.

'Here.' Nia makes a small cut at her wrist – all the magic she'd paid for today used up at the Balefire. She rubs her palms together and her hands begin to glow; she touches my face and it's like standing by a fire. Continues to apply this heat to the rest of me until I'm barely bothered by the ghost of chill. To the east, dawn is pricking the sky so we'll warm up soon enough carrying the stretcher.

'Thanks.' I dress quickly.

'Ready?' asks Nia.

One last glance upward to that tree and what looks like a broken branch. I should climb up to the ledge, examine the place where Deirdre made her final choice, look for clues – but I believe I know what happened; can imagine it all too clearly.

'Ready.'

Deirdre's dainty like her mother, but in death she's taken on the weight of all her sorrows, all her grief. We rest frequently. Perched on a rock, staring at the body, my cousin mutters. The wooded path is bright now that night's fled.

'What's that, Nia?'

'My tree-wife…' She clears her throat. 'She was perfect.'

'Yes.'

'Until—'

'The Balefire was *perfect*. The wood-witch was perfect. *Nothing* went wrong with either of those things.'

'But immediately after—'

'Not immediately—'

'Well, *soon* after! When we should have bought ourselves safety for wintertide, good fortune and prosperity for the coming year. Yet *this* is the first significant event to happen…'

My temper rises. 'You're saying it's my fault. That I'm not good enough to have organised it all. That you should have been steward – that *you* should have taken over from Maud.'

She rises, stares down at me. 'Well, it hasn't gone wrong in a hundred or more years. Not until last night.'

I stand so we're eye-to-eye. 'All I did was the orchestration, Nia. All I'm good for, remember? And we all know you couldn't organise a fuck in a brothel.' I step closer even though rage is darkening her face. 'There's nothing magical in what *I* did. *You* were the one to make the tree-witch. *You* were the one to cast the spell that lit the flames.' I hiss: 'Without Maud, *you* were the only new magical element in the equation. *You*. Not me. Gisela will look to *you* if there's any blame to go around.'

Now Nia's expression is stricken – presumably how she expected me to look when she began this fight. There's a satisfaction in that, but I also wonder whether I should simply leave Nia to her own devices. Leave my cousin to return Deirdre to her mother while I walk into the woods and never look back. But I'm too rooted in Silverton. Unsure how I'd survive without it.

Yet I can't imagine Nia would have mis-made the wood-wife. Queering her spell and attracting our grandmother's scrutiny, our community's whispers, just to spite me? No. I shouldn't be surprised that her first thought was to direct blame at me. Oddly, I'm pleased I was paired with her, because at least it's kept her away from our grandmother's ears these past hours.

'Ellie—'

'Shut up.'

I take up the weight of Deirdre once again and wait until Nia grabs the back of the stretcher before setting off.

* * *

We're sweating with exertion as we carry our burden into the northern end of Silverton, largely because I refused to rest again, determined to deprive my cousin of any further chances to bicker. There are shouts from the wooden watchtower as we're seen and a crowd gathers and follows, pouring from the poorer cottages, then the larger houses, and finally even from the mansions and townhouses. Familiar faces tell me a lot of the other search parties have already returned. I think about the number of folk roiling along behind us: most of them won't know Deirdre, not as a person. But they'll know her, now, as a tragedy, a tale to tell and warn young women about the dangers of love. They all want to watch, to witness, to gossip. I have to bite back the urge to yell at them all, to send them away with a flea in their ears, to tell them this girl is *not* to be a spectacle.

But I keep my mouth shut.

Screaming and bellowing won't do Deirdre any good, nor me. Drawing attention to myself will likely make people start thinking the way Nia did – that somehow everything is all my fault. The result of all my lacks. So, I focus on the cobbles in front of me, moving towards the Briar House rather than the infirmary and the mortuary because I just need to get poor Deirdre cleaned up before her mother sees her. I need to get this fractured creature to a place that might feel like home ever-so-slightly rather than to a cold marble slab.

We almost make it. Are almost at the garden gate of the tall wood and stone mansion. Almost inside the high hedge-fence with its tame brambles that might have hidden us from sight. Perchance someone had run to Beres, told her what we'd brought for her. Or the cries from the watchtower carried enough to bring her from her cottage.

We're so close – then the screaming begins, from the far end of the market square, a constant piercing clarion that gets louder and louder, accompanied by the beating of boots (horribly familiar), and Beres tears along the thoroughfare, coming to rest a few feet from us and the laden stretcher. She seems to hover like a hummingbird, just a little off the ground, held there by her own vibrating grief, then abruptly takes the final steps and sinks down beside her daughter's body.

'I'm so sorry,' I say, and begin to weep at last, whether for my own failure or Beres's loss or Deirdre's, I'm uncertain. All three would be acceptable, I believe.

6

My memories of my mother May are scarce; like Nia and Eira's mother – my aunt – she died the year the plague swept through. So swift and unexpected, brought in by merchants who made it as far as our town before shuffling off their mortal coil. We had no warning, were unprepared. The population was halved in a few weeks; you either got sick and died or you did not get sick at all. All but one. I was three, the other two four. Audra was six and though her mother was gravely ill, Hebe eventually recovered (the only one to do so). She lasted four years longer than ours, but was never really *right* again.

I *do* recall a day of being dressed in black, such a heavy little dress, so many petticoats and layers, so prim, and Gisela draping a veil over my head. It tickled my nose, scratched at my skin, and when I tried to remove the netting Grandmamma's fingers were firm on mine. She sat me on her knee, held me tightly and said, 'Do you know why we wear dark colours and cover our faces at funerals?'

I shook my head, aching to pull the tulle away, but mindful that Grandmamma Gisela's hands might turn to punishment at any moment. She smiled down, her own veil as yet un-affixed, still it seemed there was a pall of smoke between us.

'There was, and there was not' – she began so I would know it for a tale – 'a woman of our family called Hilla. Now, Hilla's husband was not a good man and when he died his wife had no wish to mourn. So she did not choose a grieving gown, refusing to hide from his shade behind widow's weeds – we wear black and veils so the ghosts of the dead cannot distinguish us, cannot pursue us. But Hilla' – Gisela shook her head in despair – 'oh, Hilla. She wanted to be seen, desired nothing so much as that he should know she danced with every step to and from his tomb. Hilla wore a bright crimson dress to her husband's funeral – just the sort he'd forbidden her to wear during their marriage lest any other man look at her. The mourners held their breath, waiting to see what might happen.'

'What happened?' I whispered, thinking perhaps it wouldn't be so bad, to have my mother back in whatever form she might appear. Something I do recollect is that she was kind in all things.

'Her husband's ghost followed her home and made life a misery. Banging pots and pans, throwing books and bottles, rushing up and down the stairs in the middle of the night so poor Hilla – foolish Hilla! – got no sleep whatsoever. Because' – Gisela paused, raised an instructive finger – 'ghosts are not the people we love and remember. They're changed – the good ones become bad, the bad even worse.'

'What do they want, Grandmamma?'

'To rest. Just as the living do, and just as your dear grandmamma does, so do not trouble her further by playing with your veil, Ellie.'

Clearly my cousins were more biddable in this instance for only I received this lesson. I wanted to ask what happened to

64

Hilla, but sensed that it was not the best time, and I never did find the right moment.

That was, of course, well before I learned about Gilly Briar, who'd banished the ghosts of Silverton long ago. Telling me *that* story wouldn't have induced any fear, nor convinced me to do what Gisela wished: to be a well-behaved Briar child, to follow the forms, to be proper when we were meant to be examples for everyone else's standards. Even a motherless three-year-old.

I'm thinking about that story now as I sit in front of the roaring fire in the library, freshly bathed and wrapped in the warmest robes, my feet stretched towards the flames. Would Deirdre, if she came back (if she could), make my life a misery? Make the life of her son's father a misery? Would she, regretful, name her little lad and let him rest? I'm waiting for my grandmother to return from tending to Beres, while Eira tends to Deirdre in the infirmary. Waiting for her to tell me what happens next. I imagine Gisela using that soothing voice of hers, the one she reserves for the wounded and idiots, offering Beres tea that's a mix of camomile and lemon balm and a dash of valerian; she'll hold the other woman's hand and soothingly press the pressure points to calm her. Gisela *won't* suggest heart's ease – Beres is an entirely different creature to her daughter.

When the door opens, I'm both relieved and disappointed to see Audra. She's carrying a tray with a large mug (I can smell the alcohol from here), a bowl of soup and a plate of bread.

'I don't think you got to eat anything at the Balefire before… well, before.' She places the tray on my lap, and immediately I'm starving.

'Thank you, Audra.' I start eating so I don't have to talk, but

65

my cousin doesn't take the hint. Sitting on the chair opposite, she watches me for a while. It's disconcerting to say the least.

'Ellie…'

I raise a brow.

'Ellie, what happened to Deirdre wasn't your fault.'

'When you saw her, did you think she might… that the heart's ease might…'

My cousin shakes her head emphatically. 'No.'

I blink hard. This kindness doesn't make me feel any better.

'And, Ellie, the Balefire – it wasn't spoiled. Wasn't ruined. There wasn't anything you could have done more, nothing you could have controlled or predicted. The Balefire *was* a success.'

'Easy for you to say. Gisela—'

'—Ellie—'

'I *know* Grandmamma didn't truly want me to do the Balefire. I *know* she only let me because you begged her, said it was always part of Maud's duties and should remain with the steward. She didn't want me because I'm not a witch – but a witch wasn't needed for what I did. But maybe she was right. Maybe everything went wrong because of what I'm not.' I'm babbling now, admitting what Nia accused me of, feeling the weight of it. 'If I hadn't been so stubborn, if Nia had done it, none of this would have happened.'

'Ellie! Ellie! No. Deirdre is a sad loss but you – we – did everything we could. Even if Nia had become the steward – and there's no reason she should, Maud never trained her – this would *still* have happened. It was a horrible thing and terribly timed, but everyone knows that sometimes there's nothing to be done to remedy such a situation.'

My cousin holds my hand as I bite my lip and refuse to cry. When I can speak again, I say: 'What about the baby?'

She tilts her head, considering. 'We can ask Beres to name him. She's his grandmother, there's a thread of blood, a strong one. A grandmother's almost as good as a mother – as we well know.' She grins sadly. 'It wouldn't have worked while Deirdre was alive, but now she's… and with the father unknown. Maybe it will be enough.'

'Maybe.' It might work. We must do it soon, but much will depend on Beres's state of mind. I hand the unfinished meal back to Audra. 'I've had my fill, thank you.'

My cousin leans over and kisses my cheek before taking the tray. At the door she gives an encouraging smile. 'Don't fear, Ellie, I won't let anything happen to you.'

* * *

At some point I fall asleep, waking only when someone shakes me.

Gisela waits. I was dreaming of a woman dancing in a red dress, all the way to the graveyard. I struggle to rise, disoriented, confused and not a little panicky. In spite of all Audra's assurances, I pour forth whimpering noises and unintelligible words. And I hate myself for it, for sounding like a child.

'Grandmamma, I'm so sorry, so very sorry—'

She gathers me to her, and for a while I'm that three-year-old without her mother, before it was certain I had no power, before she knew I was different and didn't belong in this house or this family, not really. When I'm calmer, Gisela sits us both down and questions me carefully about everything I did leading up to the Balefire – even though she knows it exactly because I discussed each step with her, checking and double-checking. We were both anxious that things go right. And Maud had always

67

had me by her side, learning by doing, learning by rote, every year helping with the preparations; right up until her voice was gone, eaten away by the cancer.

Gisela sighs. For a while she says nothing, and I try to divine what will come. Finally, she announces:

'Ellie, you're not to blame, my girl. You did nothing wrong, there is nothing to punish you for. You did your absolute best and I couldn't ask more of any Briar, witch or otherwise.'

'And Nia? Will Nia be alright?' I resent asking but the better part of me wants to know my cousin's also safe; that no one's found the wood-witch wanting. Gisela nods curtly. I relax as if the bones have left me. Still, I can't help but dig into the wound. 'Does Beres blame me?'

Gisela hesitates a little too long and I'm pierced by the unfairness of it all. 'Ellie Briar, Beres has just lost her only daughter, her only grandchild a week ago. Be patient. She's not a stupid woman, nor a bitter one, nor mean. Give her time.'

She's right. It doesn't hurt any less. Nor does the caveat that arrives very quickly.

'However, Ellie, I think it wise for you to undertake visits to the outlying farms.' She holds up a finger to my trembling lips. 'It's due to be done anyway before the snows set in. It's Nia's turn, but no one will think it strange if you go – you've done this before.' *Always with Maud.* 'It won't hurt for you to not be so visible for a little while, just until Beres regains her equilibrium. Just until the Balefire isn't so fresh in everyone's mind.'

She smiles, fever-bright. 'And it's a chance to visit with Liv! Won't that be wonderful? It's a while since you've seen her, isn't it?'

Nodding, I close my eyes, feeling fresh tears seep from under the lashes. Gisela's hands close over mine, tighten their grip. She whispers fiercely and I smell her breath – weariness, too much coffee, and age. I'm not even sure she means me to hear the words: 'I'll give no one else to the flames.'

7

Two days later I'm gone, just ahead of the dawn and well before Deirdre's mid-morning funeral. Gone so Beres Baines doesn't have to look at me, so no one else might get ideas. If this is *not* being blamed, then I never want to know what actual blame feels like. Somewhere behind me, Gisela is preparing for the interment with Audra beside her, learning; Eira's delivering babies; Nia's on the common holding archery practice for the vigilants.

The reins are loose in my grip. Hieronymus, the dun-coloured draught horse, plods along, drawing the small wagon that contains everything I'll need. Seven farms beyond easy reach of Silverton, but they're our people nonetheless, tending fields and growing crops that get sold at the markets, help keep us fed. Outlier children often board in town for schooling.

Seven farms and a week away. The Havards, the Dees, the Olafssons, the Treharnes, the Axelssons, the Bergs and the Holms. Large families in every case, large properties too, although varying in degrees of prosperity, breeding and education. At some, I'll stay in a guest room in the farmhouse; at others, sleeping in the comfort and security of the wagon is preferable. Especially at the Holms'.

These circuits happen every three months, at the turn of each season. I've only ever done them in Maud's company, presumably because no one wants the outliers thinking we couldn't be bothered to send a *real* witch to check on their wellbeing – but I'm the steward now and that counts for something. Or I hope so. One advantage is that there'll be no one who knows about Balefire Eve and Deirdre. At least not quite yet.

I should be grateful, to escape so lightly. For Gisela to be so adamant that what happened was not my fault. That I'm still the steward and not sent away as Maud sometimes suggested when she thought I couldn't hear (before she realised I had a use) – like a shame to be hidden (even if I *am* being sent away for a little while). Like Nia had said more than once to my face when we were small, before I learned to either hit her or report to Gisela – a decision I made carefully, always wary of being labelled a tattletale. Yet it feels like a punishment all the same. Shaking my head, I try to concentrate on the landscape, looking for distraction.

The sun's spearing through the trees like fire, burning away the mist and the frost on the ground. There's the crunch of stones beneath the wheels, and the song of birds waking with the light, the shuffling of other creatures bedding down until darkness returns. My thoughts swell, skip back to a matter I've considered these last couple of days: Dai Carabhille.

I've not spoken to him, and he's not sought me out. I've seen him in town, making deliveries, walking past the Briar House, but not giving a single glance towards its doors or windows. Not looking for me. My heart clenches and shrivels, an apple left to wither. My grandmother's observation repeats: that he's not looking at me because he's too busy looking at other faces. And the truth is that if he'd wished to find me, if he was worried for me and my fate, he would have. There was no mystery about my location, I was not in hiding. If he'd had a kind or concerned thought for me, he knew where I was.

The cold truth slides through my heart like a slow knife. I hate Gisela for being right and I hate myself for believing her. I've examined the cadaver of my feelings from every angle, poked and prodded, tried to resuscitate it, but it's got no more life than poor Deirdre and her child. Don't mistake me: it hurts. *I* hurt and ache. But if I didn't believe my grandmother then my feelings for Dai would still be warm and strong, not slowly bleeding out, creeping towards an arctic hardness. Pondering further will do me no good; best to let my mind shy away from such things.

I focus on the road ahead, rocks and dirt, the occasional rut. There were more farms here when the first Briars came, though the holdings were much smaller. But Silverton itself had shrunk by the time Gilly and Sandor rolled into the tiny village with its dying population and growing range of illnesses no one could cure. She brewed her potions and tisanes, elixirs and philtres. She brought the place and its people back to life. Sandor set up a school, helped businesses start or revive, opened the first bookstore, employing folk. The little farms joined together via marriages or disappeared through natural attrition, but they came to rely on Silverton's witches to keep them well and educated, to bring their harvest to markets, to ensure they made it through wintertide as well as the town-dwellers.

We clop over an arched stone bridge, water splashing loudly beneath; the road begins to slope, just a little. The outliers are further down the mountain range where the conditions are less harsh. Above the tops of the autumn-fire trees on either side I

72

can see the higher peaks, already fringed with snow. The further I get from home, the lighter I begin to feel. I sit straighter on the bench seat, breathe more deeply, begin humming to myself. The horse's ears flick left and right, then settle. And I know that this is a chance to see Liv. A chance to catch up with my friend, someone who'll listen to my whining and make me feel better, even if I'm being childish.

Along this route and many of the others that dot our mountainous region, there were once witch-pickets lining the way. Made of holly and laid by the first god-hound to come as our overseer, they were designed to keep the Briars from leaving the area, perhaps also to stop other witches from finding us. Over the years, however, we've removed them – or rather had lovers and friends and employees do so – and replaced them, rather cleverly we like to think, with troll pikes, iron staves topped with a twisted upside-down horseshoe. Those creatures (far more dangerous than us) appear in spring and summer, and some still roam in early autumn, but by winter they're hibernating. The troll pikes keep them away from the major roads, Silverton and surrounds. One of my tasks on this journey is to check those planted around the farmsteads; we are far more diligent in this than the god-hounds with examining their witch-pickets. The intention is to prevent children from being stolen and replaced with monstrous little changelings. There's a tale that one of the long-ago princesses of Lodellan was said to have lost a daughter in this fashion. Certainly it broke her mother's heart, although it's said her father never noticed.

Neither my cousins nor I have any idea who our fathers were; perhaps one of the wandering men who travel the roads, the tinkers and merchants, perhaps married Silverton men long dead of the same plague that took our mothers. No one's ever claimed us, which is how the Briars like it. It doesn't matter. We don't take their names, we girls. Any sons – well, there's not been a boy born into this family in generations. Grandfather Tobias was a rarity, a known father, though he never lived in the Briar House all those years he and Gisela carried on. She continued to visit him long after child-getting was a reason for her attendance, so one assumes there was love. Or at least right up until the incident with poor Aunt Hebe.

Tobias was a son of Lodellan, the latest in a long line of god-hounds sent to watch over us. This is how we exist: under the Church's sufferance. The priests' reports assure whichever Archbishop currently rules the cathedral-city that we're only using our magic to heal, not harm. That we do nothing dark or questionable, nothing wicked, nothing that's an actual exercise of power. And that we hold the border to the Darklands – a little nation, barely a county; mostly villages set around the Leech Lords' estates, some small towns, only a few cities. Small but dangerous.

The Briars had lived according to those rules – or at least not openly flouting them – for a very long time indeed.

Until Gisela.

Gisela, who'd just inherited her mantle. Who wanted more, to *do* more, who did not wish to practise her craft in darkness as if it were shameful. Gisela who chafed against the restrictions imposed by a cadre of fearful hypocrites in a far-off city.

At some point, the old priest had sensed his end approaching, and wrote to his masters: it was time for a replacement, a youngster he might train in the duties incumbent upon a defender of the church, a supervisor of witches. Alas, he met his god before the new man arrived. Had Gisela's mother, Romelia, still been alive matters might have progressed differently, but Romelia had been laid to rest around the same time as the old god-hound. So, when the handsome Father Tobias appeared, the new Briar Witch presented herself as his adviser. Gisela, who'd done a judicious audit of the old man's papers and scrolls, books of instruction and the like, and carefully cleared the hearth of the priest's house of what might have been an unseemly amount of ashes. Back then, Tobias was more trusting, more naïve, even when it came to witches. He assumed all the years of church oversight – of *domestication* – meant we'd not dare step outside of the bounds of what was *allowed*.

And Gisela, young and fiery, beautiful and wilful, with powers far greater than she was permitted to exercise, set her cap at this new priest. Knowing that love and lust would blind him and bind him. That she could get her way in all things. For a long time, she did. He fathered her children and cared enough to protect them by sending the requisite reports back to his Archbishop. Reports dictated by his lover. He wanted to please her.

This information I had from Maud, more than once over the course of my life, sometimes the story wavering a little, but the core details remaining the same. Maud with her tone so wistful and proud, bitter and longing.

For *such* a long time, things continued in this fashion.

Then the plague came, and put a crack in everything, drove a wedge into the weak points of our existence, and that was how the darkness got in.

May (my mother) and Susannah (Nia and Eira's) died quickly. Hebe, Audra's mother, the middle child, was very ill. When she rose from her sickbed (the only one of Gisela's daughters to do so) she was changed. Once a dependable young woman, she'd become fey and disconnected from reality. The old tales she and her sisters had been raised on were *real* to her. The bedtime stories she passed on to her daughter gained the weight of truth. They hid, Hebe swore, secrets that needed to be uncovered: the reign of Lady Death, the location of her kingdom; the sorceress who could change her face and live forever; and the Witches' War, when the world was remade before those three witches went *beneath*. Those witches who'd had the chance to rule yet lost their courage and left us all to the whims of childish, spiteful men – although Hebe could never give precise details of this failure.

Sometimes, on those days when my aunt thought we should all hear what she had to say, she'd gather us in the library and for a while we were transported as she conjured a tiny theatre between her fingers. Mostly it was with Audra alone that she shared these fables, strange whispered gospels, but I still recall those times when we were all witness to Hebe's wonders. Audra would be pulled away from lessons and games, even the dinner table, to listen as her mother told her such tales with the urgency of a secret, the impetus of a quest to be undertaken, the weight of a sacred vow.

And, having been thus unpicked from reality, my aunt began to use her power with no thought for its effect, drawing fire and water from the air, raising the earth into small hillocks around town and shrieking with delight as folk ran for their lives from tiny cyclones. Openly, brazenly, in front of her father, she would throw enchantments about like confetti – the red price spattering from her hands and wrists – as if he'd not been trained to take ones such as us apart. As if he was not, to his very blood and bone, still a priest. Gisela didn't pay attention – or not enough – and so, on the day when both Tobias and Hebe went missing, it was too late by the time she realised matters had gone amiss.

Something swoops in front of my face, giving me such a scare that I almost topple from the seat. I certainly let out a screech, which is echoed by the bird that flaps its wings hard and takes off into the depths of the trees. Bird? Or bat? Feathers, definitely feathers. As my heart calms, I squint, trying hard to see amongst the branches and leaves, the burns of autumn-orange, the evergreens and the mix of naked boles. Something brown and gold, I think, but it disappears so quickly I can't be sure of anything, really. There's another screech in the woods, an animal dying, plucked from the grass and undergrowth. Turned into an avian snack.

I shake my head, mentally list off the tasks at each farmstead. All going well, I can fit the Dees in today before heading to the Havards. But I need to make better time if I wish to arrive by dinner tonight; Liv Havard is the only person amongst the outliers that I'd call an actual friend.

I click my tongue at Hieronymus, and he picks up the pace with only a slight snort to register his irritation.

8

'More wine?' Liv asks. It's quiet at last, her husband having herded their seven children off to bed and left us to our own devices. The large common room is warm, the fire crackling. I like this space with its tapestries (hunting scenes) brightening the log walls, and the silver lanterns Liv brought as part of her dower, made with true O'Malley silver – the last of it, according to Edgar, who sold them to her, with the final scion of that great house disappearing a few years ago.

'Always.' I hold up my glass for a refill. My friend's dark eyes glitter with merriment.

When we were small and skipping school, Liv and I would climb trees and she'd share her plans to run away. Not because she was unhappy, but because she craved adventure and change. She'd drawn a map on a piece of parchment (stolen by me from Gisela's desk, one of the most expensive the Carabhilles produced) with all the destinations she would visit, and arrows to show the route she'd take. Said map bore, of course, no resemblance to the actual locations or the distances between them, but we were too young to know or care. Liv was going to see the ghostly wolf-hounds that guarded the cathedral in Lodellan, listen to the melodies of the rusalky on the Singing Rock outside of Bellsholm, wander the streets of the port-city of Breakwater where winged navigators once lived, and take ship from there perhaps to St Sinwin's Harbour (which is rumoured to be the last stop before the edge of the world). Perhaps become a pirate. She would visit the ruins at Cwen's Reach and bring me back one of the unloved books that were said to still litter the courtyard centuries after the Citadel's destruction. She would even (and we both trembled at the very name) cross over to the Darklands and make her way to Calder (or Caulder, depending on the age of the atlas consulted and the education of the cartographer who made it), seeking an audience with one of the Leech Lords of legend, Adlissa the Bloodless. Blood-drinkers. Soul-takers.

But then she got married, and the furthest she went was to Bedo Havard's farm.

Bedo's a kind man, older than his second wife by a decade. He's ever-patient, bearded, not unhandsome, and gentle. Something I'd always noticed, even when I was younger and visiting with Maud, was that he didn't leave the care of his five children solely to Lina, his first wife; they shared the burden and the joy. A man whose actions spoke for him and were never out of tune with what came from his mouth, which made him a rare creature indeed. No one thought he'd remarry after Lina died, but then he met Liv and, well, they have twins of their own now, and all the stepchildren call her 'Mother' with nothing but adoration. Liv's adapted spectacularly well to the demands of running such a large holding.

I've missed her in the two years she's been gone from Silverton. Her home was somewhere I'd flee to when my cousins were being particularly awful. I've often wondered if the loss of her parents a few months before she met Bedo made her more susceptible to domesticity. If all her yearning for adventure could be undone by the sudden lack of blood family. Yet I don't ask – it's one of those questions with the potential to start an unpicking that may well leave a life in tatters. Like *Are you happy?*

Upon my arrival, we got the basics out of the way – the Havards are all healthy, no trace of sniffles or colds, no long-term illnesses, only some scrapes and scratches from climbing trees. They've made little dent in my medicinal supplies, and Liv and I spent the afternoon preserving the last of their fruit and vegetables for winter, crushing herbs and roots to ensure a good stock of herbal remedies most likely to be needed in the bitter cold.

'Now,' Liv says, 'tell me everything you didn't say at dinner!'

There is gossip of course, and rumour – harmless because it's between us and has nowhere else to go. There are the plans for Eira's marriage, and my hope that Liv will be able to visit then for a few days, not least because my family will be unbearable during a wedding. Or rather I will find them unbearable. There're my usual complaints about Nia and our usual state of low-level bickering. We chatter about all the easy things, the matters that are funny or annoying or do not hurt too much, because when the trivial matters are done there are only the painful things.

I tell her about the Balefire because that event started out so well; in all other respects, it was a triumph. I'd handed Bedo wood-wife ashes, which he'd buried in front of the stoop as soon as he could, to join an accumulation of cinereal relics – the protection of the ceremony carried forth to the outlying farms. But then the tale cascades downward, to Deirdre and her death and her unnamed baby, to my conversation with Gisela and my own realisation about Dai. And I know those two losses are in no way comparable – that one is so frivolous as to be ridiculous mentioned in the same breath – but Liv is my dear friend and such friends will hear the worst selfishness from your mouth and not judge you.

'I'm sorry,' she says. And I know it's an all-encompassing 'sorry'. That she won't make it worse by picking it apart or saying 'I told you so' about Dai (even though she did warn me, for years).

'I've been an idiot.' I shrug. 'You told me enough times.'

'What did my mother used to say? We only learn to fear the fire by sticking our fingers in the embers?'

'Half the fire's luck. I didn't get *anything* stuck in me…'

We take an unseemly while to stop giggling, but I feel better. Like a canker's been lanced. Though there's still hurt, it doesn't seem quite so much like internal decay. I knew coming here would be a tonic. The Dees earlier in the day were polite but distant – they're no different when the others visit, for living out here appeals to the already insular and makes others so. We do our best not to be intrusive, only helpful. Two of their lads had colds, which I treated with a tincture of dried elderberries and honey, and they were breathing more easily by the time I set off. Hopefully they didn't regard my swift departure as too swift – but I couldn't imagine sitting with Nan Dee and her brood in such companionship as with the Havards.

'Oh, did you hear about St Ogg's?' offers Liv.

'Edgar fair sang that one to Gisela, much to her spiteful delight.'

This sets off another fit of laughter. When we're quiet again, I ask, 'Is everything well?'

She smiles but there's a hitch to it, an uncertainty. 'Liv? Tell me.'

'I'm being fanciful. Rune' – the eldest child at ten – 'found six dead deer in the woods about a month back.'

'Not uncommon. Wolves?' I know it's stupid even before the word escapes me because deer killed by wolves would never be cause for the tension in her face.

A shake of the head. 'Throats cut, sliced clean, but little trace of blood on the ground. And rabbits and foxes and badgers. Bedo found a *bear* last week.'

'Bears should be bedding down by now. Your neighbours? Any feuds?' I wonder which of them would bother to travel so far simply to leave corpses on another farm.

'Not so much as a cross word…'

'Hunters, then? Have any travellers been by?'

'None on the road, none that we've seen – except Edgar. Besides, it's not the time for them. Folk are settling into their homes, getting ready for the snow. Soon enough the ways will be impassable for a few months.'

I think of Edgar and his annual apprentices. Our gentleman-merchant prides himself on his reputation, the clientele he's built up over the years. He'd not risk his business with an ill-chosen companion; he's got a good feel for character.

'The troll pikes I checked were all intact.' I frown.

'And that's not how a troll feeds…'

'Bandits, perhaps? Edgar mentioned there'd been tell of groups making winter camps – but only to the north, not this far south.'

'Ah, it could be anything out here! Dark forests! Things that sleep beneath the mountains for decades woken by chance, the shifting of a hillside, the flooding of a stream or stirring of a lake. Mostly, they stay away from large groups and towns. But the far-flung farms? Smallholdings? Sometimes the threat doesn't seem so great; the risk and reward for a hungry belly might be balanced.'

'Be watchful. Make sure your farmhands are alert and keep the children close to home.' I tell her what she already knows. 'And send for us if anything happens.'

'Of course.' She pauses, breaks into a smile. 'But this is dreary! Better news is…' Liv pats her pretty blue gown, puffs her belly out.

'Again?! Already?' I laugh, reaching across to hold her hand.

'Don't look like that – we need some more unpaid labour!'

Once more I wonder if my friend thinks of the wondrous travels she'll never have now. I wonder if she ever thinks about running away?

Are you happy?

I believe she is.

* * *

Four days later, I'm on my way back to Silverton and missing my friend.

The Olafssons were nice enough, the family well, but the mother, Della, was pregnant yet again. Liv's twenty and strong; Della's almost fifty and exhausted from ten other children (the oldest is thirty with offspring of his own). Though I saw she was tempted by the solution I offered, she didn't accept. There would likely be difficulties when labour came, so I spoke with her daughter-in-law, left a supply of sedatives, yarrow-infused bandages and a small blue vial containing the solution Della had already refused. I thought there might quite soon come a time when Della regretted her decision.

The Treharnes were brisk to the point of rudeness when they saw I wasn't one of the witches. I treated a deep cut on the leg of a farmhand, which had begun to turn septic, and spoke sternly to Mr Treharne about letting it go so long. But their property marked my turning point – from there I was heading back towards home, with just three families remaining to visit.

My relief was short-lived.

The farmsteads of both the Axelssons and the Bergs were completely deserted.

It's not an impossible thing to happen – everyone has duties, but at least some members of a household have chores that revolve around the house itself, the kitchen. Someone is always cooking, cleaning, weaving or sewing, tending to small children, while others are out sowing or tilling the fields or hunting in the forests. And usually at least one hireling can be spotted in the shadows of barns and outbuildings, feeding animals, fixing tools, checking seed stocks.

But *no one* around? For hours? In two locations?

In the houses: clothing and shoes, hair and toothbrushes, valuables untouched. No sign of food preparation for some time either. Fresh fruit and vegetables left to ripen had begun to rot. The sheep and cattle? Gone. Horses and goats too. Which might suggest the family had left that way – except wagons remained, tack too, so no one had saddled up and ridden off. Besides, where would they have gone? Both farms were productive and profitable, no reason to walk off the land.

And no sense of chores undone, of anyone being "disappeared" in the middle of tasks.

Just... abandonment.

Both big houses with central high-ceilinged halls, rooms running around the sides and back. Hollow, the pair of them, echoing with only my footsteps and a terrible emptiness. On their doorsteps I left small sacks of Balefire ash, just in case someone returned.

I waited at the Axelssons' for two hours before setting off, and relieved I was to leave. I thought, perhaps, they might be at the Bergs'. I was sure there would be a good reason – some sort of celebration, or they'd gone to offer aid in an as-yet-unknown-and-unthought-of crisis.

But the Berg farmstead was just as empty, just as strangely tidy, just as bereft. Again, I waited a few hours until the sun began to set – lazy in its winter-orbit – then pointed Hieronymus back towards the road, towards the Holms' and my last port-of-call. I knew I'd not arrive before dark, that I'd sleep in the wagon by the side of the road, but anything was better than remaining in the emptiness of the Berg holding. I couldn't stop myself from making sure that the blackthorn baton was secure at my waist and checking on the small knife in my right boot, just in case.

A while and some distance later, when the sense of unease seemed to lift, I found a clearing. I built a fire, made soup with vegetables and dried meat, thickened with the last of the flour, toasted stale bread, drank tea sweetened with honey to help me sleep. I didn't take any of the rose-plum brandy, not wanting to be insensible should anything... occur. I left the horse's tether loose so if he took fright in the night, he could flee. He's well-trained enough to wander back when it's safe, to find me again. But I slept through, cosy in the warmth of the wagon with the latch in place. No scraping or scratching or knocking at the door.

No snuffling or sniffing or growling. Hieronymus was calm and quiet the whole night.

Now, in the interests of making a quick exit should it be required, I'm on his back, having left the wagon at the beginning of the track that winds its way up to the last farm. Something's prickling at the nape of my neck. I may well be simply spooked, Liv's tales adding to my unease. I may well be letting my imagination run away with me, but I'd rather be safe than sorry. The Holms, with their five brutish sons, are my least favourite stop, and I'm ever grateful that it's the last one. There are only a few hours between me and Silverton.

9

The Holms' holding is the smallest of the outlier properties, not as old as the others, also not as well maintained. The track leading up to the house-yard is pitted with holes and ruts. Cart wheels would have a difficult time negotiating this passage, stock and people alike might well injure themselves, so I feel doubly wise to have left the wagon by the side of the road. Astride an unsaddled Hieronymus, I'm careful where I aim him.

Grey stone foundations and dirty white wattle-and-daub walls for both the house and outbuildings, and withy fences around pens and fields. As we enter the courtyard between home and barn, I have the same sense of abandonment as at the last two stops. No sound, not even birds. No domestic animals to be seen or heard, neither alive nor dead. Hesitantly I dismount, and slip the blackthorn baton from my belt, hold it firmly. My preference is not to get close to anything dangerous, however I may not have a choice.

The farmhouse – single-storeyed and dim – is, unsurprisingly, empty. It's not only untidy, but downright unclean. There are no daughters, only boys, and Mrs Holm gave up trying to keep a proud house some years ago. Muddy boot prints mar the floorboards and rugs, a sign of men traipsing in whatever they've walked through outside. In the bedrooms: unmade beds, open wardrobes, piles of unwashed clothing in corners. The bathtub's filled with water turned stagnant and scummy, though I can still smell lily-scented soap. In the kitchen, food scraps litter the countertop, dishes and cups are unwashed on the table. That's new, at least – that the house isn't pristine in its desertion – or perhaps it's simply the usual state of this place. The sons of the house hold no pleasant spot in my memory. Whenever they came to town, they'd strut about, leering at women and provoking any man foolish enough to look sideways at them. They knew not to try their luck with witches; Sten, the oldest, had thought on one occasion that I was a good target because I couldn't set him on fire. A knee to the balls showed him the error of his ways.

I'm outside again as soon as I can be because the empty building is oppressive; I take deep breaths. The walled herb garden has withered, all the plants frost-burned. Next, the sheds: dairy, forge, pigsty, cow byre, tack room, slaughterhouse. As ever, nothing. Then there's only the barn left – the sturdiest structure, in the best condition, the wooden planks of the walls close-fit to keep out the elements.

The only light is what pours in when I open the large doors. The corners are filled with sluggish shadows. I squint. Bales of hay, equipment, shelving, some tools, sacks of seed. My grip tightens on the baton as I take a few steps in, careful to never leave the sunshine. When I can't bear the ringing silence any longer, I call:

'Hello? It's Ellie Briar. Is anyone there? I've come to

help…' At least my voice doesn't shake. I listen hard. Feeling foolish, I add: 'It's just that the Axelssons and the Bergs are missing and I was hoping someone knew…'

No response. Why am I bothering? Talking to shades and inanimate objects. When I turn to leave, there's a scrape and a crash behind me. I swing around, baton raised, a snarl lifting my lip – to see a fox, mangy and old, tearing from the shadows, past me, out the door, finally disappearing around the corner of the byre. I'm unable to stop the profanities from pouring forth but I manage not to pee myself in fright. It's a close thing.

Hieronymus, chewing on the few surviving green plants, watches me curiously.

I make one last circuit, yet there's nothing and no one about – not even a sense of being watched. The empty farms, missing families and farmhands – between fifteen and thirty people at each – and animals. At one holding, it might be possible. At two, unlikely but still possible. But three in a row?

Back to Hieronymus. Back down that rutted and ruined track. Back to the wagon, re-hitching it swiftly as the urge to get away as quickly as possible pokes at me. Back onto the road, nervous as a cat, hyper-aware of my surroundings, of the sounds of the forest – all the sounds that weren't present at the Holms', or the Bergs' or the Axelssons'.

Searching through my memories as the landscape flashes by – or as much as possible at the draft horse's top speed – I try to find a similarity, an explanation in an old tale told to me by Maud or Hebe or Gisela or the cousins. I tell them aloud as the horse's ears twitch, as if he's listening carefully to pick up something I might miss or correct a point of fact.

Far away and just as long ago, a young woman came to a village inhabited by ghosts.

No. Not at all relevant. Silverton and its surrounds have no ghosts. So, another:

Far beyond the edge of the world, a witch once drowned a village.

Again, no. No mystery there as to what happened.

There once was a town called Iserthal, where the lake froze over during winter, and one day a girl crossing the ice saw something in its depths. Another girl. Black-haired, dark-eyed, red-lipped, a drowned corpse waiting for the thaw to release it. Except every day that girl appeared to get closer to the surface as if she managed somehow to rise. When at last spring came, an arm broke the water, and the damozel was freed.

I wrack my brains: what happened next? What?

An outrage against the damozel. Yet she was no mere mortal; a child of the under-earth, the Erl-king's get and not likely to forgive. One day, she disappeared and all Iserthal's children with her. All but two. And tales of plague maidens flourished: wherever a child went missing the maiden could be blamed – how many murderers got away with their crimes under cover of such a legend?

But plague maidens don't take adults or are not reputed to do so. Another then:

Here is a story I learned from an owl. A robber-bridegroom, an outcast lord, set up camp not so far from a village that had an unnaturally large number of beautiful young women. Every so often, he'd find himself in need of a new wife, so he'd pluck one away from her family. Sometimes wooing her and the family deciding it was worth the risk to get an excess daughter married off, but mostly the girls were snatched as they returned from doing their washing by the stream or picking mushrooms in the woods or any other activity that drew attention to them. And although there was a high mortality rate for such girls as married the robber-bridegroom, the villagers seemed to accept it, for weren't young women terribly clumsy and careless? And didn't they, as a matter of course, fall into wells and drown, trip into open fireplaces and burn, be smothered by feather pillows and heavy mattresses? Generally getting themselves into fatal trouble.

Until at last the remaining young women decided they were heartily sick of waiting for their time to come, so they banded together, marched on the robber-bridegroom's mansion and set it ablaze. There is, naturally, a cost that comes with slaughtering a lord, no matter how predatory he might be, thus the villagers, with much grumbling, upped sticks and abandoned their home lest their daughters' deed be found out, and soldiers be sent by the king (a cousin of the robber-bridegroom).

Amusing, but no.

In the long ago day, a wave of villages were emptied by plague...

No. If it was disease, there would be bodies at the farms. If they'd all been ill and packed up wagons to seek aid, they'd have gone to Silverton and I'd have met them on the road.

So long ago that only the very old remember, there was a town which appeared every hundred years. The rest of the time, 'twas as deserted as a brothel on a Sundee morn.

No. Obviously not.

Once there was a girl and once there was a woman as came to a bramble fence so high it caged an empty village. Nothing but her own blood would open a path.

No, no, no.

When memory was young, there came a lad from out of the forest.
For all intents and purposes, he appeared pleasant enough and
was welcomed into homes on the understanding he'd labour for
his bed and board. Which he did diligently until the full moon
struck (regular as clockwork), when he became something other
and set about annihilating the family that had welcomed him.

Again: such creatures, like trolls, are not tidy. They do not
hide what they've done, they don't clean kitchens and make
beds post-slaughter. There is a lack of caution in them. Besides,
it's years since anyone's been troubled by a man walking on two
legs, then on four, at least in these parts, and the troll pickets
remain intact and undisturbed.

None of the stories are right.

No answers to be found there.

I just need to get home as fast as I can.

Gisela will know what to do.

* * *

We pull up at the stables after dark, but the head groom rushes
out to meet me. I hand him the reins and raise a hand when he
tries to speak. I'm aware the account for stabling our mounts is
coming due and he's a stickler for reminding me about it even
though we've never been late.

'Sorry, Severin, I have to get home quickly. I'll settle with
you first thing in the morning.'

Stiff as a board, I set off at a jog, which is the best I can
manage after hours on that bench seat. The streetlamps light my
way. There's very little noise, even the air seems subdued. When
I burst through the front door of the Briar House and stumble

into the library, where my cousins are standing as if in the middle of something. Their expressions tell me that I might look a little deranged. More than a little.

'Where's Gisela? I need to speak to her—'

'—Ellie—'

'Eira, where is she!? There's something wrong at the outlier farms – people are missing – I need to tell Gisela.'

'Ellie—'

'Shut up, Nia! Is she with Beres?'

'Ellie,' and Audra's voice pulls me up short. Something in her tone, something more than the command I know our grandmother has drilled into her over the years. 'Gisela... Grandmamma is dead, Ellie.'

10

My grandmother never truly looked old, not until now, not until the life was gone from her. She's lying in the stately little parlour (barely used except for very important guests or those we wish to intimidate), with gold-flocked wallpaper and honey-wood furnishings, including three beautifully crafted blue velvet-covered chairs so spindly they don't look like they can bear their own weight. Here's where the population come to pay their respects during the day, filing through as the Briar Witch lies in state, touching her bare feet for a blessing as if she were a saint. Old and young, appearing at the door and offering trays and dishes of grief-food, baskets of eggs and bread, so the bereaved don't have to cook. We've done this duty for others so many times, yet never thought to receive it. And with Maud… there was no viewing.

Nothing but the best for our grandmother, so she's in the death-bed Kendrick & Daughters have made for her. The wood's black and shiny, with gold locks and hinges for when we close her in; inside's padded with bright red silk that only serves to make Gisela look bloodless. As if it's the last place she'll rest. Short wooden trestles keep the coffin up off the floor, as away from vermin and other nuisances as anything can ever be. And we have no pets in this house – no cats especially – because of Gisela's wariness about shifters.

The mirrors are draped and the curtains drawn; the only light is from the candles on the mantle. No fire – we need the room to remain cool – so I'm wrapped in a thick coat as I take my turn sitting vigil with Grandmamma. The others have dealt with the full force of this sudden passing. They were *here* and I was not. I hurt no less, I mourn no less, yet somehow not being around when Gisela died… not finding her, not trying – and failing – to save her, I have a certain distance from the situation.

Dressed in her purple Balefire Eve gown, hair carefully braided by Nia to cover the hole in Gisela's skull, our grandmother looks almost like an effigy. My delicate chair's uncomfortable, designed to keep a watcher awake. I hold my grandmother's hand – an uncomfortable contortion for us both, although far less so for her – and feel how cold death has made her, how thin her fingers are (so naked without the ruby ring!), how limp she is without the animating flame of a soul. I've helped prepare others' dead for burial most of my life, but it feels so strange to sense the enormous absence of *her*. A hole in her flesh, this room, this house, this town.

This world.

'I'll miss you terribly, Grandmamma.' My voice surprises me. I'd not intended to speak aloud. 'I mean, in the usual way of things I would miss you terribly, but I fear I will miss you even more in the days to come. Things… are not right. Beyond what happened with Deirdre…'

I tell her about the outlier farms because my cousins were dismissive; none of them are taking it seriously, or so it seemed. And admittedly, our own catastrophe feels so much larger than anything else that could possibly go wrong. Overwhelming. We've suffered a loss we didn't think would come for years.

We're now truly orphans, though no one's given voice to that hard truth yet. We're in a time of change the likes of which none of us has ever witnessed – not even our mothers, for Gisela was the Briar Witch before they were born; Gisela's the longest-serving Briar Witch. There's no one to guide our next steps, no older and wiser heads to advise us. No one to turn to when we doubt ourselves. Had matters run according to expectations, Gisela would have stepped aside in a few years for Audra but continued to oversee things. But this… this is anything but a smooth transition. I *know* there were things Gisela was putting off teaching my cousin, things for which she felt Audra wasn't mature enough. I know because I could become invisible around my grandmother and great-aunt as much as around anyone and they'd talk without noticing my presence. The lives of almost two thousand folk rest in our very untested hands.

Our bellwether is gone.

A tear burns its way down my cheek, which is when Audra appears.

In mourning black, Audra fair glows – a point of light in the night is she. Even with her hair hidden beneath a lace cap she's a glory to behold. She kneels in front of me, takes my free hand, and we stare at each other.

Finally, I blurt out, 'Will we manage?' I want to say, '*How* will we manage?'

She smiles, lopsided. 'Yes. We must.'

I think about last night, how she broke the news to me. 'Nia found her the day after you left. Gisela was well enough – better than that, you know her. She's so vital. *Was*.' How she swallowed, tried not to cry; how Nia hadn't bothered to be strong, had wept and howled and Eira had joined her. 'Grandmamma attended to Deirdre's funeral, sat with Beres that night. She seemed weary, but well. We all went about our duties next morning. When Gisela didn't appear for lunch, Nia went to her room.' Louder wailing from the sisters. 'We think she fainted and fell. Hit her head on the corner of the fireplace. By the time Nia found her, she was cold.'

The frail hand now in mine is colder still.

Outside the window I hear a thud and a thump, as if something's fallen from the roof or the eaves; too heavy for a squirrel, too high for a fox. Birds would be asleep, except for owls, of course, and I can't imagine one flying *into* the building, not with their clever senses. Then comes a giggle, high and almost hysterical. I stare at my cousin. The singing starts next.

A nursery rhyme, one we all heard in our cradles, will most likely hum to our own offspring.

Mamma will protect you.
Mamma she will sing.
Mamma will buy you a golden ring.

Mamma she will hug you.
Mamma she will sigh.
Mamma will protect you though in the ground you lie.

The voice is childish and not quite right, inhuman. I want to rise and draw back the curtains, look out – and not. Very much *not*. Audra's gone almost as deathly pale as Gisela, lips trembling.

'What is that?' I hiss – harsh because I'm as afraid as I've ever been.

'It's a—' She has to clear her throat. '*The* melyne.'

Not a ghost, no, because we don't have ghosts. But a revenant, a heavy dead thing. A lifeless child left too long out of its grave, unclaimed by a parent's naming. Deirdre's little lad.

'So soon? You said—'

The singing grows fainter as the source moves off.

'Beres agreed to name him, but when we went to collect the body it was gone.' Guilt's fleeting on her features. 'Every night since the day you left it's been singing at windows, running across roofs, banging on doors.'

'I didn't hear it last night.'

'It had already made its round by the time you arrived.'

I close my eyes. If history and lore are anything to go by, this weighty little haunt will only get louder and angrier and more insistent unless it's given a name. Unless we can find where it sleeps during the day, catch it, have Beres name it or find the father, appeal to his better nature or fear. If we don't put it to rest it will become violent and enraged – the amusement it's currently taking in being creepy won't last long. There are stories of folk dying from their attentions.

'We could try salt around the houses, but I doubt our stores would last.'

'And sleet and snow will melt it soon.' She sighs. 'A good thought though, Ellie, no one else has had any. Thank you.' She smiles and I feel the warmth of approval blossom in my chest. 'Tomorrow, we bury our grandmother. Then we'll turn our minds to the issue of the melyne.'

'I'll do some reading, see if I can find some stopgap measures.' Unlikely, but there are books in the basement that haven't been touched in long years. I can but hope for a miracle.

'Nia's tried to shoot it, but—'

'No! She shouldn't do that. It'll only enrage the thing. It's already dead.'

'Too fast anyway.' Audra rises, then kisses the top of my head. 'Are you alright for the night? Shall I sit with you?'

I squeeze her hand. 'No. Get some sleep. All will be well.'

She leans over and places a soft kiss on Gisela's cheek. My cousin whispers, *Sorry*, and I feel that she's speaking for all of us. That we all somehow failed Gisela Briar.

* * *

Dressed in our blackest gowns, hair covered by ebony veils, we carry the coffin from the Briar House and straight up Main Street, through the middle of town, directly to the cemetery on the northern boundary. We refuse offers of help from burly men who should know better, should know that this is our duty and we'll not shirk it. We don't bother with the church, she never had any time for the place. Townsfolk in mourning-wear line the streets, weeping, waving roses hastily made of black crepe. They fall in behind us as we pass, so it's a long, tiring processional tail that follows us.

The wrought-iron fence around the graveyard's relatively new. This bone orchard is newer too – the oldest one is deeper in the woods, full some while ago. We weave along paths between simple headstones and larger crypts. A grave, freshly dug, catches my attention. Earth still mounded to one side, the hole not yet filled but planks of old wood covering it. Deirdre's last resting place, held open for the body of her son. Soon we're amongst the large tombs for those who can afford better than a single stone memorial. The Briar Mausoleum, black quartz shot with silver, has our name across the lintel; it and the carvings of oak and rowan and birch leaves are fresh and stark as if carved yesterday. We rest the coffin on the cold ground. Behind us the population flows out and around, spreading like a delta, finding space amongst the headstones, the carvings, the yew trees with their tinkling copper and iron bells, and white briony, hemlock and blood-bell bushes. Not everyone can find a place, and there are those still outside the fence. It'll be hard for them to hear, even though the silence is astonishing, lying like a cloak.

I lean over to Audra and say like a good steward, 'Speak loudly.'

She nods, then conducts her first funeral – her most important one – as the Briar Witch. I expect my cousin's speech to be terribly long, recounting all of Gisela's achievements. I straighten my back, plant my feet, prepare for a marathon. Instead, Audra simply says, 'Gisela Briar was the best of us and we commit her to the earth she served.'

Somehow, it seems both enough and not. I notice mourners exchanging glances, uncertain, disappointed. Perhaps confused. But no one is going to argue with the new Briar Witch at the old one's interment. None of the cousins will question Audra in public. Anyway, *this* isn't the ceremony that really counts.

I unlock the beaten copper doors with a key from my chatelaine, push them open. Nia sends a ball of fire down the stairs ahead of us, deep into the earth. It ignites the torches lining the right wall, an impressive gesture. We lift the coffin once more and follow the light. Niches on the left side hold the remains of death-beds, of skeletons big and small, witches once, now dust.

In the centre of the lowest chamber is a broad bier where Maud's urn and most of her ashes rest. We heave Gisela up beside her sister. Audra offers one last wish: that our grandmother will go safely into the beyond, the other places, that one day she might return and tread the earth again, elsewhere and in new form, part of the cycle as the trees and plants and animals are, born, living, dying, resting, returning, repeating it over again. Her voice sounds strange down here in the earth and stone, sepulchral as if we're a little dead ourselves. No one makes to leave: we are all, I think, reluctant to lose this moment.

But in the end Audra turns and ascends, then Eira and Nia, and at last I've no choice but to join them or stay in the gloom. When we surface, we will be forever changed, made anew.

As I reach the top step, I'm concentrating on Audra – marvelling at her speed, how far she's gotten so quickly, now almost at the entrance to the cemetery as if she'd run when the rest of us were still climbing the stairs – and in that moment of inattention the toe of my shoe catches in the hem of my long skirts. It tears and I try to shake off the snare.

I lose my balance and fall – forwards, thankfully – and my hands hit the rough stone, tearing palms, jarring wrists. My head hits, too, though I've enough presence of mind to turn my face and save myself a broken nose. Skin comes away from my forehead and cheek; a warm flow of red starts immediately.

I'm suddenly so tired I don't want to get up. I want to stay there and sleep.

But Nia and Eira won't allow that. They pick me up, dust me off, begin mopping the crimson from me, tutting and shushing as they do, even Nia sounding genuinely concerned. No longer any sign of Audra, who's apparently too committed to her path back home to know what's happened to me.

'Who are *they*?' I ask, slapping away hands. 'There are so many!'

'What are you talking about, Ellie?' Nia's impatient.

'All of them, all the people.' I pause. 'Who are they? Where did they come from?'

Figures have joined the crowd who accompanied us, filling impossibly slim spaces left between parents and children, husbands and wives, siblings and lovers and friends. I recognise some but… they're faded somehow, washed out… ghostly. Yet they can't be ghosts because Silverton has no ghosts.

Then one wispy head turns towards me, another and another.

A whisper runs through the spectral group, lips moving though the sound seems out of time with the motions that make it, but I hear them clearly: *She can see us?*

A speaker?

She can see us?

A speaker!

She can see us!

And the pale tide rushes in my direction, shouting with voices no one else can hear. The first one hits me and it's like a bucket of ice water. The second and third are the same, but the fourth, fifth, sixth lose their effect just as I begin to lose count. They pass through me, meeting no resistance from my flesh, in one side and out the other, leaving only a strange kind of echo, a pulse, a vibration, which soon turns into shivers, then a juddering, then I cannot stop shaking and a fit takes me.

The darkness eats everything.

11

All's silent when I wake.

The mattress beneath me is comfortable, familiar, and there's the usual smell of potpourri – roses and violets and lavender – that I keep on the dresser. The forest-green hues of my bedchamber appear black in the night, but the light-coloured wood of the furniture looks like gold against it. The fire's gone out and the room is icy, unwelcoming. I shiver my way over to the hearth, cajole the tiny embers hiding there until they give a soft and unwilling *hiss*. Add kindling, which catches quickly, greedy for large fodder, branches and split logs. My cousins would simply have used their magic to do this, yet I take pride in the ritual and skill it takes to coax by hand. Soon the heat drives me back.

Only then do I straighten and look around properly.

There's no one else here. The space is empty. Properly empty. No sign of anything untoward.

No figures fogging the air, not quite touching the floor, staring at me like I'm the beginning and the ending of all things. Something the starving would devour. I think back to how often in my life I've felt invisible – *been* invisible – either through my own will or simple habit on the part of others. That it became an ache living inside me, a parasitic yearning, to be *seen*. So much so that the moment Dai Carabhille saw me – actually *saw* me – across the Balefire had been the most intoxicating of my life. The very first time I felt properly seen.

Right up, that is, until this morning at the funeral. Right up until those fresh seconds in the graveyard, with warm blood seeping from cuts on my forehead and cheek, the grazes on my hands (I touch them now – mostly healed by dint of a cousin's magic while I slept). I knew then what it was like to be seen, completely and utterly. Ravening faces, hollow eyes and open mouths – not a wish to bed me, however, but a need and a want for something else. Something other. Something I don't understand.

Hunger, first and foremost. Starvation. *Famishment*.

I'd prefer never to be seen again.

And yet…

What were they?

They looked like every description I've ever read of ghosts in all those books in the library, all those crowing accounts. The ghosts that Silverton does not have. The ghosts that Gilly Briar banished.

Now, staring into the mirror above the mantle, I trace the lines of my reflection, the smudges where Eira's healed the grazes.

If they are indeed *ghosts*, why would *I* be able to see them? Me? Powerless, ordinary Ellie Briar? The only explanation is madness. My mind stretched too far in the past days; too many losses, too great to bear. Perhaps whatever sent Aunt Hebe mad is simply something that resides in our blood and waits. Resurges at times of illness and stress, and the weak amongst us fall by the wayside. Gods know it had happened before Hebe, though never so spectacularly. Perhaps I'm that one in this generation – I'm offended, to be honest. Who'd have thought me so feeble?

I move over to the window where the moon's hanging low in the sky. I think of the melyne, listen hard for any trace of the lullaby or the giggling. Of thuds and thumps on roofs.

Nothing. Silverton lies below, glinting in the frost affixed to shingles and chimneys and eaves. No snow quite yet. Pretty enough to look like glass has been blown across our town, and only me awake to see it gleam and glitter in the moonlight.

Only me…

…and the foggy white figures waiting below in the front garden of the Briar House.

Drifting past the fallow flowerbeds, along the alleys formed by hedges that make it look like a maze; leaning against the trunks of trees, wrapping themselves over the stone sculptures of animals and people. Two are even skating – or pretending to – on the large pond in the far left corner. All terribly calm, nothing riotous about them. Some look more solid than others, some seem even at this distance to have a trace of colour about them. They might be mistaken for the living except I can see through their bodies to what's behind them – the faintest outline of whatever solid thing is there. Faint, but certain nevertheless.

My attention's drawn to a solitary figure on the path. A man, and tall, his face turned towards my window, hands in the pockets of a frockcoat long out of style. His demeanour one of patience. His features are quite clear – he does seem kind – and he smiles up at me. Should I feel more afraid than I do? Probably. Somehow, I'm not particularly fearful. The sensation is, in spite of everything, excitement.

* * *

Wrapped in a thick coat and fur-lined slippers, I sneak out as quietly as I can, half-hoping that the garden will be empty. But it's not. I remain on the veranda, just to be safe.

He's still in the same spot. Still smiling. Hands still in his pockets.

Up closer, he seems familiar. A man in his later years, the faded hues of him show white hair, the frockcoat green with silver embroidery, grey breeches, polished riding boots with a hint of red to them. Beardless, laugh lines around his mouth, thought lines across his high forehead. Not at all threatening. Nothing to be afraid of.

Except things that don't exist.

'Hello,' he says.

'Hello.'

'It's nice to meet you at last.'

'Is it?'

'I'm sorry about before – at the funeral. It's just been such a long time since anyone's *seen* us.' One hand leaves a pocket, gestures vaguely to the forms drifting around, drifting nearer. 'They – we – got a bit excited.'

'Will it happen again? I'd prefer not.' I do my own bit of gesturing, less vague, more pointed at the approaching figures.

'Oh, no. It won't. I've spoken with them. We'll all be very well-behaved, I promise.' He sounds sincere as he glances at his fellows with a sternness that makes them stop in their tracks, retreat.

'Who are you? I mean, I don't intend to be rude, but… *what* are you?'

'Sorry, so sorry. I haven't spoken to the living in so very long. I'm out of practice – manners and so forth.'

'Well, no one's *ever* spoken to the dead in Silverton, thus we are equally adrift. I'm Ellie. Ellie Briar, a – a daughter of the house.'

'Oh, I know! I'm Sandor. Sandor Briar – a grandfather, I suspect, some ways back.' He sweeps into a deep bow, then gives a self-deprecating grin as he straightens.

I blink, touch the scar on my wrist to make sure I'm awake. 'Sandor Briar?' *Don't repeat things, Ellie.*

'Briar's what we called ourselves when we arrived here, and I was Briar longer than I was ever the surname I was born with.'

I recall the pen and ink drawings in our history books, the family tree, its branches hung with witches, and the woodcut portrait in the library. Hard to really show a fine likeness with such a blunt tool, but whoever made that did a good job. Sandor was younger when that was made, middle-aged perhaps, but there's enough of a resemblance to the man – spectre – standing before me. 'And you're a ghost?'

'So it would seem. Either that or a very old man indeed.'

'There are no ghosts in Silverton,' I point out and his face undergoes several types of grief.

'That was Gilly, my Gilly-girl. Trying to fix things…' He sighs and even though there's no breath in his lungs the misty substance of him wavers as if shifted by a breeze. So strange.

'Am I mad? Am I really seeing you?' Before I realise it, I'm down the steps, my fingers poking his chest. They meet no resistance. It's like pushing into very loosely packed snow, or densely packed fog. This close I can make out the embroidery on his collar: small books and fountain pens, joined by thorny vines.

'Not mad.' He shakes his head. 'And I'm sorry for that – it might have been easier, yes? But you're quite sane, Ellie

Briar, and I have so much to tell you…' His tone's excited and anxious and energetic.

I can't take him into the house. The other ghosts have gathered again, *clumping* at a respectful distance, trying to appear as if they're not listening. But I don't want to be seen out in the garden in the wee hours, apparently talking to myself. My name will be mentioned in the same breath as poor Aunt Hebe's.

'The priest's house is empty. We can talk in there. This lot, however' – I gesture at our audience – 'can't come in. Too crowded.' I think, briefly, that it might be nice for them to be inside, perhaps in the church, then I realise they've been roaming Silverton for who-knows-how-long, in and out of everywhere without our knowledge. They don't need protection from the elements. They'll go where they wish. But I draw the line at having them crammed into the rectory's parlour, pressing in like a pale avalanche to suffocate me.

* * *

The place is smaller than I remember, having not set foot in here forever – to the best of my knowledge none of us have. I must have been seven the last time, all of us piling in to stare at what Audra had done. To see our grandfather in what had clearly *not* been a peaceful demise. I wonder if Maud came back, again and again, finding quiet time to sit here and recall what she never had but always wanted?

A nice home, to be sure, well maintained when we had an incumbent god-hound. A-framed, the bedroom in the loft, the ground floor housing a small parlour, a larger library (for books on theology and registers of births, deaths and marriages – the most recent kept in the Briar House), a kitchen, and washroom.

And a discreet back door for those times Gisela came to visit, doing her best not to draw attention – not for her own reputation but to spare Tobias' blushes, his discomfort at his enjoyment of the sins of the flesh. Not all god-hounds share this prudishness, but Tobias seemed to be possessed of enough for several priests.

Now, the place is just as Tobias left it, though filled with dust and the smell of neglect. We use the library because there's a hearth there, none in the parlour. I lay a fire because it's so terribly cold and no one should notice smoke coming from the chimney at this hour. Sandor sits on a wooden chair that would be uncomfortable if he weren't simply floating an inch above it. It's more for the *form* of sitting, I think, the habit. The best way to tell a story. When the flames are burning brightly, the spectre holds out his hands as if they might warm him – how fascinating, the marks that living leaves long after death.

I settle into the depths of the old brown leather chair to which Grandfather Tobias was partial. His shape's still hollowed in the padding and I feel small again. He hated us sitting on it, but we'd sneak in when he was out; one of us on lookout, the others taking turns to climb onto that *throne* he'd claimed for himself. We'd impersonate him too, and Eira was always the best at mimicking his pompous tone, the self-righteous pronouncements – *Ungodly girls will burn! You lack, all of you, humility! Hoydens! Light-skirts! Guttersnipes!* – sending us into gales of hysterical laughter. I shake my head a little at the memory, then focus on Sandor the spirit, this purported ever-so-great-grandfather.

'You have stories, don't you?' he begins. 'Of us? Your forebears?'

I nod. 'Of course. You know we do – you've been listening in for almost three centuries!'

109

'Not all the time! Gods, that would be unbearable. Sometimes we're here, aware, other times… it's like sleep, I suppose? A hibernation? But we're tethered, we cannot move on. Stuck. We always "wake" after a while.'

'Oh.' A relief, of sorts, that they don't – can't – know *everything*. 'Tales, then. Gilly and Sandor Briar who found this place and saved it, and in doing so saved the Briars. Gave us a safe haven.'

'Not everyone saw us that way. The town was in a parlous state when we arrived, but the remnants of the founding family were proud and stiff-necked.'

'The Brothers Bear?'

His smile is brief and cold. 'Unhappy to accept help from anyone, let alone vagabonds like us. Even if it meant their little town died a grim death, because it would be an admission that, as leaders, they'd failed. Luckily, other folk were less committed to such an end, and we were allowed to help. It gave us good standing.'

'And we've done our best to follow that example.' Why do I sound defensive?

Sandor smiles, takes an unexpected tangent: 'Have you heard of Hilla?'

'Hilla and her red dress, dancing at her husband's funeral,' I say. 'Heedless Hilla who brought his ghost back into their home until he drove her mad.'

Sandor frowns. 'No. It wasn't like that.'

'Oh. That's what my grandmother told me when I was a child…'

'Hilla wore her red dress, certainly. And her husband was a dreadful man, but he didn't rise – there are myriad reasons why phantoms fail to rest, but he had none of them. Hilla, however, was a lightning rod for ghosts. She was a speaker for the dead.'

'I've never heard the term.' Until the funeral. Until those voices whisper-shouting *A speaker!*

Sandor sits forward. 'She could see them from her cradle, I think; we would watch her eyes move beyond us, listen to her laugh at things we couldn't see.'

'So Hilla was your—'

'—daughter. Gilly's and my oldest.' He smiles sadly. 'She found her calling in helping them. When spirits stay behind, it's often because there's something they've not done in life – made proper amends, told someone they were loved, passed on a secret... generally an omission of some kind.' A sort of a shrug. 'Or worse, something they *have* done in life.'

'And she wore red so they'd see her.'

'It's like a beacon...'

'But why me—'

'The blood. On your forehead when you fell. I can't tell you why, but I think the blow knocked something loose or made a connection, and you saw what no one else has in hundreds of years. And the blood...' He draws out the word. 'We all know the lore, we've carried such hope for so long... and when you stared directly at us, *saw* us... well, we knew.'

'So. Hilla, in her bright crimson dress...'

'...listened to their woes and helped with the things they'd left undone in life. She took apologies to those they'd wronged, told impoverished heirs where lost treasure might be found, brought confessions of ill-deeds to light and ensured any innocents unjustly accused were set free. The dead asked these things, the worst of them and the best, for it was the only way they would find peace.'

He's quiet for so long I feel the need to prompt him: 'Then, what happened? Sandor? There's no record of this, there are no tales of Hilla Briar doing such things. She's a cautionary tale about not drawing attention! No mention of her as a speaker for the dead, nothing about what made Gilly "exile" the ghosts.'

He rubs his hands over his face, again that habit of life which produces no effect now, no scratch of stubble or whisper of movement through the air. 'Gilly, my Gilly-girl. She did not like what our daughter was doing. You must understand that Gilly… she was afraid it was making Hilla strange. That she would lose her connection to reality.' He clears his throat. 'Gilly thought she was saving Hilla. And make no mistake, our eldest daughter had become fey and ungrounded, obsessed with the dead and their needs, forgetful of the living. And Gilly, thinking to do good, did a great and terrible thing instead.' He sighs.

'What *did* she do?' I can guess, though.

'Gilly thought she had banished the ghosts, made it so they could never again enter Silverton. But—'

'—but she just made them invisible. To everyone. Even Hilla?'

'Even Hilla. And my daughter, who'd had such a sense of purpose her whole life lost her reason entirely, the guyline that kept her tethered to us and the world. She'd wander the forest graveyard calling for them, singing to spectres she could no longer see. Forgetting to come home so that at the end of every day I would go and find her, bring her back, feed her dinner as if she were still a child. And then one day when I sought her… she no longer breathed.'

'Oh, Sandor.' His pain appears fresh even after all this time. 'Did you find Hilla when *you* died? Was she waiting?' And I wonder about Deirdre. I wonder about Gisela and I want to ask if they're around, out there somewhere in the cold night air, but Sandor's in the middle of a tale I need to know. Plenty of time to ask about my own dead.

He shakes his head. 'No. No sign of my dear daughter. No sign of Gilly amongst the departed either. No other Briars over the years, in fact, or none I've seen. They seem to have nothing to keep them from eternal rest.' He grins bitterly.

'And what do you want from me?'

'Be our speaker, Ellie. Make our final peace for us. Let us sleep forever. If you can, find a way to undo Gilly's mistake.'

And this is enormous. Although perhaps I shouldn't be surprised. 'Oh,' I say. 'Oh.'

'We have no hope but you, Ellie Briar.' He smiles again. 'And you'll never stop seeing us. Not a threat, never a threat, but merely an observation.'

And abruptly he looks tired, this grandsire of mine.

I've got so many questions, but through the gap in the curtains is creeping a pale ray of dawn. Outside, the sky will be lightening. I should return to my bed before someone discovers me missing, raises the alarm. I tell him this. I tell him I'll bring my answer when I've had time to consider all he's told me. He promises that all the ghosts will stay out of sight – mine – until I render my judgment.

As I leave Tobias's old abode, having made sure the fire was out, I think about my cousins. What would happen if I told them that I – empty Ellie Briar, no-magic nelly that I am – can see ghosts. Silverton's non-existent ghosts. I think of Maud – what if I could tell her that, after all the bloodletting

113

she visited upon me, it only took a bump to the head, a scratch. But my cousins…

No. Not yet. Not until I can prove my claim. Not until I can somehow show that I'm not insane, that said bump to the head hasn't sent me bonkers, nor grief driven me mad. No. I'll bide my time, learn what I can before I make any pronouncements or confessions.

Besides, I can't deny there's a part of me that wants to keep this just to myself for however long I can. This secret magic of my own, all mine, at last. I just want to enjoy it for a while.

12

'I'm sorry, Ellie.' Audra does indeed sound sorry as she twists her shining hair into a tight bun and stuffs it beneath a knitted black cap, checks her reflection in the entry-hall mirror as if someone's going to see her. 'But you know you can't come.'

I know no such thing. Eira glances away, paying particular attention to her shoelaces. Nia wears a smug look, buttoning her coat. This task is done so rarely. None of us were born when it was last performed, and it wasn't done for our mothers or Great-Aunt Maud. It's written down (in general in our history books; in particular in the grimoires), the ceremony, and mentions absolutely nothing about non-magical Briars. The fact that there never have been any before me is neither here nor there.

What I do know is that there are no rules beyond secrecy, to keep this ritual from the common folk. My cousins all know it too. The first burial is for the town, for the sake of form. This second is for the safety of Silverton and beyond, part of our covenant with the church, and keeping this secret is what the Briars – *all* of us – are charged to do.

And I also *know* that they've already performed one ceremony *without* me. When I was visiting the outliers, when Gisela died so suddenly, they didn't wait for my return to anoint Audra, even though that was my duty as steward. Nia took the pigeon's egg ruby ring from Gisela's hand, Eira putting it on Audra's finger as she swore the oath to defend our family, our kind, and the people under our protection. Swore on her own life to ensure safety and harmony for Silverton, and a future for the Briars, even if it cost her everything. Swore that the Briars would continue.

'But we didn't know when you'd return…' they'd said, as if it couldn't have waited. Indeed, I was two days early due to not having to attend to three families. Waiting would not have killed them.

Yet I *am* a Briar.

Though not a witch, I *am* a speaker for the dead, apparently, but who knows what that really means? There's a moment when I consider telling them as they prepare to depart. *Look! I'm different now. I'm just as strange as you! I belong.* As if that could wash away years of mockery, of difference, of otherness.

Yet I can't prove it. There are too many ifs, howevers and variables, too much to explain and no evidence whatsoever to support my claims. Just me insisting I can see ghosts and that oh, yes, I've been chatting with the spirit of our ever-so-great-grandsire. What tales he has to tell! That would go splendidly. Audra and Eira with their gentle pity and Nia delighted that I've distinguished my ordinariness by adding a streak of insanity.

This morning I returned to my usual duties (checking with the clerks at the townhall, delivering approved applications for building permits, refusals for others, pending queries for others still), keen to show that everything is as it should be. As it *will* be with our new Briar Witch and her steward running things.

Normal. Regular. The ghosts, true to Sandor's word, did not come near me, but I've spent the day spotting them from the corner of my eye. Peeking around corners, over high hedges, out from windows of houses where perhaps they once lived. All watching me with curiosity and hope, or maybe simple suspicion. As if I might decide to let them down.

So, tonight I say nothing, just lower my lashes and my head, as if I'm obedient. Say 'I understand' and help my cousins tuck away strands of bright hair, wrap scarves around necks, making sure they've got the right ingredients for their little spells, that the tiny knives they use to pay the red price are very sharp and clean. I survey all three in their black trews and jackets, caps, gloves. Their boots are spelled to ensure they make no sound, their attire similarly treated so the fabric doesn't whisper of their presence and give them away, and to make them nigh on impossible to see. They can move through the night, silent and shifty as cats. I, of course, can't treat my clothing this way – don't think I haven't tried but enchantment simply resists me, runs off like water on a duck's back. My cousins could do it on my behalf but won't. *Simply cannot.*

No matter.

They can struggle with their burden.

I have my own ways and means.

'We'll need the key, Ellie.' Audra waits while I unhook it from the chatelaine, forcing my movements to show no sign of reluctance.

'I understand,' I repeat. 'Gods' speed this night.'

* * *

When they're gone, slipping out the kitchen door and through the secret back gate in the high hedge-fence, I run up to Gisela's suite.

117

Whispering an apology, I open the door and step inside. Audra hasn't taken possession yet, so everything is as our grandmother left it. A red-curtained four-poster bed, walk-in wardrobe, small private washroom, a dressing table with a gold filigree mirror, and a sitting area in a corner by one of the windows furnished with a comfortable chair, a tiny coffee table inlaid with mother-of-pearl, and two low bookshelves (overflowing with fairy tales, starter spell books and more advanced, and some vaguely pornographic romances). The thick carpets look like flower meadows.

Just in case, I scan for my grandmother's shade, as if she's about to chide me. Before we parted Sandor had said that needful ghosts show themselves when they're ready. When they understand what's happened, or they're tired of waiting. Gisela might not be here yet, and she might never be – he also said that sometimes the dead go straight to their rest. She might be floating around somewhere, as yet unwilling to be seen. She might be enjoying her freedom from the importuning of all the folk whose lives have depended on her for so long. And Sandor couldn't – wouldn't – tell me if he'd seen her. Said it would be breaking the rules; that ghosts can't tell each other's secrets and apparently that includes letting anyone know they exist before they've chosen to reveal themselves to the living. Part of me wonders if Sandor is making some of these rules up.

But there's no sign of my grandmother as I go to her walk-in wardrobe (keeping my eyes from the hearthstone where she hit her head). Her clothes and the scent of roses remain. I quickly find what I'm looking for: black trousers, a shirt and coat, boots I know will almost fit me, and a soft woollen cap. While my cousins are making their way to the graveyard and wrestling a corpse from her coffin, I'm changing in a leisurely fashion. Gisela wore this outfit frequently, and it's ensorcelled just as theirs are. There's no good reason for the magic to have faded just because Gisela's gone. If magic died with witches then bridges would fall, buildings would disappear, the world would stop spinning – although there are tales of those who knitted such destructions into their spells.

There was Blodwen, who'd bargained to restore a woman's beauty, only to be betrayed and burnt. She mustn't have trusted that woman, though, for she had her revenge. The enchantment died with her, leaving the traitorous client as she'd been before.

Another witch, having given a man a cure and a promise of three fine sons, was then reported to the god-hounds by that self-same man in order to avoid paying her fee. The woman was drowned, and when the man's wife gave birth it was to a litter of wolf-cubs that promptly devoured their father.

I'm just borrowing what's been left behind.

* * *

Over there, not too far off, is a gate. It's tall and heavy, made of wood and banded with rusted iron, hinged into the rocks of the mountain pass. It opens and closes with surprising ease for those humans who travel back and forth between these lands and the Darklands. For the Leech Lords, however, the way is barred. They may stand on the other side of the border, looking through to the road to Silverton and beyond, yet never cross.

But here's the more important spot, hidden from the road and the gate: here the trees grow oh-so-very close together, with little spells to send a traveller's attention astray, to turn them around, lose themselves. Here's where only a Briar knows to tread, the pattern beneath the trunks that brings one into the circle. Only a Briar could guide a stranger in.

I climb one of the trees that surrounds the clearing, an evergreen with all its leaves still intact for good cover, and settle into the crook of a sturdy branch. It seems to take an awfully long time before my cousins arrive with their precious burden, and I'm shivering with cold by then. A stretcher between Nia and Eira, Audra walking ahead, a ball of light floating in front of her to show the way. I wonder how long she waited before setting that forth – carrying Gisela through the town with only the last of the month's moon to guide them. A little malicious glee warms me. Serves them right for excluding me. Maybe they'll remember it next time. And then *I* remember that next time means another death – Audra's – and I'm not interested in losing more of my family. The thought sobers me, pushing the malice away, or maybe just down under a rock for a while.

Just outside the stone circle, my cousins place the stretcher on the ground, then lift Gisela, carry her to the altar in the centre (where I once lay, hoping for the magic to find me). Sweat glistens on Nia's and Eira's brows while Audra remains decidedly unsweaty. She twitches a finger and the ball of light rises above her head, illuminating the whole clearing. We're far up in the higher ground, not so far from where we found Deirdre that awful night; too far to be seen from town, so close to the border with the Darklands.

Twelve monoliths of stone, between five and seven feet tall, roughly equidistant.

My cousins stand around Gisela's body, the points of a triangle. Audra holds a book – our grandmother's grimoire with its blue and silver cover – opens it, clears her throat. She begins to speak a spell, a hymn in the language of witches (which I understand but cannot use), and the others intone a refrain, arms raised above their heads. The book now floats in front of Audra as if on an invisible lectern. Everything blends into a single song, harmonious, and then the standing stones begin to move.

Shuddering, they whirl on the spot, then circle the clearing; a grinding sound fills the air as if a giant mortar and pestle are in use.

Maud told me about this a long time ago (after that abortive final attempt to make me *witch*). Took me walking up here and described her own mother's second burial, the most important one. When I asked Gisela later, she was angry until her sister said I needed to know. That of all of the grandchildren I was the most likely to keep a secret because I was the most desperate to be taken seriously. It hurt because she was right.

At this moment, however, I'm so busy watching those menhirs dance that I almost tip from the tree with dizziness. I have to grip hard at my perch, close my eyes until the world stops spinning, and I don't open them again until the grinding stops. Everything is still and it might be that nothing happened, except Gisela's body is gone, the altar bare.

I count the standing stones, find the twelve have become thirteen.

Only the Briar Witches – as opposed to witches who happen to be Briars – earn a place here. A new guardian between us and the Darklands, a new guardian to hold back the Leech Lords. And no one but us to know because who might try to destroy this magical protection if they knew its true nature? Even though there are wards around this clearing that will send the unwary – the non-Briar – astray, defend against the ill-intentioned, what if a greater, darker power were to find it?

The ball of light shrinks and lowers, waits in front of Audra like a pet. The book's in her hands again. Nia and Eira look exhausted, as does Audra, who's actually broken a sweat. Nia rolls up the stretcher and hefts it onto her shoulder, careful to avoid the bow and quiver. Without a word, the trio turn and begin to traipse back home. They'll be faster this time, without the weight of Grandmamma, but they're also tired which gives me a little extra advantage. I shinny down the trunk of the tree and set off at a jog, taking different paths.

* * *

By the time they return, I'm in front of the fire in the library. I've only been home long enough to change my clothes, hide Gisela's under my bed, then settle rather breathlessly into a seat, book on my lap; and it's only then that the adrenaline subsides enough for me to feel the sting of a cut on my cheek where a whipping branch has scratched. I pull my hair forward to cover it. Eira enters first, eyes fastening on my face. The others are thumping around in the entrance, removing boots. She crosses the room quickly, reaching out so lightning fast I think she's going to slap me. Instead, her fingers come away clutching evergreen leaves. She stuffs the evidence into her pocket, then says loudly, 'You shouldn't have stayed up so late, Ellie.'

My voice is steady as I reply: 'I wanted to know you were all safely home.'

By the time Audra and Nia appear, there's no sign of any defiance on my part. Audra smiles at me – what an obedient girl I am! I rise, pour four glasses of spring-cherry whiskey, handing them around as I ask all the right questions about their endeavours. Audra answers a little giddily, Nia chiming in to make sure I know what I missed; Eira remains silent, keeping her eyes on the tips of her own stockinged feet. I nod as if fascinated.

Apparently my performance is convincing.

'Ellie, do you think you can hold the fort? For a week or less?' Audra's change of topic wrongfoots me but I bridle at the tone. As if I'm a child of questionable abilities about to be given a sop task.

'Of course, but why?'

'I've been thinking about the outliers. I know you think we didn't take you seriously, but that's not it at all. We' – she shakes her head – '*I* needed to get tonight out of the way. To know we'd done everything for Gisela. But it's important for someone to check on the holdings, make sure everything's as it should be.'

'I can go,' pipes Nia.

'Or me.' Eira tears her attention away from her toes.

Audra shakes her head. 'It needs to be me. I'm the new Briar Witch – the outliers need to know they're not forgotten. That they matter to us.' The other two protest that she's needed here. 'Now's the perfect time. I'm not yet totally overwhelmed by work. Between the three of you, everything will be done that needs to be.'

There's no use arguing with her when she's got an idea like this, so I simply suggest, 'Will you take someone with you? A couple of Nia's biggest vigilants?'

'Yes,' says Nia. 'I'll—'

'—I'll travel faster on my own – just a horse, no wagon to drag behind. I *can* look after myself, Ellie.' She smiles to take the heat off the words, the implication that *I* couldn't. 'And as

I said, I'll be a week or less. The only thing that I'll miss is the monthly assembly. You can run that, yes?'

'Of course, Audra. It's what I've been trained to do.' *Have been doing for six months while you've been playing princess*. That thought hits out of the blue, the bitterness of it shocking me. 'And the farmers will be delighted to see you've made the effort. It'll give them confidence in you.' It doesn't hurt to remind her that she's got responsibilities outside town – and even though this is not a democracy, Gisela was always careful to keep her people contented – it made them more willing to obey, less likely to question. 'But what about the melyne?'

She bites her lip, contemplating; fidgets with the pigeon's egg ruby ring as if it feels too heavy. She'd forgotten it. 'What do *you* suggest?'

'Well,' I pause as if I haven't given it any thought until this very moment. 'I think we should search the graveyards first of all – every tomb, every crack in a headstone, every split in a tree trunk. The one in town and then the old forest one, if need be. If we find the creature, we take it to Beres for naming. Nia should lead the search – use the vigilants and any volunteers you can recruit. The thing's still quite new, and I think we have time before it gets angry, at least that's what my reading tells me.' I shake the book in my lap – *Murcianus' Guide to the Mystical and Murderous* – to show them I've been working while they've been away. I don't meet Eira's eye. 'It's a good start.'

Audra nods, as if it's precisely what she herself thought. She looks at Nia and Eira. 'See? Our Ellie has it well in hand. I'll be back before you miss me.'

When Nia and Audra go up to bed, Eira waits behind. We

sit quietly for a while, the silence stretching as I refuse to speak first. At last she rises and comes over and stuffs the evergreen leaves into my palm. 'Be careful, Ellie. Just... be careful.'

She lifts the fall of my hair away, touches my cheek, and concentrates. I feel the scratch healing, imagine her putting tiny invisible stitches in so no one will see the scrape and ask about it. Then her thumb smooths the skin and I know it'll be flawless, that her skills have grown since she repaired my wrist so long ago. And I'm spared an argument only because the others are home, and Eira doesn't want to be overheard. After she's gone, I throw the greenery on the fire, watch it curl and smoke. I know what answer I'll give Sandor.

13

The tithe-barns – there are ten, traditionally designed for the clergy to collect and store their share of the harvest but repurposed by the Briars to collect and store *our* share of the harvest for communal distribution in wintertide if required, any surplus being sold at the first spring market – are hives of activity. Shelving almost to the vaulted ceilings, thatched roofs checked every few months to ensure there's no chance of leakage, of spoiling the stocks. Each has a cellar for salted meats and fish, preserves, alcohol, cheeses, fruitcakes and the like. The clerks, twenty in all, are moving up and down the rows in pairs, one counting, one scribing, all feverish to finish the stocktake in the last barn by the end of the day.

They'll probably do it too – Maud inculcated a sense of fear into them that's powered their productivity long after her death. I thought, perhaps, when I took over as steward, they might slack off, but no. Either their own sense of pride in a job well done is too strong, or they learned not to try and trick me when I was Maud's offsider. They discovered quickly that I picked up mistakes as well as she did and demanded correction at a faster rate. They were never going to fear me for being a witch, but I'll settle for being regarded as even pickier than my great-aunt, and I spent hours practising her disapproving face in the mirror.

I've been sitting at the custodian's little desk near the front entrance, signing off on tallies all morning, but here's the first discrepancy. I feel my expression begin to curdle and Dónal, who's bringing me the completed tally sheets, stills.

'What is it, Steward Briar?' His tone's thin, as snippy as he's game to get. He was Maud's chief clerk (her third and last) and the one to whom she turned for explanations and amendments. I think he loved her – despite having interests elsewhere – but she never reciprocated. A perfect relationship, really; no chance of disappointing reality, one party always trying to impress the other.

'Last count, we had thirty bottles of that winter-plum brandy in the cellars.'

He puts a finger on the page in front of me, says, '*There*.'

'But not *here*,' I reply. 'Not the imported one – now there are only twenty-six and no record of where they've gone or who's taken them.'

'Oh.' Dónal purses his lips, goes a little pale. We both know none of the Briars would have taken them – they're far too expensive and were purchased as an investment, not for gracing the table, the glass bottles themselves worth a fortune, laced with gold and silver designs of mermaids and ships. Very distinctive. Which means either a miscalculation or theft. Either is possible, but the second is more likely, given the efficiency of this particular crew. So, theft from outside seems the logical explanation.

'Organise a recount, please. If they can't be located then I expect you to begin making enquiries about where they might have gone. Check which vigilants have been rostered on the tithe-barns. Alek Zabel's the clerk who signed off on the last stock count three months ago.' I'm aware of Zabel, somewhere down the far end of an aisle. Instead I smile at Dónal just as Maud used to when she was saying something terrible. 'No direct accusations; see what the other clerks know, see if his family have been spending more than is their habit. Let me know what you find out, and we'll proceed from there. Who knows? There might be a good reason for it.'

A curt nod. 'There's no good reason for theft, miss.'

'Ah, Dónal. Hunger and shame are always a good start. Too proud to ask for help. We'll find out soon enough.' He still looks stiff and unforgiving; he and Maud had that in common. 'Thank you, Dónal. I'll leave you to it.'

By rights, I should stay, but the last of the signing sheets will wait until tomorrow, especially now that I've given Dónal a mystery to chew on. He's subtle; it might take him a few days to dig up the truth, but I've no doubt he'll get to it. The respite gives me a chance to begin my new and secret appointment – if only I can get some time alone.

Audra left at dawn, on the fleetest horse Severin could produce, still refusing any accompaniment despite Eira's nagging. Nia went off with some of the vigilants to search the cemetery for the melyne. Eira (grumbling) went to the infirmary as she does every day, but as I exit the tithe-barn I find her pacing up the street towards me with her usual determined gait. And she's seen me, is waving at me, so it's too late to try and hide. Besides, I know what's coming.

'Ellie.' She stops in front of me.

'Hello, Eira. Are you hungry? The coffeehouse has those wonderful iced buns.'

'Where were you last night?' Hands on her hips, eyebrows drawn together in a frown, not to be distracted by the mention of buns.

'Why, Eira Briar, you know very well I was at home, waiting obediently for my beloved cousins to return.' A stilted smile props up my lips. I'd promised myself I wouldn't get annoyed.

'Ellie—'

'Eira.'

'Ellie—'

'Eira.'

She's going red in the face.

'Ellie, Audra—'

'—had no reason to leave me behind. I had every right to be there. I've as much Briar blood as the rest of you, even if no magic. Audra was being – mean.' And now I sound childish. I should have said 'petty' – that's a word for a grownup complaint. *Mean* sounds like I've had a toy denied me. 'Oh, c'mon, Eira. I – I just wanted to see Gisela one last time. There was no harm done. I broke no rule.'

'No, but you disobeyed the Briar Witch. And didn't you swear to obey her?'

'Technically, no. Because you all held that ceremony without me as well. You might remind her, when she returns, that she failed to take *my* oath.' I pout. 'I promised Gisela I'd support Audra, yes. But, Eira, the Briar Witch must act in the interests of Silverton and our family – forbidding me from going to the stone circle was neither of those things.' I pause. 'It was *petty*.'

Eira's expression softens. She touches my face. 'Just be careful. Audra... Audra can get funny if she's defied. Sometimes, she'll stay quiet, patient, then make a point later when it will have the most impact.' She licks her lips. 'Other times… remember Grandfather Tobias? How quick? How decisive?'

I nod, consider Maud's dislike of Audra, even before Audra did what she did. How Maud would mutter that Audra took too much for granted. 'But part of the steward's job is to speak truth. If the Briar Witch isn't making her best decisions, then the steward needs to speak up. It's what Maud always did whether Gisela liked it or not, for as long as she had a voice.'

'It'll be a while before Audra relaxes into her role, Ellie. Before she trusts us to do our duties the way Gisela trusted us. Before she feels secure – it's awful hard to be thrown into such a position. Maud always acted as if she might be gone in a second, so she taught you everything, made you learn by doing. Gisela… Gisela thought she always had more time, so she put things off with Audra.' My cousin smiles. 'But Audra will settle, just be patient. All I'm saying is: be careful, alright?'

I wrap my arms around her because some human contact will help convince her that I've forgiven the slight. And because some human contact might convince me to do so. 'I promise.'

* * *

I take a deep breath before pushing into the papermill shop, more nervous than I want to be and irritated at myself for it. Briefly I regret coming. Edgar will have similar things in his wagon, yet not so lovely; besides he's not around at the moment and this can't wait. But the room's empty however, the bell above the door ringing gently. Scanning the shelves, it doesn't take long: as soon as my eyes rest upon it, I know it's right. A red leather-bound book, some gold detailing on the spine and front, a design of bones and flowers intertwined. And beneath the glass of a display cabinet are a pen of pewter, engraved to look like vines and leaves, and a matching inkpot. When I spoke to Sandor this morning, in the brief moments I had alone between Audra's departure and Nia shouting that I should hurry and come for breakfast, he said I'd need such a book – a register. Even though I have such things spare at home, for this I want something beautiful and new. Something purpose-specific. Something special. *Mine.*

A new task.

A new speaker.

New implements.

There's a creak and the workshop door opens. I barely look up. The voice that had once kept me entranced doesn't stir the butterflies in my stomach but rather stills them.

'Good morrow, Ellie,' says Dai, wiping his hands meticulously on a fine blue kerchief, as if he's just come in from dirty work. He smiles. Once it would've made my heart leap, but there's only a cold and steady beat.

'I'll take the red journal and this pen and inkpot, please.' I point to my choices, then pull the small black velvet purse from my pocket and count out the silver pieces. Leave them on my side of the counter so he must reach for them. When he begins to pull lengths of pale yellow tissue paper I tell him not to bother. He watches in surprise as I slide the purchases into my satchel. 'Thank you.'

I'm out the door and closing it on his farewell. He's used to me taking my time about decisions, general queries about anything I could make up out of thin air just to have an excuse to talk to him. This brisk departure must have been a shock. Or perhaps he didn't even notice a change.

Funny, that Gisela's demise should have given me the opportunity to pursue Dai. And yet in the days since Deirdre's death, since my trip to the outliers, since Gisela's funerals, he's barely been in my thoughts. And only then to consider that he's not come anywhere near me even to ask if I am well after my grandmother's death. I can't recall seeing him at her first funeral, even in the crowds who lined the streets watching the cortege. I was so intensely alive to him before – now there's nothing.

I feel so much lighter.

* * *

Sandor, standing in front of the unlit library hearth, hands clasped behind his back, smiles when I arrive at the priest's house and it's the sweetest expression. I wonder what life might have been like for us if he'd been the grandfather we'd grown up with rather than Tobias and all his resentments.

'Oh. I didn't think to buy ink. I'm a fool.'

'There's a bottle on the desk.' He points to a small glass vessel, its contents long dried-up.

I shrug off the satchel. 'I'll go to the house—'

'There's really no need. We… we need a particular mix, my dear. I should have told you before, but I didn't want to spook you.'

I lift a brow. 'What is it?'

He looks apologetic, sincerely so. 'You – remember at the graveyard, how agitated we all became?'

'Because I could see you?'

'Yes, and because of the blood.' He gestures to himself. 'You may have noticed that some of us seem more solid than others? Easier to see, our lineaments more finely rendered.'

'I thought I'd imagined it.'

132

'The blood gives us a little more presence, shall we say? We're not leeches, I hasten to add, we cannot and do not drain the living, but a little – lick – like we took at the churchyard… well, you understand.'

'Are you saying ghosts need to *lick* me?' I can't keep the outrage out of my voice.

'Oh, no! Not at all. But there must be a link between the speaker and the dead and it's one of blood.' He points to the table. 'That will be your Book of the Dead, a record of all who pass through your care. For the ink, we need to mix some of your blood with ordinary ink.' He hastily says, 'Not much! It will become something alternate and will help you show them the path.'

'I don't even know the way myself!'

'Speak to them, hear what holds them here, write it in your great book, then help them to let go. Some simply need to be assured they're dead. Some will have small endeavours only the living can undertake for them; others much larger.'

I slump into Tobias's chair, sigh.

'Is there anything else you've failed to mention, Sandor?' He shakes his head. 'And how much blood am I expected to give up for this?'

He smiles. 'Nothing life-threatening, and once the batch is made, it never runs out, never dries up. Not until you yourself are dead – then the next speaker must create their own.'

'How cheerful.' I stare at my hands. 'Why wasn't this in any of the books in the library? I've read all my life – not everything there, but a lot. There's only ever the merest mention of ghosts and how we have none, but nothing about speakers for the dead.'

'Gilly… my wife destroyed those books. Anything that encouraged Hilla in her calling.' He shrugs. 'It made no difference that Hilla had already learned everything she needed to know. Gilly was closing the gate after the horse had bolted, but I think she felt driven to it.'

Gilly Briar, the greatest of us, leaving enormous gaps in our knowledge. When Edgar returns for his last run of the season, I'll ask him to find me tomes of the sort *I* need. About ghosts and speakers, anything and everything he can locate. On the quiet, at least for the moment. And nothing will arrive until the spring when the roads clear again, and by then I should have found a way to tell my cousins – to *prove* – what I claim. That I am what I've become.

First things first: I leave Tobias's comfy chair, wipe the layer of dust from the desk with my heavy blue skirts. The lid is stuck on the old bottle of ink, takes a few taps with the letter opener to get it off. In my satchel is a small leather roll: a very sharp knife, bandages and padding, a vial of disinfectant; the usual equipment a Briar carries as a matter of course.

Finally, I sit on the hard, straight-backed chair at the desk and glance at Sandor. He nods, encouraging, as I unbutton my left sleeve and, with the sharp bright blade, make an incision in the crook of my elbow – such a wound anywhere else would be noticed and I don't wish to explain any bandaging to my cousins. With the mouth of the bottle to the cut, the thick dark fluid oozes in to mix with the dried flakes of black ink in the bottom.

'Enough! Enough!' Sandor cries out, far sooner than I'd expected, and sounding a little distressed. I'm not at all dizzy. I put the quarter-filled bottle down, press a wad of fabric against the cut, and awkwardly wind a bandage around it. After rebuttoning my sleeve, I reach for the bottle.

It's full.

'Oh.' Surrounded by witches my whole life and *this* surprises me. 'How do you know all this, Sandor?'

'All those books Gilly burned? Who do you think collected them? As soon as Hilla began her transformation, I began my researches. The reference volumes took up a significant part of the library before... but I remember. I remember everything. I knew, somehow, that I'd need to. That someone would come.' His smile's tremulous. 'Ready?'

From the satchel I take the book, inkwell and fountain pen. Sandor whistles in admiration, reaching for the pen, but is unable to pick it up with his ghostly fingers.

I open the book and dip the nib of the pen into the bottle (I've wasted money on the inkwell). The liquid surges upward as if eager to be used. I tap the nib gently, removing the excess. On the first page I write *The Briar Book of the Dead* and the date underneath.

'Very nice,' says Sandor.

'Bring them in. Groups of no more than ten at a time so they don't swarm.'

135

14

Mistress Reynard has left our meal warming on the stove; we see her so little it's as if a ghost keeps house for us. Occasionally I have to ponder for an extra few seconds to recall her face, or remember who she is when she hails me in the marketplace to say that Nia's taken her new hunting bow out and so dinner will be a mystery. A widow, she's efficient and unobtrusive, trustworthy and paid very well to be so, and thus able to keep her family comfortably.

Tonight, we eat in the kitchen instead of in the dining room proper because anything else feels like too much trouble; like Gisela's empty place will be too much to bear. Sally Eldin's here too, to cheer Eira; they hold hands across the table. Plates piled with mashed potatoes and roast wild goose (slow moving in flying south, a perfect target for my cousin) dripping with cider gravy, we sit in silence. There's a rum cake and custard to come for dessert; Eira fills our glasses with a red imported from the newly reopened Singing Vine Vineyard. An air of exhaustion lies heavy in the room. Nia, having searched through the cemetery from sunup to sundown, has grave-dirt smears on her face and cobwebs in her hair, and I am not fool enough to point this out. The maternity ward of the infirmary was working overtime today and Eira delivered seven babies – better her than me. And I...

I'm wrung out from dealing with the sins of the departed. The palm of my hand and a small part of my brain feel... frozen is the best way I can describe it, as if an icy needle's been stuck in my head, just in that one spot. I must ask Sandor about that, if it happened to Hilla or if it's just because I'm not used to handling the dead. I was too distracted to do so this afternoon. Now, I stare at the candle flames on the table, wondering if I watch long enough might they unfreeze that icy little nub?

'Ellie!' Nia's shout pulls me from my trance.

I startle, almost tip out of my chair. Sally gives a sort of shocked laugh. I'd not heard a thing – wonder how long Nia's been talking to me. 'What?!'

'I said *What's next?*' She pulls a sour face. 'Any other boneyards you'd like me to sit in tomorrow?

'No, but you could spread manure on everyone's gardens before the snows fall?'

The outrage rises like a cloud above her; she swells like a rooster drawing itself up to crow. When Eira and Sally shriek with laughter, Nia seems to realise I'm joking, deflates – she's clearly too tired to remain offended.

'I'm sorry, Nia.' And I'm too tired to fight. 'I'm sorry it was such a waste of a day. It seemed like the rational place to look, and you've the sharpest eyes. And your vigilants are attentive, precise about their work.'

Well, some are. She grumbles, but the compliment seems to please her. 'I need to visit the orchards very soon.'

She'll check the trees, re-carve the runes into the base of their

137

trunks, spill a little of her own blood, sing incantations to ensure a healthy harvest. 'Not tonight, though – you'll be exhausted in the morning, and I'm sorry to say it, but tomorrow will need to be a search of the old forest graveyard. If the melyne's not in town, that's the next logical place for it to nest. The distance from town might explain why it appears so late?'

'Travelling,' muses Sally. Eira pats her hand like she's a clever girl.

'Do you remember the stories Maud would tell about the old graveyard?' Nia asks, refilling her wine glass.

Eira snorts. 'That the corpses would rise and dance every full moon?'

Sally gives her a sidelong look. I wonder how much she knows about us? About life within these walls? But her eyes are shining with anticipation, so maybe she wants to know more. I wonder if Audra will let Eira and Sally live in the Briar House? A new Briar Witch might make new rules.

Nia says: 'And Gisela would add, just in case we decided to go and watch, that if you saw them, your eyeballs would fall out?'

'Or that all the statues were people who'd witnessed something they shouldn't and turned to stone?'

'How every grave led below to the under-earth?' I grin. 'That was Aunt Hebe's.'

Nia nods. 'That because there were no copper or iron bells hung on the trees there, the Erl-King's daughter would come to claim naughty children like us?'

We laugh, but I remember how terrified I used to be of those tales because Nia would whisper that only witches were safe. I wonder if she recalls that too.

'Gods, they told us some stories!' Eira rises and begins to fill four bowls with dessert.

'Which one do you remember most from childhood?' Nia asks.

Eira puts her head to one side. 'I think the one about the witches?'

'That doesn't narrow things down,' I deadpan, and we giggle.

Eira returns, distributes the rum cake and custard. Sitting, she leans forward, elbows on the tabletop. 'Mother told us this one and I remember it more clearly than I remember her, to be truthful:

'Once upon a time, in a great city neither here nor there, for some reason or other, the heavy dead would not lie down to rest. Night by night – for such things can only move in darkness – they would knock upon doors and, whether the inhabitants answered or not, all those inside would fall victim to a mysterious illness. None of the physickers could do any good, and indeed most fell victim themselves, dying in their beds, in alleys, on privies and in libraries as they searched for cures, or by the gates as they tried to flee.

The city, it seemed, would become a home to bones and restless dead.

The witches came on the seventh day of the plague.

Some arrived in wagons, in groups or alone on horses. Twenty in all. Twenty for thousands. They moved through the streets and houses, from low to high, sorting the departed from the dying, ministering to those they could help, and leaving the cadavers of those they could not for later; when someone else had the leisure to bury them. And they sent the uneasy corpses running back to their graves with spells and curses and admonitions; made them sleep to never rise again.

Not a witch wore a mask – if they were meant to fall, nothing would stop that.

Not a one of them fell.'

Eira sits back with a sad smile; we'd heard that tale well before Silverton got its own plague, before we lost our mothers to it. Back when we believed every story we were told, when we thought the Briar Witches were invincible. A nice certainty as a child, to feel so safe – so hard a thing to discover was a lie, in such a brutal fashion. I can understand why Eira remembers it.

Nia nods gravely, 'And you, Ellie?'

It feels strange that she asks me, as if I matter to her, as if my opinion counts. I have to bite back the urge to demand *why*. I hesitate, then let the tale tumble from my lips.

'There once was, and there was not, a poor woman with a child. They lived far from town, in a small mean hut on windswept moors. The woman liked it there because she could breathe; no one told her what to do, or took her very few possessions from her. And her child could run wherever they wished without danger, or at least no more dangers than those provided by nature.

But one winter the child sickened and there was nothing the woman could do, not even with her spells and potions, nor all the wishing and wanting in the world. She'd never failed before, but finally she accepted that it was beyond her. So, she bundled the little one into the warmest clothes and wrapped her cloak around them both and began to walk to the nearest town, in the final desperate hope that one of the physickers there could do what she could not.

But they'd not gone terribly far before the infant rendered up their last breath. The woman had left it too late, and going out onto the ice-riven moors at night was a foolish act. The last straw for the weakened child. And the woman knew this, her grief and guilt tearing at her heart as she dropped to her knees and screamed curses to the sky.

A weeping and wailing that was a summoning, did she but know it.

A fine black carriage drawn by six great grey wish-hounds rolled up silently beside them, the blank-faced coachman crooning to the beasts. A footman appeared from nowhere, each of his atoms coalescing from the air as a mist, to open the door.

Out stepped the Lady Death, tall and pale as the moon, with burning eyes, ebony hair and lips as red as a bloody kiss. She came close. Her gown was cobwebs and smoke, and where it brushed against the woman, it clung to her skin like breath.

'Why do you weep so?' asked the Lady in the voice of the last bell.

'You took my child!'

The Lady appeared taken aback. 'Never take. Only receive. They come to me in their own time and I welcome them.'

'Return my little one. I'll pay any price.'

'Whatever might you offer?' Lady Death didn't laugh, but her tone was gentle mockery, eyes roaming the woman's beautiful face.

The object of her scrutiny noticed, even through her grief.

'Love,' she said. 'I will give you love.'

She rose, placed her lips against those of Lady Death. The goddess tasted like rot and roses, but the woman did not find this unpleasant, did not pull away. And the Lady Death, who was used to worship, but not actual affection, lost her immortal heart. There are those who are in love with death, but do not love death.

When the Lady pulled away – it was she, not the woman, who ended their first kiss – it seemed to the woman's eye that there was now a little colour in those pale cheeks, that the cold lips had taken on some warmth, that the fiery eyes blazed brighter still. The Lady Death touched the child's head, and said, 'What profit if I take you and leave the child to fend for themself? How long will they last without you?'

'Please,' said the woman. 'Let my child live.'

'I told you, I do not take.' Lady Death hooded her gaze. 'I will wait for you to come to me,' said she, and returned to her conveyance. The footman closed the door behind her and turned into mist; the coachman shouted to the wish-hounds and the carriage disappeared across the rocky, snowy moors. And the child in the woman's arms gave a cry and a shudder and breathed once more.'

I don't tell my cousins that Hebe told me this story, and it's the one I told myself when I was old enough to feel my mother as an absence. That she'd gone to serve the Lady Death, having given her own life in return for mine. That was why she left me.

'How beautiful and sad,' sighs Sally.

I clear my throat. 'And you, Nia?'

My cousin taps a nail on the table, pauses so long I think she won't answer. But then:

'Once upon a time, so long ago that no one remembers when, there were three witches who went beneath.

They may or may not have been sisters – they'd been together too long to recall themselves – but they fought like sisters and loved with the same fierce loyalty, so the truth doesn't really matter.

They may or may not have started a war, and won, changing the very nature of existence itself, of the air, the water, the earth and fire.

They may or may not have been alive when they went beneath or were perhaps simply exhausted by their existence.

Any road, one moment they were there, the next they were not.

But they left traces behind. In the trees and woods and soil, streams and snows, breezes and flames. In the veins of every woman – to varying degrees – who came after them.

And, sometimes, if a woman is in need, if she is cunning and clever, if she is quiet enough to hear the red thread in her veins, she might just be able to find those witches who went beneath.'

It seems like a strange story from Nia – it sounds like one Audra might tell if she were here, inherited from Hebe – but perhaps it's one that Nia remembers being told by our aunt when she was in an expansive mood. I think about the claim that a trace of them is in every woman and wonder why I missed out. Why the stocks ran out when I was created. I don't ask my cousins *why* – it's the sort of question that leads to greater hurt.

Sally rises and starts to clear away the dishes, and continues to do so despite our protests. Soon she's at the sink, merrily washing up. Gods, I *hope* Audra lets her and Eira live in the Briar House!

We sit in silence for a few moments, before Eira turns the discussion to more practical matters. The monthly assembly will take place on Friday and she heard at the infirmary today about complaints that will be raised by one of the guilds. Gossip and rumour are the means the Briars have long used to manage Silverton and its people. Keep your finger on the pulse, Gisela and Maud would both say, it's the best way to know when to quicken it or stop it altogether. Tomorrow, Gisela's sewing circle meets, which gives me a chance to pick up a few more details.

* * *

Only after a long bath and I've slipped into bed do I turn my mind back to the ghosts.

The ghosts were…

The ghosts were…

The ghosts were strange.

Some had grave sins weighing on their conscience, some just needed to be told by the living they were dead because no one else – no other spectre – had been able to convince them of that very troubling fact. In many ways, the latter were the easiest to deal with, and it seemed the simple act of me writing their names down in my great book – the blood-ink a covenant – made them more willing to believe me. Just like with magic, I'd paid my red price, hadn't I? I dealt with thirty souls that way. Often, they were among the oldest spirits and I did not recognise their surnames – families who'd died out or been subsumed by others. I was able to check the registers Tobias and his predecessors had kept – lists of births, deaths and marriages – and track many, but not all. I'll return to those troublesome ones when I've managed to settle the more straightforward.

Will it hurt? more than one had asked and I'd looked to Sandor for the answer. He gave a helpless sort of a shrug, so I chose to say with utter confidence, *No, merely a painless slumber*. I hope it wasn't an actual lie.

When they were ready – when they believed me – I offered my hand, which they took. And then they were gone, dissipating into a shimmering white cloud. My palm, still cold and numb, has a sheen to it even after washing.

There were others with transgressions on their conscience but no one to whom reparations could be made. Them I had to absolve, according to Sandor. Record their names, their sins, and the fact they were *sorry* – and that I, as their speaker, forgave them. In the back of my mind is the little voice demanding 'Who are *you* to forgive anyone?'

Some of those sins were very difficult to hear – if left to my own devices, I may well have withheld forgiveness – but as Sandor pointed out, if I did there'd be unhappy ghosts in Silverton, with only me to see and hear them. I can't even begin to imagine what life would be like with them hanging around, glaring at me.

The worst of the things I heard? Things I pardoned?

Aeron Owens, who killed his own child because he feared the boy was another man's.

Rhys Probert, a rich man, filled with lust for his stepdaughter, gave in to his desires one night then, fearful she would tell, held a pillow over her face until she breathed no more. He threw her body down a disused well behind his home, claimed she'd run off.

Carys Morris drowned four of her nine children to punish her husband, one for each time she found out he'd been unfaithful.

Efa Jones murdered her rival in love and let her sweetheart hang for the crime.

Ioan Kneath promised marriage to half a dozen girls but killed each one when she became pregnant because he didn't want to ruin his chances with a rich man's daughter.

Mari Llewellyn strangled three beautiful women and used their body fat to make soap because she thought it would keep her lovely as she aged.

Definitely the worst of the day's batch.

Then there were others – not sinners, but victims – and they wanted their deaths to be known even if there was no justice to be had because their killers had also passed away. But in this lot there were none wanting bodies found, inheritances located or lost items returned; easy in that respect. I asked Sandor about them because there were no corresponding killers amongst the ghosts – victims and murderers, thus far, have not met in the priest's house.

Sinners, murderers, thieves and the like, my ever-so-great-grandfather said, didn't necessarily go to a state of 'unrest'. If they had no remorse, then there was no reason for them to remain in the world, which struck me as entirely unfair. He shrugged and said that in his experience life was unfair. That his Gilly-girl felt no guilt about her actions with regard to Hilla and he'd never seen her in all his centuries – yet *he* was kept awake because he'd felt bad about something someone else had done. Conscience, Sandor said, was the waking bell that tolled – and some folk were utterly deaf to it.

When I could no longer bear the coldness on my palm or in my mind, nor the confessions of awful deeds nor the pure sadness of souls being lost for so many years, I called a halt.

Now, I whisper, 'Sandor?' as if I don't want him to hear. But he does, materialising at the foot of my bed.

'Where do they go?' I ask. 'Where do they go from here?'

'I don't know, Ellie. I only know we can't remain – or shouldn't.' He shrugs. 'Perhaps they get whatever they deserve, be it good or bad. Perhaps they go to sleep forever. Perhaps they come back to try again, if they heed the lessons this life taught them – or indeed if they didn't.' Another shrug, hands back in pockets. 'I don't know.'

'Will you stay? Just until I sleep?'

'Of course. You're my family.'

15

The big parlour's almost overheated with so many bodies in it. But this is Gisela's sewing circle and they like the room warm; Gisela is gone but I've done my best to keep everything else the same as they've been used to with my grandmother. I could tell when they arrived this morning that they were less than impressed to find Audra not in attendance – this little salon served the purpose of ensuring an important part of Gisela's spy network was kept happy. These women, in particular the older ones, took pride in being part of the Briar Witch's circle. I'm unsure whether my cousin forgot this was on or simply decided it could be skipped; either way it was a poor choice. Yet I didn't bring it up even when I questioned her decision, so I bear some blame. To be fair, Audra never attended these sessions – no interest in sewing – and I'm not sure if she's ever truly understood how much useful knowledge is to be gleaned from women's whispers.

I've never been one for knitting, couldn't pick up a stitch if you gave me a shovel (possibly because it's another form of magic), but I'm good at mending. Gisela said it was part of my nature, to fix things; Maud would snort and say it was only because I'd broken them in the first place. Nevertheless, mornings such as these I would sit between them in the large parlour and darn socks, corsets, tears in skirts and shirts and trousers, underwear and tablecloths. Whatever I was handed. With its core of older townswomen and a moveable feast of the younger ones (whose invitations depended on the usefulness of their chatter), I learned to become invisible, to listen and darn. Making myself so small and insignificant that people forgot I was there when my grandmother and great-aunt left the room to collect the morning tea and spoke even more freely. A talent that's continued even as I've grown; there's a value to being part of the scenery. Even now, sitting in Gisela's chair, I sense eyes starting to glide over me as if I'm a blank space. A gentle smile on my lips, a heavy blanket on my lap, a silver needle between my fingers, the talk floats and flows around me.

The tidbits collected here often gave hints as to issues that might be brought up at the monthly assembly, whispers of plans and discontents so we could have solutions already in mind, helping us to appear preternaturally prepared. It never hurt, Gisela always said, to have folk suspect you might be even more powerful than you actually were.

Margaret Selles, Ursley Kemp and Joan Greville are regulars – stalwarts – wives of merchants (textiles and grain) and tradesmen (head of the carpenters' guild), and Ursley has her own fabric shop; they were Grandmamma's best spies. In addition, today there's Annaple Penman, Mercy Thomson, Nery Littledean, and Cysley Redworth – a baker, apprentice butcher, weaver and potter – all younger, but learning.

'The dress is beautiful, Joan,' Ursley says admiringly, placing a stitch along the frayed edge of a tablecloth.

'Beres gave me some help with the pleating and embroidery,' says Joan, a froth of silver fabric and lace in her hands; her daughter Iris's wedding dress. 'Not my forte, as everyone knows.'

Gentle giggles around the room, but for me the mention of Beres feels like a slap. The conversation continues; there's no ill-intent, only my own guilt making me oversensitive. Beres Baines is usually here, but not today, and I can't deny a sense of relief. Having to make small talk or commiserations feels beyond me. I didn't see her at Gisela's funeral, but Eira assured me she was there, in the crowd.

'Has Aaron finished the cottage?' Nery is stitching the wedding quilt that will lie on Iris and Aaron's marital bed. It's white and soft as a cloud; she's sewn silver charms (love knots and bows, tiny horseshoes) for luck and fertility into its layers, as well as stitched stylised sprigs of apple blossom and rose and lavender and balm of Gilead into the design. Swan feathers will go into the pillows in hopes of ensuring fidelity – though given what I've heard from Silverton's ghosts I fear that might be too much to hope for. Too much of a burden for such delicate things.

'They're thatching the roof this morning.' Joan smiles. 'And Gisela laid her blessing on the doorstep before—' she breaks off abruptly, which draws unwanted attention to me.

I blink back tears, smile. 'It's alright, Joan. Life goes on, as Gisela would have said herself.'

They murmur uncomfortably.

'Gisela wouldn't want anyone to weep overmuch about her. She called you friends and would be so happy to see you continuing this tradition.' The tension dissipates. I feel proud; Gisela couldn't have done a better job of disarming them. 'Is all else well?'

'Well,' begins Margaret, then pauses.

'There is the problem of…' Cysley continues.

'…we know you're doing everything you can…' Mercy is apologetic.

'…but the melyne,' finishes Annaple. 'The noise.'

'Oh. Yes,' I say. To be honest, I've not heard it on our roof again, and have admittedly been distracted by ghosts. Had rather hoped – even though I know better, even though I've warned the others about the consequences – it would go away. That Nia, deep in the forest today searching ancient tombs and graves for the creature, might be successful – but this might prove more effective. 'Where's it been? Which houses?'

Glances are exchanged. None of theirs, as it turns out.

'It dances across roofs—' Joan begins.

'—singing and—' Margaret waves her hands.

'—and giggling—' Ursley shakes out the blanket she's working on to count her stitches.

'—and finishes at the Carabhilles',' ends Nery.

'Giulia is beside herself.' Joan bites her lip. 'I shouldn't have said anything.'

'No, no, Joan. I'm so glad you did! Nia was searching yesterday and today in the graveyards, poor thing, a terrible way to spend a day – but knowing this, we can try to locate the little thing at night. When it's active.' I smile, genuinely relieved. 'This is what we need to know! You've done us a great service.'

And Joan beams; even the silver at her temples glows with pride. I imagine the feel of a pulse beneath my fingers, this river of gab and gossip. Giulia's beside herself but she's *not* come to us.

While they continue to chatter and sew, an idea takes hold of my mind and I begin to plan.

* * *

By late morning, the parlour's empty and I'm closing the back door to the priest's house, stepping into the demands of the clamouring dead. They're excited this morning, this new batch, having realised that some of their compatriots have indeed moved on. I suspect that after so very long they were prepared for disappointment, even though I was the first to see them in centuries. But now, with hope and the promise of release, they're zipping around the small library as if at a party, giddy like tipsy guests.

There are more phantoms (alive and dead before my birth) who require me only to acknowledge their deaths, to tell me why they've remained. They're easy enough to convince since I'm not Sandor, whom several believed was a ghost lying to them – an idea some held for over a century, which proves that even death cannot cure idiocy. Others, however, would only accept the truth when showed their names in the relevant register of deaths from Tobias's shelves.

'I think,' Sandor says, 'it's time for some of the more difficult cases.'

I feel like a student who, having answered the simple questions, is about to be tested more severely.

The tales of woe begin, and their solutions are not so easy.

Wick Ablesman, blacksmith, (I remember him, remember his death too) had buried his mother-in-law's valuable plate in their back garden. Wick, however, died not long after, being kicked in the head by a horse he was shoeing. His family subsequently fell on hard times; now his widow and five children often apply to the tithe-barns to make ends meet.

'Why did you do this?' I ask.

He looks ashamed. 'I felt my wife was a spendthrift. Didn't want her to fritter her inheritance away.'

'Was she? A spendthrift?'

He shakes his head. 'No. I begrudged her any delight. I was cheap, tight with money.'

It'll be a simple enough matter to set them digging in the right spot, but more difficult to explain how *I* know any of this. I write Wick's deed into the book, offer my hand, which he takes – yet he remains. Sandor, by my side, speaks low: 'Sometimes they won't – can't – go until they see the matter dealt with.'

'Oh.' I tell Wick to wait, as if he's got a choice.

Next, Bruna Martin steps forward. She who stole from her sister's coffeehouse to gamble in the Dancing Briar Inn (nothing to do with us, merely named to flatter many years ago). She promised herself she'd pay it back when she won, little realising the innkeeper's brother cheated in all his games of chance. A few years before, Bruna, drunk after yet another night of losing at the tables, fell into the river one winter's eve, onto a patch of ice weak enough to let her through, but not so weak that she could break it again and climb out. Her body floated downstream in spring, and by that time her sister's business had crumbled. Now Ada Martin lives with her daughter and son-in-law, a tolerated source of babysitting and housekeeping. Bruna, like Wick, remains even after I've recorded her and offered my hand. Her expression is one of mild displeasure.

Tabitha White, tall and thin, anxiety twisting her face, died with her husband's pocket-watch in her hand as she returned from the jeweller who'd repaired it. When she collapsed from a heart attack in the middle of the street, the watch rolled under a building. Benjamin White developed a suspicion of the jeweller: that he'd kept it for himself. It's not a huge matter, nor even a sin, but something that's been weighing on Tabitha's mind. A last task she did not finish, a torment for a woman concerned with precision and completion. Such a small thing to keep one from one's grave, but clearly enough. I consider some I *know* have committed actual great sins – my grandfather, for one – yet there's no sign of Tobias coming to seek forgiveness, no sign of him restlessly stalking Silverton.

These three, the last of today's batch, need to be released and I need to establish if Sandor's right – that those who aren't very trusting must wait to see the final amends made. So I pack up my Briar Book and step outside with a small spectral entourage, my trio of penitents, and Sandor.

* * *

Hestia Ablesman's cottage is small for six people, and dilapidated, but failing fortunes meant the family had to move from the large home Wick had provided. Wick's four daughters are all out working, two apprenticed to spinners, one in domestic service, the last working in Eldin's Bakery for Sally's mother. The youngest child, a hulking lad of fifteen who should be 'prenticed to some tradesman or other, but's too lazy, answers. Wick, by my side, makes a sort of a growl, meaty fists clenching; his son would be getting his ears boxed if only Wick could make contact. The boy gives me an arrogant stare.

'Call your mother and get a shovel, Xander. Meet me in the backyard of your old house. Be quick about it or we'll see how you like being turned into a toad by my cousins.' To his credit, he moves swiftly. Sandor grins.

In the garden behind a three-storey townhouse two streets over – it's remained empty since the Ablesmans moved out – I watch Wick cast about for the spot, as if he's not stood over it for six years, mourning his act of meanness. He points to the base of an apple tree, and when his terribly thin widow appears, son shambling after her, he gives a sob.

'Hello, Hestia.'

'Hello, Miss Briar.'

Six months and you'd think they'd start to replace "Miss" with "Steward"; but perhaps Maud held the position too long and too definitively. I'll always be Miss Ellie Briar. I point too.

'Xander, dig.'

The lad's smart enough this time not to throw any dirty looks my way. There's a habit of obedience ingrained in Silverton folk even if some aren't happy about it. Xander sets to work, and he's barely raised a sweat by the time there's a *crunch*. The shovel's hit a wooden box, which the lad hauls up to the flat ground. It opens to a gleam of silver and gold.

'It's my mam's!' Hestia cries in wonderment, looking at me as if I've performed a miracle. 'How did you know?'

'I was going through some old papers of Gisela's and found an unopened letter. Wick must have given it to her shortly before his death and it got lost. I'm so sorry it's caused you hardship. Somehow, it's been missed all these years. Tomorrow, go to the bank – there will be a line of credit for you to draw on. I hope that'll help make amends.' A lie, a small one, but it won't hurt her memory of Wick. And the money won't make a dent in Briar fortunes, while showing that we admit and correct our mistakes. Not perfect, but it's a tiny tarnish on our reputation that I can live with.

'Thank you,' Wick Ablesman whispers, and gives a sigh of relief, fading to nothing.

'And you, Xander. Tomorrow morning, you'll present yourself at the guardhouse to begin training as a vigilant. The marshal will keep an eye on you and inform me of your progress or otherwise. Don't give me reason to regret this.' Nia won't thank me for this task, but I don't really care. Equally, I'm pleased she didn't hear me speak of her as if she's my inferior. There are lines it's unwise to cross.

Sandor mutters, 'Well done,' as if he must keep his voice low. 'Next?'

* * *

In the large common room of the Dancing Briar, Garvan Brody, he who offers the games of chance, is manning the counter. Or rather leaning against it, giving his various nieces orders about how to do their jobs. From their resigned expressions I can tell this is a daily occurrence, one with which they're long bored.

'Afternoon, Ellie Briar, what can I do for you?' He grins when he sees me, barely straightening up. His body language displaying a similar degree of disdain as Xander's earlier.

'A private matter, Mr Brody.' With a leer, he shows me (and my train of ghosts) to one of the back rooms, little cupboards, really, designed for assignations and intimate dinners.

'I'd be delighted to render *any* kind of assistance to *you*.' As

155

if I'd be interested in his fat gut, balding pate and scent of sour rye. I smile coldly.

'I'm here in my capacity as steward, Mr Brody, to collect a gambling debt. Every single coin you took from Bruna Martin when she spent her time here in ill-chosen pursuits.'

His features remain in their usual constellation – as if he's an honest merchant – but the blood's draining from his ruddy face. 'Now, now, Ellie Briar. There's no need for that. Bruna knew what she was doing and accepted the risk. It's not my fault—'

'It is your fault when you mark cards, palm the more desirable ones, use trick dice, put weights on the roulette wheel.' All the things Bruna realised after her death, in the years she's had to observe unseen and unheard as she shouted at Garvan Brody for his perfidy. She's standing behind him now, dancing, yelling again, somewhat distracting. 'We don't mind the gambling, we know folk need some amusements, but you will clean up your act. You will stop cheating and those you know to have no self-control? You'll refuse to let them play beyond a certain point. If I hear of any more poverty caused by your actions, I will come for you and you will not enjoy the experience. I will remove your brother's licence to run an inn and he'll have you to thank for that. I'll make it impossible for you and yours to make a living, and you'll know exactly what it's like to be one of the families you've cheated.'

'You can't know—'

Then I name the precise figure he extorted from Bruna Martin, and his mouth drops open. 'And, *Garvan*, I know you watched her fall. Watched Bruna go beneath the ice and you didn't help her.'

'Oh, a nice touch,' Sandor observes. I can't prove it, of course, but Garvan doesn't know that, doesn't know how I came by any of my information, so he shuts up because he's not willing to push his luck. It's enough that I *do* know.

I wait while he collects the funds, hands them to me in a heavy pouch, which I deliver to Ada Martin. Her sister hovers nearby, trying to touch her shoulder, hand passing through the solid flesh. I explain that Garvan felt bad about her situation, that he'd let her sister gamble far too frequently; I don't mention the cheating – that's something to keep in reserve. I say his conscience has bothered him though he's been slow to act upon it. There's enough money for her to move out of her daughter's house, if she so wishes. Bruna gives up the ghost with a sigh and evaporates.

* * *

Tabitha White drifts in front of me. When she stops by the wooden steps leading up to a small cottage set in the backstreets of town, I get down on my hands and knees with a sigh, feeling very put-upon. Praying not to disturb any spiders, I reach under the porch and dig into the loose earth. Just before despair sets in my fingers close around a cold hard object. I sit back on my heels and examine the find: dirt-encrusted, a long chain snaking between my fingers. I brush away the filth to expose an engraved silver pocket-watch.

In his shoe store I tell an astonished Benjamin White that the gleam caught my eye as I walked along the street where his wife fell. That I knew he would be glad to have it returned. A very happy coincidence. Tabitha smiles fondly at her husband, then she's gone.

Outside in the fresh air once more, with only one ghost beside me, I tell Sandor I've had enough for today, and other things require my attention. Apart from that (and the cold palm, the icy point in my mind), these are sufficient miracles and out-of-the-ordinary occurrences for folk to discuss in connection with my name. He raises a discontented eyebrow but asks if I'd like some company.

'Yes,' I decide.

'Where are we going? We don't appear to be heading back into town…'

'We're not. We going to where Deirdre Baines breathed her last.'

16

The journey up the mountain is easier this time because it's daylight and I know where I'm going. There's no searching a night-time landscape, seeking an injured woman off the beaten path. Much faster too because I can generally use existing roads and trails. It doesn't, however, remove my low-level irritation at how effortless Sandor's gait is; the fact that nothing will tire him while I, in my prime, still need to rest on occasion. There are advantages, it seems, to being dead.

'How did you and Gilly meet?' I ask as I sit on a rock, trying to get my breath back after a particularly steep stretch. There's no history of this in the library, or at least not that I've found, only the fact of their being together. 'Was it love at first sight?'

He laughs at that. 'Absolutely not. She was interested in another, but I was fortunate that her mother liked me and pressed my suit. Plus that other – a wastrel – tried to burn her mother as a witch. I'm glad to say my Gilly-girl was clever enough not to give him what he was after.'

'We seldom choose the ones our mothers like, you know. You were a father of daughters…'

'I think that's because mothers want for their daughters the sort of men they wished they'd chosen for themselves in their youth. But daughters don't want their choices made for them, and wisdom only comes with experience… and so…'

'A vicious circle.' I look at the trees, those that have lost their leaves, those that are evergreen. I think about Gisela, not urging me towards someone but away, yet offering no alternative that might have distracted me. I wonder if her later life choice would have been to have no one at all? What of Great-Aunt Maud? She made no choice in her youth except to moon over the man her sister had; in later life she still yearned toward him. 'So. Gilly did not like you.'

'She liked me fine, but there was no interest. I was not *interesting*.' He grins, does a little jig. 'I did not cut a dash, I was neither bold nor exciting, I did not bend or break rules. I was not rich, merely the son of a man who ran a bookstore.'

'Then what happened?'

'A god-hound came to Edda's Meadow, which was a town like most others, with any witches mostly given to hiding what they were, or claiming to be nothing more than healers. That seemed safest, but often they were the first to be accused of wrongdoing. Helping people obviously being a precursor to injuring them.' He shakes his head. 'Gilly and her mother – foster-mother, in fact – it was all very complicated and Gilly never told me everything, but in the end they ran. Had to. And I ran with them, or with Gilly anyway – we parted company with her mother to make it harder for us all to be tracked. I was there for Gilly, I was solid and dependable when everything else in our world was uncertain and dangerous. I was safe.' He shrugs. 'And my rival was dead, so that helped.'

I snort a laugh.

'And you found Silverton.'

'By sheer accident. We were just moving north, our only plan to avoid god-hounds. We stumbled on this place – dying village it was then – and we were able to help.' His smile's sad. 'We were so young, and even in danger we thought ourselves immortal. Couldn't imagine death… We made a good life, for a long while, and then…'

'And then you became a ghost?'

'Something like that.'

A thought occurs. 'The melyne? They've appeared before in the town, not often admittedly, but they *have* appeared, so obviously never hidden by Gilly's spell. They're heavy things, can be seen and heard, they affect the world around them, sometimes murderously. It's dead, as are you, so why are you a ghost and the melyne isn't?'

'Why do you think?' He tilts his head, regards me expectantly. Silverton's first school master will demand I puzzle it out myself.

'Well. It's never been alive, has it? It hadn't drawn breath – had nothing to give up, no spirit. Is that what makes it a heavy haunt? All that wasted potential? Going bad like a spoiled fruit?'

He nods. 'Wasted potential doesn't dissipate. It rots.'

'Did you see her?' I ask. 'Deirdre? Did you ever see who she met?'

He shakes his head. 'I know it's hard to believe when we've got nothing else to do, but ghosts don't constantly watch the living, Ellie. I saw her that night, sneaking out of town – saw her pass beneath the shadows of the northern watchtower while your vigilants ate and drank. But the girl was of no interest to me or any of my fellows. There was no reason to watch her.'

Rising, I set off at a brisk pace. 'We'd best get a move on. I want to be there and back before darkness falls.'

* * *

I recognise the pond where Nia and I found Deirdre. I look up to the edge of the small cliff where the waterfall flows from and see the tree. A piece of broken wood was tangled in the noose around Deirdre's neck. She had to have jumped from somewhere, but it was too late and too cold and too dark that night to investigate further, and a good chance I'd end up broken on the rocks much the same as her if I'd tried. Now, I find a series of hand- and footholds cut into the stone of the cliff. I wonder if Deirdre used them or took the longer path, up higher and around and through the woods.

I tuck my skirts into my waistband and climb. While it's not effortless, it's also not overly difficult and Deirdre could have done it. Would have done it – and did. I heave myself over the ledge and lie on the damp ground for a few moments. Sandor, with irksome ease, floats up.

'It's hard not to hate you right now.'

When I get my breath back, I go to the tree. A lower branch has been broken. In the darkness she wouldn't have seen how rotted it was or she just wasn't paying attention. It couldn't take her weight; I wonder how long she hung there, suffocating? Before she hit the rocks, and her head was stove in. Did she drown a little too? All three events contributing to her demise? All painful and awful. Poison would have been quicker, easier. Yet that's not how her mind would have been working. The worst possible reaction to heart's ease. I should have known the risk was too great. That Deirdre was too fragile to bear it. I should never have asked Audra to do it. I swallow a sob.

At the foot of the tree is a small pile of belongings. A lantern, its reservoir dry. A pair of leather clogs, not especially hardy or warm, but some last-minute rationality at least made her slip them on before going into the night. They're resting on top of a folded cloak, a pretty thing of plaited ribbons lined with fur that Beres had made especially for her, something others have envied. I pick up the shoes, looking for a note, hoping for a record of Deirdre's son's name.

No.

Nothing.

Nothing except the shifting of an item in one of the clogs, a slight change in the heft of it. In the left, I find it.

A silver chain from which hangs a silver medallion engraved with a stylised book. A small thing, but distinct. A piece I'd chosen specially from Edgar's trove of treasures. The same one that I gave to Dai for his birthday not a month ago. The same one that's meant to be worn under his shirt and close to his heart.

* * *

I've been crouching outside the Carabhilles' tall townhouse – just inside the stone fence – for far too long for comfort. It's cold and dark and I sent Sandor away because I knew I'd be tempted to talk to him, which might well attract attention. Might as easily scare off the one I want to come. But it's well after midnight now and I don't know how much longer I can last.

Staring up at the unlit windows of the second storey, where only a sliver of a moon's reflected, I try to put out of my mind those times in spring and summer when it was so warm and I would take a walk past of an evening, hoping that Dai might be sitting on the veranda. And some nights he was, cleaning his nails fastidiously, and I'd drift over to chat. Ask questions about paper and its making, about the creation of the finer, more expensive products, about the construction of books and journals, the differences between a cover of leather and one of silk, of board or fur – and the truly incredible ones of stone, and others of glass. Once, Dai had said, there was even one of emerald – engraved by a woman, a jeweller in Able's Croft – but she'd lost her gift and could no longer do any such thing. They'd yet to find another craftsperson capable of replacing her.

The trick, I'd learned, was to keep him talking about things of interest to *him*. On a good night he might ask *Are you well, Ellie Briar?* and those rare occurrences seemed like miracles. The sort of occurrences that made me buy little gifts (having to ask money of Maud, begging, bearing the roll of her eyes, the cynical expression) whenever Edgar came through with new things in his wagon, like that medallion I'd chosen months and months before Dai's birthday. Then waiting impatiently to give it to him on just such an evening, not in front of anyone, no, but when it was just us and he had nothing else to do with his time. *Why thank you, Ellie Briar, what a fine thing!*

What I should have taken away from those nights, however, was the true knowledge of how boring paper could be. Of how self-obsessed young men are, and how young men such as he would never change. It's a truly bitter pill to know with utter certainty that Gisela was right about Dai Carabhille. That he'd not finished looking elsewhere.

A series of noises: thuds and thumps as something leaps from roof to roof, then a scrabble and a scramble just outside the low stone fence, then giggling, that horrible childish creepy sound. It's what I've been waiting for, yet my mouth dries up; I don't want to see that awful thing. There's no choice though. If we don't finish this soon – *now* – the melyne will become something we cannot control. It will get angrier and angrier; no more giggling, only rage at not being owned or claimed or named by those who should love it.

I've laid out sugar lollies on top of the wall, to lead it along. What child can resist a sweetie? Shifting, muscles aching after long stillness, I peek from behind a bush. There's a silhouette, baby-shaped and plump, but moving quickly and with more agility than an infant should display. On all fours – not hands and knees, not with the palms to the ground but the knuckles and, at the back, high up on the toes, little calves and thighs bulging with energy. A nerve in my left eyelid begins to flicker, flutter. I don't want to see this thing, truly I do not.

But it's coming towards me whether I wish it or not.

It stops at each lure, sits and gobbles the treat down, then begins its forward motion again. The last sweet is closest to me and the melyne is almost there. I clear my throat and begin to sing, softly so as not to startle it, sing the lullaby with which it's been keeping the town awake, and add the final stanza.

Mamma will protect you.
Mamma she will sing.
Mamma will buy you a golden ring.

Mamma she will hug you.
Mamma she will sigh.
Mamma will protect you though in the ground you lie.

165

Mamma she will rock you.
Mamma she will cry.
Mamma she will name you before you say goodbye.

The wee cold lad pauses, one hand and one foot raised, and I fear he might bolt. That all this waiting in the icy black will be for naught.

No. He shifts once more, nimble and almost anxious, scampering towards me faster and faster. I rise, slowly, my legs protesting, and present a much bigger target.

It leaps.

Hits my stomach like a frog on a stone, making a similar sound, suckering on as if it's got sticky pads on fingertips and toes. Climbs to my chest, holds itself out from me a little and stares into my eyes – then buries its face into my neck, purring like a kitten.

Gods, it's so cold, this little thing that never drew breath. And beneath the moonlight its skin is the blue of decay, of blood that doesn't pump around a body; it smells like meat that's gone off and it's all I can do not to gag. It's just a baby, after all, and none of these things are its – *his* – fault.

'Hush,' I say and he cuddles closer as I take the steps up to the Carabhilles' yellow front door, and knock loudly. The noise makes the child shudder. 'Hush, all will be well.'

Almost immediately there's activity inside, the flare of light, which tells me someone's been sitting up, waiting for the melyne to visit once again. The door flies open; lanterns held high show Dai, Hari and their father, all with cudgels raised – as if this tiny monster presented such a threat to three grown men. As if it would announce itself by knocking.

'Ellie,' says Dai, and they lower their weapons. 'You've caught it?'

And I look down again and see the details of the face staring fearfully up at me. Mottled and dead, but with black curls and blue eyes just like his father. I swallow again. 'You need to name him, Dai. You need to name your child.'

Mr Carabhille looks at his oldest son, shocked. Hari doesn't look at his brother at all, glances away, goes red, which tells me *he* knew – siblings are often the closest confidantes – and he said nothing. I think less of him. Behind the men of the house stands Giulia Carabhille, hands over her face, so thin and pale. Did she suspect?

Dai's shaking his head. 'It's not mine. Don't be stupid!'

His voice rises, as does his bluster. The child trembles against me. 'You don't have to touch him, Dai, you just need to name him. Give him peace.'

'I can't name what's not mine! I won't! As if I'd touch Deirdre Baines!'

In answer, I reach into the pocket of my coat, find what I'm looking for, and draw it forth. 'I found it where she'd hung herself.'

The silver medallion dangles between us, hypnotic as a pendulum. This gift from me to him, him to her. For a moment I think he's going to brazen it out, claim Deirdre stole it. But then a shiver goes through his face, as if the bones underneath are cracking and shifting with the earth, and he hangs his head.

'Drystan,' he mutters. I nod.

Dai looks up, and his gaze flicks past me. From the darkness Nia and Eira and Beres will be stepping. They waited in the parlour of Joan Greville's home across the road – too cold for

Beres to be outside at night – and it had to be me in the blackness because, well, Audra left me in charge, didn't she?

I go down to meet them and Beres reaches for her grandchild, this poor woman deprived of family. As I offer him I can feel the change already; no less icy yet somehow lighter, movements ceasing. What I put into her hands is a child as pale and white as a swan's feather and smelling sweet as lilies. Dead, but named. Dead but claimed. Owned. Belonging.

'Will you see them home?' I ask Eira because I'm at the end of what I can make myself do, and she nods. I avoid looking at Nia. Tomorrow, Deirdre's grave will be finally filled in, the wee lad laid to rest with his mother. Tonight, Beres can sit with her grandchild. Eira and Nia herd her and her beloved burden away. Weariness rushes through the very sinews of me and I just want to sleep, but I look back to the townhouse, to the Carabhilles who still stand in the doorway. Shame on the faces of Giulia and Cane, and Hari's too. Absolute rage on Dai's as he glares at me.

Without a word, I turn and head for home.

17

The grandfather clock in the library is ticking, a reminder that I need to go to the priest's house and set more ghosts to rest, but I can't quite force myself from the chair. Instead, I spent the morning going over invoices approving payment for work done and goods received, as well as ensuring my clerks' salaries include a bonus for finishing the stocktake ahead of time – even though Dónal reluctantly reported that he's yet to find where the missing winter-plum brandy has gone. That he's at a loss as to who even had the opportunity to take it. I wonder again if it was Gisela, setting it aside for some purpose of her own, but it seems so unlikely; she'd have told me.

I should have woken with a sense of achievement after yesterday, but I can't shake a sense of gloom. Thoughts of what a fool I've been about Dai – not that he made a fool of me, but that I let it happen; that I made it so easy. The fight I had with Nia last night before we set out to lay in wait for the melyne. And the feeling of cold in my hands, against my neck and chest where I held the little monster – *Drystan*, I correct. The absence of Audra, who should be helping me deal with these things.

Staring at my hands, palms down, fingers splayed on the desk, on the blotter that still bears Gisela's scribbles and ink spills. Audra's not yet changed it, hasn't begun to make her mark in this room that still smells of our grandmother's perfume. Someone else will need to buy more blotter sheets from the Carabhilles; I'll not be able (or willing) to show my face there for some time.

I could be in Maud's office next door – *my* office – but this is where the Briar Witch sits, and for all intents and purposes, I am her proxy. I can't recall Maud ever doing this on those occasions when Gisela visited the outliers. It's not a bid for power, although I've a sneaky image of myself as a cat curling onto a forbidden couch. I shake the idea away.

My hands.

Even after the child took on its humanity in proper death, became lighter, my palms felt strange. Still do. Am I imagining it? Or is this one of the side-effects of handling the unquiet dead? That cold spot in the mind, the numbness of the hands whenever life intersects with death? Will it get worse? Did Hilla become this way the more she spoke for those who no longer lived? Would her purpose have resulted in the same end that she met when it was taken away?

Will I finish as untethered as she?

Or like Aunt Hebe, my reason completely removed? Unable to distinguish between reality and a childhood fairy story? Finding truth in fables? Will someone, at the last, treat me the way Tobias did his own daughter on that awful day?

There's a knock at the library door and Nia's voice calling, 'Ellie?'

I suppress a sigh which, if heard, would likely start another fight. Last night after she and Eira returned from seeing to Beres, they'd paused outside my bedroom and whispered my name. I pretended to be asleep. I'm tempted to do it again, hide under the desk, but she knows I'm in here. Unusual, though, for her to knock so politely. I bid her to enter, and lean back in the chair, happy to have the desk between us. 'What?'

'Last night… you… Yesterday afternoon… I… What I mean to say… you…'

Her recriminations still sting. After I'd returned from finding Deirdre's things I'd told my cousins about the medallion, about the logical conclusion. There was no choice – I could hardly level an accusation without proof.

Nia shouted that I'd been blind and stupid and childish. That I was a liability to the Briars. When she said *Why didn't you listen to Gisela?* I knew our grandmother had discussed these matters with my cousins behind my back well before she'd said anything to me. That burns still. As if there wasn't enough humiliation in knowing the man I'd loved was a liar, a wastrel, a waste of breath and bone. Nia's barrage only stopped when Eira yelled at her to leave me be, to let me tell them what we had to do. That there'd be plenty of time for arguments later.

Now, Nia's staring at me, her fingers fiddling with the pockets of the overalls she wears for physical labour – she's been supervising the stockpiling of firewood. Her mouth opens. Here it comes: *You're an idiot. How could you have set your cap at him? You must have known what he was like!* Except I didn't. I only knew what I *thought* he was like. What I wanted him to be like. So, perhaps I'm an even bigger idiot.

'Last night, Ellie, you did very well. I just wanted to say.' Nia smiles crookedly. I manage not to give a surprised *Oh!* 'And I'm sorry for what I said.'

'I wish I'd known sooner, I could have done something sooner.'

'No one else found the truth. You were the one.' She stops smiling, drops into the chair on the other side of the desk. 'And I'm sorry *he* was such a disappointment.'

I shrug. 'Gisela warned me.'

'I know that doesn't make it any better.' She looks down at her hands. 'I also wanted to tell you about the forest graveyard.'

She'd been too busy shouting the day before. 'It doesn't matter, does it? And I'm sorry you wasted your time.'

'That's just it. I'm not sure it was a waste.' She shakes her head.

I gesture for her to go on.

'We came across bones.'

'It's a graveyard?'

'Piles of small animal bones. Piles of them, Ellie. Hundreds of bones in little cairns. None of them looked new, but they're not ancient.'

'No one's used that cemetery for years, more than a century. A predator's—'

'There are no teeth marks on the bones – bears or wolves would have cracked them open. No knife marks either.'

'Any sign of anyone being there recently?'

'None that I could see. And no sign the melyne had been hiding there, so can't blame it.'

'I wonder… if it was Aunt Hebe? If that was where she would go, before she lost any sense of inhibition about her magic? Perhaps that was her place, when she knew enough to hide what she was doing?'

'Maybe.' She shrugs, rising. 'I just thought I should tell you.'

'Thank you.'

After she's gone, I look at my hands again, front and back. Crack the knuckles, massage the joints. A little bit of warmth returns to them. Perhaps the numbness is just because I've been dealing with so many spectres at the one time? If I'd been doing this all my life, had rest periods in between, maybe I'd hardly notice? I should ask Sandor; I wish I could speak with Hilla.

I think about Aunt Hebe again, how she became. Remind myself that it was the plague not the sorcery that turned her mind.

I can't deny she'd become a danger, to herself and others, for all magic demands a red price. The smaller the spell, the smaller the amount of blood – the Briars have tiny cuts on the backs of their hands from their everyday magics. Larger scars elsewhere. Witchcraft is about a balance, a give and take; it requires ritual and preparation. One thing the Briars began to do long ago was find a way to pay ahead of time – every morning they spill a little blood to start the day, to gain credit for whatever magic they might use. But because it takes blood, a witch must exercise restraint in the spells she casts – small things might take small tithes, but they add up. However…

In the usual way of things, you use your own blood to pay for your own power but the blood *doesn't* have to come from the witch – in fact for bigger, darker sorceries it's best if it doesn't – what profit if you create a great enchantment but expire from blood loss? Animals can be the source… or other people. Hebe, becoming more and more open and free with her conjury, chaotic and promiscuous in its use, had progressed from cutting herself to using lambs and calves and foals and baby goats and leaving their bodies wherever she'd used them up. Not bothering to hide the evidence for she didn't consider she was doing wrong. Then larger animals were found, treated in the same manner. Prized oxen and horses, rams and she-goats. The younger the blood, the more innocence to spend; the older the blood, the more experience – the difference the age of the sacrifice made was the sort of power you might draw from it.

What if, before that, she was using wild animals out in the woods? When she still had the sense to hide what she was doing?

I do remember, small though I was at the time, the arguments at mealtimes and more frequent intervals. I remember Grandfather Tobias storming towards the Briar House and throwing the door open, seeking Hebe and only ever – or for the longest time – finding Gisela barring his way. Defending her broken child, their sole remaining daughter.

Until the day Gisela was not there.

Until the day Tobias had seen Hebe taking a child by the hand and leading him out of the market square, into the woods in the murky dusk-light.

All that's been pieced together is fragments: what others saw, what Tobias admitted. That he'd intercepted his daughter and sent the stray child back home. That he'd taken Hebe's hand and led her up and up and up to the stone circle – and she showed him the way in without thought or caution – because what better place to make his point, make his stand, to make it clear he wouldn't put up with this witch's nonsense any longer. And, before he set her alight, he slit her throat with the very knife she was carrying, let his daughter's blood pour onto the altar, profaning the clearing.

Maud told me, when I dared to ask years later, that it was the only witch-burning Silverton had ever seen (and remained so right up until six months ago). Even in the years before the

Briars arrived, when the place was little more than ten tiny shacks left over from the time of the Three Brothers Bear – creatures themselves of magic, although there's none of that left in their few descendants nowadays.

No one had seen what Tobias did, and we only knew because he returned to the Briar House and proudly announced it, eyes bright with religious fervour. That he'd restored himself to his priestly vows, had finally redeemed himself in the sight of his god. Taken back what Gisela had stolen from him – his self-respect. That he had shown the witches, at last, who was in charge.

And I remember him that night, standing there in the front room of the house, fist raised to the heavens as if he would call down fire on the rest of us if we didn't buckle under and obey His Word. I'm not sure Gisela learned even then that keeping someone beneath your heel their whole life isn't a good idea. Yet she couldn't bring herself to deal with him – she still loved him and that had tied her in the sort of knots she'd sought to entrap him with all those years before.

Then our grandfather went back to his little house to celebrate his victory.

And Audra, now motherless as the rest of us, at ten years of age, took his meal over that night, stopping on the way in our garden and plucking leaves of nightshade to add to his salad greens. And he wouldn't have noticed them on his plate because he'd never really bothered to learn much about or from us – we were, after all, only witches and women.

Audra had known for some time she would be the next Briar Witch – her mother wasn't fit, and neither Nia nor Eira, and certainly not me, could have taken that place. So, she told Gisela

175

in the aftermath that she'd made the decision for the safety of the family, and no one could fault her on that. Who knew when Tobias might have decided that another of us needed a fiery lesson? So, our grandfather ceased to be part of our every day. Only Maud truly missed him, but I didn't realise that until later; certainly not for the months and months of nights when Audra would come to my room and weep. We would hold hands, motherless mites, and she'd tell me tales of Hebe and I would agree that yes, her memories were correct. That, in memories, her mother could still be held. As the years passed, those visits grew fewer, only stopping when I was fifteen and she eighteen and found other friends and places to spend her evenings.

I blink, pull myself up from the reverie. My hands, still there, although clenched. I relax them, lie them flat again. The feeling is returning more and more. I force my breathing to slow and remind myself that I've fixed what had been broken. The father found, the child named, the village freed of nightly incursions and the threat of worse. I did it on my own, without magic. Without Audra's help or Gisela's or Maud's.

I've proven myself, even Nia acknowledged it.

It still doesn't absolve me of my guilt about Deirdre. I could be bitter about her and Dai, but I was never with Dai, was I? It was all in my imagination. I think of the place where I'd held him and all my hopes for so long, tap my chest, find it hollow.

But I wonder, once again, why Deirdre never said who the father was.

* * *

In my own office, I read over the letter to the Archbishop of Lodellan once more. There's nothing to change, nothing to add, and I recognise this as mere nervousness. Edgar will be coming this way in a day or three, back from his foray into the Darklands. I wonder, yet again, how long we can get away with this? When will someone begin to question Tobias's longevity, tot up the years since his birth? A god-hound with a comfortable home, decent diet and no natural enemies can last for years and years – unless poisoned by a granddaughter. The priests who've watched over the Briars in the past tended to remain here most of their lives, replaced only at the last moment, taking time to train their successor – an unbroken line right up until my grandfather.

Re-folding the letter and stuffing it into the envelope, I return it to the bottom drawer of the desk. When Audra's back, we'll need to plan how to deal with the inevitability of queries being made at best, an inquisitor arriving at worst. We can't afford to ignore the possibility any longer.

I find I'm feeling better, happier. Whether the funk's passed as a result of Nia's unexpected apology or the sense of self-satisfaction, I don't know. But it's enough to get me to leave the house, game to face the ghosts again. But as soon as I set foot outside the hedge-fence, I'm beset.

Every few steps someone's offering thanks and well wishes for my actions last night. About what I did and how well I did it. And people who've barely bothered to hide their disappointment when I've been sent to check on their ailments now ask me about those very same ailments, seek my advice on treatments. This… this is new. I've become a magnet for eyes, and it's discomfiting for someone who's taken such refuge in her invisibility. I'm almost free of the market square when Iris Greville and her betrothed Aaron Hansen accost me in the politest possible way, apologetically, as if they realise they've caught me just as I'm gathering steam to flee.

'Steward Briar, just a moment, please?' *Steward?* Iris has big brown eyes and a smile like the sun; she's going to shine in the wedding dress her mother's made. Aaron's quiet, a plain lad, kind.

'Of course. How may I help?'

'Well, when Mother said Audra was away, we thought to postpone the wedding this Saturday – but now we're hoping you might officiate for us?'

Audra forgot this. I'd written it in Gisela's diary months ago and my cousin should have checked our grandmother's schedule to ensure she didn't miss any commitments like this. But Audra forgot. I'd assumed she'd made arrangements with them. I suppose I share some blame for foolishly assuming. When my cousin returns, we need to sit down and get her organised.

'Yes, of course, Iris. It would be an honour.' I'll need to read up on the ceremony; I've never done it before.

And they're beaming as they leave.

It still takes a while to reach my destination, a longer while still to sneak around the back without being seen. It's better for me to be unlocatable for some time than have anyone notice me going in *here* and ask why I keep returning. No one looking in would see my companions, but they would see me writing and talking animatedly, seemingly to myself. Having only just become acquainted with the sensation of being accepted and valued, I don't want to lose it so very soon.

18

The cottage looks like, well, a witch's cottage.

Or what one might think a witch's cottage would look like: a roundish building with tiny diamond-paned windows along the weathered birch walls and a high conical thatched roof. To add to the impression, it's not in town, but out in the forest – not so far from the oldest cemetery, as a matter of fact. In the yard, both back and front, are small white boxes. I'm standing just outside the picket fence, a basket in each hand (one full and heavy, one empty and not), and I'm here because Agnes Grieve has not delivered the honey.

I'd planned to spend the morning with the ghosts, then the afternoon reading over the documents for the next assembly sitting – boundary disputes, claims of poor-quality goods, orders not filled as promised, drunk-and-disorderly, property damage and theft. But at breakfast Mistress Reynard reported that we were out of honey, which meant that something was wrong because Agnes Grieve *never* forgets to bring our honey order. Hence the empty basket.

When I'd wandered into the entry hall not long after, I almost ran into Eira, one of the brown leather 'birthing' bags slung over her shoulder – everything a Briar needs to attend a labour.

'Oh, Ellie. Sari Dane's baby's coming early. Can you check on Ezekiel Perry? He's one of Audra's old folk' – our cousin's adopted a range of difficult oldies with no family to care for them – 'she's been taking him a basket of food every week. He likes her well enough, but it doesn't stop him from having a tantrum whenever she knocks on his door – it's the pale green one, by the way, the only one – and I was meant to do so this morning, but…' She shrugs to indicate *everything*. 'Of course,' I said, relieved not to be attending another birth. The last lying-in was Deirdre's.

Hence the full basket.

So here I am, in the woods to the west, having foolishly chosen to see Agnes first before I circle back via Ezekiel Perry's home on the outskirts. I push the gate open with my foot. The closer I get, the louder is the buzzing. *The hives*, I think, then realise it's coming from the cottage. I've been here before, mostly with Maud, to deliver things, to pay for the special medicinal honey Agnes would blend for us. I've never heard this sort of noise.

I put both baskets on the stoop and raise my fist to knock; the buzzing grows even louder. It sounds decidedly unhappy, but what am I going to do? Stand out here until Agnes happens upon me? Still, I hesitate – then knock. Immediately the noise ceases. Well, that's torn it.

The door opens to the sight of a woman – old, even older than Gisela – and short and indignant. A tawny dress with black petticoats poking beneath the hems, hair the colour of old amber. Her skin's lined, shimmering with a dusting of… pollen? Around her head, maybe a dozen bees, as if she's a flower. They don't look any happier than she does, if a bee could be said to *look* unhappy.

'Well?' Agnes glances up and down, then squints hard into my face. 'Where's the other one?'

'Which one? There are four of us.' I'm bored with being a disappointment for not being one of my cousins, and that comes through in my tone.

The tiny woman draws herself up and the buzzing resumes so loudly that I can feel it as a vibration on the air. 'The new one, the one who should have come to tell me about the Briar Witch! About the death! So I could tell the bees as was right and proper.' She leans forward, as if she's about to strike or spit at me. 'Instead of the bees telling *me*!'

Oh. Oh no. Oh gods, no. I have to resist the urge to fidget with the satchel strap across my chest, resist shifting my feet like a scolded schoolchild.

Audra.

Audra didn't let the beekeeper know about Gisela's death. She knew she had to – it's always been one of the new Briar Witch's first tasks, and Gisela brought her here just after my mother and Aunt Susannah died and Hebe was still bedridden. To tell Agnes so she could inform the bees, so the bees would remain in their hives for bees are strange little creatures, creatures that observe strict etiquette and don't take well to rudeness or laxity in manners or the disrespect of pecking orders. While it may seem a silly thing, the loss of the hives would affect our economy, the life of the entire town. Sugar is expensive to import, so honey takes its place; and we export Mistress Grieve's various creations to various cities and ports. And honey is a healthful thing; we use it in many cures and treatments, from coughs and colds to open wounds.

But Audra, who arranged the funeral as the new Briar Witch should – without me there to help – had insisted she'd done all that needed doing. And I trusted her. More fool me.

I'm instantly contrite. 'Oh, Agnes. Mistress Grieve. I'm so very sorry. I hadn't realised.' Wrack my brain for a memory of her at the funeral, find none; to be fair, I was quite distracted. 'There's no excuse. We' – I'd love to blame Audra but laying it at her feet won't help matters – 'were so overwrought. It's a reason, not an excuse.'

She narrows her eyes, spies the empty basket. 'And the only reason you came today is because you wanted your honey.' A triumphant expression, no surprise, a grim satisfaction at confirmation of how untried and ignorant we fresh Briars are without Gisela.

'That's true. Ignorance not malice. I'm truly sorry, I didn't realise Audra hadn't been here to tell you, Agnes. I am so very sorry. What can we do to make it right?'

Maud said once that Agnes Grieve was a sort of a witch herself, the way she charmed the bees, kept them happy and producing, that she could whisper to them which flowers to take nectar from so the flavours were different from the usual run. But Agnes is also aware that there's only so far she can push the Briars, even if we're in the wrong. Behind her the hum calms; I wonder how many bees she's got in there? Maud also said that in wintertide Agnes herds them all into the house and they sleep in the conical roof until spring when she sends them back out into her garden and the forest. But I've never been inside and thought it was a joke. Part of me wants to see them there, part of me prefers to stay in the open.

'Will the bees stay?' I ask quietly.

Slowly, she nods, then stomps back into the dim interior, reappears to hand me a single small bottle of honey. A punishment, not a forgiveness. She says, 'We'll discuss reparations in spring,' and I wonder what form it will take.

But I accept gratefully and thank her.

'There'll be a wedding, on Saturday,' I tell her, half-apologetically.

'I know. Iris Greville told me. Made a special trip.' She closes the door with a snap to make her point.

Audra and I are going to have a talk upon her return.

* * *

As I'm approaching the row of homes on the northern boundary, Maundy's Mile, the poorer ones with only narrow yards between them and where the woods begin, past the old well no one uses since we plumbed the houses, Sandor appears beside me. He's not best pleased.

'I thought you were going to attend to your ghosts first thing this morning.' A tone of reproof, a little reminiscent of Tobias, and I've already been treated like a badly behaved child today.

'It might have escaped your notice, but I have other duties to attend to. The living need me as much as, if not more than, the dead. And if I neglect my job as steward, the living will notice.'

He makes a noise, a harrumph, doesn't disappear.

The house with the pale green door looks mean. Its picket fence has a lean and several palings are missing. The little gate is entirely off its hinges, lying in the neglected garden bed, tendrils of some weed already wrapping around it. Nia should have had someone here to do repairs. Then again, much though I'd like to blame Nia, Audra's been coming here regularly, so she must know the state of it; *she* should have told Nia. Mentally, I add

183

another item to the list of things to discuss with my cousins: a tour of the whole town, noting what needs doing in terms of the buildings and streets so that we don't have slums developing. This is exactly the sort of project the guilds could send their apprentices to work on. The marshal will need to schedule it, and it won't hurt the Briar Witch to be reminded how broad is the scope of the remit of her rule.

Sandor floats beside me up to the narrow porch and the front door, which is closed. Dusty-looking curtains inside the window, cobwebs like lace frosting the glass. An old rocking chair in the lee where two walls create a corner, also covered in cobwebs and dust. I shiver beneath my coat as I set the baskets down.

'Goose walking over your grave?' asks Sandor.

I snort. 'Or a ghost.'

Sandor settles onto the chair, sets up a rocking. I knock, sage paint peeling away under my knuckles.

'Mr Perry? It's Ellie Briar. I've brought a basket of food. Audra asked me to look in on you while she's away.' Close enough to the truth – if his temper's as bad as Eira said, he'll not care who it is. 'Mr Perry?'

Knocking more loudly, I put my ear close to the wood, listen for any movement. Not even a scurrying of mice or insects. At the windows, I press my face against cold glass, trying to find gaps in the curtains – but if there are any, it doesn't matter because it's entirely dark inside. Is there another entrance?

Around the back of the cottage is a tiny yard; where it meets the forest the fence is entirely gone. There are very narrow paths worn out into the trees; animals – fox and badger, I imagine – made them. Kitchen windows look out over the spartan space, but there's no door, and again no sign of light or life inside.

On the porch, Sandor's not changed position, is just giving me a curiously irksome stare from the rocking chair.

'Well, can't *you* go in?' I ask, aware that I'm whining. 'See if he's home?'

'I could, but it's terribly rude.'

'You're telling me you've never been into people's houses because *it's rude*?' I stare at him. He shrugs, doesn't answer; I'm being punished for being tardy.

Frustrated, I fiddle with the sash window, which shifts with a groan. Hiking up my skirts, I clamber over the sill, heave myself into the darkness, try not to get smothered by the heavy curtains, and not get the satchel caught. Behind me, I hear *Rude*.

Black as a goat's guts. I reef the drapes back so the weak winter light can sneak in, showing a tiny sitting room with a single armchair in front of a hearth (a full wood box next to a set of fireplace tools), three thick tallow candles on the mantle. A few long steps take me into a small kitchen with a round table and two chairs, a sideboard with some plates and tin mugs. Everything's wearing a thin layer of dust. The whole place smells of unwashed old man; sweat and bitterness and barely suppressed rage.

The gloom remains a constant even with the curtains open. I use a sulphur match (I must restock) from the chatelaine tinderbox to light one of the candles. A dark thin corridor runs off to the left, and I hold my light high as I step into it. On the right is a washroom, so cramped you'd need to go outside to change your mind. No one in there.

A few more paces and I'm in a square bedroom, the bed

neatly made but the stink no less pungent. I open the cupboard, check under the bed. Nothing and nobody.

It's only when I return to the sitting room that I see him at last.

Ezekiel Perry – or at least I assume it's him – is no more than four feet tall, dressed in patched trousers and shirtsleeves, a stubbly beard, furrowed forehead and deep lines either side of a thin-lipped mouth from which protrudes a pipe, unlit. Bald pate, a hedge of silver hair around the skull. Overly large ears. An expression of absolute ire.

And even though I know – or should – that he can't hurt me, when his lips open wider and wider and wider and a scream of fury exits, and he flies at me, I throw myself backwards, hitting the edge of the doorframe and falling.

I don't know if I scream, but Sandor is suddenly there, between me and the other ghost, shouting even more loudly at Mr Perry, who looks shocked and not a little fearful. The old man, still with his living habits, stumbles away to land on his backside, staring up at Sandor. The stench of him is incredibly strong.

'Where are you?' I ask. 'Mr Perry, where are you?'

'In my own fecking home! What are you doing in here, you dozy bint?' Fright isn't enough to make him pleasant.

'I came to check on you. I mean, where's your body?'

'What do you—'

I crawl over and poke a hand right through his chest. It's like putting my fingers into sleet. He gasps as if I've pushed the breath from him.

'You're dead,' I say, probably less kindly than I might. 'Where did you die?' Thinking his body must be out in the woods, but his spirit's come back here, to the place it knows best.

He's still staring. 'Dead?'

'Dead.' Sandor's giving me a stern stare, but he isn't the one who almost soiled himself. I can feel the bruises rising on my back where I hit the doorframe. 'Do you have anything to confess?'

'Confess?' Perry looks at me as if I'm mad. This is easily the most unpleasant ghost I've had to deal with so far – even those with terrible transgressions holding them in place have had better manners. Probably in hopes of forgiveness, but still: a modicum of politeness goes a long way.

'Mr Perry, you're a ghost.'

'But there are no ghosts in Silverton.' The tone's scornful, but his delivery's uncertain – what with my fingers having so recently been in his chest.

'I'm the speaker for the dead, and my duty is to help you move on to your rest.' All of which sounds rather more grand than it should from someone still crouched on their haunches. 'If you've got something you wish fixed – an apology made, a reparation that's in order – before you can pass on, that's something I can do. But you didn't know you were dead – sometimes all you need is to be told that you are.'

'What? And then off I pop?'

'Well, yes.' I look up at Sandor for help. 'Once I write you into the book.'

Sandor sighs, then produces a booming voice such as might be heard in a Lodellan pulpit: 'Ezekiel Perry, what holds you to this earth?'

And the old man blinks, shakes his head. 'Nothing undone.'

'Where did you breathe your last?'

'Am I not here? The... rest of me?'

187

'No,' Sandor and I say at the same time.

Perry frowns, concentrating, slowly shakes his head. 'I can't recall. One moment I was in the kitchen, making a cup of tea, the next... you were trespassing.'

But just because it's the last thing he remembers doing, doesn't mean it actually was the last thing he did. Sandor's said in the past few days that the memories of ghosts can be as unreliable as those of the living, whether through wilfulness or forgetfulness. 'Mr Perry, I promise I'll find your body. If you've nothing to confess.'

Once again, he looks at Sandor for confirmation – my great grandsire clearly the more reputable of us. 'Nothing. No. Nothing.'

I set up at the table, opening the book and writing down his name, the date and his lack of anything to admit. Sandor watches as I offer my hand to Ezekiel Perry. The old man takes it without hesitation, and just like that begins to fade. In a few moments he's gone.

And I'm left with an empty house, and no body, and all I can report back to Eira is that he's missing because I can't tell her about the ghosts.

19

'So, you can see, Steward Briar, you *can see* that these eggs are not of a comparable size.'

The only thing in Berthold Lloyd's favour is the fact that he calls me "Steward Briar" instead of just plain old "Ellie Briar" like I'm still a little girl. There's been an agonising thirty-minute complaint from him about the eggs supplied to him by one of the market stallholders, whose eyes have rolled back in her head so many times that I'm concerned they'll not appear again. The size of the eggs is neither here nor there – a little on the small size two of them are, but not worth thirty minutes' of my time.

'I see you've found it vexing, Mr Lloyd. I'm sure Mistress Tyler regrets letting matters get to this point.' She gives a sharp nod – she regrets ever meeting Mr Lloyd, I suspect. 'Mistress Tyler, you will allow Mr Lloyd to choose his own perfectly-matched-or-as-close-thereto dozen eggs as soon as you both leave this meeting.' The man looks smug, the woman irked. 'And, Mr Lloyd, you will never again shop at Mistress Tyler's stall' – his mouth begins to open but I continue – 'as I would hate to ever see you before me again with a similar complaint, which might be construed as wasting time. I trust such a thing will never get this far again.'

'Oh. No, Steward Briar, no indeed.' He's still shaking his head as he leaves, a basket of unsatisfactory eggs clutched in his arms. Mistress Tyler trails behind him, turns at the door and gives me a nod and a grin. Replacing the eggs is a small price to pay for never having to deal with Mr Lloyd again.

'Nicely done,' says Dónal. In the usual way of things, the Briar Witch would be in this fine and heavy chair, and I in Dónal's smaller and less heavy one, but today I don't have to take notes because he is. And what a blessed relief it is. We're sitting in the assembly room of the townhall – the biggest open space with its vaulted wooden ceiling and row of coloured glass in the high windows to let in a rainbow of light – surrounded by a warren of poky offices to house a variety of clerks and functionaries, a registry as well; below, in the cellar, are jail cells. Rows of benches stretch out in front of us, but thankfully we've been through most of the complaints and there was only a gathering of about forty today (and some of those are just the onlookers with nowhere else to be who bring their knitting along).

The monthly assembly is where townsfolk can air any grievances, ask questions, propose changes, request access to the tithe-barns, changes to guild regulations or to put a case for new ones, ask for fresh apprentices, or coal-biters to help around the house. It's also the Briars' chance to set the town's schedule, for planting and harvesting, bottling, bagging, stacking, sewing, repairing, building, etcetera – even though some of those events have been in place for decades and have no reason to change – ritual and habit have value in people's lives, make them feel safe and stable. There's also something about feeling heard (a veneer of democracy) that makes them better behaved, more willing to toe the line; routine is a comfort and renders them more biddable. Every so often, Gisela would say, you make a concession on an issue you seemed to have been firmly wedded to – all the better to negotiate later for something you truly want. *It's important, Ellie, that they feel we're a very benevolent dictatorship. It means we can get away with more.*

They know we look after them, that the powers of the Briars are used in the pursuance of their wellbeing, so they're inclined to gratitude and obedience.

Of course, it's not foolproof, but it *is* fortuitous that I've put the matter of the melyne to rest so recently and effectively, and aided more than one person by showing them where long-lost family treasures were hidden or ensuring overdue debts were paid. The Balefire Eve is now being remembered for the successful festival it was, and Deirdre's demise as a sad misfortune related to Dai's malfeasance rather than any fault of mine.

My stomach's rumbling. In addition to Mr Lloyd's egg problem, I've settled three arguments about bad faith bargains or unfulfilled oaths, one boundary dispute, approved four requests for access to the tithe-barns, and decreased or ceased ten families' shares due to a shrinking number of mouths to feed (deaths, children leaving home), accepted requests from the carpenters' guild to admit three new apprentices – Nia will ultimately decide on them – and a building application from an ambitious young woman who, freshly minted as a miller, wishes to build a new mill. I refused, much to its maker's displeasure, an application to set up a gambling parlour – Gisela had done so before on the grounds that the Dancing Briar Inn provides enough opportunities for people to beggar themselves. Xander Ablesman received his green and silver vigilant's uniform from me, too, unsure whether to be grateful and proud or surly and proud.

Sweat is creeping down the snaking line of my spine, partly because we're seated in front of a fireplace, and partly because Sandor is stalking around the edges of the room, staring pointedly at me. Reminding me of my other duties, to which I am failing to attend. So I don't let my impatience show, I look up as if in thought, to the beams of the ceiling curved like the ribs of the world.

'Next?' I ask Dónal.

'Rowella Bisbee of the school on Adalind's Row.' Dónal's got the trick of raising his voice just enough that it serves to answer my question and encourage Rowella to step forward. She looks nervous and young, one hand pressing her grey skirts as if to flatten any creases, the other hidden behind her.

'What can we do for you, Miss Bisbee?' I ask.

She clears her throat, speaks a little too loudly, voice breaking. 'I need to talk to you about the books.'

'What books?' Dónal asks. 'Please be specific.'

That tone's not going to help matters.

'Speak freely, Rowella, please.' I smile encouragement at her.

'The exercise books. They're falling apart, the paper barely sticks together, the ink spreads like a blot no matter how careful the children are, and the covers come off at the slightest pressure.'

I frown; I know where the books come from. 'That doesn't sound right.'

I can see her hands shake from here.

'Calm down, Rowella, I'm not disbelieving you. Do you have an example?'

'Yes!' She comes forward, bringing the other hand from

behind her back. She's holding one of the blank-paged notebooks the Carabhilles make specifically for the schools; the thing's a wreck. It's fair crumbling in her palm. Poorly constructed and certainly not what's ordered or required.

'Is this a new delivery?' Dónal asks.

She nods, shyly.

'Dónal, this afternoon, please accompany Miss Bisbee to the papermill. Take the offending books back and have them replaced. Let the Carabhilles know that their invoices will be paid then. Thank you for speaking up, Rowella.' I can tell she didn't want to say anything because of who the Carabhilles are, their position. I'd love to think this is just a mistake, an oversight. I'm sure Dónal will let me know soon enough.

'Nothing more?' I ask.

'Nothing more,' the chief clerk replies, so I thank folk for their attendance and their patience and remind them to keep a look out for Ezekiel Perry, who is officially 'missing'. Nia's directing a search party even now, looking for the living man, and I hate knowing it's a waste of time, but for the moment I can't justify not doing it. As time passes, hope will lessen and wintertide will fasten its grip, the risk to searchers will be too great. There's no family to care; however, his body needs finding and I did make him a promise.

Sandor's still pacing in his ghostly way up the aisle, the soles of his shoes not quite touching the floor. Hands clasped behind his back, he stops occasionally to inspect someone or other. I understand his impatience yet the delay's not a wilful slowness on my part. I have my own duties plus those Audra has entrusted to me and I *want* my cousin to know I can be relied upon. That I've done a good job in her absence – that just because I'm not a witch doesn't mean I'm less capable of running things. If I'm honest, this desire is a little desperate, and hard to avoid when I've felt not good enough my entire life.

I know there's a room filled with anxious spectres, some of the more difficult ones – more difficult to release, that is. Those with only some of their memories – all murdered, but they don't necessarily know by whom. Either the recollection's been wiped out by death or they didn't know what happened in the first place. Some have divots in their skulls, others believe themselves to have been poisoned. The long-term dead are harder to help in terms of finding out what actually happened, but they're often the most willing to go without knowing everything. Eternity is a long time to maintain a rage.

But right now, Sandor has stopped in his tracks and is staring hard at a middle-aged man in a red embroidered waistcoat, well-made trousers and a fine gold frockcoat that's too light for the season, but which I presume he, peacock-like, simply cannot bear to hide. A thick neck in a too-tight collar, light brown hair, thinning and grey at the temples. Shoes with silver buckles on them, not the sort of functional boot that most of us are wearing with the cold. Thin lips.

Lowen Jernigan, importer of silks and glass beads, runs an emporium, or part of one with a collective of other merchants, each with their own particular sort of goods – and the gentleman who wanted to open a gaming parlour. Who didn't depart after my refusal but has sat there glowering. Sandor is standing over him, and I think if my very-great-grandsire could have any physical effect on the living, Master Jernigan would be an extremely unhappy man indeed.

Sandor turns wide eyes on me. I remain impassive. He throws meaningful looks at Jernigan, but there's nothing about the man that takes my attention. Then Sandor sits on the man's lap. Sinks into him. Then through him. Jernigan shudders, looks around, rubs at his arms to warm up. Sandor is sort of puddled on the floor, discontented.

'Steward Briar?' Dónal's awfully deferential and I realise I've missed my cue.

'Ah. Oh.' I gather my thoughts. 'Well, if there are no further matters for discussion?' Shaking heads, shuffling of feet as folk rise. 'Then I declare this assembly—'

'I have business.'

A quiet voice, gentle, a tremble to it not of fear but rage. At the back of the hall, just inside the doors, is Beres Baines, black mourning gown impeccable, hair covered with an ebony silk scarf. My heart begins to beat faster and harder, and my cheeks heat up. Will I ever be able to see this woman and not feel guilty?

I clear my throat, doing my best to not appear to do so. 'Yes, Beres?'

'I've given you time since your grandmother's funeral. Now, I demand restitution from Dai Carabhille for my daughter Deirdre. For her death. For her child. For the ordeal of the melyne. For not doing what was best for this community.' Gasps and murmurs from those looking on, positively delighted intakes of breath from the knitters.

She's entirely within her rights. Clever, too, to mention the effect on the community; remind folk she wasn't the only one affected. She's entirely entitled. I'd wondered, these past few days, if she would do this. Part of me dreaded it and part of me longed for it, and I know myself well enough to recognise that I want to punish Dai. As much for the hurt he did me, for the lack of attention, as for what he did to Deirdre. Perhaps more. I want to hurt him for being a coward, for causing a young woman such despair that she took her own life when the promise of her child was gone. I want to hurt him for proving my grandmother was right about him. For ensuring I might never trust my own feelings again.

None of which changes the fact that Beres Baines has this right, so I nod. I assure myself I can be fair and impartial. That it's only justice, and if I enjoy his pain that's merely an unintended benefit, nothing I can be blamed for. An unpleasant side of me, but there it is. And haven't I earned it? Just a little?

'Yes, Beres, you are owed. We'll discuss the details this evening, in private.'

Perhaps she wants to object, wants everyone to know what will happen, but I think she's also been disarmed by my swift agreement. The lack of argument takes the wind from her sails, leaves her nothing to push against. She knows his shame will be public – and his family will bear it too because their neighbours will whisper about whether they knew and how much. They'll give all the Carabhilles sidelong glances and murmur behind their hands as they pass in the streets, and the papermakers' elevated position won't be enough to save them from this indignity. It won't last forever, but it will sting while it does.

'Join us for dinner,' I say and Beres nods once then leaves. Other attendees rise and follow her swiftly. I've been clutching at the armrests of my chair (Gisela's chair, Audra's chair) and they're aching, the knuckles white. I release them, shake them. I catch Dónal giving me a look.

'What?' I say, and it comes out far louder than intended. 'She deserves some sort of retribution.'

The chief clerk holds his palms up to pacify me. 'No doubt, no doubt. But my, won't that put a cat amongst the pigeons? The Carabhilles' pride and joy getting his comeuppance? What exactly will you do?'

I shrug. '*That* is a problem for later. Presumably like the current whereabouts of those bottles of imported winter-plum brandy?'

'Point taken.'

'You're the one going with Miss Bisbee to enquire as to the state of those books. Good luck.'

He gives me what can best be described as a filthy look before collecting Rowella and exiting.

The hall's empty now, and no sign of Sandor. I wonder if my great-great-great-grandfather is following Lowen Jernigan. I'm sure I'll find out later, but for now I really need to figure how to punish Dai. I should be grateful, I suppose, that Agnes Grieve and her discontented bees did not make a showing.

20

'What good do you think can come of this?!'

Five minutes ago, Nia entered the library yelling and hasn't stopped since. Eira, following her, hasn't managed to get a word in edgewise. Someone told them about today's assembly before they got home. I'm waiting for my cousin to run out of puff. I keep my face neutral, remain seated behind Gisela's (Audra's) desk, forcing my hands to stay relaxed on the armrests of the chair. Internally, my temper's boiling.

It feels as if the nascent goodwill between us has been burned. When Nia pauses for breath, I ask, 'Are you quite finished?'

Before Nia can flare up again, Eira intercedes. 'Let Ellie speak, Nia. She will have some plan – you know she's not given to precipitous actions, unlike some.'

Her sister reddens. I clasp my hands on the desk, better to hide the shaking. 'Beres is entitled to retribution. Restitution. Inflicting a punishment. If we deny that, people will start looking askance at us. Gisela always said that part of our power rests in the fact that folk know we respect the laws as well as they do. It gives us legitimacy. It's the only way we can enforce them.'

'That's all well and good and very high-minded, but they

obey us because they're afraid. Not much, just enough to keep them thinking twice about disobeying.' She sneers, paces back and forth in front of the hearth.

'That's a tiny part of it, certainly, but not all of it. They know we look after them – their health, homes, education, living. They know that no one starves here, not even the poorest. It's in their own best interests for us to be around – and when they forget those interests, that's when the fear is useful. Gives them second thoughts about making trouble.'

Nia gives a noise of dissatisfaction, a mix of a teakettle coming to the boil and a bull venting its frustration. A sure sign I've made sense, against which she has no defence. Eira's mouth quirks up in a grin.

'Ellie. The Carabhilles won't be happy.'

'The Carabhilles aren't above anyone else!' I shout. Both cousins look shocked. I generally don't give vent to anger, or at least not so quickly.

Nia draws back. 'But you—'

'I what?'

'You won't look impartial in all of this, Ellie.' Her hands go to her hips. 'Everyone knows—'

'Knows what?' I demand.

'About Dai, how you felt.' A distant part of my mind notes her tone; it's neither mean nor unkind, though heat still suffuses my skin. 'Ellie, it's better if you leave it until Audra gets back. Let her decide, let her take the brunt of it.'

'It's not going to appear any more impartial to wait for Audra,' I say evenly. 'I'm not an idiot, Nia.'

'But Audra—'

'If I don't make this decision and stand by it, then all I'll show is that I can't be left in charge. Then what's the point of me?' Nia rears back. I've shouted at her again. I lick my lips. 'I might only be acting in Audra's stead but I *am* the steward. If I can't make hard decisions, I'm nothing more than a servant in the Briar House. Is that what you think I am, Nia?'

She doesn't answer.

Eira says, 'Nia. Ellie's right. She's got to do this. Consequences and all.'

* * *

'I want him whipped and branded.'

Beres, in the same mourning gown (letting us know we don't warrant a change of attire), arrived at precisely six pm and remained mostly silent, but for *please* and *thank you*, throughout the meal (Mrs Reynard's very fine potato and cheddar soup with white rolls, followed by roast duck and vegetables). We three Briars chatted about things that did not hurt. As soon as the dessert bowls (a trifle mess of meringue, cream, cake and fruit – ugly but delicious) were empty, Beres made her claim.

Eira and Nia go very still. I don't pause or spurt as I drink from my wine glass (filled with water so I keep a clear head). I nod, and swallow slowly to buy some time; to keep myself from shouting *Yes*.

Yes, and everyone else be damned. Drag him to the common and chain him to the ground, let Beres take the whip or choose a champion for herself – probably one of the blacksmiths or the brawny lads from the sawmill. Let Dai be whipped until the leather turns red; let a brand be heated in front of him, then burned into his shoulder to show him for a murderer, because in Beres's mind that's what he is. His selfishness left Deirdre in despair, and who knows what he said to her? Why she never told anyone about him? Why she kept his secret? His lack of care for the community was clear. As far as Beres is concerned, and I cannot say she's wrong, Dai Carabhille is the reason she's all alone in the world with no one to carry on her future.

But… does the punishment fit the crime? I can order it, but will there be an outcry? That it's too much, that the Briars are being ill-considered in their decisions? Dangerously dictatorial? What I said to Nia was true: we rule because Silverton's folk know we're fair. How will *I* look to order such a retribution? Spurned? Rejected? Vengeful? I go to reply, but I've waited too long.

Nia reaches across the table for Beres's hand but the distance is too great, so she ends up tapping the tablecloth instead. It looks like she's trying to make the other woman see reason rather than sympathise with her, comfort her. So, Nia's words fall in a different fashion to her intention: 'Wouldn't it be better, Beres, to make them pay a blood fee? Something that can help keep you in the coming years?'

Beres Baines – one of the gentlest souls I've ever known – rears up, the chair crashing behind her. Nia's managed to do what she feared I would: make a horrible mess. Before our guest can release a stream of invective, let my cousin know exactly what she thinks of her, I say very clearly, 'Whispering.'

Everyone stares at me.

'As I said I would,' – make them remember I'm a woman of my word – 'I spent the afternoon researching precedents, Beres, all the minutes of previous assemblies over the years and decisions made by the Briar Witches. It's been a long while since there was a melyne, but there've been other shameful acts. Girls deserted by supposed beloveds, wives cast aside for younger lovers, folk avoiding their duties to loved ones. Those actions threatening lives.'

The rage in her face is seeping away, replaced by curiosity.

I continue: 'This particular punishment involves a reparation payment, but also the plaintiff and offender sit together in the market square, and you whisper to him.'

'What?' all three ask.

'Everything and anything. What he's taken from you, how much you hate him, what you'd do to him if you were allowed. Tell tales of your child as she was, all the hopes you had for her, everything that's been lost with your grandchild – the universe he would have been and now will never. Tell Dai what he's lost in casting aside Deirdre and their son, in denying that little boy a name for so long. The reputation and respect that's gone because of his disregard for the town. Tell him the shame he's brought upon his family – who'll look upon his and his brother's marriage suits with favour now? Who'll patronise their business in the lean months when no trade can come in or out? Who'll look at him with pride and love?' I hold my hands, palms up. 'No one will hear except him, but he'll bear the weight of your words and knowing that folk are wondering what you said – that this will make the town gossip longer and harder than they otherwise would have. That what he thinks of as a little *peccadillo* won't simply die away quickly from memory. That his neighbours – his betters and his lessers – will be sniggering behind his back. That it'll be written down in our records.'

'What if he gets up and leaves?'

'Oh, we chain him in place, never fear.' I wasn't going to let the chaining part go. 'We'll set you up on the platform near the fountain. He doesn't get to go until you're done with him.' I shake my head. 'He doesn't get to walk away from the fight. We'll speak next week and arrange a time for it all to be done.'

Beres Baines considers me for a long second, weighing up what I'm offering, before giving a slow nod. She doesn't right her chair, doesn't sit down, just looks straight at me with admiration, then walks out. The front door opens and closes, the sound of her little footsteps on the veranda and stairs grows fainter and fainter.

There's a moment of silence before Nia breathes: 'Well, fuck me.' But there's no heat in her words, it's a relieved sigh.

Eira's staring. She says, 'Whispering?'

I nod.

'That's torture.'

'A form of it.'

'Without any physical marks.'

'Not a one.' I glance at Nia. 'And no one can say it's out of proportion with his sin. No one will look at us' – at *me* – 'and say we Briars were excessive or overly cruel or failing to be impartial.'

'But it *will* hurt him!' she says.

'Oh, how it will burn and pluck and cut the very pride of him. There'll be not a bruise on him, yet he'll remember it was me who put this invisible mark on him forever.'

Beres Baines might speak the words she's owed, but I'll find my own satisfaction in them too. And I can't say I'm not pleased with myself. I know it's childish, but…

'Now I'm going to bed. It's been a long day and I've more than done my part. You two can deal with the dishes.'

* * *

The next morning, I rise late and sit around in my nightgown reading a book of fairy tales until lunchtime, when I finally have a long bath and get ready for Iris Greville and Aaron Hansen's wedding.

I wear Maud's red dress, the Balefire dress. I wear red because it's joyful and vibrant, and I think of Hilla when I put it on, wanting to draw attention, to be seen. There's a strand of rubies that was my mother's and Eira weaves it through my hair. Fasten the chatelaine around my waist, and slip, because I'd feel naked without it, my blackthorn baton into the deep right pocket. Neither she nor Nia are invited, though they could attend if they wished, but Eira wants to spend her time with Sally, planning their own wedding, and Nia's taken her bow and gone hunting – I suspect she's had more than her fill of people for the week.

The assembly hall's been repurposed, hung with garlands of lace flowers and all the crocheted charms that women make and pass down to their daughters. Iris glows in the dress her mother made and Aaron, handsome with happiness, keeps stealing shy looks at her as if he's not just about to marry her. They exchange rings, I say the words over their hands, and the silver ribbon that binds them. Simple. It's a smallish wedding, but when the ceremony finishes, everyone spills out to the just-warm-enough sunshine of the market square, now set up with benches and trestle tables covered in yellow cloth and hung with more silver ribbons. Food and drink are supplied by a myriad of aunts and sisters and grandmothers, and a cow's turning on a spit over one of the firepits a butcher generally uses. By the fountain musicians play jigs and reels, and after a time those not invited stop by to give their congratulations and to bear away a piece of cake.

I wedge myself on the veranda railing of the townhall to watch, planning to stay perhaps an hour at most. Then Joan Greville hands me a plate of roast meat dripping with juices. Bread appears and baked potatoes, wedges of cheese. Next, a tankard of mead, which is sweet and strong. After refusing a third invitation to dance, I begin plotting how best to sneak away, just across the square and into the backdoor of the priest's house. See if Sandor's recovered his good humour or is still sulking.

Next a large chunk of cake appears and it would be rude to say no to that, so it's a while later still that I'm licking icing from my fingers when a voice from my left says, 'What a lovely celebration.'

Turning, I see a smiling young man not much older than myself, and just a bit taller. While I don't recognise his face, what *is* horribly familiar is his garb: a god-hound's brown robe beneath a thick black woollen cloak. He pulls the hood back to show red hair cropped short, eyes green and clever, a wide mouth. Dust and mud cover his hems, grubby boots peek out from beneath. I wonder how far he's walked and if he'd convinced some carter or tinker to take him over the worst of the roads – doing a good service for his soul and improving his chances of a better afterlife. Just past him I can see at the bottom of the steps of the priest's house a large pack, a ragged thing that seems held together with little more than dirt and good wishes.

I stare, dumbfounded, trying to keep the apprehension from my gaze. Let it all look like pleasant confusion. Does he carry a holly-tree baton like so many of his kind? It won't bother me – unless he hits me over the head with it – but it will make my family unwell. Grandfather Tobias had one when he came here, kept it too, until Gisela managed to make it disappear. Around us, I sense heads turning, curiosity flaring at the sight of this new distinctive presence who's not even got the good manners to blend in.

I still can't get any words out, but it doesn't seem to bother him. A bright open smile, guileless gaze, and he reaches for my hand. 'I'm Father Huw, here to visit Father Tobias and learn from him.'

21

'Father Huw.' I manage not to make it a question, forcing my lips into a welcoming smile; offer a hand (slightly sticky from icing), which is enveloped by something the size of a bear paw. The festivities continue unabated, and I'd like that not to change. I switch my grip and use it as leverage to spin the god-hound around, unbalance him into step with me. 'Come along, we'll get you settled. You must be exhausted after such a long journey.'

He doesn't resist though he's taller and broader than me and certainly could if he wanted. I slip my arm into his, joining us at the elbow.

'Very weary indeed,' he agrees, 'although I was fortunate to get a lift the last few leagues with a gentleman-merchant who's a regular visitor.'

That would be our Edgar, back right on schedule. I'll be hunting him down as soon as I can to establish why this god-hound is *here* when Maud sent her last report off safely. Barely pausing as Father Huw bends to retrieve his pack, I propel him up the steps.

'Unlocked?' he asks with a lift of surprise when I push the door open.

'Surely a priest's house has no need of locks?' The interior is, thankfully, ghost-free as well as considerably more dust-free than a few days ago.

He laughs, surveying the space with approval. It's humble enough to please a certain sort of priest, but pleasant enough to keep another kind happy. How fortunate I'd cleaned it for my own benefit! In the kitchen, I set about lighting the woodfire stove. 'In Lodellan, it's required more frequently than I'd like to admit.'

'Well, Father, this is *not* Lodellan.' Mind you, some of the things I've heard confessed recently dampen my pride in our rural honesty. 'Please make yourself comfortable and rest. I'll have a meal sent over. There's a washroom through that door, and the water should run warm in about half an hour if you can bear to wait.'

'That's terribly kind and most appreciated.' He puts the backpack down just inside the door. Like a guest, not making a claim, though he does remove his cloak and fold it over the pack. At his belt, no holly baton, but a silver canteen. 'I am very anxious to meet with Father Tobias. This is his home?'

'Well, it was.' I do my best to achieve an expression both pious and sad. 'But he passed away. So, I'm afraid you've missed him.'

His features rearrange themselves in an odd sort of way. There's... a lack of surprise. Curious. He seems to realise this and tries to inject something approaching shock. 'Ah. Oh. How unfortunate. I had hoped to train with him before relieving him of his duties. He's been here so very long, I'm sure a restful retirement would have been welcome.'

I laugh at that and can't stop from blurting, 'Do you really think he'd have been pleased at some wet-behind-the-ears god-pup appearing in his home to tell him he's no longer required?'

Father Huw looks as if I've slapped him, bright colour rising in his cheeks, almost as red as his hair.

I should pour oil on troubled waters, but I don't. 'I knew Father Tobias all my life, and I can *guarantee* he would not have welcomed your presence.' *Any more than we do.* I'm starting to panic – this priest presents a huge problem. For me. He should *not* be here. Yet wasn't this exactly the sort of event I'd dreaded? Just this sort of arrival? Again, I force a smile, trying to soften the blow of my words. 'I'm sorry for speaking so bluntly. Silverton has experienced several tragedies recently and this simply feels like another upheaval. Although I'm sure your intention is not to disrupt our lives.'

'Indeed not.' He sounds apologetic when I was fully expecting him to remind me of the terms of the Briars' survival. 'Yet there are matters that must be discussed…'

'Certainly,' I say. 'But you'll need to await the return of the Briar Witch.'

'You're not she?'

I shake my head. 'My cousin, Audra. I'm the steward, acting in her stead. But she's due very soon, so if you'd be patient, I'm sure she'll make it a priority to meet with you.' I'm surprised – or am I? – at my willingness to palm this task off. More than anything, it's a decision for the Briar Witch – we've no higher authority – because whatever she decides, we'll have to live with. 'I suppose you'll be wanting to inspect the church?'

'Oh, time enough for that later.'

I wonder, ever so briefly, if I should just hit him over the head with my blackthorn baton now, make sure it's properly stove-in, then have Nia bury him in an unmarked grave. Would she and Eira see it as an act purely designed to keep us safe, for a little while longer at least? Or that I'm overstepping? Could I find something in that battered pack bearing his writing style, signature, to copy? Start writing letters to the Archbishop in Father Huw's name. How much longer might we get out of such an action? We've lived for years without proper church supervision, all thanks to Gisela's cunning. Will we lose all that freedom now she's gone? Worse: will we have to deal with the consequences of having *taken* that freedom? Finally pay the piper?

In all honesty, I don't think I could do it and certainly couldn't rest in peace if I did. Murder someone in cold blood – my ghost would spend eternity wandering, trying to find someone to give it absolution. What if no one comes after me? No other speakers to lay the dead to rest? And I become like Sandor, floating about. Having to listen to what a disappointment I am in death as well as life.

'Sorry?' He's speaking again and I wasn't listening. 'What was that?'

'Your name. I asked your name.'

'Oh. Ellie. Ellie Briar. I… organise things around here. Ensure the Briar Witch's will is done and Silverton runs smoothly.' I shrug. 'Steward Briar.'

He smiles. 'An administrator.'

'For my sins,' I reply. 'And my duties are calling. If you're going to stay here, you may wish to hire someone to do for you.'

'*Do*?'

'Housework – cooking, cleaning, laundry. I can recommend someone if you wish?'

'Oh, thank you. I'll consider it.' He smiles, friendly. 'And if I need anything in the meantime? Where do I find you?'

'I'm *not* available for domestic duties.' Part of me rebels at the idea of telling him, but he'll find out soon enough, won't he? 'The Briar House is directly across the square. You can't miss it. Audra will send for you when she returns.' I hope this last will prevent him from dropping in whenever he feels like it. 'Good day.'

* * *

Garvan Brody (he of the crooked games of chance) spies me as soon as I step into the Dancing Briar Inn, and scampers out back, leaving Aine and Grace, two of his nieces, to deal with the large afternoon crowd. He's not the one I'm looking for and I've no quarrel with the girls. However, I feel sick to my stomach, rage and fear warring for prominence. Scanning the common room, I locate my quarry at his usual corner table, a little island of calm around him where no one sits when he doesn't want them to. It's quite the talent.

'Edgar.'

The tinker's iron-grey head comes up and he squints at me, nearsighted and already swaying. A goblet and a jug of something red sit on the table. He's clearly been drinking with determination while I've been talking to the priest. His face relaxes when he recognises me.

'Hello, Ellie Briar. Care to join me?' His moustache and goatee have been tidied up and freshly waxed, if I'm not mistaken.

And yes, I *do* need a drink. It feels like a year since that mead. I nod and he signals towards the bar. I slump onto the seat across from him and take a moment to gather the reins of my self-control.

'Edgar.' I'm ashamed to hear my voice shaking. I try again. 'Edgar. The letter. The last letter Maud gave you for Lodellan? For the Archbishop?'

211

He eyes me, as if trying to remember when that was. Tugs at the collar of his red shirt, adjusts the brown velvet coat – must be his courting clothes for whichever widow takes his fancy.

I speak very clearly: 'When you were here in spring, the last time you saw her, before she was' – *burned* – 'did you deliver it?'

'No need to talk to me as though I'm an idiot, Ellie Briar. Drunk yes, idiot no.'

A goblet clunks down on the table and a fresh jug of wine. Then Aine slides a plate of meat and gravy and bread in front of Edgar. He thanks her. When Aine's gone, I pull the plate away from him to get his attention, but he manages to grab the bread, and there's only so far I can remove his dinner unless I get up again. 'Edgar? The letter?'

The tinker tears off a hunk of bread and dips it in the gravy; I give up, push the plate back over to him. One raised finger bids me be patient. He chews and swallows in a leisurely fashion. 'Edgar, I swear I will break that digit off and shove it up your arse if you don't answer me *now*.'

'No letter,' he says around his food, then shakes his head. 'Maud didn't give me a letter last time, Ellie Briar.'

It seems my heart stops beating long enough for me to become dizzy, for spots to appear on the edge of my vision; reluctantly, it starts again, sluggish. 'What?'

'I went to her that time since she'd not sought me out like she usually did. Saw her in her office. Asked for the letter like a good and faithful servant. She said there wasn't one. *No letter this time, Edgar me lad.* Nothing to worry about. No need anymore.'

'And you didn't think to check with Gisela?' I drop my head into my hands, feel the heat flushing through my skin.

'Why would I?' He sounds defensive. 'I've only ever dealt with Maud about those reports all these years – why would I start questioning the steward?'

I pour red wine into my goblet, right to the top; I drink it all without pausing. Then I do it again, grateful for the meal foisted upon me at the wedding. I can't really fault Edgar. Maud *was* Gisela's right hand. Why would anyone query her actions? All Gisela got from Edgar was his gossip; Maud gave his orders. Edgar leans across the table, concerned. Around us, the noise rises as folk relax and drink, get boisterous. Grace is lighting the wall sconces, preparing for the earlier dark of wintertide.

'Did I do wrong, Ellie Briar? Is something amiss?' His features are wreathed in wrinkles, his skin tanned and cracked by exposure to the elements. Kind dark eyes, a sharp nose, sagging jowls, a wide mouth. I've known him forever. Gisela says he could have set up house anywhere many times over, lived a prosperous life, but he loves the travel. He looks positively mournful at the idea of having let us down.

'No, Edgar. Nothing's wrong.' *Except everything.* I pour another drink, go more slowly with it. 'Where's your apprentice?'

'Idiot lad. Got himself caught up with a girl in Calder. Jumped ship, so to speak.' He's irritated, but there's also a degree of understanding in his demeanour. 'Told him the dangers of being unmarked' – Calder's Leech Lords put tattoos on their folk, so no other lord will feed off them – 'of not belonging. The young never listen.'

'You could replace him with that bloody god-hound you've dropped on my doorstep,' I grump, taking another drink. 'Take him away again.'

He grins. 'Seems a nice young fella, you know, for his sort. Religious and all.'

'Yes, I'm sure he's an absolute bloody delight.' I rub my face. 'Couldn't just leave him for bandits by the roadside?'

'Didn't see any this time.' He grins.

'You told Gisela there were rumours of camps? Or a camp?'

'Heard rumours, saw nothing. Two different things.' His eyes narrow as if he's deciding whether to say anything or not. 'But the roads... they were strange this time, Ellie Briar. There were spots, though, where it was awful quiet – unnaturally so, no birdsong or even the noises of creatures in the undergrowth.' I think about the deathly silence at those outlier farms and shiver. I think of Liv talking about the dead animals in the woods. 'But then, I suppose any bandit worth his salt's going to know how to hide, yes?'

'I suppose so.' My head's feeling light, I should slow down.

Again, he's giving me that considering look, deciding whether or not to tell me something. 'Spit it out, Edgar.'

'You'll be thinking I'm mad...'

'Too late.'

'Obnoxious.'

'Oh, tell me.' I take another drink. At least the god-hound doesn't feel like quite such an issue. In the morning, it will be a different matter altogether; for the moment, I'm enjoying the oncoming numbness. 'C'mon.'

'You know how many years I've travelled these parts – should know it like the back of my hand, wouldn't you think?'

'None know them better,' I say. *Except possibly bandits.*

'Well, when I collected that priest of yours – and he's a chatterbox when the mood takes him – he's busy telling me about a waterfall he's just seen, not far from where I found him. So I tell him there's no waterfall where he says there is – never has been. The river doesn't run that way, winds off to the west it does.' He scratches his hair. 'But he's so insistent about it, so bloody earnest, that I turn the wagon around. Follow his directions, and sure enough, there it is, just past the Havard farm, in fact.'

I stare at him. 'Edgar, there's no waterfall there. I did the outlier circuit only just over a week ago.'

He nods. 'I know. And there it was.' He chews through another few mouthfuls. 'Told you it was odd. Ask the priest.'

Oh, joy, speaking with the god-hound again. 'Did you see the Havards? Ask Liv or Bedo about it?'

He shakes his head. 'I'm a bit behind schedule anyway, what with losing that apprentice and days wasted before I found him in that girl's bed.'

'Didn't happen to pass Audra on the road?'

'No. But she could have been anywhere – at one of the holdings and I'd never have known. Easy enough to miss someone.'

He's right, but I feel a sense of unease for my cousin that hasn't reared its head before – she's the most powerful of us. She should be home soon. I'll feel better when she's back, when we're a team and can face things together. When we can establish a routine for ourselves and the town.

We order more wine. Edgar shares further tales of his travels, some sound even more unbelievable than the suddenly-appearing waterfall, but he tells them with such conviction it's hard to scoff. At last, I'm half-drunk, and remember there's a wedding that I left quite precipitously. I should show my face briefly before I go home. Perhaps a final drink.

Rising, hands on the tabletop for support, I say, 'Don't stay in town too long, Edgar, the snows aren't far off and you don't want to get trapped here.' Part of me also thinks he shouldn't be here when Audra hears about the letter.

'Will you have a letter for me?' he asks, eyebrow raised, circling back to the source of my stress, just in case I'd been able to forget.

'Eventually, yes,' I say. When we've worked out what to do. I think with regret about that beautiful forgery of Tobias's handwriting in the bottom drawer of my desk, all that time and energy gone into perfecting it. I think of Maud and all her effort in coaching me to do it – and yet, *she'd* thrown it all away. Had she been ill by then? Was that it? The cancer eating at her throat that would soon take her voice, had it also turned her mind? 'But nothing to take this time.'

'And, Ellie Briar?'

'Yes, Edgar?'

'I'm sorry about your grandmother,' he says and raises his mug, a toast to Gisela. But he doesn't say that about Maud.

22

Something isn't right.

The light is wrong, the air smells wrong (not a hint of potpourri), the mattress feels wrong. And the body pressed against my back is also wrong.

This is not my bed.

I open my eyes, careful not to move lest I wake whoever's here with me. Complete silence apart from someone's steady sleepy breathing. No sound of my cousins going about their morning ablutions. Terribly quiet inside and out, the sort of silence that falls after a very big celebratory night. Vague recollections of the wedding party growing and growing as the evening wore on. There was more drinking (even if I couldn't remember that, the ache in my skull told me), there was dancing. I drank a *lot*. I danced a *lot*. There was… bright red hair in the torchlight, bright green eyes staring into mine.

Oh.

Oh no.

Don't think about it now, don't get distracted (plenty of time for self-recrimination later). Just slide out of bed, find your red dress – and your shoes (no, don't put *them* on) – down the stairs (avoiding numbers nine, five and two because they creak). Slip out the back, run through the shadow-filled alleys and narrow defiles between buildings (the ground is cold and frosty, biting at your feet), until you come to the secret gate in the hedge-fence at the rear of the Briar House. Crunch over the grass that feels like glass, slither in the kitchen door like a cat. Up the stairs on tiptoes, along the carpeted hallway, into your bedroom and kiss the door closed.

Only then do I breathe.

Only then do I think about the last glimpse I had of the loft bedroom in the priest's house, of the tousled red hair on the pillow, the pale skin over lean muscle, the broad shoulders and deep chest previously hidden by the nondescript brown robe. Certain parts of me want to turn around and go back to the warmth of that bed which isn't mine.

I shake my head and immediately regret doing so. My stomach rebels and it's all I can do to make it to my washroom in time.

* * *

It's lunchtime when I finally surface. My head pounds less after a tonic of lemon, sarsaparilla, and meadowsweet, although my tongue is still a bit dry and swollen, and despite endless brushing of teeth and gargling, my breath could kill at twenty paces. I'd best not breathe near any open flames.

When I enter the kitchen, Eira and Nia are at the table, discussing the unsuccessful search for Ezekiel Perry, with what appear to be mutton and cheese sandwiches in front of them, pickles on the side. The very thought makes my stomach turn a somersault. Apparently I look sufficiently terrible that Eira rises, presses me into a chair, then sets about serving me a bowl of porridge (plain, no cream or stewed fruits, just a little salt) and a mug of black coffee. When I've halfway emptied the bowl, Nia pipes up: 'Got that out of your system?'

There's a vague recollection of seeing her last night as I danced, glaring at me from one of the tables. Had she come to find me because I'd not made it home? And had I told her, rudely, to leave me be? Did I or just wish I had? No, I think I definitely *did*. But there's the question of what *she* saw – oh yes, there's the memory of her stomping away back to the Briar House as I continued to reel from arm to arm. And Eira would have been canoodling with Sally in their little cottage. If anyone else had seen anything untoward, my cousins would have heard about it by now, what with the speed of rumour being more fleet than a bird on the wing.

'I *heard*,' Eira says carefully, 'that there was a god-hound arrived yesterday.'

'And that you showed him into the priest's house?' Nia's tone can barely contain her anger. 'Why would you do that? He can stay at the inn like any other travelling mendicant. Are you an idiot?'

I have another mouthful of porridge, another swig of coffee, take my sweet time. Then I tell them everything (or almost) that transpired yesterday afternoon and eve. How all my efforts had seemed to pay off. Of the beautiful moments between *before* and *after*. Of Father Huw's appearance at the wedding. Of the revelation by Edgar of Maud's perfidy. Of the avalanche of consequences I envisage rushing towards us – of the life Gilly and Sandor built for us, maintained by centuries of Briars, and all about to fall apart as soon as I was left in charge. It doesn't matter that Maud's choice was no fault of mine – the mess will still drop into my lap. I don't mention how wonderful it felt for so brief a span to be needed and admired; to feel I belonged to this family.

And my cousins stare at me in open-mouthed horror.

'And so, dearest Nia, that priest is not your common or garden god-hound. He's not a'wandering through our lovely little town. He's Tobias's replacement, here to stay, and very soon he's going to ask how our grandfather, who's been dead over a decade, has religiously sent two reports a year assuring the Archbishop that the Briar witches are behaving themselves nicely, thank you very much.'

'But why would Maud do that to us?'

'Why indeed?' Even if Maud didn't like Audra and saw me as no more than a useful functionary, she did at least seem to love Nia and Eira. And Gisela. What was on our great-aunt's mind?

'What will Audra say?' Eira asks.

'I can barely wait to find out.' I rise, still a bit unsteady, and help myself to more coffee, then slump back in my chair. I don't mention the very least of my problems, which is needing a new venue for dealing with Silverton's restless dead. And I definitely do not mention that I spent last night drunkenly entwined with said troublesome priest who's now the source of, if not all, then very definitely a lot of our problems.

'I'm sure Audra would have handled it perfectly,' I mumble. 'She'd not have hesitated to kill the god-hound. Dream up a clever solution. Keep us alive for another generation or two. No, it takes me, the useless Briar, to bring destruction upon us all. Or at least let it get close enough to hover in the vicinity.'

I consider laying my head down on the tabletop and going back to sleep until everything either crumbles to ruin or is miraculously fixed.

'Planning on giving up then?' Eira asks.

'Unless you've got a better idea,' I grumble.

'Ellie Briar, I never thought I'd see the day when you gave up so easily.' That's Nia, to my surprise.

'Well, if you continue to think about it, you might realise that these circumstances are rather more challenging than usual.' I straighten. 'What do you want me to do? March over there and whack him on the head?'

Probably should have done that when I first thought about it yesterday.

'Don't be an idiot. You were right not to harm him – we don't know enough yet; we don't know precisely why he's been sent, what the mood of the current Archbishop is. If they suspect anything – although if they did, I don't think there'd be just one god-hound. And, Ellie, never forget that we serve a purpose *here*. Briars guard the border, we watch the way. We keep the lands safe. We're not so easily disposed of.'

Eira's right; I'd never thought of it like that. Everything that's been drummed into me by Gisela and Maud has emphasised that we exist at the pleasure and tolerance of the cathedral-city so the letters must be perfect, they must be sent on time. To ensure that the princes of the church never discover what happened to Tobias – either that he fathered children with the Briar Witch, or that his granddaughter killed him. The fact of him burning his own daughter has never been something that would bother the god-hounds, not given her nature.

But we *are* essential. There have been no incursions by the Leech Lords of the Darklands since the Briars arrived. The stone circle begun by Gilly's daughters, turning her body into the first

221

of the monoliths, and adding to it every time a Briar Witch died. We maintain the secret of it, making the defence stronger with every death, with every corpse. They closed the way so those who rule in the Darklands can't cross over. In the years after the menhirs were raised, hunts were coordinated for those leeches that had already entered. So few remain now that they're barely a danger, though the church is even more vigilant about dealing with them than witches. At least witches might be put to a better use. Tinkers and merchants like Edgar travel back and forth, marking themselves out either with a traders' gold pin or by adopting the sigil of one of the Darklands great houses, because if they don't, if they appear to be "unowned", random strays, free-range bleeders-on-the-hoof, they may well be fed upon. Death is a bad enough result, but turning into a leech means they can't come back home, cannot breach the border – although *becoming* one is not a simple process, involves a willingness by both feeder and bleeder. It's not an accidental thing.

So, if – *when* – our deceit becomes known, there will surely be a punishment, a fine, new restrictions. But we won't be wiped out. Only a fool would slaughter us all and risk a tide of leeches pouring through.

I sit back, nodding slowly so my head doesn't hurt. Nia asks, 'Then, Ellie Briar, what's your plan?'

'Get to know him. Get at his secrets.' *Good start, Ellie.* 'Do my best to control what he learns. Make sure Edgar leaves as soon as possible so the god-hound doesn't give him a letter to carry to the Archbishop of Lodellan. That buys us all of wintertide – the priest's unlikely to be foolish enough to set off in the snow and sleet.' I rap my knuckles on the table. 'We can always kill him later.'

222

'That's the spirit.' A familiar voice – we turn. Audra stands in the doorway, bright as hope, bright as a new gold piece. None of us heard her arrive. 'Now, cousins, who aren't we killing today?'

* * *

In the library, not much later, I'm sitting across from Audra and feeling considerably better. There's someone else to make (or at least share) weighty decisions, and if I feel a spark of resentment at seeing her in the chair I've so recently occupied, it's a very small one.

My cousin's elbows balance on the desktop, fingers steepled in front of her face. Audra looks tired, and the little lines around her mouth and on her forehead weren't in evidence before. She's also grubby with leaves, twigs and pin feathers in her hair (low-hanging trees, she says as I pick them out), smudges of dirt on her cheeks, small rents in her jacket and shirt, but I suspect I looked the same when I returned from days on the road. Her usual glow, however, is undiminished, perhaps stronger even. Yet she listens attentively while I relay (almost) everything that's happened since she left the town in my stewardship. She congratulates me on handling the melyne, is shocked at Dai Carabhille's culpability, impressed at the idea of Whispering him rather than mutilating him, laughs about Berthold Lloyd and his issue with eggs, is irritated about the school books, sad at the news Ezekiel Perry is missing, stunned at Maud's treason and deeply worried by the arrival of the god-hound.

'You were right to leave him alone, this priest. Did he present any papers?'

It's a slap in the face, though I don't think that's her intent. I'd not even thought about such a thing – a piece of parchment embossed with golden seals, written in ecclesiastical purple ink, such as still take up shelf space in the priest's house. A god-hound's passport, with his rank and first name (for they no longer need a last when they join the church, and only reclaim it upon reaching the title of Archbishop) and posting location; his licence to do as he will. Guilty that we've been breaking the rules for so long, it didn't occur to me to demand proof of who he was. On the one hand, it makes my heart soar. If he's a fraud, he's easily dealt with. But on the other, I'm still an idiot who didn't ask the right questions when I should have. I blurt all of this out to Audra, who shakes her head.

'It's alright, Ellie, don't fear. I'd likely have forgotten too – I'm only thinking of it now because I've had time – and been more inclined to dispose of him. It wasn't an easy situation and certainly not one Gisela envisaged, *and* neither Eira nor Nia would have known what to do.' I appreciate the acerbic tone; it's our little circle of two again, the *proper* orphans when our cousins always had each other. She bites her bottom lip, considering. 'Keep an eye on him. Invite him to dinner tomorrow night. We'll see what information we can get out of him. We may yet find a use for him.'

I nod. *Oh, wonderful.*

Audra leans forward, smiling, reaching for me, and says quietly, 'Ellie, you've done brilliantly in my stead. I had no doubt you would. With or without magic, you are more than capable, and I need you by my side.'

I take her hand, feel how warm the fingers are, how strong when she squeezes. Tears heat my eyes; I shouldn't feel so grateful. I should feel embarrassed to be so moved by something so small. I'm tempted to tell her about the ghosts, about Sandor, but the voice inside overrules: *Not yet.*

224

'Thank you. But we must discuss a schedule, Audra, so we're not missing things.' *You're not missing things.* 'Iris and Aaron's wedding? And you'd not told Agnes Grieve about Gisela – she wasn't best pleased.' My cousin's face flares red, and I'm unsure if it's embarrassment or annoyance. Probably both. I say hastily, 'It's understandable, we've had a lot of disruption, but from this point on we need to be in concert.'

'You're right of course, Ellie. I'll pay more attention.' Contrite.

'I'm here to support you, so we can all do our best for Silverton.' I won't mention the dissatisfaction at the sewing circle about her going away so soon after Gisela's death. No point in provoking her.

She smiles suddenly. 'Liv and Bedo send love.'

'They were well? What did you find on the other holdings?' Curious that we've only just gotten to this topic, given that it was the whole point of her trip. I noticed she dodged questions from Nia and Eira earlier; I didn't push then as I figured it boded ill, that she wanted to talk to me first. 'Safe?'

She nods vigorously. 'And the Dees, Olafssons, Treharnes, Axelssons, Bergs and Holms!'

'Really? All of them?' I'm pleased, but can't keep a hint of disbelief from my tone.

'All of them! The Axelssons, Bergs and Holms were together – they'd organised a hunt for whatever's been killing animals in the woods – didn't Liv tell you about that?'

'Only about the dead deer…' *And foxes and badgers and the bear…*

'There were even more around the other farms. The families didn't want to leave their little ones and women behind, so they set up a camp down by Cariad's Falls; safety in numbers, Mr Berg said.'

'Did they find anything?'

She shakes her head. 'Nothing more than troll spoor but the trail ran cold.'

'I checked all the troll-pikes…'

'Perhaps you missed one?' She says it blithely, as though it's a likelihood. Perhaps she's right: I missed three entire families and any sign of them making for a place less than an hour from the Bergs' farm. Nia would have no trouble believing it.

'I warned the outliers to keep a lookout and send for us if they needed vigilants or got wind of anything untoward. Liv was hoping she'd see you soon, although I'm not sure when I'll be able to spare you again, Ellie. I really do need you.'

'Two of the children are due to start school in spring – we should have her to stay when she brings them in.' I shake my head, frustrated. 'I'm glad everyone's safe. I can't believe I—'

'Ellie, it's not beyond the realms of possibility that this happened – it's very unlikely but not impossible. And better that you raised the alarm and we investigated, don't you think?'

I nod, still feeling foolish.

'Now,' she says, 'I hear that you've developed a talent for finding things?'

Audra smiles and leans back, withdrawing from contact. I realise that before she came back to the house she'd wandered through the village. Did her rounds, asking those she met how things had been while she'd been away. Checking up on me.

It was inevitable that she'd learn something about my locating long-lost treasures, hidden inheritances, buried secrets, putting

226

matters to rights. I didn't think it would be so soon, however. I keep myself from shrugging. Smile. 'Simply a matter of luck, Audra. I went to write Gisela's death in the register' – *Do not mention she'd failed to do it* – 'and found some papers and old letters. Fortunate that I was able to help people.'

'Would you mind using this luck in my favour?'

'Isn't that the entire purpose of my existence?' I laugh, and she joins in. 'What do you need, Audra?'

'There's a book my mother used to mention. Gilly Briar's grimoire – *The Bitterwood Bible*, I think she called it.'

'I remember. It held the greatest and most powerful spells any witch had ever conjured. And Gilly hid it, if I recall correctly, so no one would be tempted by all that power.' Which, I think, shows very little trust in her descendants.

She nods. 'Find it for me. Imagine of what we could do with that tome. How we could protect ourselves…' Her eyes shine.

'What from?'

'Acts of nature – famine, pestilence – a plague like the one that took your mother and, ultimately, mine. From god-hounds that might march upon us.' She spreads her hands wide, fingers splayed in the air, expansive, inviting me to *see*, to *imagine* the possibilities. 'Attack by bandits like those who destroyed St Ogg's.'

I consider telling her what Edgar said, about seeing no encampments (perhaps about that strange change in the landscape) but decide it can wait; don't remind her of Romelia and her sisters' great act, how no bandit in their right mind would try to raid Silverton. 'I'll do my best. I'll start up here, then down in the storage rooms.'

She smiles, contented. 'Thank you, my darling Ellie. Now, if you can bear to be me for one more afternoon, I'll go and bathe, then sleep! I'm exhausted.'

I grin. 'I can probably manage it.'

'You're my strength, dearest cousin.'

And we can, I think, survive without Gisela and Maud in this world. Audra and I can keep Silverton safe.

23

The next day, my head considerably clearer although my conscience definitely less so, I knock on the priest's door. The god-hound answers quickly, as if he's been waiting for just such a moment. I glance past him; no waiting ghosts. Oh, gods, were there any the other night? Watching?

'Good day, Ellie.' He sounds chipper, looks refreshed and happy, and I hate him more than a little. Not a hint of a leer, so there's that in his favour.

I do my best to keep a neutral expression, pleasant is too much to ask for. 'Hello. My cousin Audra asks that you dine with us this eve.'

'Would you like to come in?'

'Dinner. Tonight.' That's infinitely worse – it sounds like an invitation from *me*. 'The Briar Witch requests it.'

He seems to be considering. 'Well…'

'Are you telling me you've got something better to do? In town five minutes and you've already had other offers?' No one invited Tobias to dinner except Gisela; at least not after his tendency to harangue people during meals showed itself.

'Three invitations as it happens.' He grins. 'Your folk are most welcoming of strangers.'

Yes, but not generally of god-hounds. Previous priests have, on occasion, been frozen out of the community unless the Briar Witch gave her approval. 'Think carefully about offending the witches.' I begin to turn away. 'But the choice is of course your own.'

I'm at the bottom of the stairs when he calls, 'What time?'

'Six-thirty.'

'Ellie?' His tone stops me, makes me turn. He's got something in his hand. My blackthorn baton, which I've not been able to find since the wedding. 'Would you like to take this with you? Or I could bring it to dinner?'

I shoot back up the steps, snatch it from him; hook it onto my belt. Glare at his laughing face. 'You...'

'Would you like to come in and tell me what you think of me?' His voice drops an octave, and the worst thing is that I *would*. I could also shriek at him on the doorstep for everyone to hear. But I won't; I do have that much self-control. I retreat to the street.

When he calls, 'Whatever shall I wear?' a laugh shoots out of me, but I don't look around.

* * *

In the townhall, I sit with Dónal in his corner office (no larger than the others but it has a window), and we painstakingly go through the records looking for something we've missed in regard to the imported brandy. It seems like a lot of time to spend on something trivial, but Maud taught me that good organisation lay in being picky. And if we can't trace this theft – if theft it is – then who knows what else will go missing? Dónal, bless him, is as perplexed as I, so doesn't complain.

'Just so you know, Miss Bisbee and I attended at the papermill.'

'And how did that go?' I ask as if I don't care, but I've stopped scanning the columns of numbers in the ledger in front of me.

'Badly at first because Dai – who's looking worse for wear, by the by – was in the shop. Then worse and more loudly worse. Until his father appeared and sent him away.'

'Oh dear.'

'Indeed. Miss Bisbee remained remarkably calm.'

'If you spend your day with children, I think it's a fine character trait.'

'She presented the offending books, explained the problems.'

'And.'

'Master Carabhille the Elder was most apologetic and confused as to how such a mistake had been made. Supplied two more boxes of exercise books and assured me there would be no invoice for them. Undertook to check with the other schoolteachers to ensure the error had not been replicated.'

'The "errors" were delivered after the night the melyne found its father, weren't they?'

'Indeed they were.'

'Dai might have thought twice about such a petty act had he known what Beres would do.' Audra is heading over to the Carabhilles' townhouse this afternoon to advise the family about their pride and joy's forthcoming punishment. It's interesting he targeted the Adalind's Row school, the one closest to us, the one Audra seems to favour.

'Can you supervise the tithe-barns this afternoon, Dónal?' It's distribution day but I have somewhere else to be.

'As you wish, Steward Briar,' in a tone that implies I might be shirking my duty just a little.

231

* * *

Ezekiel Perry's cottage remains empty and dark. I've roamed Silverton, chatting, taking note of buildings and structures that need work, listening to a variety of complaints and compliments, but mostly I've been looking for ghosts. I've not seen a one since the assembly, and I haven't called for Sandor because, well, I was annoyed with his performance there. Huw's arrival and all it entailed felt like the last straw. I assume Sandor's been sulking; perhaps he'd simply taken a dislike to Lowen Jernigan's fancy waistcoat.

Now that the priest's house has a more weighty occupant, I thought maybe my many-times-great-grandfather had taken refuge here. As the house is empty, it wouldn't qualify as *rude* to go inside. The other ghosts… well, there are fewer now, perhaps fifty? Sixty? And it's not like they need a "somewhere" to hide when they can blink themselves out of even my sight. But as I've observed, the habits of *life* remain strongly ingrained. Feeling stupid, I knock before entering.

No misty figures or foggy blurs. No whispers. Just the same smell of old unwashed Ezekiel, although weaker; I must open a window. I light one of the candles, then wander through the few rooms to find no one, barely a breath of air in the tiny bedroom.

'Sandor?' I say and it comes out small, a little croaky; I sound like a child fearful of rebuke. I clear my throat and call properly: 'Sandor? Where are you?'

I wait, poised, holding the candle up like I'm a statue built purely for this purpose. Still nothing, and I'm surprised by the sense of loneliness that overwhelms me. My forefather's been in my life a scant week and this absence feels like a horrible loss. 'Sandor, please—'

A heavy hand falls on my shoulder and I scream. Undignified, almost dropping the taper. I turn so fast it makes my head spin, and the guttering flame shows a hulking shape, a face made terrifying by shadows and troughs, a shouting mouth.

'Ellie! You have to stop them!'

Dai Carabhille.

The only thing I recognise through my panic is his voice, a voice I once loved to hear. Now it grates on my nerves. You'd think these past days of dealing with the dead would have made me less prone to fright, wouldn't you? But then, he's not dead, is he?

'Dai! What do you want? Why are you here? Why are you sneaking up on me?' I don't bother to strip the anger out, to sweeten my tone; my voice is a naked blade.

'Ellie, the whole fucking town is talking! Whispering! Blaming! And my father… my father… looked at me like…'

I blink and peer closely, wonder what I ever saw in him. To my eyes he's no longer well-made, but a lumbering liar bent by a weight he's never had to bear: responsibility. And he is indeed unkempt. Hair shaggy, clothing crumpled, yellow marks on the shirt collar. He smells like damp sawdust, and there's a line of black under his nails that's never been there before.

'And what are they talking about, Dai?'

'Deirdre and that… thing.'

'Your child. Drystan.'

He shakes his head, swats at his hair. 'Saying it's all my fault. That I'm a coward.'

'Why do you think that is?' Not that long ago, I could never have imagined this core of ice in my heart. Apparently nor could he: deprived of sympathy, worship, Dai swells up, even taller, looming like a storm cloud.

'No one's coming into the store. Wherever I go, they stare' – once, he'd never have complained about the attention – 'and my mother can barely get anyone to serve her at the markets.'

'I'm sorry for your mother.' I am, she's a nice woman. 'But there's nothing I can do.'

'They'll listen to you! Tell them to stop! Tell them it wasn't me!'

'But it was you! You bedded her, then left her to suffer on her own when she got pregnant! And you didn't even do the decent thing when the melyne appeared – you could have admitted it, named the babe and no one would have thought worse of you!' *I would.* 'It happens, Dai, it's not uncommon, and you would have done what was needed for the sake of the community.' I shake my head. 'Instead, you kept your mouth shut and let that creature roam. It was pure luck that I stopped it when I did. It wouldn't have gone away! It would have turned murderous, and someone would have died!'

His hands are curling into fists at his sides. 'It's that you're jealous, isn't it?'

'Are you a complete idiot?' An image of that night with the god-hound springs to mind (blush-making), of doing all the things I'd once imagined doing with Dai – and now I can't even imagine *wanting* to do them with him.

'This is your petty revenge because I didn't want you.' He grins and it's the ugliest thing I've ever seen.

I spit at him: 'If you'd been honest about it all? At least

that would have been something I could admire about you. But none of this is my fault. And jealousy doesn't even enter into it.' *Only a tiny bit.*

'You're going to let that old Baines bitch humiliate me in public.' He wraps a huge fist around my upper arm and pulls me to him. 'What about now? If I fuck you now, Ellie Briar, will that make up for it? Is that your price for making this all go away? Or do I need to appeal to a higher authority?'

He's going to leave bruises. 'Get your hands off me!'

I kick out wildly, connect with his shin and he lets go, swearing. I stumble, trying to regain my balance, groping for the blackthorn baton. But instead of advancing, Dai bends over, begins to puff. Soon he's trying desperately to breathe.

Suddenly I can see why.

The white fog of spectres boils around him, pressing at him, some pushing their fingers into his mouth, others passing their hands through his chest. Sandor, expression terrifying, has hold of Dai's throat. And I let them continue thus for a few seconds longer, to teach him a lesson, to enjoy his terror when he was so happy to visit it upon me. To enjoy the feeling that someone's on my side even if it's only because without me they're doomed to wander forever. I don't care.

'Let him go,' I say at last. They obey, some a little reluctantly. Dai's gasping, straightening up, looking around to see who I'm talking to. 'Promise you won't try to harm me again. Nor follow me!'

His head's swivelling like it's on a stick, searching the dark corners of the bedroom, eyes almost all white like a panicked horse.

235

'For your own good, promise.' The ghosts look eager, as if they hope he won't. One of them strokes the nape of his neck and he screeches, spinning, a dog chasing a phantom tail.

'I promise!'

'Now, get out. And keep this to yourself lest I send them for you in the night.'

At the door he pauses, gives me one last horrified glare and says, 'I thought you weren't like the rest of them,' and he's gone from the little room, the sound of the front door opening and thudding closed behind him.

I should have told him he was imagining things. That the shortness of breath was merely a sign of stress, of anger. I should have told him not to worry. I could have slipped so easily back into Calm Ellie, Kind Ellie, Desperate Unloved Ellie, and he'd not have given it a second thought; would've assumed my time and gentleness were his due.

But I want him to be afraid of me. I want him to feel the world pulled from beneath his feet, just as poor Deirdre must have when he cast her aside. What did he say to her to stop her from telling anyone it was him? How afraid of him was she?

I go into the sitting room and Sandor follows, comes to stand beside me as I sag into the dusty armchair. 'Are you alright, Ellie?'

'Thank you,' I say, watching the shape of Dai Carabhille through the grubby window, running and stumbling and not looking back. I wonder if he'll say anything, who he'll tell. Will anyone listen to him if he does? 'Where have you been, Sandor?'

He gives a sigh. 'Sulking.'

Ha! 'I'm sorry if you feel I've not been attentive enough. But

Audra's returned and I'll have more time. The priest's house is, however, occupied.'

'I know.' Should have known he'd be watching.

'I don't suppose you've been inside spying on the god-hound?' Oh, please no, not Saturday night! Sandor gives me an offended look. Of course not. The house was occupied; it would be rude.

'We try to be good ghosts.'

'I get the phantoms with principles.' I sigh.

He gives a little bow.

'Sandor.' I swallow hard. 'Are you changing?'

He tilts his head, quizzical.

'I mean, before you said you've never been able to affect the world around you, but Dai… That was quite some effect.'

His eyes widen – he'd not realised himself; had forgotten, I think, what he couldn't do when the rage at what was being done rose. Instinct made him leap to my defence, the others probably just followed suit. He nods. 'I think you must have done something to Gilly's spell – seeing us, releasing us. You've weakened it. I can still feel its constraints, but not as strongly. I wonder if it might break entirely?'

He sounds so hopeful I can't bear to disappoint him, can't bring myself to ask, *Oh, how could I ever break a spell cast by the greatest Briar Witch of them all?* Instead I say, 'Perhaps. I'm glad you're back. I missed you.'

'I'm sorry I was childish.' He gives a courtly bow.

'Tomorrow, let's begin again. We may as well use this place – it's awful and dim, it smells, but no one else will come here. Dai certainly won't.'

'Aren't you worried about him?'

'What will he do? Tell the other witches there's a new witch? One they know to be as powerless as a newborn kitten? When he's currently in such trouble for being a liar?' I shake my head. 'No one will believe him. I'll deny it, all wide-eyed and bewildered.'

He shrugs. 'Perhaps you're right.'

'Besides, I think he's too afraid.' I look around. The place will need cleaning if I'm to spend extended time here. 'Oh, what were you trying to tell me about Lowen Jernigan? And why-oh-why did you sit in his lap?'

24

Audra, always naturally charming, appears to be going out of her way to be even more so with Father Huw, who'd politely presented his papers of appointment before dinner was served.

It's probably a good thing as Nia, Eira and I are definitely not trying very hard at all. We might also be sulking because she insisted we dress up like grand ladies waiting on a visiting prince. Fancy uncomfortable gowns, all for a god-hound in a brown robe (a clean one, thankfully, not the travel-stained thing he arrived in), and he'd polished his boots. He himself smelled freshly bathed when he appeared at our door.

Dinner conversation is stilted. You can hardly blame us: the only god-hound we've ever seen at this table was our grandfather, and that was a rare phenomenon indeed. Those were no gentle family meals, but rather an opportunity for that dusty old sod to point out our many faults (we were loud and disrespectful, opinionated and unladylike, lacking in humility to boot) and harangue Gisela for the wickedness of her ways (mind you, some of those ways were ones he'd been only too happy to participate in). Maud alone would escape criticism, possibly because she was the one who generally took him his meals (but for that fateful day) and sat front and centre in the church every Sunday with his sparse congregation, listening to his sermons (in which she had no belief).

Make no mistake: it didn't change *her* witching ways either, but I think he found something very compelling in her complete attention. And she? I think Maud, more and more, wanted what Gisela had – what came to her younger sister so seemingly easily. It took me a long time to realise that the looks my great-aunt gave Tobias were probably the same ones I'd given Dai Carabhille. And at this very moment, Audra is gazing at Huw in a very similar manner. For someone whose mother was murdered by the one and only priest we ever knew, she's being *spectacularly* charming.

'My mother used to tell me that Lodellan Cathedral was guarded by spectral wolves. Is that true, Father Huw?' She slants her eyes at him, looking up through long lashes. He, however, seems immune to the flirtatious tone. And I feel heat rising in my cheeks.

'It is, although they're very ancient and hardly visible nowadays. Sometimes you'll hear a growl behind you, feel something cold brush past your legs, but there's not much force left in them.' He's eating with gusto and it occurs to me that he might have starved a little on his way through the mountains. 'There was a major theft from the cathedral a few years ago and the wolves had no power to stop it. But there's a tale oft-repeated of how they once tore apart a troll-wife foolish enough to trespass. Sadly, nothing lasts forever, I suppose.'

'Indeed not. As we were reminded recently by our grandmother's death.'

I give her a sideways look and notice Eira and Nia doing the same thing. Audra ignores us, all her focus on the god-hound.

'You'll be wondering, no doubt, about the reports that have been received in Lodellan even though Father Tobias has been gone from us for some time.' She sounds positively pious – doesn't mention *how* long ago – and I want to laugh out loud, but that wouldn't make me popular. Audra will have a plan, she'll have been thinking about this since her return; she can be good at planning when the requirement's pointed out to her.

Huw nods, brow furrowed, yet doing his best not to look judgmental. 'It does seem rather a peculiar circumstance. I'm well aware that the witches of Silverton have particular conditions under which they rule.'

What he means is *under which they survive*.

Audra nods, serious. 'You find us at an… interesting point, Father Huw. We've lived all our lives beneath the yoke of our grandmother Gisela, the previous Briar Witch, and it has not been an easy existence.'

Around the table, Nia and Eira and I freeze for a second, then just as quickly continue with our meals. Nia quaffs wine from her goblet, Eira cuts the venison on her plate with precision, I oversalt my potatoes. Huw's gaze is fixed on Audra's lovely face, filled with nothing more than curiosity. 'I'm sorry to hear it.'

'You must understand that when Father Tobias died' – she doesn't mention he was our grandfather – 'blessed be his memory – Gisela made the decision to continue writing and sending reports in his name. She felt we'd had sufficient oversight from the church after almost three centuries.' She smiles apologetically, as if our grandmother's idea was radical and insane and nothing *we'd* ever have a part of if given a choice. 'So, *she* perpetrated this deception.'

'I see.'

'Please rest assured that my cousins and I don't share her beliefs. We welcome your presence – the people of Silverton will blossom under the ecclesiastical guidance only you can provide. You'll be a welcome addition to town life, and if you will consent, an advisor to we Briars. An unbiased eye and a fearless voice are always appreciated.' Audra gives a wide smile, positively blinding; or perhaps that's the effect of the lights reflecting off her golden gown. 'It's our first taste of freedom, making such decisions for ourselves.'

Which is when Eira begins to choke on her food. She rises, chair scraping back, and rushes from the dining room. I should stay and listen, but Nia's showing no sign of going to her sister – she looks entranced at the scene playing out – so I excuse myself and follow Eira.

In the kitchen, she's curled over the sink, hacking and spluttering, although thankfully not throwing up. When she calms and straightens, I hand her a cup of water. As soon as she's able she hisses, 'What the fuck is Audra playing at? Why is she saying such things about Gisela? Our grandmother *bought* us years of freedom, seducing Tobias, having his children, seeing to it that our safety was important to him.'

'Well, until he burned Aunt Hebe.' I raise my hands at her expression. 'I agree! I agree. But Audra's being quite brilliant. She needs to tell him something to allay his suspicions. Yes, it seems very disloyal to Gisela, but she's not around to complain and she'd be the first one to tell us we must survive at all costs.' I touch Eira's shoulder. 'Audra's buying us time in her own way, just as Gisela did. We need to know more about him before we decide what to do. If he thinks us innocent victims of the former Briar Witch? It keeps us safe a while longer.'

Slowly, Eira nods, still unhappy but seeing the wisdom of my words. I can't say I'm not incensed on our grandmother's behalf, annoyed that Audra didn't share her plan with me at least. But our cousin *is* clever and this strategy is considerably better than my first instinct to murder the new god-hound and also, probably, my second instinct to bed him. By the time we return bearing dessert there's only Nia left at the table, head in hands, muttering that the priest has excused himself on the grounds of travel-related exhaustion. I restrain myself from observing that the walk between our houses is indeed a long one. Eira and I follow the sound of laughter and peek into the entry hall where Audra and Father Huw are saying their goodbyes.

There's a moment when our beautiful cousin leans toward the young priest, almost to press herself to him – and he leaps away as if scalded.

Eira and I backpedal to the table at equal speed, lest Audra realise we witnessed this rejection. We don't look at each other. I busy myself cutting depression-sized slices of apple and raspberry pie, which Eira covers in warm custard.

Audra returns and sits. If I'd not seen it happen, I'd never have known she'd been rebuffed by the god-hound. Her colour's only a little pink, but that might otherwise have been from the wine at dinner. She's so calm, and I can't help but admire her. Such poise. Yet I also can't help but wonder how she's truly feeling: Audra's never in her life been deprived of what she wanted. It was one of Maud's complaints about her; our great-aunt regarded it as a terrible flaw, one of the reasons she didn't like her bright and beautiful niece.

* * *

Later, when everyone's gone to bed, lanterns extinguished and the muted murmur of Nia's snoring is the only sound to be heard, I slip into Gisela's empty bedroom. Audra still hasn't moved her things in. If anyone finds me, I'll simply say I was looking for a book; if it's Audra I'll say it's *The Bitterwood Bible*. That this seemed as good a place as any to search because it's been the suite of the Briar Witch all these long centuries. Not that there's any reason for me not to be here – *don't overcomplicate things, Ellie Briar, you could simply say* sadness *and that would be enough*.

But in truth, I'm seeking what Sandor told me this afternoon would be missing. Lowen Jernigan had caught his attention at the assembly – or rather something the man was wearing. A ring – a thick band of reddish gold, plain but for the repeated engraved motif of a briar round it.

Inside Gisela's walk-in wardrobe a large ebony wood box sits on a shelf, and inside the box is part of the Briar trove of jewellery and heirlooms – things that can be easily concealed, sewn into the hems of dresses and coats and cloaks should a quick getaway be required – even after three hundred years, we're prepared to run. We all have small trinkets we've inherited, but the major items, the most expensive ones, the oldest things, are kept here.

The ring, Sandor said, had been a gift from his Gilly-girl when they'd settled, become established, had more than two copper bits to rub together. To honour the new surname they'd chosen to cut themselves loose from their past. To give their daughters an identity, a connection to their new home. I've a vague memory of the piece he means – no one's worn it in ages, but I remember playing with it when I was small, when Gisela used to let us sit on her bed and go through all those shiny things. It should, said Sandor with considerable umbrage, have been buried with him. I'd replied that Briars haven't gotten ahead in the world by putting gold back in the ground, and although he grumbled a bit, he did concede the point. I think he's still embarrassed about trying to possess Jernigan – that was the sitting-in-his-lap thing, trying to settle into another's body, but there was nothing for him to latch onto.

Now, sitting on the floor of the wardrobe with the box's contents on the boards in front of me, a lantern carefully placed to show everything, I have to admit that the ring is gone. Absentmindedly, I rub at my arm, at the bruises left by Dai Carabhille, already turning dark, and wince. I put everything back, then wrap one of Gisela's dark cloaks around myself, sneak downstairs and out of the house. Once past the hedge-fence, I say Sandor's name. He appears immediately.

'How was your dinner, Ellie Briar?' He eyes my fine emerald dress peeking out from the cloak as I walk.

'Like sitting naked on a throne of nettles: painful and hopefully never to be repeated. Sandor, your ring wasn't there.'

'I knew it!'

'So: how did Lowen Jernigan get it? Only a fool would steal from witches. *Obedience* is a habit in Silverton. Besides which, he couldn't know how old it is, how seldom anyone sees it, or that it's unlikely to be missed. He *couldn't* know. There are other pieces clearly of greater value. How did he get it? And why?'

Sandor clears his throat. 'If it *couldn't* have been theft…'

'…that means…'

'…he might have been given it.'

'Why and by whom?'

'Payment? A bribe?'

'But *why*? We have everything we require, we don't need to bribe anyone.'

'Can you honestly say that neither your grandmother nor your great-aunt might have had plans of their own? Or your cousins?'

I start to protest – then I recall Maud and the letter that was not sent. What else might she have done? 'We don't know when it went missing. And I can't prove that it's ours – yours – because I can't bring you in as a witness or to claim possession. Gisela or Maud might have done it years ago.'

'Can't you just demand it back?'

Above us, but a little too close for comfort, there's a shifting of the air. Looking up I see dark wings barely visible against the night sky. Bat? Bird.

'Sandor… whoever's taken the ring, or given it away, thought it was something no one would go looking for. That it wouldn't be noticed on Jernigan's hand. If it was either Gisela or Maud, well, they're dead now. However, what if it wasn't? If I make a fuss then I show my cards, alert whoever it is about… whatever it is. *If*, and it's a big *if*, this is a recent theft, gift, bribe, whatever it is.' I sigh. 'I'll make an opportunity to speak with Lowen Jernigan – perhaps discuss the details of his failed gaming-parlour proposal. Bring it up subtly.'

'How will you do that, Ellie Briar?' Sandor asks.

'That is tomorrow's problem. Or one of them. Now, Grandfather, I'm tired and I need my beauty sleep.'

He gives me a look that says he knows where I'm going, but he's too polite to say anything. He's gone before I arrive at the priest's house. In spite of my better judgment, I can't resist the overwhelming urge to reclaim what certain parts of me insist is mine.

25

Audra's spending the day with Eira at the infirmary, something Gisela did twice a week, helping with the newborns and their mothers, overseeing Eira's trainee nurses, checking on the more difficult patients, those whose illnesses don't seem to be shifting as they should. Nia and an increasingly shrinking detail of vigilants are out looking for Ezekiel Perry again; I suspect the searches will be called off soon.

Buying myself time, I set Dónal to working out a plan for the tour I want to do with Audra of Silverton's buildings – the most efficient path through the town to view all public and private structures and decide on a programme of maintenance. Nia, as marshal, should probably come too, but I'm not sure I want her trailing along and complaining. Maybe I'll just present her with its *doneness* afterwards, a list of work she needs to supervise. Tempting.

With my day freed up, I devote the morning to methodically looking through the library for Gilly's grimoire. I'm grateful, as I pull each volume out and examine it, that Mrs Reynard dusts regularly.

I check the obvious location first, with the other accumulated grimoires of generations past and then the general books of magic (histories, technical tracts, experimental journals – all the tomes that would cause the Archbishop of Lodellan to clutch at his heart and keel over). I open each volume, ensure that the table of contents (if there is one) matches the actual contents, that the cover isn't simply a decoy, a camouflage. I make sure that endpapers are secure and not hiding anything untoward, and I flick through pages in case any marginalia might contain a clue. I also poke and prod along the backs of the bookcases just in case it's fallen behind other books or been hidden with intent. Of course, it was never going to be that easy, so now it's on to the less obvious spots, the less obvious subject areas.

In these bookcases are many spines with the golden embossed *M* of Murcianus. Fables and folktales, books on medicine and healing, atlases of lands known and otherwise, geographies of places I've never heard of, old encyclopaedias, memoires and biographies, books on the art of war and the price of peace, cookbooks, notebooks, religious tracts, novels and novellas and novelettes, collections and anthologies. Books on painting and sculpture, on games and weaponry, make-up and beauty, haircare and bodily adornment, the lore of gemstones and histories of jewellers and their wares. Tomes on tapestries and how knitting might be used as a form of magic (*Aha! I knew it*); on building and breaking all manner of things, breathing life into golems and drawing it out. Some bound between thick covers and thin, one that feels awfully like human skin, others nothing more than slim folios rolled into leather tubes.

But none of them *The Bitterwood Bible*…

All the Briars have their own grimoires – although mine is no better than a recipe book for potions and powders – but

Gilly's grimoire was the stuff of legend. One story says it was the first and greatest work of the Blessed Wanderer Murciana – whom certain sorts insist was a mendicant friar, Murcianus – who ended her years and days in the Citadel at Cwen's Reach. A home of books, knowledge and the Order of the Little Sisters of St Florian, it perished under the sustained attack of a mage who sought *The Bitterwood Bible*. It's said that the volumes deemed most important were sent forth, scattered across the world in the care of the Sisters, who flew away like birds.

Others maintain the tome in question was already gone before the Citadel's ruination – stolen many years before by a traitorous Sister, the mage's efforts all in vain. Another tale would have it lost through carelessness, yet found decades later by chance in a badger den, then traded to a bookbinder in a far-off city.

Aunt Hebe believed faithfully and forcefully that it came from the Three Who Went Beneath, those women who either started or ended (or both) the Witches' War. Hebe swore it contained their greatest secrets: how to change the very world itself, how to perform magic without paying the red price, turn day to night and back again against the will of the sky or the seasons or even time itself. There's no hint, however, in any of this as to how it came to Gilly's hands…

And no proof of its actual existence.

Me?

I don't hold with the idea it was ever one single book. I think the legend of what's been gathered together like dust to a sticky skein of spiderweb are the tales of several volumes. Perhaps all copies of that fearsome original but made at different times with additions and amendments and erasures, so none was ever

249

a perfect facsimile. While the actual *Bitterwood Bible*, the first of its kind, grew and changed and adapted with each owner, its replicas were all different, added to in different ways by diverse hands, lesser children of a strange parent.

But, thus far, I've not found the *true Bitterwood Bible*.

This room is *full*, the task will take me weeks – and then there's the extra storage in the cellar. Ah, well, a few shelves a day in between my other duties will be progress enough. There's no hurry.

* * *

'Hello, Ellie.'

I roll my eyes, think about not stopping, but I don't believe for one moment that will make the priest disappear. Not after last night, my own fault really. He's fallen into step, matching me as I increase my pace; the contents of the silver flask at his belt makes swishing sounds as he walks.

'Good afternoon.'

'May I ask you a question?'

'Does that one count?'

'Ha ha. Where are you going in such a hurry?'

I hold up the basket filled with freshly baked biscuits. 'To the school on Adalind's Row.'

His nose twitches like a rabbit's. I don't take pity on him, but I do stop and stare expectantly. 'Won't the other schools get jealous?'

'They get theirs, never fear. We have a schedule.'

'Ah.'

'Well?'

'Oh, yes. I've been talking to people and they've been—'

'—gossiping?'

'—sharing information about recent happenings and the like.'

'Gossiping.' I'm caught between impatience and suspicion.

'Well, yes.' He glances at the basket again. 'There was a young woman who died?'

'Hmmm.'

'Not long ago?'

'Hmmm.'

'Deirdre?'

'Hmmm.' *Who's been talking?*

'Did she kill herself?'

We told no one that. Neither Nia nor I and certainly not Gisela. Beres knew, of course she knew – hadn't she been dreading it for days? – but she'd not have told anyone what her daughter did. We simply said she'd drowned; had removed the rope from her neck before bringing her back. Who's been stirring up trouble? And what will this god-hound do about this girl he didn't know? Demand she be dug up from the churchyard, removed from consecrated earth like any other self-murderer in the cities? Is he preparing a sermon about just such a thing? The first he'll give in Silverton? Has he set foot in the church yet?

'No,' I say firmly. 'No, she did not kill herself. She'd been ill, was still weak. She went to collect rare flowers for a healing tea; they grow on the steep rocky slopes above one of the lakes. I fear her strength failed and she fell.' I clear my throat. 'She was alone and, I believe, hit her head and went into the water. She couldn't save herself and tumbled from the waterfall onto the rocks below.'

'If she was alone, how do you—'

'What do you want, Huw? Deirdre was grieving, she was distressed, but she had no reason to kill herself.' I lean close to him. 'And what would you do if she had? You can't punish her now, only her mother who's already suffered enough. Why would you want to inflict more pain? I didn't take you for cruel.'

He has the good grace to look away.

'Who's spoken to you?' I ask, clutching the basket's handle so tightly the wicker's imprinting on my palm.

'Mrs Carabhille. She said her son—'

Ah. 'You'd do well not to interfere in the life of a place you don't know. Giulia's son committed his own sins, so take his mother's words with a grain of salt. Dai Carabhille got Deirdre pregnant, then cast her off. Ask others what happened next, what they think of him. You've been here all of five seconds – do not deign to tell us how to deal with people we've been caring for for hundreds of years.' He doesn't reply, pale skin flushing very red. I glare for a few moments longer, then fish a biscuit from the basket. A peace offering. After a slight hesitation he takes it – who wouldn't? 'Now, be a good lad and run along.'

I resume my path towards the school, feel certain he'll leave me be for a while at least. Then he says, 'You never call me by my name.'

'Yes, I do.'

'But not when we—'

'No. I don't.'

* * *

Rowella Bisbee smiles when I appear at the gate of the schoolyard – it's breaktime and the children are out in the sun, some playing jump rope or tag, others chattering or singing, asking rhyming riddles. There's a delighted squeal when they spot me handing the basket over, and she tasks one of the older girls with distributing the bounty. Behind me, I can hear the god-hound still following me. I should never have fed him.

'Thank you, Miss Briar.' Rowella smiles broadly. I wonder if she'll stay in Silverton all her life, or if she'll work the agreed-upon five years and leave. Was a taste of the university town of Whitebarrow something to draw her back, away from home again? To a different life? I don't ask because I don't want her to think we're worrying about it, about our investment. Make her self-conscious.

'No trouble at all. Dónal tells me the Carabhilles promised to make good on their… mistake?'

She nods, hesitates. 'Mr Carabhille was most apologetic and new books were delivered to my home that same afternoon. But…'

'His son was not.' It confirms for me that Dai had done it on purpose – supplying poor goods in a moment of spite and resentment after his misdeeds had been exposed.

'I appreciate that you took care of it so quickly.'

'Well, let me know if it happens again – or anything untoward.' I doubt Rowella will be a target; it wasn't about her or the school. It was about me, thumbing a nose at me, at the Briars. 'Would you do me an enormous favour? Go and distract Father Huw for a few minutes? Just so I can sneak off. He's being a bother.'

'Consider it done,' she says and smiles. The children go back to playing and she heads towards the gate and the priest. I go around the school building and nip out the back gate.

* * *

Sandor's got four spectres into Ezekiel's cottage, all having assumed various positions of despair, hope or general moping. Junia Curnow's in the kitchen staring through the window. Branwen Kendrick, draped in the armchair by the cold fireplace, appears to have died of ennui. Enyon Cadwaladr was leaning arrogantly against the doorframe when I entered and unwilling to move so I simply stepped through him and hung my coat on the hook by the door. Costentyn Pugh is pacing from the hearth to the bedroom and back again, and again and again.

Relatively recent decedents, all known to me in their lives and, I'd have thought, relatively harmless, though Enyon's obnoxious with enough alcohol in him, which if I recall correctly was the source of his demise. He picked a fight with an enormous blacksmith, was punched no more than was necessary but tripped and fell, hitting his head. He never woke up. The blacksmith paid a hefty fine to Enyon's family and pledged one of his own sons to take up the place that Enyon would have occupied in the Cadwaladr timber mill. Mr Cadwaladr, though sad at the loss of his son, had freely admitted that young Tynon worked three times as hard as his layabout lad and made no trouble.

At the tiny table, I lay out my Book of the Dead, pen and ink, steel myself for whatever's to come, and Sandor nods to the first phantom.

Branwen, not from Silverton but married in, bringing a child with her. She fell in love with Ardal Kendrick, bore him five children before dying in childbed with the sixth. The lad she'd claimed to be her own, Branwen confesses, was not. She stole him, thinking herself barren. Now, she wants him told the truth, but he's only ten and thinks he's in a family of half-siblings. I talk to her about the difference between salving her own conscience and causing greater harm. *Does it really matter*, I say, *if he never knows? You've told me. The truth has been spoken without hurting him – let him have his family.* She doesn't take much persuading. I write her name and deed in the book, take her hand and bid her farewell. She's quickly gone.

Costentyn's wife was ill for a long while – not even Gisela had been able to cure her – and her husband couldn't bear to watch any longer. He put poison in her tea and his own ale, and they were found by their daughters one morning. He doesn't want his children told of what he did; he's avoided them since his death lest he hear them speak ill of him. I'm gentle when I point out that the bottle was in his fingers when they discovered him. His girls knew and, I reassure him, they forgave him. At the touch of my hand he smiles as he disperses.

Enyon resentfully presents himself and confesses: he was wont, in life, to spend his evenings picking pockets in whichever inn would let him through its doors to drink to excess. His father had ceased to pay his debts and Enyon thought it enterprising to make others do so in whatever way possible. I write him into the book and send him on his way – to be honest, this is far better than I'd hoped for with him, although I don't like the sensation of his skin against mine.

At last, I call, 'Junia?' but she doesn't move from the window. I rise and go to her. 'Junia, are you ready?'

'Who's that outside?' she asks, pointing. A figure in white moves between the trees, stumbling but swiftly coming closer, breaking into the small backyard. I squint.

Pale, oh so pale, there is Liv Havard limping to a stop. Her hair's in disarray, there are dark marks on her dress and apron. And she doesn't look well. More than that, worse than that, I can see the shapes of the trees *through* her.

I'm out the front door, running around back, calling. Ignoring Sandor, who's also calling, something urgent in his tone.

'Liv! Liv!' I hold my arms open even though she's dead, nothing but vapour, mist. My throat closes over. She turns at the sound of my voice, and her bewildered expression becoming pure fury.

Liv Havard, my friend, flies at me, shrieking. I don't pull back, because she can't hurt me, can have no effect on me – except when she hits it's like a thousand razors passing through my left shoulder. I remember, *then*, the ghosts almost choking Dai, Sandor in the rocking chair. I remember that Gilly's spell is coming undone, and clearly unravelling faster every time I let more spirits go. But I'd never have thought it would be like *this*.

I fall backwards onto the cold, hard ground. Though the fabric of my yellow woollen dress remains intact, blood's seeping from the inside out. I scramble around, watch Liv's spectre flying towards the trees until she loses enough momentum to turn, then she comes at me again. I'm not sure I'll survive a more direct blow, but all I can do is stare.

Just before the next impact, it starts to rain. No, not rain, but liquid definitely, dropping from the sky, passing through the substance of Liv's form. Lukewarm, blood-warm, not cold as a winter shower should be. Someone's shouting a curse – something Tobias used to yell at us when we were small and being (in his opinion) particularly trying. An exhortation of anathema ending with the word 'begone' and abruptly Liv becomes a puff of smoke.

I lie back, stare up at the sky, and the face of Father Huw, holding the obviously-now-empty silver flask from his belt.

26

'Who are you?' I ask as the god-hound helps me settle into the kitchen chair. He lights a fire in the old stove, runs the tap until the water's clear, fills a copper kettle, and puts it on to boil. Sandor hovers as I peel off my dress, loosen the laces of my quilted corset. The blood's a shocking stain, oozing rather than spurting, and an ache creeps through my shoulder and down my arm, the same sort of iciness I've felt handling the dead. Except without the numbness, unfortunately. Sandor, hands waving ineffectually, demands, 'Ellie! Why didn't you listen to me? Ellie, are you alright?'

Ignoring the silly question and gritting my teeth, I ask again: '*Who* are you?'

'Just a common or garden priest.' Unconsciously throwing my own phrase at me, Huw bends and peers at the wound.

'Oh, don't make me hate you any more than I already do.' A lesser man would've melted beneath my glare but the bastard just grins. I hesitate, then whisper, 'Can you see them?'

His grin fades. 'Not entirely. It's a bit like shadows? But the one that attacked you? It seemed more… solid. I can't make out features, just shapes, really. A woman?'

'A friend.' The word makes my heart contract. I look at Sandor and Junia. 'The more I send off, the weaker the spell becomes?'

Sandor says, 'She wasn't the same as us, Ellie. I sensed no reason, she was pure rage – as if everything else she'd been was stripped away.'

'I thought you couldn't do magic?' Huw mistakes the question as being for him.

'I was… talking to someone else. It's not magic.' I point to the two spectres. 'Can you see *them*?

Huw squints, but ultimately shakes his head. 'Just a tall shadow, and a shorter one – it's mostly like they're not really there. If I hadn't seen what I did, I probably wouldn't notice this pair – wouldn't be looking for them. Who are they?'

'My— How did you know I can't do magic?'

'I asked around. Hard to get information out of Briars, but your folk really are terrible gossips.'

'And how did you know to use…' I point at the flask now sitting on the countertop.

'Holy water? It just seemed like a good idea. I had a vague memory of classes about exorcisms – bell, book, candle and what-have-you.'

'Very effective. In my satchel – over there, by the hearth – you'll find bandages and antiseptic. Needles and thread too, but I don't think they're quite needed.' I could go home but if I asked my cousins for help, I'd have to explain too much.

'That's very prepared,' he observes as he retrieves the roll of leather, unlaces it and lays the contents on the table.

'Says the man carrying holy water *just in case*.'

258

'Can you trust him?' Sandor asks, frowning. 'Holy water banishes ghosts entirely – I don't know where, but there's no chance for redemption, no asking for help with a solution like that.'

And here's the thing: I haven't really, not up until now. Not even when I've gone to his bed. Especially not when I've gone to his bed. But he's just saved me from worse harm when he could have stood by and let one of the wicked Briars get her comeuppance. Liv was my friend, but there's no doubt in my mind she – or whatever remained of her – was trying to kill me. The thought makes me ache.

'I don't know,' I reply, 'but I can always kill him later.'

'I can hear you, you know that?' The kettle begins to boil, and Huw pours hot water into a bowl from under the sink, then adds drops of lavender wash, muttering: 'Unfriendly. And ungrateful.'

'Did you follow me? I could have sworn I got rid of you.'

'You did and it was a nice touch setting the schoolteacher on me – I had to answer children's questions about why the sky's blue. I escaped and just wandered until I saw you bolting out the door. Pure chance, really.' He dips a cotton pad into the water, gingerly shakes off the excess, and begins to clean the wound. The heat stings and the lavender relieves in equal measure. When he's done, it's clear the cuts aren't as bad as I feared. Shallow and straight, almost like someone took a cutthroat razor to me, and they stop bleeding fairly quickly. Huw's gentle as he dabs on the cream and applies the bandages. The cold is seeping away.

Job done, he takes in the Book of the Dead, left lying open beside me. Running a finger along the list of names, he reads out a few and their sins, the dates. 'You haven't been able to see them for long?'

'Only since my grandmother's funeral.' He sits in the other chair, and I tell him about the fall, about Sandor, about becoming a speaker for the departed. I don't mention Gilly and her spell. He doesn't need to know everything. 'And now, *Father Huw*, I'll ask again: who are you?'

He looks as if he's weighing up whether he can trust me or not, and for the very first time his face is without that harmless, helpful, wide-open expression. The I-have-no-secrets expression. The expression I've distrusted. At last, he makes a decision. 'Once upon a time…'

'An appropriate beginning.'

'It'll be the ending too if you don't mind your manners.'

I hold my hands up in surrender, wincing as my injury jars.

'Once upon a time, there was a young woman who wanted more from life than a remote mountain town could offer. Her family didn't understand, didn't want her to leave, so one day she pretended to go for a walk, then simply kept going. She saw a lot of places, witnessed many strange things, lived in tiny villages, bigger cities. Sometimes she found huts in the forest, always deserted, some with their roofs falling in, but inside there would be books with script she couldn't read, dried herbs, pickled meats and preserved fruits, the kinds of things that might be left for those needing somewhere to hide. She thought that, because of the books, they'd been or still were safe houses for witches – and she was very familiar with witches. Whenever she could locate such places that was where she sheltered.'

I look away, my eyes growing hot. I've read enough tales in our library of the days, weeks and months Gilly and Sandor spent fleeing, the days spent in hiding in such tiny huts, staying quiet as mice because, though the shelters were hidden, noises would still draw unwanted attention, perhaps bring a god-hound sniffing and snuffling right up to a door he'd not otherwise have seen. Sandor's expression says he's recalling that time far too well.

'After perhaps a year, perhaps two, perhaps more, she came at last to the great city with a great cathedral. To Lodellan, where God and His Opponent hold hands according to one account, are locked in eternal battle according to another. Where some streets are lined with gold, others with shit, still others with books, and yet others with men and women for sale. Where the priesthood has its deepest foundation, the place where the greatest Archbishop (each archbishop of course being the greatest in his own reign and mind) sits on a throne and wields power equal to or greater than that of the local prince.'

I don't say anything, nor do I look at him; I just listen, trying to detect by some tone how he feels about all of this, to divine some note true or false. But his timbre is steady, uninflected by emotion as he goes on.

'And the young woman who wandered into Lodellan seeking something more found it, though it wasn't anything she'd thought to get. She caught the eye of the Archbishop Janus Morrow. He was generous and she had his favour long enough to develop a taste for a way of life, to think she was better than she was, to get pregnant, and to find that although Archbishops might father children, they, unlike some of the lesser clergy, did not marry. Their hearts belonged to God alone, even when their cocks were another matter. Morrow wasn't a bad man, not entirely; he set her up in a house of her own and visited her, although less and less frequently as time went on. He saw his son on occasion, too, so the boy knew who he was. And when the woman who'd wanted so much more came to her dying, the one thing she cried out for was the home and family she'd left. When she was dead, priests came and reclaimed the house, which had been Church property, and they brought the boy to the Archbishop because they figured he too was Church property.

'Janus Morrow looked at the boy, who was nine by then, and asked, "Do you believe in God?" And the boy said, "Yes," though he believed in other things, many more things for his mother had told him wonderful tales about the place she'd been born. How it was ruled by women, tremendous women, who held great power and wielded incredible magics, who cared for the people in their charge and did all that was needed in times of crisis and calm. These women who let everyone worship as they wished, though there was a priest in the town, a man beloved by the most powerful of the witches.'

He leans forward, and I lean forward and our faces almost touch, so close I can feel his breath when he says, 'But the boy didn't tell his father that.'

'Wise,' I say, and we stay like that for long moments, and I think about kissing him, but instead whisper, 'And then?'

He leans back, stretches. 'And the boy grew up in the Archbishop's palace, with tutors galore. He saw his father sometimes. He excelled at his lessons, but what he loved best were books and the making of them, specifically the writing of them, the scribing and the calligraphy. So when his training was done a place was found for him in the Archives – a building almost as magnificent as the Archbishop's palace, which is in an eternal state of improvements and additions, adding spires, gargoyles, widow's walks, chimneys, sculptures, wings, outbuildings – but because it's an old city, so very old, there's no room to build out so they must go up – where was I?'

'A position in the Archives.'

'Ah, yes. The Archives, a perfect place for an unenthusiastic sort of cleric, and where he might have quite happily spent his days, reading and writing, receiving letters from far-flung parishes about the State of Things, and passing them on to men more significant than he, so they could Make Recommendations, which is a very important job. He read a lot of letters and reports, but his favourite came from a place very far away; he looked forward to these twice-yearly missives – so impressive in their regularity. And although he occasionally marvelled at the longevity of the priest signing said letters – the young god-hound was the third successive archivist to receive them – he didn't really give it too much thought until one day the next scheduled letter failed to arrive. Then, the young man heard rumblings: *Father Tobias is surely too old by now. He needs an assistant, an offsider, an apprentice to ensure The Word continues in places like Silverton long after he passes. So the witches remain subjugated. Obedient.*

'And the young man knew as surely as night follows day that a new god-hound would be bad news for the witches, because there'd been talk amongst the princes of the church that those women needed to recall to whom they owed their survival. That a reminder was due. He knew that these women, the ones his mother spoke of, his fairy godmothers, his wonderful witches, must be kept safe.

'And so, he begged his father for the honour of being sent to Silverton. He had, he said, lived his life not in the truest service of God, but hiding in darkened rooms and in the pages of books. He'd had a calling, been shown the way, and knew it was time for him to go forth.'

I laugh. Delighted, hysterical. Crying because I can't help myself. Whatever Maud's plan, it was not *this*.

'And, overjoyed at his son's fervent vocation, Archbishop Janus Morrow gave his permission.'

'And here you are.'

'And here I am.'

'To save us.'

'If I can.'

'Because your mother told you marvellous tales.'

'She did.'

'What was her name? Your mother.'

'Seren,' he says quietly. 'Seren Baines.'

Oh. Time stops, just for a sliver of a moment, a speck of a second. Sandor says, 'Ellie, be wary.'

'I think,' I say slowly. 'I think there's someone you should meet.'

27

It's been a very long day.

After leaving Huw and Beres to become acquainted, I'd returned to the cottage and sent Junia Curnow on her way. She'd stolen from her parents, just small amounts to buy tiny things – sparks of joy in an otherwise miserable life. I remember seeing her when I was a child and she always looked sad. No one suffered, she only took from a surplus that those parents were unwilling to share with her even as she cared for them, waiting on them hand and foot, never allowed to marry or have an independent life. She didn't hurry them on their way even though many would have done so and not without good reason. It's no chore to give her absolution.

At dinner (in a fresh dress, the yellow blood-stained one hidden), I manage to smile and chat over venison steaks – deer brought down by Nia's bow. I tell my cousins Huw's story, or an agreed-upon version of it, just enough for them to realise he's no threat to us. That he'll be a comfort to Beres, which is needed, and relieves our concerns about her being left alone in the world. I do not tell them *how* or *why* I learned this story, about Liv's ghost and all my other ghosts. I still don't understand that myself. I wonder, though, how she died and when – clearly after Audra left the Havards' holding. I wonder about the pregnancy, if something went horribly wrong even though she'd showed no sign of being anything but perfectly healthy when I examined her. I wonder about whatever is stalking the woods around the outlier farms and remember the dark marks on her clothing but not the sort that a tearing and clawing wild beast would inflict. I wonder if I can send someone to check on the farms again in case something happened after Audra's return, one of the vigilants, perhaps, but Nia would demand to know why I was depriving her of one of her force. Something doesn't feel right, but I've nothing to prove anything is wrong; the ghosts might be becoming stronger, more visible, but no one's noticed except Huw. I'd achieve nothing but pitying looks and a hefty dose of dwale or poppy milk to make me sleep if I insisted on being, well, insistent.

I remind my cousins that there remains the matter of Dai Carabhille and the Whispering to be arranged and suggest that Audra might visit the Carabhilles tomorrow. She nods, but suggests in return that perhaps, with Huw here, Beres might become a little less focused on Dai's punishment. Or at least there might be a little extra time for Dai to come to terms with his fate. To realise it could have been far, far worse. I tell her I doubt either of those things, but there's always the possibility of a miracle.

After dinner, when I'm heading up to bed, Audra catches me on the stairs.

'Had any luck, Ellie? With the book?' She speaks so quietly the others couldn't hear, and I wonder why it's a secret. Then again, Audra's probably trying to avoid a discussion with Eira, who would surely have strong opinions about looking for something that was no doubt hidden, to her mind, for a good reason.

'Not yet,' I reply. 'I'll do a little each day, in between other things.'

My cousin's lips compress into an impatient line, and I feel that old sense flowing up from the bottom of my stomach – that I'm a disappointment, not good enough, I'm the poorest Briar there's ever been. That I've let my darling cousin down. I manage not to stammer: 'Is there some hurry, Audra?'

She frowns, then smiles. 'Oh, no. I'm just worried, Ellie, about whatever attacked the outlier farms. What if it comes for us next? What if we're not prepared?'

I think about Liv again, about the rest of the families on those far-flung properties, and the voices in my head are at war: tell Audra about the ghosts and come clean; but no, because I can't prove anything, and I'm already suspect among my family – adding insanity to being unbearably ordinary feels like a final straw.

'You're right, of course. I'm sorry, Audra, I've let you down.' I fight back tears, but she doesn't know they're of frustration rather than shame. And a grief to which I can't give voice.

'No, Ellie, you haven't! Don't ever think that. I just…' she touches my hand, '…I just want us all to be safe.'

'I'll do my best.'

'I know you will, Ellie.'

* * *

In my room, standing at the window, dressed for bed but unable to sleep and staring idly down at the garden, I see Audra leave the house. I watch a while, thinking she might be going to the priest's house, but she veers off, heading into the maze of big houses inhabited by the rich. A visit for port, the cachet of the Briar Witch dropping in after dinner, perhaps the chance to canvass agreements or new business proposals. Has Audra already looked for *The Bitterwood Bible* herself without success? I wonder that she can't try some spell to make it leap from its hiding place, right into her elegant palm. Then again, if Gilly went to the trouble of concealing the damned thing, she'd almost certainly have gone to the trouble of laying counter-spells to prevent it being found by such easy means.

'Sandor?' I whisper. 'Sandor?'

And my very-great-grandfather appears next to me.

'Things are changing,' I say, 'more and more.'

He nods.

'Liv's ghost, why was she different to the rest of you? She didn't want to talk…'

'I'm not sure she could. She hated you.'

'But she was my friend!'

'My dear, it certainly didn't seem that way.' His hands lift. 'She was… I felt her approach but until I saw her I didn't know what it was. Does that make sense? There was nothing recognisable in her, nothing like a person. She was all rage held together in a vaguely human shape. Utter fury. Completely unhinged, Ellie.' He looks down at his hands, perplexed. 'I'm not sure she recognised you or if it was just that you were the only living person in sight.'

'But surely ghosts get angry?'

'Of course. But most can be spoken to, if not reasoned with. That thing—'

'—Liv—'

'—Liv was no longer there, Ellie. I could detect no core of a person in that storm. How much worse might it have been if she'd stumbled across someone else? And how much worse for you if that god-hound hadn't been snooping?'

'I know.' I rub my hands over my face; the movement causes a twinge in my shoulder. 'She lives – lived – on one of the outlier farms. How did she get here?'

'We sometimes wander. Some died far from their birthplace, yet they return. Perhaps that was it?'

'Perhaps. But she had nothing to confess or tell?'

'Again, Ellie, there was nothing of *her* left. Sometimes it's nothing more than habit, like a bird following migratory patterns.' He sighs. 'At some point, you're going to have to tell your family at the very least what you can see, do.'

'Well, yes but… not yet.' I wrap my arms around my body, try to make myself smaller, trying for the comfort of compactness – of not being such a big target. Then a thought hits, and for a moment I feel so clever that my face must glow; then so stupid I can't believe I can breathe and walk at the same time. How can I have taken this long to think of it? 'Sandor! Do you know where Gilly hid her grimoire?'

He looks confused. 'Gilly's grimoire?'

'*The Bitterwood Bible* – you know, the one she used all her life, the one she brought to Silverton. The greatest grimoire a witch has ever held.'

He shakes his head. 'Gilly had no such thing. There was just her notebook of herbs and their uses, a recipe book, really.'

'That can't be right.'

'Gilly was no witch to need a grimoire.' He's sounding a little short now. 'Gilly was *no* witch.'

'But… Gilly Briar was the greatest of us all. Gilly Briar who came to Silverton and saved us and it. Gilly Briar who won the dispensation from the princes of the church and allowed us to live in safety. Gilly Briar who hid *The Bitterwood Bible* so no one would be tempted to misuse it.' I spread my fingers as if that will convince him. '*Gilly Briar, Gilly Briar, she'll set you on fire.* We used to sing that when we were little.'

Sandor's fiercely shaking his head. 'Gilly's foster-mother, Patience Gideon, had a grimoire. I don't know if she named it or not, although it doesn't seem like the sort of thing she'd do. She'd consider it ridiculous.' He makes an exasperated noise. 'Gilly would regale me with tales of that book, of all the magic Patience could work. And every time she spoke of it, I could hear the envy in her voice. Patience was so powerful and Gilly… Gilly was not.'

'Like me.'

'Even worse – you can see the dead, speak to them, help them. You have your own sort of magic. Gilly – to add insult to injury, all seven of our daughters *were* witches. Witch-blood chooses wildly. Patience said it ran differently in every vein.'

I feel like the ground should be shaking, the walls tumbling around me as this house falls apart with this erosion of my history, of everything my family's believed and passed down. So much of it lies.

But Sandor's continuing: 'I think, sometimes, that's why she did what she did to Hilla. Took away that magic – it was the one thing she could do.'

'But how? If she couldn't do magic?'

'How could she hide the ghosts?'

He looks away as if reluctant to tell me.

'Sandor. I need to know.'

'You must understand, Ellie, what it is like to have no magic when it's all you've dreamed of. How it twists the heart and mind and you can convince yourself that what you do is from pure altruism when it's... self-seeking.'

'Sandor,' I say, and he realises to whom he's speaking.

'I'm sorry, my dear. You know that all magic demands a price. Intent, ritual and a red price. The bigger the magic, the higher the cost to pay for it. Some will use the blood of others – animals and sometimes people. I think perhaps when you hit your head, bled in the tomb, you paid your red price.' Sandor shrugs. 'I truly do not know, Ellie, but that's my theory.'

'What about Gilly? How did she convince people she was a witch?'

'Ellie, the Briars as they are today are very different. You've been fairly untroubled by the sorts of trials that afflict most women of your sort. In the general way of things, witches do not gather. Do not create communes or communities – not openly, at any rate. They hide what they are in order to survive. They run. Fear is a constant and that can stunt not only life, but also ability. Different witches, different powers, different degrees of prowess. It's why Gilly could pass as a witch in an earlier time: all she had to do was brew a good potion and folk were willing to believe it was based in power. The Briars, *now*, practise in the open, don't think twice about it. It's a privilege to do so, to not consider whether it will get you killed. You've been trained and guided and given a chance to grow. Many witches were not so lucky.'

I think about the daily ritual, bloodletting for whatever spells my family might cast that day. The crimson tithe paid in advance, paid just in case. 'But how did Gilly...'

'What a non-witch *can* do is buy or borrow or be gifted another's magic in the form of an object a witch has stored an enchantment inside. Like... a bottle of poison – even if you didn't make it, you could still use it.' I nod to show I've understood. 'So, the witch imbues a particular talisman or totem with some of her own puissance and gives the non-witch a word to ignite it, for want of a better description. But it's not something lightly or easily done. The cost is always high and seldom worth it.'

'Then who did Gilly pay? Not one of your daughters?' I think of myself borrowing Gisela's clothes with the concealment spells in them; not quite the same.

'No! A woman passed through on her way to elsewhere, but she'd sought us out. A powerful witch, she brought the Archbishop Narcissus Marsh's dispensation and the secret of closing the border with the Darklands. And my Gilly... made the bargain with her and kept the thing hidden for years, hoarding that little piece of power like a miser. I didn't know anything about it until it was too late. Until she'd taken the very thing that gave Hilla's life meaning.'

'The dispensation? Didn't Gilly—'

'Patience again. No detail of how it was obtained, but only the assurance that it would stand up to scrutiny and Gilly and hers could survive.' He grins. 'I don't know how Patience knew where we were, but *she* was a witch of witches. And I don't know how she got that dispensation, but news arrived later that Marsh had died a strange death – drowning from drinking wine.' He shrugged. 'Something Patience had managed before. Whatever she did, however she did it, that dispensation has never been questioned. It was only later that the first god-hound arrived to begin his watch. I was dead by then, so was my Gilly. Our youngest daughter Bea was Briar Witch and she had a wise head on her. Let him stay, had the church and priest's house built. Kept peace with him.'

I realise I'm picking skin from the side of my thumb, drawing blood. 'And you don't know where *The Bitterwood Bible* might be?'

Sandor shakes his head. 'Wherever Patience Gideon breathed her last, I would imagine.'

I think about Gilly, who did such a great and terrible thing to her own child; who seeded a river of untruths through our generations. I wonder how I'm going to tell Audra. Then I wonder how I'm going to avoid it. I wonder how long I can pretend to search for the book. How long before I have to admit everything and how I know these new things – all the truths and all the lies?

'How many ghosts do we have left, Sandor?' I can hear the weariness in my voice.

Apparently so can Sandor, for he says soothingly, 'Not so many.'

I nod. 'I'm very tired. I really need to consider what's going to happen when they're all gone.'

'And me. When I'm gone.'

That startles me. I'd forgotten, for however short a time, that my grandsire would disappear too. That he would want his rest when all the others were at peace.

'Oh. Yes.' I list on my fingers. 'Then what happens to Gilly's spell? Because it's definitely weakening. How long before I must tell my family and the townsfolk? What happens when I'm gone? Will there be another speaker to take my place?'

'Perhaps that last one is planning a little too far ahead?' He smiles fondly. 'You're very young, my dear.'

But we both know that's no proof against death.

'Thank you, Sandor. I think I'm ready to sleep now.'

'Shall I wait until you drift off?' he asks.

I'm distracted by a flash at the window – an owl, fast and feathered, a blur of movement as it hunts something small in the darkness below.

'Yes, please. If you don't mind.'

'I don't mind at all.'

I climb into bed and for the second time, Sandor stands guard over my slumber. I let my mind drift, seeking distraction from all I've learned, from everything churning in my brain.

I think of owls. A memory of a voice from long ago – perhaps Gisela, perhaps my mother – telling me tales of their creation. That they were made of flowers and spiderwebs and moonlight. That they kept themselves apart from other birds, considering them to be made of base matter when the owls were so exalted. That they kept their own counsel, discussing which creatures might be hunted with impunity and which presented a danger too great. That an owl always knew where a dreadful event would occur and would be waiting there as a witness. That, if you wanted to know the secrets of the night, you must bribe the owl to tell you, but its price for such treasure was always high. That to dream of one was a portent of misfortune. That their own feathers might be used against them. That, given half a chance, they ate the souls of the dead.

Tomorrow, I'll regroup, I tell myself. Tomorrow, things will be better.

28

But tomorrow, to my considerable irritation, brings further unravelling.

My simple plan was to deliver a basket to one of Audra's old folk (while she attended a morning tea with the Lazars, the Tremaines, the Elliotts and the Urwins – fancy folk), then present myself at Lowen Jernigan's Emporium on the pretext of discussing his application for a gaming parlour (as if he might have some hope the next time) and compliment him on the gold ring that I know was my ever-so-great grandfather's. After that, checking on Dónal and his planning endeavours, and after *that* more ghosts to be dealt with.

However, there's a crowd gathered around the fountain as I'm walking through the marketplace, food basket on one arm. They draw my attention because the muttering, whispering and expressions of uncertainty become louder as I approach. No one's looking at me, though, and when I'm close enough I can see what's causing the consternation.

Spectres.

Three spectres to be precise.

Or, to be even more precise, the very vague outline of three spectres draping themselves over the formidable bronzed shapes of the Three Brothers Bear. So vague, in fact, that it's hard to tell they're there at all. *I* know they're there. The townsfolk? They're just seeing scraps and hints. Echoes and impressions coming through the skin of Gilly Briar's "purchased" (and apparently rapidly weakening) magic.

I recognise the miserable Verlaine sisters, who lived in the same house after their parents' passing, remaining spinsters not through any real choice but because, driven by petty jealousy, each one would ruin the others' romances. Eventually no suitor would go near them – even before their beauty was spent. They were so purely fractious and unpleasant that no man could ever inspire a level of love that could overcome their own enthusiasm for spiting each other. When one finally died, the other two limped along for a short while until another shuffled off her mortal coil. The last gave up the ghost upon finding herself with no one to fight.

The thing to be thankful for, I suppose, is that they're not bickering, nor making a noise that might be heard either as a sibilant breeze or the same sort of ruckus that issued forth from their home most days and nights. Alvina, Bedelia and Clover are definitely posing, yet they've not chosen to appear as they did in their youth. Perhaps it didn't occur. Or perhaps they don't really know they're almost visible.

Ursley Kemp, one of the sewing circle, stands terribly still as if frozen from the neck down, staring upward. She keeps moving her head in tiny increments as if that will help her see whatever might be there. I touch her arm to distract her, and she shakes herself as if coming-to. While she's thus occupied, I glare at the

Verlaines so they can't possibly mistake my displeasure. With a resentful look, they shrug and disappear.

Those gathered seem to wake as one, all snapped to attention and staring about as if wondering why they're here, what they were doing before they drifted off. Like someone who can't remember why they went into another room. 'Are you quite well, Ursley?'

'Ellie.' She blinks, nods reluctantly. 'I saw… thought I saw…'

'You're rather pale. Shall I help you home?'

'Oh. No.' Embarrassed now. 'Thank you, Ellie, you're so kind. I'll be fine.'

And she hurries off down Leatherworkers Lane – whether that's where she was going in the first place is anyone's guess. I smile at those around me; they nod uncertainly and gradually drift away. By the afternoon the incident will either be forcibly forgotten, put out of mind, or something they mention only to their nearest-and-dearest. Something the recounting of which will trail off with 'Oh, but that's silly. I just imagined it.'

At some point, they'll have to be told, won't they?

Will they?

The problem with telling them everything – or even just parts of everything – is that it means admitting one of the Briars (the greatest of us!) condemned their loved ones to a wandering purgatory three hundred years ago. That some – although not all, there is that tiny saving grace – have been tethered to Earth by guilt, real or imagined, or a sense of unease, of *unfinishedness*, or even just unawareness of their death having occurred. That a Briar *hid* them from the eyes of those who might have helped. How long can I put that off? How long can I avoid telling my cousins? Have *they* seen anything? No one's brought it up at the dining table…

277

I should get on. Standing around the marketplace watching folk will draw attention. People are moving back and forth again in their usual fashion, no more suspicious glances at the fountain, although some are giving it a wide berth. Then again, my own stillness works in my favour – it's as if no one can see me, no one's looking *at me*. Ah, just like the old days.

Something I've been pondering recently is that not only did the Briars have no record or memory of a speaker for the dead, no one else in Silverton seemed to either. How long did it take to be forgotten? For the idea to die? Or if not die, then go into hibernation. What did Gilly say? That she'd banished the ghosts and there'd be no need ever again for someone like Hilla? No need for a speaker? I suppose with no one able to see or hear the ghosts – to even know they were there – the very idea of a speaker fell out of fashion and mention. Lying dormant until an accident – an unpredictable result of my own clumsiness – changed me. It wasn't really a banishment, was it? More like casting a veil over them; they could see us, yet never appear to us; we could never see or hear them; they couldn't affect us or the world around them. Like locking them in a vacuum.

Now, that veil's thinning and the dead can break through, if only a little at the moment. Soon, I imagine, they'll be rattling chains and slamming doors, turning rooms chilly with their displeasure, shifting furniture around at their whim. Letting all and sundry know they're here and they're unhappy.

All these ghosts we notoriously do not have.

I shake my head; it's a problem for another day. I push away from the fountain, startling the couple walking by as if I've jumped out at them.

'Where'd you come from?' huffs the male, then realises who it is. 'Apologies, Steward Briar. Didn't see you there.'

I smile, gracious, begin to tell him not to worry when a movement catches my eye. In the mouth of a narrow alley between two buildings I spot Dai and Nia, standing close. He's red in the face but isn't making any threatening movements. She's got her palms against his chest, as if to soothe him; I'm imagining her using a softer tone than is her habit. An unusual… alliance? Is this why Nia was so against a punishment for Dai? So worried about the Carabhilles? Was this why Dai cast Deirdre aside? Examining my feelings, I find only curiosity. But it'll have to be another problem for another day because I'm currently fully stocked.

I take a different route so they don't see me, duck down a side street, keep going in this subversive fashion to discourage any possible pursuit (how paranoid have I become?) until I emerge onto Peyton's Pavement, a street away from Ezekiel Perry's cottage. My first stop, however, is a different small mean house. This is a street of them, quite a few empty. Perhaps we should be encouraging newlywed young couples to move here, bring some life back to it, and who might check on their older neighbours.

The widowed Madlyn Wilson lives alone. She's got no family left, is of an unpleasant disposition and no one but the Briars bother with her – rather like Ezekiel. Her home's in better condition than his, though, is a little bigger and looks cleaner outside, and the red door is freshly painted. Said door is also hanging open, as if she just disappeared inside a moment ago. I take the two short steps up to the tiny porch, and knock.

'Mistress Wilson? It's Ellie Briar.' I wait a few moments but there's no answer. I knock again, call again, more loudly.

The creeping sense of unease begins at the base of my spine. I put the basket down by the barren window-box where brightly coloured flowers will bloom in spring, then unhitch the baton from my belt.

Moving through the rooms I make enough noise to ensure the old lady won't be spooked if I happen upon her. She's hard of hearing, and her sight's not the best. In any other house, I wouldn't be so worried – I'd tell myself she's gone out to the markets, to visit a friend or family. Except she doesn't have any. The two bedrooms are empty, as are the bathroom, kitchen and sitting room. The beds are made. The place is tidy; there's not the same air of neglect as Ezekiel's, but there *is* the same sense of utter emptiness. It's a hollow home. And it all feels very familiar.

Closing the door firmly behind me, I continue on to Ezekiel's cottage.

Sandor is visible in the window – I wonder if others can see him if they pass by? Or is he still like the Verlaines, a hint of a suggestion in the air? An uncertainty? His eyes, when I step inside, go immediately to the basket on my arm, and his brow creases in understanding.

'Another?' he asks, though he doesn't need to.

I nod. 'I—'

'Will you tell someone?'

'That another old person's missing? Yes. But I don't know what's happened to her – there's no sign of her ghost. Have *you* seen anything? Anything otherworldly? I know you don't like to tell tales—'

'—I can't—'

'—but surely you must have seen something?'

280

'Nothing. Ellie, that's something I *would* tell you – it doesn't pertain to another spectre's private choices. And I can't be everywhere all at once. I can't see everything, nor can any of the others.' He jerks a thumb over his shoulder at the sad little group waiting for my attention. 'Do they look like they're noticing much at all?'

They do not. I sink into a chair. 'This could all be a coincidence. Liv's death – poor Bedo! The children…' I blink back tears. 'Old people die, they wander off, get lost. Not even my phantoms see anything. What can I tell Audra? All these things I know that I can't prove; even things like finding the treasure Wick Ablesman buried can be dismissed. And, Sandor, at this point… I've told so many lies to cover up what's happened, the ghosts, Gilly, everything. Why would Audra put any store in anything I say when she realises?'

He's silent for a moment, then hesitant when he finally speaks. 'What if you could present her with *The Bitterwood Bible*?'

'Well, I'd still be a liar, but she mightn't hate me quite so much.' I tug at my hair in frustration. 'But you said Gilly had no grimoire. Was no witch.'

'But her foster-mother was.'

'Sandor—'

'No, listen to me: Patience owned the book. I know Gilly didn't have it – but Patience might be able to tell you where she last had it.' He shrugs. 'It would be a very small needle in a very large haystack, but you could get a hint of where to look next. The way Gilly spoke of it… Patience was very careful with that book, she wouldn't have lost it. You might be able to track it down.'

'Which is all very well, but Patience Gideon has been dead for almost three hundred years.'

'Summon her.' He waves his hands about. 'If you can call her she might tell you where it is…'

'Aren't you forgetting, Sandor, that I'm a broken vessel? I can't even do card tricks let alone actual magic.' I shake my head yet again.

'Ellie, you call me, don't you?'

'But—'

'Do you think I'm just floating around at your shoulder all day and night, waiting to make myself visible? I'm elsewhere, child, but when you summon me I feel it and respond. You *might* even be able to bind ghosts to remain in your presence. We have a blood connection, yes, but I think it may go beyond that.'

I stare at him.

'Ellie, my dear girl, here's the thing: I believe you're different. Not a witch like the others, most definitely not. But you *are* a speaker for the dead – might they not speak *with* you as well? If you were to call? If you were able to tell Audra where the book might be… that might mitigate things.'

'How would I…?'

'You've got an entire library at your disposal, Ellie Briar. Do your research.'

'Sandor Briar, in a town with no ghosts, and with no books about ghosts, where would I find a spell to summon a ghost?'

He sucks on his bottom lip, makes a noise. 'Summon a *memoria* – or a sliver of a person at a particular time. You'll only get their memories of that age and before, but that should do the trick.'

'You know an awful lot about witchcraft, old man.'

'I've been surrounded by witches for centuries, whether they knew it or not. One can't help picking up a few tips here and there.' His tone's uppity.

'Do you want to see her? Patience? Be there when I try…'

He's already shaking his head. 'It's been too long, Ellie. I've spent my death mired in the past. Patience Gideon, fond though I was of her, would just be another straw on the camel's back.'

I understand. It's like the weight of family, and sometimes I wish I could refuse all the little extra burdens and obligations that go with it. Return it with a polite *no thank you*.

But his idea of a *memoria* isn't a bad one. It might even work. I puff out a breath and nod, then change the topic. 'What I do need you to do is tell your compatriots to *stop* showing themselves. I'm sure it's a novelty after all these years, but they're making things difficult for me. I need the town calm while I get this work finished. Then I'll figure out how to let the populace know that the Briars have been lying to them for centuries.'

'Fair.'

'And let's start with the Verlaine sisters – I have a feeling they'll be the worst offenders the longer they're left to their own devices.'

'Agreed.'

I lay out my implements, then dig around in Mistress Wilson's basket. This will be another long day and there's no point letting the food go to waste. Chatting with Lowen Jernigan will need to wait – the sooner I get rid of these meddlesome phantoms, the better.

29

'Did Mrs Wilson send her empty back?'

I thought I was clever sneaking in through the kitchen door; Eira's there and by her tone she's not happy. I, of course, forgot to grab it from the kitchen bench when I left the abandoned cottage, and the new one is still at Ezekiel's. I knocked on Huw's door on my way home, but received no answer, so I'm not especially happy either.

'Oh. I'm sorry. I forgot. Tomorrow. Promise.' I try to escape, but she darts around the table and cuts me off from the door. What I want to do is search the library shelves, not for the object of Audra's desire, but for a book of magic, one with the simplest summoning ritual – so simple even I couldn't make it go wrong.

'Honestly, Ellie. What's wrong with you? You're so distracted. You and Audra both. The pair of you are meant to be running this town but you can't seem to remember the most basic things.' Her hands are flapping and pointing, and her colour's high.

'Is this about baskets or did you have a spat with Sally?' It's intended as a distraction but my cousin bursts into tears. Such a rare event that I'm taken off guard. 'Oh, Eira. I'm sorry. What happened?'

I pull out a chair and sit her down, then set about making tea. Eira snuffles, blows her nose, bites her lip. 'I asked Audra about a date for the wedding. It's time for us, me and Sally. Gisela promised it would be soon.'

'What did Audra say?' Audra's no fan of Sally Eldin, but there's no good reason to stand in the way of Eira's happiness.

'That it needs to be postponed *for a respectable period of mourning*.' Eira's swinging between anger and sadness. 'And she said' – more tears – 'Sally wasn't allowed to visit the house anymore. No one should be wandering in and out who's not a Briar.' She looks desperate. 'But Sally will be a Briar, Ellie. She will!'

I'm surprised at Audra. Then again, maybe she's just being petty, trying to establish her control. Like forbidding me from going to Gisela's second burial. I think about Eira urging me to be careful then.

My tone's mild when I say, 'Audra's struggling, I think, to come to terms with everything. Gisela hadn't finished her training, and as you said she thought she had more time. We've been in a state of turmoil for weeks now. Audra doesn't know what sort of Briar Witch she'll be – it was Gisela's position for so long, and we've only ever known one leader. Audra... Audra needs to find her own shape, her own style.' I put a cup of tea in front of her, then the canister of her own biscuits. 'She'll work it out soon, I promise, but you know her first instinct is to be controlling. We just need to be patient.'

Eira looks at me with a painfully hopeful gaze. 'You could talk to her! She'll listen to you, Ellie. You're her right hand – she'll listen just as Gisela listened to Maud.'

Until Maud had no voice.

'Eira—'

'Please, Ellie!'

And because I'm not used to my cousins begging me for anything, I'm not used to having something they need, and because I'm a fool desperate for approval from my family, I say: 'Of course I'll talk to her.'

She hugs me hard. 'She's in the library…'

I'd not planned it to be so soon. It's not quite dinner time, but I want a bath. I want to massage the warmth back into my hands, to change the bandages on my shoulder and take something to numb the ache. I want a rest before I try and convince Audra to do something she doesn't want to do. But Eira's so devastated.

Far too soon, I'm standing outside the library door, steeling myself. Deep breaths. *Knock, knock, knock.* A pause before she bids me enter. Audra's smile is warm when she sees the tea tray I'm carrying.

'Perfect timing.' On the desk in front of her is a map with red circles, her own grimoire, black with gold-embossed sunbursts blooming across the cover. A pen and inkpot sit beside it and her fingertips are smudged. She sprinkles some pounce onto the page, and hastily closes it, puts it on top of the map so I can set the tray down and serve. There's a prickle along my spine, seeing her ensconced in this room, and I'm unsure if it's anticipation at the beginning of our partnership proper – or envy that she's in the seat I found so comfortable.

Cheerfully, only a little forced, I ask: 'New spells?'

'I'm experimenting with some of Gisela's.' She nods to the lectern where our grandmother's great book sits open. 'Different herbs and chants, to see how effects might become more powerful.'

286

I hand her a cup, take my own, and sit. 'Now you're settling in, we must start having daily meetings like Gisela and Maud, which means I'd best start baking more frequently.'

'Ooh! Melting moments for Monday, caramel tarts on Tuesday, cherry cake on Wednesday…'

'Well, that's the most important order of business sorted.' We laugh. 'Of course we'll be the size of churches by Friday.'

'That priest,' she says, eyes narrowing. A terribly swift shift, as if he's been at the forefront of her mind.

'Yes?' My tone's even. I like to think I've been careful.

'He's not coming when I call.'

Laughing, I say: 'Well, he's not a dog. God-hound, yes; actual dog, no.'

She looks insulted, then snorts. 'I mean, I've invited him to discuss his position. Told him my door's always open' – and I imagine she'll have been going out of her way to run into him – 'but no appearance thus far.'

'He's a bit dim, Audra, probably hasn't realised that what sounded like a casual comment was actually a polite demand – remember he's not from here. At the moment, he's just getting acquainted with his aunt, and Beres is so happy to have him around. He'll never replace what she's lost, but he's family. They'll make their way together.' I look into the dark liquid in my cup. 'I'm sure he'll be available soon.'

'Poor Beres. I haven't spoken to her in months. Such a terrible time for her,' she muses briefly, then switches again: 'So, you don't think the priest's going to be trouble?'

'We've none of us any reason to like god-hounds, but he's made himself useful. People seem to like and accept him – Tobias was barely tolerated even after decades, even with Gisela's intervention. Huw's helpful and kind. And he's not, miraculously, preaching. Hasn't threatened a sermon yet. We're lucky he is who he is – it could have been so much worse. I don't believe he's a hazard to us.'

There's a long pause while she sips at her tea, then she nods. 'We'll leave him be for the moment. I'm relying on you to keep an eye on him.'

I hope the relief doesn't show in my voice when I say: 'Consider it done.'

'Next order of business?' She smiles as if we're children playing in our grandmother's office. In many ways we are; in some ways we always will be.

'Eira—' I hold a forefinger up to forestall whatever she's about to say. 'Hear me out. She's very upset. Don't you think that perhaps, after all we've been through recently, a wedding might help lift spirits? Iris and Aaron's did so on a small scale for their family and friends. A Briar wedding would bring the *whole* town together. You would preside over this first celebratory event of your rule – lay to rest any concerns folk might have about these past weeks and all our troubles.' *And their discontent at your recent absence.* 'I know you don't like Sally, but there's no harm in her and she's good for Eira, makes her happy – and doesn't Eira deserve some happiness? Don't make her bitter.' Audra's pouting; she wants to argue, but knows I'm making sense. 'I'm not trying to interfere with your decisions or gainsay you, cousin, I'm just being your advisor. The steward to your Briar Witch, as Maud did for Gisela.'

'And look at what Gisela did to Maud.' She tries to say it

lightly, yet the comment falls flat. The words *And look what Maud did to us all* don't leave my lips but hover there. Or tried to do. We were only saved by the pure luck of Huw being who he was. Otherwise we might be toasting over a pyre with some new god-hound chanting prayers for our eternal damnation while all of Silverton looks on.

'I'm sorry, Ellie. I don't know what I was thinking. I'm still so tired.' Audra rubs her face with both hands and a sigh leaks out from between her fingers. 'Tell Eira to make her plans. She may marry whenever she wishes.'

'She will be pleased.'

'Anything else?' she asks.

There's a moment when the tale of the ghosts is on the tip of my tongue. My changed nature. A moment when the urge to confess is almost unbearable. But I can't quite get the words out. Instead, I shake my head, and she asks the inevitable next question.

'Any sign of *The Bitterwood Bible*? Any luck?'

The book is not here. Gilly Briar was a liar. I'll never be able to find it.

All I can do is tell the literal truth. 'Not yet. I'm a third of the way done in here. I'll look through Gisela's bedroom tomorrow so you can move in – I should have done it earlier, I'm sorry.'

'I won't be moving into Grandmother's room,' she says curtly.

'Why—'

'I don't want to. I like my own room.' She sounds so petulant it's like hearing her at age seven. Briar Witches have used that suite forever. She forces a smile. 'There've been so many changes, Ellie. I just… I just need *something* to stay the same.'

And I suppose I understand that from her perspective – most of her life has always been exactly what she wanted because she was always exactly what Gisela wanted. But now she'll need to put others first, and that will be an adjustment. I finish my tea, rise. 'Our first daily meeting, at eight tomorrow morning then?'

'Oh. Day after – you'll be pleased to know I'm meeting with the Carabhilles tomorrow morning and I think it's going to take some time to reach an agreement.'

'Aha. Well, I'll not offer to go with you. Wednesday it is.'

* * *

I'm in Eldin's Bakery trying to choose between one creamy pastry and another. I've just sat with Dónal for three hours this morning, discussing, proposing and arguing about his draft schedule for the public works tour. The only thing that will revive me for an afternoon of dealing with ghosts is a sweet treat. Sally's behind the counter but it becomes clear she's not paying attention to me.

'Sally?'

'Oh! Sorry, Ellie. There's something going on out there.' She juts her chin towards the door. I look around and notice through the shopwindow a cluster of bodies just across Bakers' Lane and down a little. There's a growing noise coming in the doorway.

Please, please don't let it be the ghosts.

'Is it a fight?'

Please, please let it be a fight!

'Please put both aside, Sally. I'll be back in a moment.'

All those moving bodies – mostly men – shifting and shuffling only as they do when there's a battle raging in an arena they've created by their very presence. A few women in there too, but mostly not. I get close enough to elbow my way through the pack – and folk respectfully step away when they spot me – and see two men, scuffling. Although that's definitely too gentle a word: it's a brawl and one of them is getting the worst of it.

Huw.

Huw is getting the worst of it.

Dai sits astride him, punching repeatedly. His own face is covered in blood, so it looks as if it didn't start out so unequally. Hari Carabhille's on the edge of the crowd, yelling at his brother, but I can't tell if it's encouragement or a warning. I don't think, don't shout, don't try to be reasonable. I pluck the blackthorn baton from my belt and wade forward.

The stick makes a satisfying *thwack* against the side of Dai Carabhille's head.

He falls sideways, stunned, and howls. Xander Ablesman, surprisingly neat and respectable in his vigilant's uniform, stumbles through the press, drawn by the noises, I assume. Two more of his fellow peace-officers follow, tall women who tower over Xander; older heads, wise guides for him. I point at Huw.

'Xander, take the priest to his home,' I say between gritted teeth, then turn my attention to Dai.

I swing the baton and he scrambles backwards, only just avoiding the swipes; the motion is pulling at my healing shoulder wound. I don't care if I hit him or not, but when he finally has to stop against the wall of a building, has nowhere else to go, I pull the baton back and high, pause.

'How dare you?!' I scream; I'm sitting outside myself as if driven out by rage, watching this creature of incandescent fury wearing my face. 'How dare you?'

He's staring up in fear – either at the sight of me or a memory of the last time he came after me, the ghosts at my beck and call. I don't need them today.

'Well?' I demand and he's got no answer. Just his mouth going small then large as he tries to gulp in air. I lean in, press the tip of the baton up under his chin. 'If you ever touch him or anyone else again, I will make you regret it.'

His brother rushes at last to aid him, but I yell, 'Stay back, Hari.' Then to the vigilants, 'Throw him in a cell.' They move forward, take Dai by his arms and heave him upward. I feel a grin around my mouth. 'Run home to your mummy, Hari.'

I push through the crowd that fall back like the petals of a dying flower, and head towards the priest's house. I think how Audra was visiting the Carabhilles today – clearly Dai didn't take that warning seriously. A night in a cell might make a difference.

Xander's made himself useful, put the kettle on to boil, and laid Huw out on the long couch instead of trying to heave him up to the loft and bed. I thank him and shoo him out, locking the door behind him. I prepare the lavender wash and bandages, just as Huw did for me not many days since. His eyes are closed, one hand across his brow. There's a lot of blood and one eye is already beginning to puff and bruise. I sit beside him, gently lift his hand away.

'Ouch.'

'What were you thinking? He's the size of a bear.'

'What sort of sympathy is that?'

'He's a head taller than you, twice as broad and weighs—'

'Yes, thank you very much, all shortcomings noted.'

'That's not what I meant. Only that he's the biggest man in the entire town—'

'Well, it wasn't actually my choice.' He opens the eye that's not swollen shut. 'He went for me the moment he saw me. And in case you're not clear on things like this, brawling isn't exactly on the curriculum at the seminary.'

'No, just burning women.' Which is a low blow, I'll admit. I dip one of the cotton pads into the water and begin cleaning him up.

'Your bedside manner leaves a lot to be desired.'

'Why did he attack you?' I'm careful to be gentle. My hands are shaking now the shock is setting in.

'He said to me right before the first punch, and I quote, "Stay the fuck away from her."'

I touch his nose.

'Ow! Ellie, please.'

'Sorry, sorry.' I give it another prod, gentler this time. 'Well, it's not broken. That's lucky. Nothing's broken, which is a small miracle in itself.' His bottom lip is split and oozing red. I dab it clean, but the red quickly returns.

'Oh, how lucky I feel.'

30

The Briar House is finally quiet – much quieter than last night when it echoed with argument.

Beres had come knocking on the door of the priest's house, not long after Huw had fallen asleep from a hefty dose of poppy milk. With his wounds cleaned and those that needed it bandaged, he didn't look too bad. Of course, he didn't look too good either, and Beres had heard what had happened.

'You have to do something!' she yelled at me after one glance at her nephew. She could've yelled even louder, he wouldn't have woken. 'Dai Carabhille is—'

'I know exactly what he is, Beres. He's in a cell beneath the townhall tonight, and we'll see how he likes that. I'll speak to Audra – she was making arrangements this morning for the Whispering' – although I wonder how well that went – 'and we'll be adding an extra punishment for this assault.'

Her lips pulled back in contempt. 'What use are the Briars if they can't keep one man from injuring others at his whim?'

And I didn't have an answer, so I left her to take care of her nephew and went home.

Audra and Nia were in the library and the moment I opened

my mouth I realised that my temper was still too hot to touch, because I shouted. I shouted at Audra because she'd been ineffectual in her duty – the Carabhilles were not taking her seriously as Briar Witch. That meant they weren't taking the Briars seriously – Dai had simply ignored whatever she'd said to him. His first act after being told one punishment was to go out and assault the local priest. Audra's face grew bright red, but I was reckless and didn't care about her reaction. We seemed eons away from the previous evening's promising partnership.

'If they think they're above us, then how much longer before the next fine family thinks that way? How long before the consortium of merchants decides to go against our decisions because they don't *like* them and we're just little girls with no weight?'

Nia tried to interrupt, 'But, Ellie—'

'Don't you say anything. I saw *you* talking to Dai Carabhille, all very cosy and comforting. Whose side are you on, Nia?' And I watch as Audra's gaze on our cousin gets very intense indeed.

Nia stammered, stuttered. 'I was just trying to calm him down—'

'And since when did you care about how Dai Carabhille felt, Nia?' I turned my attention back to Audra. 'Gisela always said that fear is a tool to be used judiciously. If they don't fear the consequences of going against us, they will not obey. And as I've said before, we hold this position as much from their fear of what we might and can do as from the benefits they derive from our rule. If we fail to act now, to bring this bastard to heel, our family will fall. How long before we're being used as kindling next Balefire Eve?'

And my cousin, who a moment ago looked as if she might set me alight herself, appeared terrified. Just for a moment, but

I saw the fleeting terror on her lovely face and knew I'd gotten through to her. She'd remember that I spoke so harshly, but for that moment I'd made my point, and at least no one was saying I was malicious because he'd spurned me.

'We'll increase the reparations—' Audra began.

'The Carabhilles have money – fines mean nothing to them. They'll pay those without qualm. But injuries to their reputation? That's what hurts them. The idea that their eldest isn't quite the paragon of virtue, the fine scion of their house that everyone thought? That's what hurts them. That's the way to teach them a lesson.'

'Ellie's right,' Nia mumbled. She looks as if I've bruised her. A rare moment, to have wounded Nia Briar.

I pushed my advantage: '*And* it's looking as if Dai's got a particular set against the Baines family. And even more as if we're just letting him do it.'

Audra, thin-voiced, said: 'He stays in a cell this night. That might teach him a lesson. And we will double the reparation payment. And both he and Hari are forbidden from presenting themselves as suitors for a year.'

'Two years,' I say.

'Eighteen months,' she counters.

I nodded, as if it was up to me. 'You can't be anything but strong, Audra. Not now. If people start to see us as lambs, we'll be devoured.'

* * *

Now, I've rolled back the library rug to expose the carving in the floorboards. A five-pointed star inside a circle, made long ago. I've seen the others use it, but never done it myself. In a child's grimoire – a tiny beginner's book – I found the simplest of summoning spells. I have the ingredients, it requires very little preparation, and if I fail there'll not be too much clean-up.

I checked on Huw first thing this morning, then saw Audra and Nia off on a tour of the charcoal-burning operations – while I don't envy Audra the boredom, it'll be a good lesson in taking her job seriously and a penance. With Eira at the infirmary and then going with Sally to pick out wedding-dress fabrics at Ursley's shop and visiting Beres at the priest's house for their making, I'll be uninterrupted for several hours at least.

I have more questions than answers, and Sandor was right: if I can find *The Bitterwood Bible*, or even just its location, then I can present that information to Audra. It will soften the blow when I confess all my own obfuscations and outright lies. It might even help her forgive how I spoke to her last night.

I'd thought about trying to summon Gilly Briar – asking her the truth about everything. The *why* of it all and *how* did she manage to leave behind a reputation as a witch – yet she'd never owned *The Bitterwood Bible* and couldn't have used it even if she had. There's the temptation, too, to call her simply to find out what it had cost to purchase someone else's magic. How that other witch had imbued the talisman – but I'm smart enough to recognise that's a path leading to madness. Even if I asked my cousins, would they be willing to do it? And what price would be demanded?

Perhaps, if I'd not become the speaker for the dead, I'd have been properly tempted – or irresistibly so. If I'd remained as I was, desperate to be like any other Briar. But now? I don't feel like such a blank. A lack. A lacuna. A loss.

So, not Gilly.

The person who actually *owned* the grimoire in question was Patience Gideon. The spell says I need an anchor, a tuning fork of a thing – something the one to be summoned owned or touched. I'm mindful that I can call Sandor to me, but we have shared blood – Patience, a foster-mother only to Gilly, isn't part of our line. Without that or an anchor it might not work at all. Or might go horribly wrong. But Sandor swears she was responsible for the dispensation.

It takes a while to get that off the wall, gently pry the document from the frame, peel it from the matting, and decide which corner to slice off – then I put everything back together so the mutilation won't be seen, and because Maud taught me to clean as I go. The sliver of parchment goes into a mortar and is crushed along with sandalwood for clarity of mind, other wood powders for ignition, and amber resin for protection just in case Patience Gideon proves to be unfriendly. I'd also thought about taking Huw's flask of holy water but I baulked; something feels wrong about it. I think of Liv Havard sent on her way with no chance for redemption or peace. Just blinking out like a light plucked from the sky, a candle flame snuffed. So, I'll take my chances.

Finally, I place the mortar at the centre of the star – the safest place to stand – prick a finger and urge a single drop of blood into it – too much and the mixture will not light. But this is the price, the crimson tithe all magic demands. I'm no witch, but I'm a speaker for the dead. I am strange and other, and I will send my summons forth on a wing and a prayer, and a breath of flame.

I light a sulphur match, touch it to the contents of the mortar, watch the flame catch with a hiss and a crack, and a huge puff of smoke rises, far larger than the small vessel should be able to produce. I'm almost too distracted to make my demand, but my voice is strong when I speak. 'I summon thee, Patience Gideon. I call thee forth to answer the speaker for the dead.'

The smoke remains inert for a moment or five, and I assume I've failed. Who do I think I am? I've not been able to make the simplest enchantment work all my nineteen years – why would that change now? Just because I'm at the beck and call of the departed? Suddenly, the cloud reshapes itself, becomes less smoke, more mist, not ghostly at all, quite solid-looking. But she's not a ghost, is she? Just something I've conjured, a *memoria*. Me, hollow Ellie Briar. A tall woman, perhaps a young-looking fifty (fine lines around the mouth and across her forehead), with clear green gaze and dark hair. A forest-hued dress wrapped around an hourglass figure. Not at all wispy, mostly solid. Looking at me, around the room, eyes landing and widening at the sight of the mantlepiece – or more particularly the woodcut and the dispensation.

'Patience Gideon?' I say, throat dry. My fingers seek the scar on my wrist, that physical sign of all my failures; I think of Maud and her knife, all that blood. I shake the image away, say again, 'Patience Gideon?'

She looks taken aback. 'Oh. Haven't heard that name in a very long time.'

'Well, you've been…'

'Dead? Obviously. Why am I here now?' She raises a brow, looks around the room again, comes back to me. 'Did you do this? Stupid question, of course you did, there's no one else here.'

'…dead a long time.'

'How long?'

I blink, realise that I don't precisely know. 'A touch over three hundred years? Perhaps? *When* did you die?'

A puzzled expression settles on her face. 'I... don't know. I was very old, I remember that much.'

'You don't look old.'

'And aren't you the sweetest thing?' She smiles, peers at herself in the obsidian scrying mirror over the mantle, tilting her head left and right, a hand to the neck checking for wrinkles. 'I suspect, m'dear, that I look the way I did when I liked myself the most. When I was content with myself and my life.' She looks contemplative and wise – then surprised. 'Oh. But you've summoned me as a *memoria*.'

'From the time whenever you touched...' I gesture at the dispensation. Her expression clears.

'Ah! Clever. Then it's how I looked when I held *that*.' She strokes her face, moving her head so she can study herself properly in the mirror. 'Certainly more beautiful in my youth, but so seldom happy.'

'I'm sorry.'

'Don't be. We learn more through sadness than we ever do through happiness. Happiness makes us heedless.' She examines her hands. 'An unexpected return at any rate. And, young lady, if I remember such things correctly, you've got me for a limited span, and this sort of thing can't be done again. You've pulled me from... somewhere.' She frowns again, that confusion. 'Wherever that was. So, don't waste time: what do you want?'

Patience Gideon squints as if only now seeing me properly. Then in a second she's an inch from my face, peering, peering, peering. 'Oh. Oh. Look at you, little thing. No magic but... Did you *borrow*?' She looks suspicious, vaguely horrified.

I shake my head. 'I'm something else. A speaker for the dead.'

Her eyes go wide. 'Oh, my. Rare, really.'

'Really?'

'My dear, if your sort were common there'd be no ghosts, or at least considerably fewer of them. Well done, you. But,' she points to the clock, 'tick tock.'

'*The Bitterwood Bible*. Your grimoire.'

'Never called it that. Silly idea, as if a book of shadows needs another name.'

'Gilly did. Your foster daughter. Gilly Briar.'

Her features soften into fondness and regret. 'My Gilly-girl.'

'I'm one of her descendants. Ellie Briar of Silverton.' Talking quickly in case she disappears. 'One of our tales is that the grimoire was Gilly's and before her death she hid it.'

Patience, expression moving between stunned bewilderment, utter outrage and back again, finally mutters, 'Oh, Gilly, what did you do?'

'I've been told by Sandor Briar' – she smiles at his name – 'that Gilly was like me. Not a witch's bootstrap.'

'No power in her at all. Nothing. Didn't make any weight on the witches' scale. Poor girl. It always tormented her. I thought she'd come to terms with it…'

Should I mention Hilla and what Gilly did to her own daughter? I choose *not*. 'Patience, your grimoire. If it's not here, then where?'

'It was burned, Ellie Briar. In a village where they tried and failed to kill me they threw it onto the pyre with an eidolon they thought was me. That great book passed down from my mother, from her mother and hers and hers – originally stolen and stolen again, I think – was turned into cinders and ash by a bunch of idiots in a place called Edda's Meadow.'

I feel a pang for something I've never had and could never have used, but also a huge sense of relief that it's no longer in existence. That it *can't* be used. Then I remember I'll have to tell Audra.

Patience is speaking again. 'My Gilly… I found her by the roadside when she was a child. She could never accept her lack of power. A yearning that can never be satisfied turns the heart and head.'

And I still don't tell her about Hilla; it would only be pain to carry away. She is, I notice, growing less solid. I wrack my brain, seeking any last questions.

'The dispensation – how did you get it?'

She laughs. 'There was an Archbishop, Narcissus Marsh – a notorious witch-hunter even though he'd taken a witch for a lover. He sent his god-hounds after her when she fled him. Selke had sought refuge in my home and – ah! So much happened, but she saved me from a burning and that creates a debt. I knew she'd have no peace as long as he lived, and that Gilly would be hunted too because of the mess we'd left behind in Edda's Meadow. Although the god-hounds didn't know I still lived, they knew Gilly'd run. Didn't care she was no witch, would have burned her just as cheerfully.' She smiles bitterly.

'I went to Lodellan, settled there, got to know the city. My home again became a safe haven for refugee witches, and some had encountered Gilly and Sandor on their travels so I knew where they'd washed up. But I also knew that if I could find them, so could the god-hounds. In those days, there were still incursions from the Darklands, not just raiding parties to fatten their larders but hunting parties that left entire villages wiped out. All those leeches in that tiny little county, surrounded by mountains, with that one gateway in and out, and not so very far from my Gilly-girl.' She begins to pace, waving her hands.

'I firmly believe that any piece of knowledge might one day save you, so I made a point of learning something from every witch who passed through my house. One woman told me that the Leech Lords did not like witches – that she'd seen them be repelled by her very presence. That got me thinking, and one evening I walked in the Archbishop's dreams.'

'Can you really do that?'

She snorts. 'Some can. I can't. No, disguised myself as a servant, snuck into his palace and drugged his wine. Told him I was a messenger from his vengeful God, that if he didn't heed and obey he'd be dead three days hence. Highly suggestible, priests. That in a tiny place far to the north there was a family of witches who could cast enchantments to close the gateway to and from the Darklands. Closed to the leeches alone – wouldn't want to restrict trade routes. Only a fool would tell him the power lay in our very bodies – can you imagine the crusade the church would unleash, witch-hides tied to shields, our bones turned into weapons?' There's a tremor in her, as if she blinked out for a second.

'All it required, I said, was for him to grant those few witches their lives and *employment*. Then he and all of Lodellan – all the souls there and elsewhere – all those precious souls the church loves to count like misers – would be kept safe. From the leeches, at least.' She seems to feel herself fading too, as she speaks faster and faster. 'Told him a herald would collect it the next morning – *my* guest – and when she left, she took the dispensation and instructions.'

'We have a stone circle, all the bodies of the Briar Witches, to hold them back.' She nods, and I don't tell her that the woman she sent told Gilly other things, gave her more and worse knowledge. 'But you didn't spare him? Narcissus Marsh?'

'Of course not. No more pity for him than he'd ever given to my kind! But I waited, waited until my courier was well out of the city, waited three weeks, then visited the Archbishop again, bringing him a special vintage.' She laughs. 'Two copies of the dispensation: one for the bearer, one for the Cathedral Archives. I knew his reputation was so great, his devotion to keeping us in check, that no one would question what he'd ordered, not even after death. They might add something to it but wouldn't disobey.'

'A god-hound sent to watch over us.'

She snorts. I wish I had time to tell her everything, all our history, all we've achieved because she made it possible. I want her to know that we are her line whether blood joins us or not. She's not real, just a *memoria*, but still. On impulse I ask, 'The Witches' War? Do you know of it?'

But it's too late, she's thin as a sheet of water, colourless as one too. Her mouth opens, lips move, yet I can't hear a word.

'Goodbye,' I say, and Patience Gideon's gone. I can't help but feel I've squandered my time with her. I should have told her more. Asked her more.

That was magic, a voice in my head says, drawing attention. *You did* – committed – *magic*. I touch the scar on my wrist, think *I did it, Maud, I did it.*

But I don't think I really did. It didn't feel like I always thought it would. There wasn't even the same rush I felt on Balefire Eve when the wood-wife went up in flames. There wasn't that sensation I've always hungered for... believed I was missing out on. Expectation and reality are two different things.

But I am completely exhausted – drained and barely able to move. I'd dearly like to lie down and sleep on the floor, but instead force myself to erase any last sign of what I've done, finally rolling the rug over the pentacle. When I'm finished, I look around the library, checking that nothing remains to give me away. The lectern needs to be moved back into place on the rug. I shuffle it until it covers the indentation its weight has left over the years. I should shelve Gisela's blue and silver leather grimoire alongside those of all the other Briar grimoires, yet that will feel very final indeed. Being able to see it here daily, as if waiting for her to use it, somehow eases the loss. It's the same urge, I suppose, that makes Audra not want to move into our grandmother's bedchamber.

Running my fingers over the worn cover, tracing the silver foil. It almost feels warm. Idly I play with the silk ribbon to mark place, then flip it open. Curiosity, nothing more. A page with multiple creases in it – one of those meant to remain hidden, carefully folded to hide a particular spell. This one left flat, presumably in haste, not refolded again.

Briar Tongue (Alt: briar-tongue, thorn-tongue).

A tea with rosehips and thorns, berry juice – any one, to cover the taste.

To silence your enemies.

An incantation to recite.

A rhyme to ensure the object of your enchantment would not – could not – speak your secret until the hex was removed. At first the spell would silence them only when they tried to speak

305

of the matter of concern. If they persisted, the thorn would grow in the tongue, sewing shut the voice until they could not speak at all. They wouldn't even be able to write, couldn't pass messages, nothing. Unable to communicate. Shut in.

Thorn-tongue.

Briar-tongue.

The last spell Gisela used? But on whom? Or simply a random page, looked at and discarded? Its concealment forgotten when the reader was interrupted? Why would my grandmother be looking at such a thing? How long ago?

Slowly, I close the book, leaving it just as I found it – I've enough unpleasant family secrets to unravel. Later on, I'll work out what to do next. For now, I go to my room and collapse into a deep slumber even though it's still broad daylight.

31

I'm awake if not exactly alert by the time my cousins arrive home for dinner. I do my best to listen to the tales of their days. Audra mentions in passing that they had Dai released before leaving for the coppices where the charcoal kilns are located. Both she and Nia smell of woodsmoke. Eira talks about dresses and place settings, where best to hold the wedding to accommodate the largest number of attendees – the common will fit everyone but if she's not prepared to wait until spring, we'll need to arrange a village of marquees there so no one freezes to death. Nia doesn't say much. I excuse myself after dessert to go check on Huw and relieve Beres.

Beres is gleeful about Dai's night in a cell, even if it was only one. Even more pleased when I tell her about Audra banning both Carabhille sons from courtship for a year and a half. She doesn't care about the reparation payments – *What do I need with money*, she scoffs? She's always earned her own, will continue to do so. What she wants to know is when will this all be public knowledge. Friday, I say, Audra's calling a town meeting. You've only a couple of days to wait, I say, and send her off to her own home. I'll sit with him. She says she'll come back in a few hours. I climb up to the loft where Huw's been relocated to bed. His bruises and cuts are healing, though they remain vivid even with the best of my creams and potions. He's still drugged, a poppy-influenced slumber, and I'm suddenly exhausted once again. I slip in beside him and am quickly asleep.

* * *

In the dream, Liv's shoving her fingers down my throat, and I'm unsure if she's trying to pull my tongue out or dig deeper, into the heart and lungs. Take the very core of me, as if I'm responsible for her death. And just maybe I am. I should have gone back, should have checked on the Havards and the other outliers. They were under my charge and I did not make sure they were safe. I ran home like a scared child. I'm freezing. Open my eyes, realise I've kicked off the covers.

Outside the window, dawn's fleeing and I should return to the Briar House.

Down in the parlour, Beres is curled in Tobias's old brown chair, a blanket over her. I wonder if she came upstairs and saw us. I wonder if she'll tell anyone about us. I doubt it. Not yet anyway. She's had enough of people knowing her family's business for quite a while, I suspect.

It's my own fault: I should have waited in that very chair, then she'd have woken me when she came back last night and sent me home. I tiptoe so as not to disturb her, to avoid any uncomfortable conversation for a while longer. I'm tired and unfocused, and I do something I haven't done any morning since Huw's arrival: I leave by the front door.

Of course, that's when Audra's waiting for me, isn't it?

And my cousin has clearly been there for a while, prepared, wrapped in a long fox-fur cloak against the cold. Loitering with intent. No surprise on her face, perhaps just a hint of satisfaction at a suspicion confirmed. Her lips lift at the corners in what should be a smile.

'No wonder he's not interested in me,' says she. Her tone's light, but there's something underlying that's very heavy indeed.

'Audra—' I begin; the natural panic starts to rise, of every child who's not good enough. Then I remind myself I've nothing to feel guilty about. I'd slept with Huw before she returned; I did not steal a beloved from her. I simply hadn't told her I'd already laid claim. Perhaps I should have, but I didn't regard her actions – running into him in the street, giving an open invitation to the Briar House – as a matter of the heart. Mind you, she's not been nursing him, not even dropped over to see how he's recovering. Yes, I enjoyed having a secret, liked having something that was mine alone. Something my magical cousin did not get to take or have handed to her purely because of who she is.

'How long has this been going on?' she asks, examining the fingernails on one hand.

I join her in the street. 'Before you returned from the outlier farms. When he'd just arrived.'

Her brows rise. 'You certainly recovered quickly from your previous disappointment. Who'd have thought you had it in you, Ellie Briar?'

'I've had it in me quite a lot, Audra.' Raucous laughter breaks the early-morning quiet and the tension dissipates. 'I'm sorry I didn't tell you. I just… I just wanted something for myself, just for a while.' I shake my head. 'You're not too heartbroken, are you?'

She snorts. 'It merely seemed convenient, to take him to bed like Gisela did Tobias and bring him closer to us. But no matter, whether it's you or me or even Nia who does that isn't really relevant. As long as he's in thrall to the Briars.'

I hardly think Huw's the "in thrall" type but I don't tell her that. Easier for him, though, if she thinks him a tame god-hound on a string at least for a while. We start towards home. 'Audra, I've been thinking I should go and check on the outlier farms again. Take some of the vigilants—'

Audra's shaking her head before I even finish.

'There's no need, Ellie, they're all perfectly fine – besides it's too close to the snows and I need you here. There are enough outliers to look after themselves. I need you beside me because I'm still too uncertain of myself' – she looks embarrassed to admit it – 'you said so yourself that I've been less than stellar in my leadership. While that stung, you were right. I need you keeping things running while I get a handle on everything – and I *need* you to find that book.'

Again, I almost tell her about the ghosts. I almost tell her about seeing Liv. I almost tell her about summoning Patience. That the book is nothing but embers and ash. But somehow it feels like on top of learning about Huw and me… it might be a bridge too far. That I've been keeping too much from her and my cousin might feel she can no longer trust me.

And I don't know when I might be able to start sharing these things with her… if ever. Do I simply wrap them inside and never let them out?

'There's nothing can be done for them now, anyway,' she says and catches my startled look. 'Until spring. Until it's safer for us to go there. Don't worry, Ellie, the outliers will be fine. We have enough to worry about with tomorrow's meeting.'

Our boots crunch across the frost-covered ground. 'Dai needs to learn he's answerable to us. To the town. His parents won't be happy, but they're aware he's brought them into disrepute. Giulia might still try and protect him, but Cane knows better. And this is about more than just teaching Dai a lesson – it's a reminder to Silverton that we are in charge.'

Audra nods. 'I need to think about what I'll say. If I write something, will you read it?'

'Of course. But you can't read it out to them – it must have immediacy, not feel like a prepared speech.'

'You're right, of course.' She looks at me, a little in wonder, a little in irritation. 'How did you learn all these things, Ellie Briar? All these clever little ways?'

'I watched Gisela and I listened to Maud. Gisela always practised her addresses in front of Maud so they looked completely natural. And I was quiet all the time, people forgot I was there. When you're invisible, they show themselves for who they truly are – so, when I watched Gisela, I also watched those to whom she spoke. Watched their reactions, watched how her words affected them for good or ill.'

She shakes her head with a grin, linking her arm with mine. 'If you weren't on my side I'd have to be very suspicious of you.'

* * *

Lowen Jernigan's emporium on Silk Merchants Way is a tall wooden building, four storeys high, each crammed with a plethora of luxury goods: fabrics, perfumery, furniture, bed linen and table settings, confectionary, tapestries, curtains, ladies and gentlemen's finest attire fit for a court visit (I have yet to work out who buys those when we so lack a court, but there's never the same ones on display each month), paintings, servants' livery,

311

carved ebony clothing chests, specially made limited-edition notebooks from Carabhilles that cannot be commonly bought. There's even a black marble bath – on the ground floor, no one's foolish enough to take it to a higher level – but thus far no one's found its asking price acceptable. The top floor contains offices, for Mr Jernigan and his consortium partners. I wait for a minute in the corridor at the top of the stairs in order to catch my breath and order my thoughts – those interesting details Dónal shared this morning – before letting myself in.

The reception area is a little dingy, lit by lanterns even though it's daylight outside – this space has no windows, is walled in by the other rooms around it. The anxious-looking young man sitting at the desk, pouring over ledgers, glances up nervously, does a double-take and rises.

'Miss – Steward Briar.'

I don't know his name, but he's the one I've heard about – part of the reason I'm here – so I smile. 'Good afternoon. I'm hoping to see Mr Jernigan?'

'You don't have an appointment – but then you don't need one, do you? Of course not.' He's busy pulling on a black frockcoat over his plain black waistcoat, tidying his hair. I realise it's not for me when he shuffles around his desk and goes to the door with a brass nameplate bearing Lowen Jernigan's name. He pauses, clears his throat, lifts his fist to knock, takes a deep breath, then gives three precise sharp raps. A habit, a ritual. What's required.

What comes from inside the next room is little more than a snarl, and the young aide's voice goes up a notch as he calls, 'I'm sorry to disturb you, sir, but Steward Briar is here to see you.'

I half expect to hear him saying I should come back when I've got an appointment, but after a moment the door opens, and I'm treated to a cool smile. The same tall puffy man with wispy brown hair and thin lips, today he's wearing black velvet trousers, a green and gold waistcoat, and the same gold frockcoat and fancy shoes as at the assembly. The same finely made but slightly too-tight clothing.

'I do apologise, Mr Jernigan. I did want to ask you some further questions about your proposal for a gaming parlour – to see if we might come to some arrangement.'

A spark of self-interest lights his face and he waves me in. I note he doesn't tell his offsider to bring coffee or tea.

The room is cold, the fire unlit, whether it's preference or parsimony I'm not sure, but this is where the light is, streaming through tall arched windows that take up one whole wall. There's a vast desk in a pale wood, almost white; the rest of the furnishings match, with some gilding on fittings and edges. A large red rug on the floor, two armchairs in front of the hearth, between them a small bronze table bearing cut-crystal glasses and an impressive-looking bottle three-quarters full of purplish-amber liquid. Jernigan points me towards a chair.

Making myself comfortable, I take in the painting above the fireplace: a forest scene, autumn-toned, a blaze of orange in the trees, a clearing around a small cabin. Three burly bearded men standing by a well.

'The Three Brothers Bear,' my host says, noticing my interest.

'Oh,' I say. 'How strange – I've always pictured them like the fountain.'

Jernigan gives me a chilly brief thing that's meant to pass for a smile. 'The original house in the woods, before they came here, founded Silverton.'

The weight of the unspoken: before it fell to ruin, before a witch came and took it over. I choose not to have that conversation. 'Your ancestors, Mr Jernigan?'

'A long way back, yes. Bloodlines still matter.' He reaches for the bottle on the bronze table and waggles it at me. It's laced with gold and silver designs of mermaids and ships. Very distinctive. I nod. He hands me a glass.

I take a sip. 'My, that's very fine. *Distinctive.*'

'How can I help you, Steward Briar?' He peers at me over the lip of his own glass.

'Your games parlour, Mr Jernigan. I was wondering why you chose such a venture.'

He looks away, furtive. 'I – that is, we, my partners and I – felt it was a good investment. A new place for people to go and enjoy themselves. You, clearly, do not feel the same.'

'I feel that the Dancing Briar Inn already provides sufficient diversions of this nature. And it's come to my attention recently that Garvan Brody, who runs those diversions, has been less than honest in doing so.'

'People know the risks—'

'The problem is that there are folk who have no control over themselves when it comes to games of chance, and a proprietor with no scruples won't care if someone's family ends up destitute as long as a business is making a profit, honest or otherwise.'

'Are you suggesting I—'

'I'm suggesting nothing. I know for a fact that you were having meetings with Garvan Brody.' Information Dónal shared with me this morning; Garvan, looking to return to his illegal ways in a new location. 'I know his name did not appear on your proposal yet I'm willing to bet he's been advising you on how to make games of chance spin in your favour.' I take another sip of my drink.

He gives a dismissive wave and a band of thick reddish gold on his middle finger catches the light. It's just as Sandor described, just as I remember, the briar pattern engraved around it. Quick as can be, I take his hand, much to his startlement.

'My! What an unusual ring, Mr Jernigan.' I turn the limb this way and that, as if admiring. I can feel from the tension in his arm that he's resisting pulling away. 'Where did you get it?'

'A family heirloom,' he says.

'What a coincidence. My family had one just like it.' And I smile up into his face, stare into his eyes and I know he's lying to me. 'But then, you know that.'

He splutters. 'I don't know what you mean! What exactly are you insinuating?'

'How did you come to be in possession of a Briar heirloom, Mr Jernigan? It's such a distinctive thing – just like this brandy, which I know for a fact was imported by the Briars for our exclusive use. And of which four bottles are missing from the tithe-barns.' He pulls away finally. 'Did you pay some foolish thief to come into my home? Did you think no one would notice? Was it the same thief who crept into the tithe-barns?'

'I think you should leave, *Miss* Briar. You are making accusations you cannot prove. I would never steal—'

He's right. I've got no proof. Only my vague memory of the thing being amongst Gisela's gems, and the word of a ghost. But then, I don't have to prove it. I just need to rattle him.

'Who gave it to you?' I ask and there's a flicker in his expression; the tic of an eyelid says I've hit a nerve.

'Please leave my office at once.'

And I go, with a knowing grin even though I barely know any more than I did when I arrived, but it'll be good to tell Dónal where the brandy went, and nice to confirm for Sandor that he's right about the ring. I smile politely as I pass the young man at the desk, whose dalliance with Dónal gave me an excuse to visit, and even though my questions remain unanswered I've put the wind up Mr Jernigan, as Maud would have said. It might curtail some of his activities for a while at least. I could have him hauled in front of Audra at the next assembly, but for the moment I still don't know *how* he got that bottle – or where the other three are.

'Ellie?'

Outside the emporium, a quiet voice but one I'd rather not deal with. Still and all, I turn around. Hari Carabhille looks nervous. Last I saw him he was watching his brother get dragged away by the guardsmen. I raise a brow, in no mood to be personable. 'What?'

'I'm just the messenger, Ellie. Dai asked me to give you this.' He holds out a slip of creamy paper. Reluctantly, I take it. It's not even a full sheet, but a torn sliver; blocky handwriting undeniably Dai's glares out at me.

You need to speak to me, Ellie Briar. There are things you need to know. Things only I can tell you. Meet me today, a place and time of your choosing – just not that *place. Keep your monsters away.*

'Well?' Hari asks. 'He said for me to bring your answer.'

'Maybe,' I say, annoyed and knowing that I'll go. What does he think? He's going to talk me out of having him punished? 'Six this evening. The widow Madlyn Wilson's cottage on Peyton's Pavement. It's the only one with a red door.'

316

32

Dónal and I, sitting at his desk, are discussing how Jernigan got his hands on the brandy. My chief clerk has been keeping an eye on Alek Zabel, the clerk who signed the bottles out, but has so far found no sign of any circumstance that might account for a theft. His family appears happy and well cared for.

'Can't we send the marshal and vigilants to the emporium?' he asks wistfully.

'Ah, he'll have hidden the bottle by now, and all the others. Even if he hasn't, he can always say it was his – he's an importer, after all.'

'But the cost to anyone else…'

'He can claim it was a trade.' I sigh. 'No, I need something more concrete before I go to Audra about this. But I don't think we'll see a resubmission of his games-parlour proposal for a while at least.'

There's a ruckus outside in the registry, a door thudding into a wall, rapid footsteps. I reach for my blackthorn baton, then remember it's not there, that I couldn't find it this morning when I dressed, must have left it at Huw's again. A few moments later Eira bursts into the little office. She's trying to look calm, but I know her too well. Not to mention she's shaking all over.

'What's wrong?' I ask.

'Ellie, I need you to come with me.'

I nod to Dónal, snatch up my satchel and join my cousin. When we're properly out of the townhall, she says: 'Sally's not well.'

'Oh no. We should get Audra—' But: Eira's the town physicker, so why-oh-why is she coming to me?

'No! No. Audra already doesn't like her – if we – if she – you need to come, Ellie.'

'What about Nia?'

'Nia can't help. Nia can't keep her mouth shut.' The acerbic tone for her sister surprises me. Eira wrings her hands as we stride briskly along Gilly's Way. 'We were planning the wedding, when... she just started screaming, and fainted. I just don't know what to do. She's pale and cold, but sweating, fast pulse, shallow breathing, all signs of shock – but nothing happened, Ellie!' Her voice breaks.

Primrose Cottage is nestled between two much larger houses, but it doesn't look out of place. Pristine white, diamond-pane windows, the thatched roof cut into a decorative pattern, a well-tended garden, all behind a sturdy white picket fence. Inside, it's a surprisingly tasteful mix of pale yellows and stronger pinks. Sally's lying on a fuchsia velvet fainting couch, a crocheted blanket over her. Lips a little blue as she smiles at us and she's shivering.

'Mint tea, Eira?' I don't ask why she hadn't already done it; she's in a panic herself. Silverton's physicker, who can be trusted in every medical emergency, is falling apart now her beloved is unwell. While Eira busies herself in the kitchen, I prop some pillows under Sally's feet, then drag a chair over for myself, putting my satchel on the little polished wood coffee table. Sally stares at me with dilated pupils.

'What happened?'

She starts to speak, and gives up three times before getting out, 'You'll think I'm mad.'

'Probably not. If you don't want Eira to know, I won't say anything. But talk fast.'

'I thought I saw…'

I raise my brows, encouraging.

'I thought I saw my father. At the table right there, glaring at us.' Sally's hands and voice shake. 'He was hissing at me, saying I could never marry, that I… I was…' She chokes on whatever she was going to say. 'Am I going mad?'

I ponder Estyn Eldin. He's been dead for years but hasn't been amongst the crowd of Silverton's spectres. Sandor said they come when they want to, when they're ready. Estyn obviously isn't ready. He's been skulking out of sight until now, when, like the rest of them, he's gaining heft and influence on the world that hasn't seen him for so long. Seeing how much mischief and grief he can cause his poor daughter.

And I…

I can't wait any longer to tell someone about what I've become. If I simply make him go, Sally, poor Sally, will be left with this awful terror and I can see how it's got its claws in her. In all good conscience, I can't let her think she's insane, or let Eira think her beloved is ill or falling apart.

'Sally, you're perfectly sane.' I pat her hand. Eira returns from the kitchen, a teacup and saucer in one hand. There's a gentle rattling to show my cousin's nerves are stretched. 'Eira, sit. I have something to tell you.'

She wriggles under Sally's blanketed legs. I take a deep breath and I tell them almost everything. Eira doesn't believe me, so I tell them again. And again. A constant cycle of questions, reminding me there's a very good reason not to tell anyone anything. Huw at least believed me, for which I've never had the decency to thank him. Must rectify.

Finally, I say, 'Eira, enough.'

'But—'

'Haven't you seen anything?'

'I... well, I'm not... Ursley Kemp said she thought she'd seen something at the fountain the other day, then decided it must have been fog or a reflection from the water. Xander Ablesman told Nia that the day you found his mother's inheritance you were strange, talking to yourself.' *And there's me thinking I've been so subtle.* She shakes her head. 'Sometimes I've thought I could see figures from the corner of my eye but I'm... I'm just tired.'

'No, you're not. I mean, you're tired but that's not it.' I wrack my brain for how to convince her. 'Sally, do you have any idea what might be keeping your father here? Do you think your mother might have seen him too?'

And Sally looks away. From me to stare at Eira, who doesn't flinch, and I realise that whatever the secret is, Sally's already told my cousin. And I can imagine what it might be. The clock on the wall says there's still a while before I'm meeting Dai. I open my satchel and lay *The Briar Book of the Dead* out on the little coffee table, the bottle of ink and the pen beside it – and a little silver canister Huw gave me despite my objections.

I speak firmly: 'Estyn Eldin. Show yourself.'

Nothing. Only Eira and Sally staring at me in gravest doubt – which is a bit unfair from Sally, given what brought me here.

'Estyn Eldin, I am the speaker for the dead and I will not be defied. Appear. Now!' I'm a little shocked by the command in my voice; so are Eira and Sally, and Estyn Eldin because he pops into the corner of the parlour. 'Come here.'

He was a big man, broad and powerful, rather like his daughter in looks. He slinks closer, and I'm trying to remember if I ever thought him so lowly in life. Perhaps he held himself differently then, knowing his sins were his own, that they were secret. A man's comportment changes when his shame is on display. He sneers, 'Yes?'

I face Sally and Eira, take in their expressions. 'Can you see him?'

Sally nods. Eira says, 'I can see something. It's like a man made of mist.'

'As speaker for the dead, I bind you here.' Sandor said that might work; we'll see soon enough. I point at the Book of the Dead. 'It's time for you to go, Mr Eldin. Time for your sins to be confessed and writ down. For you to beg forgiveness.'

'I don't want to. Don't want to go. Won't go.' His eyes slide to his daughter and my cousin, filled with spite.

'The choice is yours,' I reply, and he gives me a surprised look. 'You have two.'

'What? Stay or go?' he scoffs.

'Oh no. Go or go, the manner is the only variable. You can confess and be set free. Or I can send you away without forgiveness, but you won't haunt your daughter any longer.'

'And how are you going to do that?'

'You've not been watching me the past weeks, have you? Seeing what I can do? No, too busy leering at your own child.' He hisses. 'That silver bottle contains holy water. You'll simply be gone, no rest or peace. I don't know where you'll go, but it won't be gentle.' He's straining to get away, but it's like invisible chains are holding him in place. 'It's that or the other. Which is it to be?'

Finally, he chooses confession. He tells me what he did to his daughter from age ten to thirteen, how it only stopped because he died. I write it in the book, then I take his hand though all I'm longing to do is throw the holy water at him, send him wherever to suffer. But I don't. He doesn't deserve gentleness, but Sally does. Poor Sally. Then Estyn Eldin is gone at last.

I'm exhausted when I sit back in the chair and let the pen drop. My palm feels icy again, and I'm starting to see a correlation between the severity of the sin and the effect its forgiveness has on me. I'm coming to the idea that forgiveness isn't about a kindness. It's a hard thing to do, not easy, not simple. That it's a price as much as blood is for magic. Forgiveness has a cost.

After extracting promises from them both to keep their newfound knowledge to themselves until I can break the news to Audra and Nia – Eira doesn't even argue – I pack my things. I consider dropping in at the priest's house to locate my baton, but the chances of me leaving there quickly, or even wanting to, are very slim. No, if I go straight to the Widow Wilson's deserted cottage, speak with Dai and find out what he thinks I need to know, I can be back in Huw's bed within the hour. If Dai's idiot enough to get aggressive, I'll call for Sandor.

I'm almost at my destination when something swoops by my face, the lightest of touches but immediately it stings. My hand comes away wet. A long cut. A claw? A barely visible puff of feathers now far away and climbing into the night sky.

Just as it was the last time, the red door's open, although I could've sworn I'd closed it when I left. Perhaps Dai's just sloppy. But there's no light inside, nothing flowing from behind the curtains, and there are very few streetlamps along Peyton's Pavement. I locate the tinderbox on my chatelaine, strike one of the sulphur matches.

Step inside.

And almost immediately trip over something. I recover my balance only after an undignified dance. There were candles on the mantle if I remember correctly, and I desperately shield the guttering match as I cross the sitting room. Just in time, the flame catches the wicks and light blooms. I turn towards the doorway.

A large man, lying on his back. The biggest man in all of Silverton. Black hair sticky and shiny with rapidly congealing red blood, white bone fragments around the crater in his skull. Part of his face has been stove in too, but there's no mistaking those blue, blue eyes in the once-handsome face. On the floor beside him, a blackthorn baton, slick with blood. I touch my face again; it comes away red, tacky and already congealing.

No sign of a ghost, no spirit rising from the body or floating bewildered around the cottage. Dai Carabhille, it seems, died with no sense that he'd committed a sin, no need for forgiveness; still considering himself the injured party in all that had happened. Typical.

One of his hands is curled on his chest, something white and brown sticking from between the fingers. I pry at it, and his body's still warm, still limber – not long since his death.

I pluck it out and stare.

I'm still staring at it when there's the sound of more than one set of boots from the doorway, and a voice says, 'Oh, Ellie. What have you done?'

33

That I am currently languishing somewhere lately occupied by Dai Carabhille is an irony not lost on me. While Silverton's lock-up isn't the most salubrious of locations, which I suppose it's not meant to be, it is at least clean. Because our crime is generally dealt with by fines and retributions, we have very little of it, so the vault in the bowels of the townhall doesn't get a huge amount of use. Admittedly, some of our more over-enthusiastic drinkers are quite familiar with the place and even have preferred cells. There's fresh straw on the stone floor, and the pallet mattresses are changed every week, the blankets washed, the ablutions buckets emptied and disinfected daily. And tonight, there's no one to share the space with.

Still.

No windows and I can't tell how long I've been here. I'm starving. It's cold. Nia at least handed me an extra blanket before she left, but she didn't look at me and I didn't try to persuade her of my innocence. She's the one person I'll never beg. Audra took my chatelaine so I can neither start a fire for warmth nor try to use one of the handy attachments in a late-career change from disgraced steward to clueless lockpicker.

'We can't be seen to be anything but even-handed, Ellie,

I'm sure you understand,' Audra had said tenderly as I'd been marched from the Widow Wilson's home to the townhall. As if she wasn't locking me up for something I didn't do. As if my cousin had suddenly decided I was the sort of person who would beat a man to death because he'd rejected me. As if this wouldn't damage my reputation even if I were to be found not guilty. 'And weren't you heard threatening him in Bakers' Lane? As you've observed, we can't be ineffectual in our duty, and we hold our position in part through folk having a fear of consequences – so those consequences must also be seen to affect us.'

How kind of her to quote my own words at me. Should have known she'd never let a lecture go. The hours and minutes seem to crawl by. I've nothing to read or write with because Audra took my satchel and it's only a matter of time before she opens it, reads the Book of the Dead. No sign of Eira or Huw. I can't sleep either, all I can do is jump from thought to thought, imagining any number of scenarios, none of which end well for me.

And I argued with Audra. Oh, how I argued, though I stopped short of telling her about Silverton's ghosts – because a woman crouching over a murdered man and shouting about ghosts would have made matters look even worse. I told her I'd been with Eira and Sally, but not why – Sally's past is private – but it didn't matter because Dai was still warm. Had he been stiff and cold, I might have been able to convince her I'd just stumbled upon the body. But there I was and there was my baton. Telling her it had been missing, that I'd been looking for it – admitting I'd been careless with it did nothing except erode the very memory of everything I've achieved these past weeks.

More than that: the memory of all the support I've given her not just as the Briar Witch, but *forever*. Who did she come to when her mother had been murdered? Not Nia, not Eira, because they still had each other. *Me*. Who comforted her and dried her tears? Who suggested that she, as the Witch Apparent, would suffer no consequences from a righteous act of retribution? And who suggested the nightshade leaves in the garden? And didn't she keep her mouth shut all those years, never once telling Gisela or Maud that we shared the blame for Tobias's death?

Yet none of that seemed to matter anymore.

'Can't she just come home, Audra?' Nia had asked, a request that surprised me. 'Ellie could stay in her room, we could lock the door—'

And Audra shook her head.

'Do you really think, Audra, I'd do this?' Pointing at the dead thing. 'That I wanted revenge for so petty a reason?'

But my cousin simply kept her reasonable tone, while Nia watched on, and in the end it was either go quietly and with some dignity, in the darkness when no one else could see my humiliation, or start shouting and punching, which would have looked like an admission of guilt.

So, here I am.

I haven't called for Sandor. Not yet. I'll need to speak to him, but there are things I'm trying to figure out. Things that don't fit together. I'm pacing back and forth, trying to pick things apart, fit them where they're meant to go.

Yearning, I say, 'Grandmamma, I wish to the gods you were here.'

There's the overwhelming sense I'm no longer alone. No sound, no creak of the door to the stairs opening, and certainly not of the cell door. Just a chill shifting across the room, and a mist that begins to take shape just inside the bars.

I think of spirits getting lost, of them not knowing they're dead, or refusing to believe it. I wonder what Gisela thought when she realised that she was one of the ghosts that Silverton didn't have? Gisela, the first Briar ghost I've seen apart from Sandor.

All the ghosts I've dealt with, seen, have appeared as they remember themselves in life.

Gisela looks neither happy nor contented. She doesn't look how I last saw her, neat and tidy in her death-bed, head wound covered, makeup on her cheeks and lips. Gisela looks the way she died: white as a sheet, blood dripping dark and shining from the hole in her left temple, running down her neck and staining her pale lilac dress. There's more colour to her; Gilly's spell is getting weaker and weaker. No one would think her alive, up close. At a distance, in the dusk or early morning when the light does strange things? The illusion might stick for a wee while. She's got her hands out to me, palms up, blood on them too.

Did my grandmother rise after she fell, all unsteady, see herself like *this* in the mirror… then what? Fall for the last time?

'Grandmamma.' I want to hold her, but I know better. 'Gisela.'

There's a strange, brief delight that I can tell her how much I loved her, miss her. Tell her what's happened to put me in this parlous position. Listen as she tells me all will be well. Except she doesn't say anything.

Gisela points to her mouth.

'What's wrong?' More frantically, she points, opens her mouth more, fingers going in as if to make herself sick. She comes closer and I resist the urge to step away; hold my ground as her mouth opens wider, wider, wider rather like Ezekiel Perry's did that day. But there's no sense of threat, just desperation.

So, I gather my courage and step forward to meet her, follow the direction of her fingers, peer into that gaping maw, down that elongated throat, right at the back of the tongue, and see...

And see...

And see something that looks solid, though it shouldn't be. I force myself to reach in, until the tip of my finger touches it. I recoil. Hard. Not quite wooden. Fibrous. Wet. Smelling faintly of roses. I look even closer: something's stitched through the meat of the ghostly tongue, looking like nothing so much as a sea serpent's body, in and out of the water, in and out. And at the tip, a sharp protrusion.

A thorn.

A briar-tongue.

The spell from Gisela's grimoire.

My grandmother points again, urgently, like she's choking. Drowning in her own throat. But I think I know how to solve this at the very least: think about the girl who used her own blood to unlock a cage of brambles wrapped around a village. Briars and blood, blood and briars; blood to open the way, seal a promise, buy the heart's desire, blood for belonging and whatever magic great or small it might contain. I push my index finger back into her mouth and prick it on the sharp tip.

Almost immediately the thorn begins to dissolve. Soon Gisela is puffing out smoke like a dragon. She bends over, hands on her knees and breathes – or makes a mimic of it – *'Fuck!'*

And I don't believe I've ever heard my grandmother swear before.

Maud used to do it regularly, I think in defiance of her perfect sister. Gisela straightens and flies at me, tries to enfold me in a hug, but merely passes through me, wet and cold. It leaves me coughing.

'Grandmamma, we have ghosts. Silverton has ghosts.' She gives me precisely the look that comment deserves. 'Have you spoken with Sandor?'

'Sandor?' From her confusion it's clear not.

'You haven't seen him or any of the other phantoms? Sandor, Gilly's husband, he's been stuck here for hundreds of years – so many have. Gilly did something, a spell that rendered them invisible, unable to communicate, unable to move on – not all, only some.' I'm talking so fast, babbling. 'But I can help them. I have been helping. At your funeral, I had an accident. I can see them, speak to them. I take their confessions and send them to their rest. I can help you too.' Except I don't have my Book of the Dead with me, nor the pen and blood-ink to seal the transaction. 'Why are you still here, Grandmamma? What remains unfinished?'

She's shaking her head; too much information all at once, I assume. She says 'Murder.'

'Whose?'

'Mine. And the one I committed.' She scrubs at her hands, trying to remove the old blood, but the stain remains.

'Who?'

'Maud.' She paces the cell, in and out of the bars, then back to me, through me. A little sob: 'My own sister.'

'Gisela, stop. Tell me about Maud.'

'Maud wasn't going to keep her mouth shut any longer. I'd begged, oh, how I begged. Told her that she needed to stay silent or we would fall. Everything the Briars had built would come apart. Our safe haven would be gone. I told her that for the greater good, she needed to look the other way.'

'From what? Why?'

'But she'd promise she'd stop! She was so sorry. Wept. How could I not forgive her? My beautiful clever girl. The sum of all our hopes. She just… needed to learn.'

'What are you talking about. Who?' If I could I'd shake her.

'But Maud. She'd never really forgiven what happened to Tobias' – my cheeks flame with guilt – 'yet she understood it, understood the pain.' She shakes her head. Blood droplets flick off, float in the air, almost as if she's in water. 'But not long ago, she started finding the animals. All she was trying to do was practise. She confessed she'd gone too far, promised she'd never do it again—'

'Gisela!' I yell and she stops in shock. 'Too many *shes*. Who? Who had Maud seen? Who had promised?'

'Audra. My Audra. Maud never trusted her, not after Tobias. Never liked her even before, thought she was too assured, entitled – too much like I'd been. So, Maud would follow her sometimes. She saw Audra with that boy – Dai. Saw them together. And she saw what Audra was doing with the blood of animals, feeding and growing her power. Just like her mother had done all those years ago. And Maud told me. And I confronted Audra. And Audra promised me she would stop – that she just wanted to be as powerful as she could be to protect us, the town. Maud said I was a fool to believe her, said she'd tell all of you, all the prominent citizens, anyone who might raise an objection to Audra becoming the next Briar Witch.'

'What did you do, Gisela?'

She looks away but keeps talking. 'I gave her the thorn-tongue tea. It… only affects you if you try to speak of what's forbidden, try to write of it. It gets worse the more you try until the voice is gone entirely.'

I blink, feel dizzy. 'And then you told us she was sick, her voice gone. And you let no one else attend to her, told us she'd decided to go to the flames. That it was her choice, she'd rather that than succumb to the cancer in her throat. That others had done it before and it was a way of not wasting all that power in her, that some of her ashes could be kept for spells. And we followed you into the woods and watched you burn your sister.'

Another sob, but I don't have much sympathy left for my grandmother.

'And you'd have put her under a compulsion so she'd obey, because Maud would never have gone willingly to her death even if you had stolen her voice.' I recall my great-aunt, supposedly a willing sacrifice, walking into the pyre Gisela had lit for her outside the menhirs.

'I thought… I thought it was over. Could be forgotten.' She swallows. 'But I realised Audra hadn't stopped with the bigger blood magics. And she was still seeing Dai Carabhille. He'd gotten poor Deirdre pregnant. Audra couldn't bear that he'd done that – been unfaithful to her, made a fool of her.'

I think of all the times I'd confided to my cousin, my almost-sister, how I felt about Dai Carabhille. How kindly she'd listened. How gently she'd teased. How consistently she'd encouraged me. All so I'd look a fool. All so she could take what I'd loved behind my back. How often has she said 'the performance is part of the pleasure'? Dai's dead. Audra was *with* Dai. Everything Gisela said to me went double for Audra because she was actually *with* him. I think of him yelling at Huw in the market that day, punching the priest's head: *Stay the fuck away from her. Her.* Audra. Not me. *Her.* The Briar Witch who'd been seen talking to, flirting with, the handsome god-hound.

'Gisela.' I stagger back and sit on one of the pallets.

My grandmother comes closer and closer. If she still had breath I'd feel it upon my cheeks. Gods, I wish she'd stop talking, I don't want to know any more.

'After Deirdre's death... I confronted her again. She'd brought tea to my bedroom and I drank it like a fool. I said harsh things, hurtful. Then my throat began to... I turned my back on her. I felt a push. Terrible pain in my head.' One hand goes to the wound. 'I rose and she pushed me down again. A pillow over my face. Terrible darkness.'

I remember Audra whispering *Sorry* to Gisela as I sat vigil with our grandmother's corpse. 'Why silence you only to kill you?'

'I don't think she intended murder at first. Just wanted to convince me of her good intentions as she always had before. But I was angry and cruel and I think she lost her temper, and Audra...'

'Audra makes bad decisions when she's angry.'

There's the sound of boots on the steps outside the door.

Frantically, I ask: 'Have you been near her?'

Gisela shakes her head. 'I've tried. Ever since I woke to *this.* But something pushes me away.'

The clank of a key on a ring of more of its kind.

'Why is she doing this, Grandmamma? Why?'

The creak of the hinges. I look to the entrance, at the shape appearing there, then back at Gisela, only to see her blink out of sight.

34

Eira stops dead in her tracks and stares, balancing a tray on one hand. I half expect Audra to step from behind her, keen to make sure I don't start making accusations. But I suspect Audra thinks no matter what I say, I would just sound hysterical. Except Audra doesn't know what I know, all my evidence from the mouths of ghosts. Audra doesn't think I know anything. Audra thinks I'm an idiot, a dupe, a pawn. As long as she keeps thinking that, all the better for me.

Eira looks back up the stairs, then carefully closes the door. Checking. Paces over to my cell, hovers away a little from the bars.

'What?' I sneer. 'Think I'm going to reach through and grab you? Monster that I am?'

'Ellie,' she says, hurt. 'No. Of course not.'

'Everyone else seems to find it easy to believe.' I rise and kick at one of the beds, send it flying. 'Audra. Nia.'

And I don't know why it hurts that Nia should believe it too.

'Was – was… were you talking to Gisela?' Her voice trips a little.

'At least you know I'm not lying about the ghosts.'

'Ellie, if I tell Audra about the—'

'Oh, no. Don't tell her anything, especially not about the ghosts. Gisela—'

'What did she say?'

'That she was murdered. That Audra did it.' All colour drains from Eira's face.

'But why would Audra…'

I tell her what Gisela told me, about Audra and her magic, about Maud's threats and her murder by her sister, about the briar-tongue. Eira jerks at that, stammering, 'Nia's stopped speaking. Last night. She won't answer me.'

'Oh. No.' I close my eyes. What did Nia do, what questions did she ask? I tell Eira what to do, how to cure it. 'But make sure she doesn't let Audra know. If Audra's silenced her, there's a reason. She can't kill all of us off, or not all at once, but she'll do her best to shut us up.'

'Why's she doing it? What's she want?'

'Something… bigger. She asked me to find Gilly Briar's grimoire, said it contained spells to protect us. But even if she's got all this magic, what can she do with it here?' My stomach rumbles. 'Is that for me?'

'Oh.' She puts the tray down just outside the bars, sits behind it. I sit too, reaching through to grab the bread and cheese, eating with one hand, the other dipping the hem of my skirt into the cup of water and wiping away the dried crust of blood on my cheek. It feels as if it's almost healed. I wish I could say the same for my shoulder, which is still aching and itching where the wounds are pulling together.

'What time is it?'

'Almost eight in the morning.'

'What's Audra said?'

'She's going to use the town meeting that was meant to be for Dai's sentencing to dig your grave. I've been listening at the library door; she's practising her speech, asking everyone to remember the good you've done. Saying you were heart-broken and unable to control yourself. That you'd been acting strangely since Deirdre's death. Implied you might have played a part in that too – incompetence, not malice. Saying that you're terribly sorry and will accept the best judgment of the Briar Witch.'

Oh well, at least she's taking my advice about practising her speeches.

'Did you know about Audra and Dai?' Her expression says she didn't. 'Making such a fuss about her rebellious years being behind her, having a better class of friends. She just got better at hiding what she did.'

I reach for the cup, lift it, smell it. Not coffee. Rosehip tea. I put it on the floor beside me, tip it so it hits the flags with a *chink*, and the liquid soaks into the cracks between the stones.

Eira stares. 'Is that…?'

'Can I suggest you don't drink anything Audra offers? Gods, she didn't touch the bread or cheese, did she?'

'No, no. Just made the tea, saying how much you'd be in need of it.'

I run my fingers through my hair. 'What about Huw? What's she told him?' *And does he believe it of me?*

'Kept that quiet, didn't you? All those secrets you've got, Ellie Briar.' She raises a brow. 'He came by looking for you. I said you were unwell. Audra overheard, came out and told him the truth – or her version of it.' She shrugs helplessly. 'He didn't argue with her, but that might simply be prudence.'

'Oh, I hope so. Eira, tell him to go and stay with Beres if he's not already there. They should keep an eye on each other.' I share something I left out yesterday – about the outliers and Liv's ghost, about Ezekiel Perry and the empty cottages at the north end of town. I tell her that I'm starting to fear all these missing people are connected to Audra. 'What if… what if the red price from animals isn't enough for her?'

Eira stares at me in horror. 'What's… what's she want it all for? All that power? We're in the middle of nowhere, what could she possibly…' She trails off. 'What can I do, Ellie? She doesn't suspect me, I don't think.'

'Audra… Audra likes to see what she expects to see, so just go about your duties, don't ask questions. Stay with Sally, don't go to the Briar House. I need you to speak with Lowen Jernigan.'

'The merchant? But—'

'It's important. He knows something. He's wearing a ring that used to belong to Sandor Briar. Do you remember it? Rose-gold, a briar pattern around it. It was in Gisela's jewellery box and now it's gone. Unless he found a very brave or stupid thief, someone gave it to him, and it had to be one of us. Had to be Audra.' I tell her about the winter-plum brandy too.

'But, Ellie, Jernigan's dead. He was found in his office this morning when his aide arrived. It looked like he'd been there all night.'

'Will she try and blame me for that too?'

'I don't think even she would be able to make that stick. *I* asked around. You were with people all afternoon after you left

337

him, and he was seen alive by several people after you were frogmarched through the streets.'

'Small mercies.' I rub hard at my face. 'He had to know something, Eira. He didn't get that ring without an exchange – that was payment for something.'

'What can I do?'

I bend down and pull something long and delicate from my boot, the thing I'd plucked from Dai's dead hand – Audra didn't find it because she knows I keep the knife in my right one and, Audra being Audra, didn't bother to check the left. I hand it over to Eira and tell her who to give it to and what to do with it.

She eyes me speculatively. 'Anything else?'

'Get me out of here before she decides to burn me.'

* * *

When Eira's gone, I call for Sandor.

My great-grandsire looks at me, at the bars, the cell. 'Well, this is a pretty pickle.'

'My cousin Audra has taken a set against me.'

'Clearly.'

'As a result, all ghost-related activities are suspended – indefinitely if she disposes of me.' Then again, I've not told her about *The Bitterwood Bible*. I wonder how much longer that might keep me safe.

'Then how are you going to get out of here?'

'I thought you were getting more solid, having more effect on the world? No lockpicking skills?'

'Not hardly. Ellie, this is—'

'Serious. Yes, I am very well aware. I need you to do

338

something. Lowen Jernigan? The dandy with your ring? I hear he's met a precipitous end.'

'He has indeed and he is not happy about it.'

'I'm so glad to hear he's still about. Be a good ever-so-great grandfather and make him tell you how he got that ring. I believe it was my cousin Audra.'

'Why would she do that?' But I notice he's no longer claiming he simply can't share other ghosts' information. Progress.

'I think she paid him for something – but Briars nowadays don't have their own money.' He raises both brows. 'Minerva Briar, a hundred years ago, ran away with a large chunk of the family fortune. So, everything we need, all bills, are paid for from a common bank account accessed only by the steward, and if the others want pin money, they have to ask me. Which means—'

'—if Audra needed funds for something and didn't want you to know about it—'

'—she would take something of value that, in the usual run of things, wouldn't be missed. Or at least not for a long while. Your ring and the very expensive winter-plum brandy. So, my dear Sandor, extract whatever information Mr Jernigan has and we will be on our way to solving at least one mystery.'

'What about you? You can't stay here.'

'And I don't intend to – escape is well in hand.' I exaggerate, showing more confidence than I actually feel. 'But I need you to go and—'

'—scare it out of Jernigan.'

'Any way you like. Quickly, Sandor, so quickly. And if there's any chance you can spy on Audra, see what she's up to? If you don't consider it too *rude*?'

339

'I would but I can't get near her. Haven't been able to get in the house when she's there either.' He shakes his head. 'There's something about her.'

I consider this. It might work in my favour. While the ghosts are becoming more visible to certain folk, even if Audra is sensitive enough to see them, if they can't get close to her, she'll not recognise them from a distance. And why would she even think about ghosts? Why would any Briar, given our history, our upbringing? Then I remember my Book of the Dead, in the satchel that Audra took from me when they dragged me from Madlyn Wilson's home, and my heart sinks.

'Right. You know what to do, then come back to me.'

* * *

Having finally fallen asleep at some point, all my nervous energy expended, I'm not sure what wakes me. I don't think it's a noise. I roll over on the palette, notice the lamps are burning low. Outside the cell, someone's sitting on a chair brought down especially. There's the sound of clicking, fingers snapping and a halo of fire ignites around the figure. It's impressive. It makes Audra utterly luminous. It takes a lot of power; a lot of blood, but there's no sign of a cut on her hands. Yet she's pulling the magic from somewhere, paying for it somehow, but not with her own little bloodlettings, not with the usual morning ritual the Briars perform daily.

There's something on her lap. I roll up to standing, move towards the bars. One of her hands is stroking a page, thick creamy parchment inscribed with reddish ink, held within a red leather cover embossed with golden bones and flowers. A book. My book. *My* Briar Book of the Dead. When Audra looks up at me it's with an intense curiosity. A perplexity, as if I've confounded her expectations.

'Tell me, Ellie Briar, what have you been doing behind my back?' At her feet, a mug from which steam is rising.

'I might ask you the very same question, Audra Briar.'

She grins, crookedly; a hand gestures to the page and its list of names, dates and sins. 'A book of dead people, no less.'

'We have ghosts. We always have had. Gilly Briar didn't banish them, she just hid them. Made them invisible, so no one's been able to help them. Not for a very long time.'

'And *you* can see them?' There's mockery in her voice, but a tremor in her tone.

'They come to me. They want to be at peace.'

'Tell me you've at least asked one of them about my *Bitterwood Bible*.'

'Tell me why you want it. Truthfully.'

She looks at me consideringly.

'My mother told me one of its spells will resurrect the dead.'

'And?'

'I want my mother back. I want her beside me. I need her knowledge of the old tales. It wasn't fair, what happened to her. It wasn't fair that I lost her. You know that, Ellie, you agreed with me then. The nightshade was your idea. Simple, elegant. Organised.' I almost don't recognise her voice.

'Does it not occur to you that the very scarcity of a resurrection spell, the fact of it being hidden and rare, might be for a very good reason? That we're not meant to bring back the dead? There's a reason Lady Death cannot be found?'

'Oh, Ellie. Wouldn't you do it? What wouldn't you do to have your mother back?'

'I wouldn't kill my grandmother. I wouldn't steal my cousin's heart's desire.' Audra's eyes have gone flat and cold, like a fire gone out. 'And I wouldn't murder a poor girl silly enough to get pregnant to a vain selfish idiot of a man.'

'I didn't touch Deirdre!' Interesting that's what sets her off.

'You said you hadn't spoken to Beres in months. You said *months*.'

'What of it?'

'But you said you'd go and see Deirdre. The day I asked you. You promised. That you'd perform heart's ease on her so she'd name the baby. So she'd survive. And then you said you'd done it.'

'Beres wasn't—'

'Beres was there. She told me, when I asked her where she thought Deirdre might be, that Balefire Eve. She wouldn't have left her daughter alone – she'd had Ursley sit with her in the morning when she went for groceries. Then she stayed with her, didn't even consider coming down to the Balefire. When Deirdre disappeared Beres thought she was asleep in her room, but she'd been gone a long while.' I shake my head, irritated at my own blindness. 'You didn't go. Why?'

I don't mention the briar-tongue, the spell she'd taken from Gisela's book. No doubt she'd love to silence me as she had Gisela. As Gisela had Maud, to protect Audra, the bright one upon whom all our grandmother's hopes rested.

'Why should I!?' A rage. A rage flaring from my cousin like the day her mother was murdered, so powerful that it had infected me too. Her fury, her pain, the loss of Aunt Hebe who'd been a strange mother to us all, a sort of playmate, the source of the best tales. Tales that seemed almost real. Tales that had apparently become to Audra as real as they'd been to her mother.

'Why should I help her? Stupid girl, seducing him. Getting pregnant. Taking what I'd chosen for myself.' She shakes her head, a frantic motion as if to remove rattlesome thoughts. 'And he… he was a boy, Ellie, and not fit to marry a Briar.'

Those words sound familiar, yet I can't quite place them. 'But you didn't display him! Walk out with him or show your intentions! Didn't want to marry him. Just wanted to take him away from…'

'Well, he's gone now.' A laugh rips from her mouth, near-hysteric. She covers her lips, suddenly self-conscious.

'You did that too, didn't you? Used my baton, left it there.' I close my eyes. 'What would you have done to *me*? If Dai had found me at all pleasing? If it had been me carrying his child?'

'Why would he have bedded *you*? He used to laugh about you, Ellie!' She sneers and the flagstones beneath my feet begin to tremble, shift upward – I dance backward until I'm standing on the pallet, watching a localised earthquake. It stops, the flags returning to their places and Audra laughs, drops her hand from the gestures she'd been making. I feel tears threatening, raise a hand to wipe my eyes, stop myself, rest my fingers on the scratch on my cheek instead. Audra gives a strange, tiny smile.

'Did you make her lose the baby?' I ask in a very small voice. 'All out of spite?'

'No, you answer *my* question. Have your ghosts told you where to find my book? Have you found it in the library, wherever old Gilly Briar hid it?'

343

And I should keep my mouth shut. I should play for time. But with a surge of malicious delight I say, '*The Bitterwood Bible* doesn't exist. It was never Gilly's to begin with. She was no witch. She was no better than *me*. The grimoire belonged to her foster-mother and it was *burned.* Burned on a pyre in Edda's Meadow when the Briars fled. It doesn't exist – like all your mother's tales, it's just a *lie.*'

If I was looking for devastation, I'm disappointed.

'I think you're lying, Ellie Briar. I think you just want to hurt me. But you should know that I will get what I want. I will get it whether you help or hinder me.'

'Haven't you seen them, Audra? The ghosts.' I frown.

'I think that you've spent so long not belonging that *this*,' she holds up the book, 'is a very elaborate fantasy. To make yourself feel *special*. To make the people of Silverton think they need you.'

That doesn't hurt the way she wants it to, but what if she burns my book? Audra doesn't, hasn't, can't see the ghosts. 'What did you do to the outliers? What did you do to Liv?'

She closes my Book of the Dead slowly, pushes the steaming mug towards the bars with the toe of her shoe. 'You should drink your tea, Ellie, before it goes cold.'

'I've quite lost my taste for it.'

344

35

I'm still awake when Huw arrives some while later. Too paranoid to sleep lest Audra sneak in again, right into my cell, drawing a knife across my neck or, worse, forcing a rosehip tea down my throat. I'm so stupidly relieved to see him that I want to cry. I keep blinking at him, stunned as a night bird in the dawn light. He looks, all things considered, not too bad despite the still-swollen eye and the yellowing bruises.

'Time to go, Ellie. Got your things?' he says, pulling a jangle of keys from his priestly cloak. They look suspiciously like the ones that hang on the wall behind Dónal's desk upstairs.

'Go where? Not that I'm complaining.' I shift my weight from foot to foot. 'Why are you here?'

'Things,' says he, trying and discarding one key after another, 'are not going well. Audra decided after talking to you, I assume, that matters could not wait until Friday to be discussed. She brought the meeting forward, sent the vigilants out to shout in the streets – hear ye, hear ye and all that. Too many folk to fit into the assembly hall, so they went down to the common, which is where your cousin announced you'd be burned.'

'Oh.'

'She was at pains to emphasise that no one was above the law – *her* law, is how she phrased it.'

'Oh.'

Huw nods. 'It was impressively ill-chosen and poorly pitched. It seems a very large number of Silvertonians really rather like you. Despite Audra's claims of your guilt and the admission thereof, people are most unwilling to believe it.'

'Really?'

'Much muttering of "Surely there's been some mistake" and the like. Very loud muttering, in fact,' says Huw, still trying to find the right key for the cell. 'Even Giulia Carabhille argued that it seemed very unlikely.'

'Now *that* seems unlikely.'

'It seems that, on balance, your time acting *in loco hexerus* is being adjudged more of a success than Audra's as Briar Witch. Her cause was not helped by going to visit the outliers at a time when the town was being terrorized by, what was it? A melyne. Which you caught – well done by the way. In addition, your fortunate findings of treasures and truths from the recent or otherwise dead has generally made quite a few lives better. Ha!' The lock finally clicks and I all but fall out. Huw catches me, and we hold each other too tightly for our respective injuries, but it doesn't seem to matter. He touches the scratch on my cheek, I gently kiss his split lip.

'Now put this on,' he says, pushing me away to remove his black priest's cloak, which he then wraps around my shoulders, tying it tight at the neck, pulling the hood up to shadow my face. Then he steps into the cell and pulls the door shut. 'In the pocket's something you might just need.'

I draw said thing out: a bronze tube. 'Thank you?'

'Holly,' he says, exasperated. 'Twist the top, there's a holly baton inside.'

Not blackthorn. Holly. Something to make a witch quite unwell, mute her powers. Bronze to dampen the effect. Something he's had the very good sense to conceal since his arrival – its existence might have been taken as a hostility. Something that won't bother me a jot.

'A thoughtful accessory, thank you. Don't suppose you found my chatelaine on your travels?'

'No, Audra's kept firm hold on that by all accounts.'

'Of course. But what are you doing?!'

'The thing is, Eira says, if Audra can't get rid of you openly then, knowing Audra as you all do – although apparently not as well as you'd thought – she'll try to get rid of you behind closed doors. Her little meeting ended with her agreeing to reconsider your fate, based on "her people's wishes". Eira said, and I quote, "I swear, it was painful to watch, her talking like a duchess, Gisela never put on such airs".' He reaches through the bars, turns the key awkwardly in the lock, then removes it and steps away from the cell door. 'Which means you might have a day or five, but she'll find a way to get you if you stay here. So, you have to go.'

'But what about you? She'll know you didn't magically appear in here.'

'No, that's why I need the keys, so it looks like I acted alone. Upstairs are four vigilants. They're on the largeish side but not very bright as I was able to talk them into letting me, a god-hound, offer you, a sort-of witch, "spiritual comfort". They've seen me come in. They must see me *or* someone wearing my cloak leave.'

'Huw—'

'Ellie, please go. Go quickly. I don't want to see you hurt and someone's got to be free to work out what to do about Audra.'

'Won't you be in trouble?'

He grins. 'Seems to be the safest place for me at the moment. Your cousin doesn't give up easily.'

I turn, head for the door, glance back briefly. The last I see of him, he's stretching out on the pallet, hands behind his head, staring at the ceiling.

Up the stairs, up, up, up past two vigilants at the desk that counts as a guard station – who don't even glance at me – then into the ratway of corridors, then the assembly hall itself, and all those paces to the front door and the last two vigilants waiting there, standing at attention. I bow my head, drop the hood further over my features and hold my breath. One of them wanders away, presumably for ablutions or just to stretch her legs (honestly, Nia needs to retrain these idiots). I'm so close…

The other one's hand shoots out and grabs my arm. Startled, I look up, straight into the face of Xander Ablesman. His eyes widen, mouth opens.

He releases me, says, 'Goodnight, Father Huw.'

And I step out into the night, heart thudding so hard I fear it must be heard.

I cross the marketplace, trying to keep my pace steady, unhurried, until I'm swallowed by the shadows of a narrow alley. For three whole seconds, I relax – until a hand grabs my arm again and I give a strangled cry. A voice hisses for me to be quiet. In a splash of light from someone's window I see Eira's face, pale and strained. She puts a finger to her lips and drags me

348

on, darting through the darkest, slenderest alleys, scampering along Peyton's Pavement until we stumble out onto Maundy's Mile, and fetch up near Ezekiel's cottage. That's where I assert my will and pull Eira towards it.

'What are you doing?'

'It won't take a second.' In a moment, we're inside, only the watery moonlight coming through the open curtains. No movement. Nothing. 'Sandor? Sandor?'

For a moment, nothing happens.

'Ellie, we've got to get you away—'

'Sandor!'

'There's no need to shout.' He appears at Eira's elbow and she bites back a scream; he's quick to apologise. 'I'm so sorry, my dear.'

'You can see him, now? Properly?' I ask, and my cousin nods. 'Hear him?'

'Not really. It's like a whispering. Not clear.'

'Still some of Gilly's spell around then.'

'Or she's simply not sensitive enough. Not everyone is. Not everyone will see us even when the spell's run its course.'

'Audra can't see any of you.'

'Interesting.'

'Ellie. We don't have time!' Eira's beginning to panic.

'One second. Did you find him, Sandor? Jernigan?'

'Yes. And very unpleasant it was too.' He adjusts the front of his waistcoat as if dusting off an undesirable experience. 'He said your cousin wanted – needed money. And she asked for contact with some of his less savoury associates.'

'Such as?'

'Bandits. She needed minions who'd be unquestioning no matter what she asked of them.'

'And because Briars have no personal funds and all expenditure must be approved by me, she had to barter your ring and the imported brandy. Thank you, Sandor. Anything else?'

'Nothing of use.'

'Ellie, we have to go.' Eira's peering out the windows, watching for pursuit.

'You're leaving?' Sandor sounds affronted.

'Discretion being the better part of valour, think of this as a strategic retreat. A brief departure is better, I think you'll agree, than Audra killing me and you all waiting out eternity in this cottage. I'll be back, Sandor, soon as I can.'

Eira grabs my hand again and doesn't take no for an answer. Out the front door, around the back, through the overgrown garden and the fallen down fence, into the blackness of the woods. We run, stepping high to avoid tripping over tree roots, risking fox holes and our ankles with every step. Until at last we break out onto one of the roads that run to the north of town. She halts and so do I. We gasp for breath.

'Eira—'

'Wait, just wait.'

'Is Nia alright?'

She nods, still trying to catch her breath. The moon comes out from behind a cloud, illuminates her face. 'So far she's managed to hide that she can speak again. But she said she'd told Audra you wouldn't kill anyone in a million years, that there had to be something wrong. That's when she got the tea. Audra said when she'd learned to hold her tongue and serve the

Briar Witch better, then she'd get her voice back.'

'Gods. Beg her to hold her tongue. Audra's too strong. I don't know where she's drawing power from, but it's not herself.' I don't tell Eira about Audra wanting to bring her mother back from the dead, because why tempt another motherless girl with the idea? Before more questions start, there's the creak of wagon wheels and the nicker of horses unhappy to be outside in the cold and dark so late.

'All in what's getting in.' Edgar's voice; Edgar who'd clearly not left town. 'I'd like to be very far from here very quickly.'

Eira shoves something into my hand. 'This is to pay your way.' Then hugs me hard. 'Stay away.'

'I'll return when I can.' I breathe deeply. 'Don't antagonise her. Keep yourselves and Huw safe. I promise I'll be back.'

I climb up beside Edgar, and when I look down again, there's no sign of Eira. It's as if she was never there. My driver gestures behind us, to a little curtained doorway through which I'm meant to go. An excess of caution, but I don't complain. Instead, I crawl into the wagon proper, burrow into a soft little narrow bed. Edgar gees up the horses and we move off. I fall asleep to the rhythm of the road.

* * *

It's bright and sunny and brittle-cold when I wake, though I'm warm under the blankets. The sunlight makes the curtains translucent. We're still in motion and I wonder if Edgar rested at all last night. I clamber out, sit next to him. He looks exhausted.

'Good morning. Where are we?'

'Well beyond Silverton's outskirts – and reasonable reach,' he replies, urging the horses off the road and into a tree-fringed clearing. There's a stream beside it, still running despite the weather. 'So, time to stop for some breakfast, yes?'

I nod. 'I'm starving.'

'Get us some water, I'll start a fire.'

Coffee, bacon and toast later, I'm feeling considerably better – the threat of death being less imminent helps. Sitting on a three-legged stool, I lift my face to the warm sunshine, enjoying the sounds of the morning: Edgar humming, the stream singing, birds talking at each other, unseen beasties scratching in the undergrowth. In one of the pockets of Huw's cloak is the weight of the pouch Eira pushed at me last night. I pull it out, open it, spill the contents onto my skirt.

A glittering hoard. Well, a small glittering hoard. Some pieces I recognise from my recent rummaging through Gisela's jewellery box. Of course, Eira couldn't get any coin from the bank, not without my say-so, and she's taken a cunning leaf from Audra's book – steal the family treasure. Who would notice? I resolve, if I ever return to the Briar House, to lock up our gems more securely.

'That's a queen's ransom,' says Edgar.

'Indeed.' I choose an emerald brooch, toss it to him; he catches it easily. 'Will that cover the inconvenience of mounting a rescue and going out of your way? I'm assuming you know someone who knows someone who can turn that into coin.'

'More than. In fact, this is good for another two rescues.' He holds it up to the light, admiring. 'Possibly also the commissioning of one robbery.'

'Useful to know.' I pick out a ring, a small thing meant for a finger much tinier than mine. Possibly a child, a baby Briar. A silver band with a black stone, striated, rectangular, no bigger than half the size of the fingernail on my pinkie finger. The same sort of stone, I think, as Audra's necklace; the one that had belonged to her mother Hebe.

'Tourmaline,' says Edgar. 'Black tourmaline.'

'Good for grounding and grieving, devouring dark energies, reputed to help circulation,' I recite, a memory from some book or other.

'And to ward off ghosts.'

I frown. 'Really? Never heard that before.'

And why would I? In a place that has no ghosts.

Then something clicks. Audra's not seen the ghosts. Audra may well not be sensitive enough to do so, but Audra also always wears her mother's pendant, that huge chunk of black tourmaline. Both Gisela and Sandor said they couldn't get near her…

I examine the ring. Its gemstone is so much smaller. Eira was holding the pouch when we were in Ezekiel's cottage – was that what stopped her from hearing Sandor clearly? The piece was insufficiently large to keep him away, but just large enough to "muffle" him. And the only time Sandor was actually inside the Briar House? Audra was away, going to "check on" the outliers, or out for a meeting with leading citizens.

I think back to Sandor's report on Lowen Jernigan: that Audra traded him the ring and the brandy in exchange for money and unsavoury contacts. The ring was worth a lot; Lowen was probably meant to resell it but had decided to keep it instead. Perhaps he liked that it was something of ours; just as the Briars had taken Silverton from his ancestors, he'd taken something of value from us. And the brandy, of Alek Zabel's signature in the ledger – no wrongdoing on the clerk's part, merely fulfilling a request from the Briar Witch…

'Edgar,' I say slowly, 'you said you've seen no bandit camps recently?'

'None,' he says, picking bacon shards from his teeth, pocketing the emerald brooch.

'But that doesn't mean they're not around, correct? Like you said, it just means they're better concealed.'

'I suppose so.'

'Do you know the whereabouts of the first cottage of the Three Brothers Bear?' One by one, I drop each piece of jewellery back into the pouch, every single one making a small sound of protest.

He nods.

'Is it far out of your way?'

'Ellie Briar, it's fair to say that I'm already so far out of my way and off schedule that it hardly matters.' He shrugs. 'What's one more diversion?'

36

Mid-journey, Edgar asks, casually, politely, what I did to upset Audra.

'Didn't Eira tell you?'

'No. I only left Silverton yesterday morning – luckily, I wasn't hurrying anywhere else. That young priest came haring after me, said I was needed. So I looped back and waited where he told me to wait.'

I hesitate – what to tell him? How much to tell him? The truth of the Briars? How many murders we've committed? About the ghosts? Gisela liked Edgar, I think Maud trusted him. I'd hate to ever feel willing to brew him a rosehip tea to keep his mouth shut – then again Edgar wouldn't have lasted this long if he were careless with secrets.

So, I tell him little pieces. The ghosts and how I came to see them but not why they'd been invisible. I tell him about Gisela and Maud, about Dai and Deirdre, about Audra and the burned book she's seeking. I tell him about Jernigan and Sandor's ring. I tell him how magic runs in the blood, works in the blood, costs in blood. He gives me a look to say I'm an idiot and why would I think he doesn't know *that*? In the end, I think I've told him almost everything, or at least enough.

'*Anyway*,' I say, 'my point is that Audra always was the strongest of us, streaks ahead of the others. Eira would pull water from the air, but Audra would freeze it into a perfect flower. Nia would light up a darkened room with tiny flames, but Audra would make them dance. And Audra is charming, and she has heart's ease, to help…' I swallow. 'Greater power, a greater cost. Gisela said it was animals at first, and Liv said they'd found slaughtered deer in the woods around their holding. Then those outlier farms being empty – I don't believe they were safe. I don't believe Audra saw them safe and sound.'

'How would she get out there though? To those farms, then back again? On the fastest horse, it's still a matter of days.'

I have my suspicions but don't share them. 'And the disappearances in town, the empty cottages. Whatever deal she's done with Jernigan for his unsavoury contacts? It's more than trying to bring her mother back.' I scratch my head, stare out at the passing scenery, autumn colours and flashes of evergreen, white peaks beyond. I haven't been this way before. There was no call to do so. 'She's been curled in the bosom of our family, given every advantage, taking it for granted and now…' A lump in my throat silences me.

'Mr Jernigan has – had – a reputation for getting things done by hook or by crook,' observes Edgar.

'Meaning?'

'Meaning his unsavoury contacts. There are groups of bandits known to kidnap people for money – either holding them for ransom or keeping them locked away until they're no longer a threat to whoever ordered their kidnapping. It's a typical bandit sort of activity, I'll admit. But there are others – worse – who'll take whole families, whole villages to Calder and sell them to the Leech Lords. To the sort who aren't so picky about their obligations to those who work their land and aren't so interested in conserving their *resources* if you get my drift.'

My stomach flips in on itself and I feel ill. I close my eyes for a moment, wishing it all away.

'Why, do you think, would Audra be interested in such bandits. I mean, if it's the worst sort?'

I just shake my head. We travel on in silence for almost another hour before Edgar says, 'This is the path, here.'

At first, I can't see where he means, then I realise that what looks like a perfectly ordinary bit of foliage is actually a weave of offcuts. Fallen branches lashed together to create a screen. Edgar halts the horses, and I climb down to lift the screen aside and reveal a broad well-used road. I look back at Edgar. 'Stay here. There'll be no turning the wagon about and making a quick escape.'

I grab Huw's holly baton, leaving it in its bronze case for extra heft, and set off along the track. It's not long before I hear footsteps behind me, and Edgar muttering, 'If I lose you now I can never show my face in Silverton again – Eira and that god-hound will have my guts for garters.'

'If I get out of this alive, Edgar, I promise that any time you want to settle down, there'll be a place for you in Silverton. A nice little house. A big house. Whatever you want.' I shrug. 'Of course, if I don't survive then no, I would not advise returning to town.'

The route is easy, well-maintained, just a slight slope downwards. The trees to either side are close-set, and seem to go on forever.

'Can you hear that?' Edgar asks after a few minutes.

'You mean the nothingness? The complete lack of sound?' Just like the deserted outlier farms.

'Exactly that.' He walks a little faster – not to get to our destination more quickly, but to move closer to me. As if I'm much of a defence.

'Can you smell smoke?' I say and he nods. 'Be careful and quiet. If worse comes to worst, we just need to outrun them.'

'Well, I just need to outrun *you*.'

'You are not filling me with confidence or fellow feeling.'

We creep on, more slowly, staying closest to the trees at the side in case we need to hide. At the end of the road, everything opens out into an extensive yard; we hang back, hiding behind boles and brush. At its centre is what can best be described as a conglomeration, several buildings of wood and stone all clustered together around a small cottage. A cottage that I recognise from the painting on the wall of Lowen Jernigan's office. The original cottage of the Three Brothers Bear, but added to, connecting corridors running between the structures. The same old well sits out front.

Still no sound to be heard. A thin plume rises from somewhere behind the complex; the chimneys are bereft of smoke. The cottage windows have no curtains, the door is closed, no lights inside; it might as easily be inhabited as deserted. The front garden is churned as if by many boots. To the left, a large free-standing set of stables and a carriage house.

'Stay hidden here. You'll know soon enough if I'm in trouble.'

'And what'll I do then?'

I sigh. 'Run.'

First, I check the stables and carriage house. No horses in

the former although the stalls contain manure, no one's mucked them out seemingly in days; the latter's home to a selection of covered drays, all unoccupied. I make my way around the yard: no trace of any animal life, no stock, no pets, an empty chickencoop. No cattle grazing in the homefield.

I try the door of the cottage. Unlocked.

Inside, there's just enough sunlight coming in to show a thin fall of dust on everything; roughhewn chairs and tables, shelving. Bedrooms have bunks or mattresses on the bare floorboards, banded trunks, pisspots in corners. No sign of any recent meals in the tiny kitchen. I come to a doorway, and into one of those corridors linking the cottage with other parts of the structure. A short walk and I step into a series of jail cells. Dank straw on the dirt floor, no windows, no pallets, foetid buckets, making Silverton's lockup seem positively luxurious. The cell doors are all open.

How many prisoners were they keeping at any one time? Were the outlier families brought here? Gods, was this where Liv died? Bedo? Their children? I recall Audra swearing all the outliers were safe – saying that my friend had sent love, lying to my face when Liv was either already dead or on her way to being so – and have to lean against a wall until the dizziness passes.

I find no one in the entire complex, which curves around and brings me back into the cottage. Out front once more, I gesture for Edgar to join me.

'Not a soul to be seen,' I say before he asks.

We make our way around to the back of the buildings. Again, no one and nothing, but again there are signs that at one point perhaps not so long ago there was a lot of activity. A trail in the churned earth where many feet were forced to a final destination.

The crater is perhaps a quarter of a league in circumference, sloping to a deep nadir. The plume of smoke rises from the middle. As I draw closer I feel heat coming in waves from the ground. Not a fierce new burning, but one that's been cooling for some time. It's still impressive, you'd still be able to cook eggs on the rock. I run my fingers over the scar on my wrist, feel my own blood running, running, running...

It looks as if something hit the earth at great speed or there was an explosion. It smells... it smells like cooked meat. I kneel. Brown-red is burnt onto the dirt and stones, like congealed blood applied to heat. No scraps of clothing or flesh, no bone shards, no shoes, no leftover limbs, nor pieces of jewellery shining up through the muck. I remember my promise to Ezekiel, that I'd locate his body – but, somehow, I don't think there'll be anything to find. That Audra's magic has become such that it eats *everything*. I spy what look like a couple of logs around the perimeter and closer examination shows they're fenceposts.

'They herded them,' I say. 'Confined them into a huge pen so they wouldn't run.'

'Those covered drays in the carriage house? Exactly the sort that have been reported as taking folk towards Calder whether they wish it or no. Valuable things. Not something to be abandoned so easily.'

'Edgar, I wonder... I wonder if the bandits reached the end of their usefulness...'

'And met the same fate as their kidnap victims?' It's not really a question, though his voice goes up at the end.

'What if these bandits were the ones who cleared the outlier holdings? Took travellers from the road. Anyone else they could find. Didn't take them to Calder, but here. For my cousin's purposes.'

'What might those be?'

'This much blood and flesh? If I'm right about what happened here. This much… currency to pay the red price? Gods, Edgar, what's she going to do with it all?' But Edgar doesn't have an answer or isn't game to venture one.

The walk back to Edgar's wagon is silent, except for the few moments when my stomach rebels and I have to throw up everything I ate for breakfast and whatever else my innards can find. The gentleman-merchant holds my hair. Up on the bench seat, he gathers the reins but doesn't do anything with them, just stares. At the horses, their ears, the road away and the road that returns to Silverton.

'You said… when you were drunk, you said there was a river out of its course. A waterfall over by the Havards' farm?' He nods. 'What if that was her 'prentice work? To see what she *could* do? How many other spots has she shifted the earth, the waters, levelled mountains, then created her own new ones?'

'Wouldn't that use up all the currency?'

'We don't know how much she's got. How long she's been… storing it.' I bury my face in my hands. 'We have to go back, Edgar. *I* have to go back.'

He gives a great sigh, the sort you give to an idiot who's suggested something monumentally idiotic. But he shakes the reins, clicks his tongue and turns the horses in the right direction.

After a while, I find my voice again. 'Edgar?'

'Hmmm?'

'Have you ever heard any tales of the Witches' War?'

He gives me a sidelong look, considering, and then begins to speak.

'I only know what I was told by my old granny, who'd heard it from her granny, who'd heard it from – well, you know. A tale passed along forever.' Edgar gees the horses along, a little faster. 'I think it's one of those stories that got lost – repressed. Repeating it got you burned or hung or drowned, so it's become a whisper, only shared in the darkness.'

He presses his lips together, as if considering. Only by the greatest restraint do I stop myself from saying, *Well?*

37

Once upon a time, there were three women.

No 'once there was and there was not'.

Their names are lost but they most definitely were.

And they began as neglected wives and ended as destroyers of the world.

But first: the beginning.

From their very cradles, they could do things. Make things so or otherwise, as was their will. They might have been sisters, or not. It made their mother – or mothers – fearful, for she or they knew all too well what happened to girls with wills of their own. She – or they – tried to teach those daughters to hide what they were, what they could do. Urged them never to let a man know that they were cleverer, stronger, had a power that couldn't be shared or taken, tamed or trammelled. Don't laugh too loudly, don't speak too loudly, don't express a contradictory opinion. She – they – taught that independence would be the ruination of them. Tried to teach that all they were, and all they could be, should be suppressed in the hunt for a husband – and the only safety in the world was under the hand of one of those – and even after said husband had been acquired, never let him see the truth of you.

The risk was too great.

The lessons were all the same, the mothers all sang an identical mournful tune. Passed the same wisdom of self-preservation, self-negation.

And for many years, the women-daughters-sisters listened, or tried to. Did well enough at it – this untruth to self – that they all found husbands with position and sufficient gold to make life comfortable. They had children, gave their husbands sons, and tried to teach their own daughters the same lessons they'd been given.

Except the words began to stick in their throats, gluggy as badly made bread. Poisonous as ergot. Strangling as a hand around the neck.

So, they began to use new words, sing new songs, teach new lessons.

That a woman's only true value was the one she held for herself.

And they began to show their magic without fear. Began to change things, opinions, people, places, the very world.

But there was resistance.

Of course there was.

They were hunted, pursued like foxes from one safe place to another until there was nowhere left to hide. Nothing except their power between them and death at the hands of the church and all its men. Even Abbesses had hidden them, in their time, though that risked the dissolution of their abbeys and death for the inhabitants. Ordinary women helped them along their way, women high- and low-born. Not all women – some didn't want change, didn't want the uncertainty that came with it. Liked having their lives run for them – it never occurred to them they weren't being asked to give that up, just that some women didn't want masters. Should be given the choice.

Any road, they came to an end, these three who might have been sisters. To a place called Bittersweet Bay and there they made their stand. They released the greatest magics they could conjure, into the sky and the earth and the sea. They left an imprint in every woman who lived, and some of the men. Both gifts and plagues were thus freed. They changed the world forever, marked it no matter what else might happen to them.

The men who'd hunted them did not survive, which caused them little grief, but there were others caught in the wave of destruction to whom the witches wouldn't have wished ill. They could, at that moment, have stepped into the breach they'd caused in existence, made themselves gods. But they knew, each of them, that power corrupts, and when you feel like a god – or a need to be one – that's the time to step back from whatever you're doing.

They took hold of the strands of darkness and light they'd loosed and began to weave. Breathing life into what both was and was not between their fingers they created something new.

But there was no place for them after what they'd done. Even though they fixed it – mended it, amended it, stitched everything back together – they'd done such a thing that the earth would no longer hold them.

And so, they went to a place called The Barrow. And so, they went beneath.

Edgar's voice trails away, and I can't quite tell how I feel about the tale. There's a yearning, certainly, for it to be true; and a fear also. It dovetails, in places, with the shorter version Nia told at dinner that night – oh, how long ago it feels! How did she finish it? *'And, sometimes, if a woman is in need, if she is cunning and clever, if she is quiet enough to hear the red thread in her veins, she might just be able to find those witches who went beneath.'* Edgar's version, however, departs from that other, the one we first heard from Aunt Hebe – this one contains warnings.

We rattle over a stone bridge, past a travellers' hut for those caught on the road overnight. The door's ajar and two grey squirrels scamper out. The stream sounds loud, the flood fuller than it should be when everything is beginning to slow down with ice... I think about the river put out of its course by an unknown force, about the displacement of so much earth back at the cottage of the Three Brothers Bear, of the smell of cooked flesh and blood.

'What are you thinking, Ellie Briar?'

'I'm thinking about the amount of blood the three who went beneath had to spill for the sort of magic in that story.' I rub my face. 'I'm thinking about the oceans of crimson they paid in tithe. I'm thinking that was why the world couldn't – wouldn't – hold them anymore.'

'And?'

'And while I'm sure much less was needed to put a river out of its course, to cause a crater like the one we left, I'm also sure it's enough to have Audra either feeling like a god or needing to be one.' I imagine my cousin as she was in the cells below the townhall, a halo of fire around her, a smile on her lips; I add lightning at her fingertips.

'Do you think she'll step back from the edge on her own?'

'Do you know any other witches, Edgar?'

'None like you. Most have to hide themselves at one point or another, just to survive. But you lot have been able to grow wild as you will even with occasional supervision. Mostly, you're without fear – the sort of constant fear others are branded by. So, no. I don't think your cousin'll step back on her own.'

To Edgar's consternation, I shout for Sandor and Gisela. My voice rings through the trees and the clear cold air. Neither appears, which suggests the distance remains too great for a simple calling, even with a bond of blood, and I don't have what's needed for a proper summoning.

'Sorry,' I say to Edgar, 'just testing a theory.'

'And here's me thinking you're the sanest one of the lot.'

'Rude.'

'What are you going to do when you get back?'

'Don't you mean *we*?'

'Nope. *You*. I'm out of there as soon as I return you where I found you.'

'Unfriendly.'

'Well?'

'Honestly? No idea.' I settle against the seat, wedge myself into the curve of the wagon body and let the gentle rattling motion lull me. Seems like a good idea to sleep while I can.

* * *

I think I wake in darkness, but then I realise I've not woken at all.

I'm at the top of a stone staircase, my feet bare and cold, on steps circling down and down and down. I take careful quiet paces. Below: three figures, tall and straight in the manner of those who refuse to bow to time. Sitting amongst a mess of books and papers scattered across myriad desks and shelves, the soft lights of lanterns floating in the air around them. Black dresses, white hair, white feathery eyebrows. The closer I get, the clearer they are: women, old. Palest beldams who've seen no sun since they went beneath – for surely this is them. Those ones, those women, the witches, the Three Who Changed Everything.

And though I'm trying so hard to be silent, they glance up, all at once.

'Look at you, hollow thing,' one says.

'How strange! Not seen one of those in years,' chimes the other.

'Not empty, sisters. No. She has her purpose… not yet fulfilled.'

'Why are you waiting, child?' calls one. 'Come down to us.'

'We can help, if you are in need.'

One, two, three reaching up towards me, arms and fingers lengthening, lengthening, lengthening. 'Let us fill you with—'

And that's when I wake.

Startled and shouting and lashing out, bursting with fear of becoming something else, something I don't recognise, something that's not me – becoming something I've always thought I longed to be.

'Bad dreams?' asks Edgar after we both calm down.

'The worst,' I say, and wonder if that's true or not, because there's the tiniest feeling that I might have thrown away something I needed.

Audra wouldn't have hesitated to take what was offered. She'd have gone straight to them, taken it as if it was her due. Probably, she'd have demanded more.

38

It's well and truly dark by the time Edgar leaves me in roughly the same spot where he collected me a little over twenty-four hours ago. We sit for a while, the horses snorting gently, me reluctant to go and do what I must. Perhaps he just as reluctant to let me go. Finally, I can't put it off any longer.

My boots touch the earth and it feels like a mistake. Like I should climb up again and tell Edgar he's got a new business partner and let's head towards wherever is furthest from Silverton and its witches. It's not too late.

Except it *is* too late.

My cousin – my cousins – are my responsibility.

Silverton is my responsibility.

To save whoever I can.

However I can.

I reach up, pat Edgar's hands. 'Thank you for helping. For taking me away and bringing me back. I hope to see you again.'

'Take care, Ellie Briar, and don't get yourself killed. We don't want another witches' war.' He whips up the horses, tearing away into the black with a terrible clatter I'd have preferred hadn't been made.

The night's moonless or close to and I can barely see the path as I make my way through the trees. Mind you, if anyone's out seeking me – if Audra thinks I'd be stupid enough to still be in the vicinity – oh, and look! I am! – then her search parties will have lanterns, and I'll see them before they see me. As long as I don't trip and break a leg for someone to find in the morning. Or not be found at all, dying in the forest. Alone.

Well, that was cheerful.

When I get to Ezekiel's cottage, I crouch in the woods for a while, watching for any sign of an ambush, someone lying in wait. But unless Huw told them, no one would know I've been using this place as a base. If anything, they'd keep an eye on the Widow Wilson's abode – the scene of my "crime". I'm as still and quiet as I've ever been, but there's nothing, no one moving.

I creep from the tree line and around to the front door, let myself in, then draw all the curtains tight. Deprived of the tinderbox on my chatelaine, I have to rummage through the kitchen drawers to find Ezekiel's old fire-steel; soon I've a single candle lit. It's cold and I'd dearly love a fire, but it feels like too much of a risk, so I content myself with wrapping Huw's cloak more tightly around me and finding a not-too-musty-not-too-Ezekiely blanket. In the kitchen is the basket intended for the Widow Wilson; the bread's stale but there's cheese and slices of meat that are fine in the cold weather, a fruit pie, and the bottle of lemon-whiskey. I eat, curl into Ezekiel's old armchair, trying to make myself as small as I can, and finally call for Sandor once more.

My very great-great-grandsire appears immediately, staring at me in surprise. 'That was swift.'

'And I missed you too.' I run a hand through my hair. 'What's been happening?'

He lifts a finger, twitches it, and one of the kitchen chairs scratches its way along the floor to stop in front of me. Sandor sits. 'Not a great deal, as far as I can tell. Well, with the living.'

'And the dead? The chair-moving is impressive.'

'Well, everyone's very unhappy with our speaker leaving us in the lurch.'

'You did tell them why, didn't you?'

'Of course. And I assured them you'd be returning just as soon as you could, and oh, what's a few more days after all these years?'

'But still?'

'Still. Lucky for your cousin Audra none of us can get near her.'

'Her necklace – black tourmaline. Keeps your kind at bay.'

'Impolite.' He shakes his head. 'That explains a lot.'

'What about the other ghosts?'

He rolls his eyes. 'Well, they're haunting as they've never been able to. Haunting Silverton with a vengeance. Their own families, their enemies, anyone they feel hard done by, or just don't like the look of. Rattling doors and throwing furniture around. Sitting in pantries until the milk sours and the flour develops weevils. Turning meat into maggots.'

'Unpleasant. How many are left for me to—?'

'About twenty? Thirty? They're disappearing when I get near…'

'And they won't listen to you?'

'No. My stocks are very low; after all my promises, after the majority got to go to their rest – well, those left behind aren't feeling very understanding.'

'Well, I can't do anything about that until I get my book and ink back.' I bite my lip in thought. 'If you can, tell them to keep it up, don't tell them to be reasonable. Oh, no actual damage to people, please, but have them keep the chaos rolling.'

'Why?' He looks frustrated.

'I know it goes against your every headmasterly instinct, but even though the phantoms can't get near Audra, they're creating havoc for the people who depend on her to protect them. They'll be complaining long and loud and that's going to distract her. See if they'll do their worst in the homes of the rich and influential.' I grin at the thought. 'Has she stopped searching for me?'

'I've not seen any hunters about since midday. I think she decided you weren't so foolish as to remain.'

'Little does she know how foolish I am,' I mutter. 'And Huw? Is he safe?'

'He's still locked up if that's what you mean. He said Audra considers him to be "misguided" and believes that a few days in isolation contemplating his sins will do them both good.'

'He can hear you now?'

'He seemed quite sensitive before, and growing more so. Not everyone is, Ellie. You've almost dismantled Gilly's spell, and it's most definitely continued to erode in the last day.'

'And Eira and Nia?'

'I've only seen them at a distance – always in the company of the Briar Witch, so I can't get any closer.'

And I wonder if she's keeping them near for a reason. If Nia's managed to keep her mouth closed. If Eira's avoided suspicion. I share what Edgar and I discovered, the tinker's tale of the Witches' War, of Audra's amassing of power, and that I don't truly know what she's going to do with it. But that it will be awful. 'I need to speak to Eira.'

'You can't go to the Briar House – there are guards posted outside.'

'No, I can't. But I suspect Eira isn't there either.'

* * *

Primrose Cottage looks dark and deserted in the hour just before dawn, except when I creep to the door, I spot a crack of light from lanterns inside. I knock very quietly and wait. I knock again. And a third time, cursing under my breath. At last, there's a creak and Sally's face appears. As soon as she sees me, bless her, she drags me inside, then re-engages the lock.

Standing in the middle of the parlour, Eira's anxiously wringing her hands. At the sight of me, she says, 'No!' and rushes over to grab me in the hardest hug.

'You're not meant to be here! It's not safe – gods, she was so angry when she found you gone! Oh, Ellie, why didn't you stay away?' Eira's weeping, making it hard to follow, but the gist is clear. I'm in trouble.

'I know, I know, but I couldn't. Audra's going to do something, Eira. Something terrible.'

'What?'

'I don't really know.' Quickly, I tell her everything: what I know, what I suspect, and what I need to do right now. I warn her to brace herself, as this won't be easy to see. And then I call on Gisela. I call on Gisela because if anything happens to me, someone else needs to know as much as I do.

I know Eira saw our grandmother's dead body, helped to

373

wash and dress her, was so careful to make sure that her hair was free of congealed blood, that the terrible wound in Gisela's head was concealed, and then briefly in the jail. But that's not how Gisela's appearing in her afterlife, and if anything, she looks worse than when I last saw her.

Sally turns positively green, staring at Gisela in her little parlour; Eira's positively pallid.

'Sally, why don't you go to bed? No need for you to be here,' I say it gently, but don't know if it sounds that way. Sally looks to Eira for permission – not wanting to desert her lover – and Eira nods. I remember the pouch in my pocket; even the smallest piece of tourmaline could interfere with the ghosts. 'Oh, Sally, put this somewhere safe, please.'

'Audra's threatened her,' my cousin says after Sally disappears down the short hallway. 'Told me not to see Sally, to stay at home.'

'Obedience runs in the family, I can see.' I grin in spite of everything.

'Grandmamma,' says Eira longingly, and tries to take Gisela in her arms. All it does is interrupt the ghost's being, wafting it about like wet fog. Eira steps back and Gisela strokes a hand down my cousin's face, as if that might feel the same.

'Gisela,' I say, demanding her attention. 'You know what Audra's planning?'

She nods. 'Lodellan. The cathedral city. The very home of the church. She wants to destroy it.'

It's not hard to understand the urge, given what happened to her mother at the hands of a god-hound. But that Audra, our bright beautiful Audra, should have thought it reasonable to buy the means to do so at the cost of all those lives. All that blood, all the flesh and bone. A monstrous magical rendering of all those souls were, could be and would have been.

'How?' Eira and I cry at the same moment.

'She believes she can use the menhirs to do so. Use them to focus and direct the power she's been amassing.' Gisela has a hand to her chest, as if it hurts, as if her heart's bothering her. I suppose it is.

'Oh. Gods,' says Eira, and half-sits, half-collapses onto the couch.

'What?' I say louder than I should.

'Audra's taking the children from the Adalind's Row School on a picnic in the woods today. As a treat.'

She's had the blood of children before – the outliers' offspring – she'd have noticed the difference. Innocent blood isn't necessarily more powerful, but it's more… malleable, suggestible, adaptable. Audra's trying magic that's not been done before – or at least not by us, not by any witch since the Witches' War – and the children's blood will be compliant and flexible to her commands.

'She won't have them yet, it's hardly even dawn. I'll go to the school now, tell Rowella to hide the children.' I'm thinking fast, trying not to panic, trying to organise, to be a good steward. 'Eira, get Nia and Huw. Bring them here. I'll return soon. Then we can work out what to do next.'

'But, Ellie—'

'Don't argue with me – just do it! I'll need both you and Nia, and you might not like what I'm going to ask.'

* * *

So, I'm running through the town with less caution than I probably should, but I don't think anyone's going to stop me.

From inside the houses I pass I can hear the sounds of crashing and breaking, sobbing and screaming and shouting. The few folk outside are being dived at by phantoms pulling horrible faces and making terrible noises. The living and the dead are too busy to notice me.

I swiftly reach Adalind's Row and bear down on the schoolyard and the little teacher's cottage in the grounds. Except I notice the door to the schoolhouse is open despite the very early hour, so I change direction.

Into the classroom with its rows of desks and chairs, maps and charts on the walls, students' artwork, bookshelves, a large blackboard up the front, just behind the teacher's desk. High windows, light and airy. No sound except a rhythmic, frantic *thud-thud-thud* from somewhere further inside. Through the doorway that leads into the backroom, where oddments are stored – and several overturned picnic baskets – I find another door, a cupboard, a key in the lock. I twist it, open the door, and Rowella Bisbee tumbles out. Forehead and nose bloodied, but she's very much alive. And very much angry.

'Where's—'

'Audra! That bitch hit me! Shoved me in there!'

'Why are you here so early?'

'She asked me to have them ready before dawn so they could see the sunrise. Said it would be perfect for the stories she planned to tell.' Rowella spits blood on the floor as I try to wipe her face with my sleeve. I bet they didn't teach that at Mater Hardgrace's. 'I was checking the baskets out here, and she said she'd take them on her own. I asked why, and she just hit me. Threw me in the cupboard.'

376

Didn't kill her though. Stopped at that. Which tells me Audra's either panicking, or perhaps being wise. If she wants the children to follow her willingly and quietly – who could make the forest more magical than a pretty witch who tells you fairy stories – then killing their teacher in front of them would be counter-productive. But having Miss Bisbee around would interfere with her plans.

Now, Audra is somewhere in the dark woods, fifty trusting children in tow, all of them filled with innocent new blood – the shiniest, richest coin with which one might pay the red price.

'Go to Primrose Cottage, tell Eira what's happened. She'll know what to do.'

And then I set off at a run yet again.

39

Huw's god-hound cloak billows behind me like wings, the holly baton in the pocket *thud-thud-thudding* against my side. I tear though the town, past laughing-howling ghosts and terrified folk. Into the woods, doing my best to avoid roots and branches and hollows. Taking the trails and roads, as Audra would have had to do with the children, will be too slow. A shortcut is my best chance of getting to the stone circle in time. I hope.

A long time ago, Maud told me she had a theory about the menhirs and I, of course, had shared it with my bright beautiful cousin on one of those nights when we talked about Hebe and magic and stories, and how one day Audra would be the Briar Witch. Everything, Maud said, had its own energy that radiated outwards or drew inwards – like lodestones. Witches have more – or different – energy than most, and the leeches felt it too keenly, it interfered with their own, repelling them. Magic is energy too, or the use of it, a kind of a transmission. The standing stones, filled with the energy still in the bodies of the Briar Witches, radiated outwards. Pushed the things of the Darklands back, away. The stones transmit magic and potency just as illnesses are transmitted from body to body. Just as the black tourmaline keeps the ghosts at bay.

Audra has gathered so much energy into herself, has bought it with a red price paid for by others. And she has those children, all that innocent blood so full of puissance. The circle, each stone a Briar Witch, the most powerful of us, even in death. If Audra uses it to send a burst of that energy – that magic, that sheer dark power coming as it does from murder and hate and fear – towards Lodellan, what damage might she do?

The first salvo in her new Witches' War…

I think back to that day in the library, to the map on her desk marked in red as she wrote new spells in her grimoire. The map to help her locate her objective – more than one city encircled too, but I didn't pay sufficient attention. But I imagine all those burning buildings, the tumbled cathedral façade, limbs poking from beneath fallen masonry, and the wailing chorus of terror and pain. The city that's stood for so long, resisted invaders and armies, avaricious princes and enraged mother superiors who marched their Battle Abbey nuns against it. All its inhabitants, the innocent as well as the guilty, the sinned-against and the sinning.

And if Audra does this, uses the standing stones for such a purpose, what might happen to *them*? What if the circle's destroyed? If the border no longer holds and the creatures of the Darklands can pour through? All those voracious Leech Lords who'll view the folk of the lands beyond as their own, as so much cattle? The lands as new feeding grounds.

And here's me, good-for-nothing, to stand in the way of the Briar Witch.

No magic.

No craft.

Not even an object imbued with enchantment, something I've bought from an actual witch. Here's me with nothing but a holly baton, now unsheathed, rushing onward.

This is quite high on my list of Very Bad Ideas.

On the clear winter air I can hear children's voices. Almost there. They sound… concerned. I slow down, making less noise as I veer away from the great wooden gate, pick my way through the clever little maze until I'm just outside the circle, peering between two trees. Trying to get my breathing – my gasping – under control. The children are huddled (crammed) in the circle, some at its edge, hands raised and pressed hard against a wall of light – barely visible but for an iridescent shimmer.

'Be calm, little ones,' comes Audra's ringing tone, pure as a crystal bell. 'It won't take long and it won't hurt at all, and you'll be part of something wonderful.'

The children, however, don't believe her. Several begin crying, wailing and howling. The older ones are banging on the walls of their prison and shouting. The glimmering light bulges out under the pressure but doesn't break.

I finally spot my cousin, on the far side of the clearing. Floating in front of her is her grimoire and a piece of yellow parchment. The map. And at her waist, my silver chatelaine – another insult to injury.

I sidle in her direction. I was rather hoping to sneak up and whack her over the head, but I fear I've got less time than required. I step out from the tree line and call, 'Audra!'

She looks up, startled. The dome over the children wavers. She's never been good at doing several things at once. 'Ellie. You should have stayed away.'

'What are you doing? So much blood, Audra. *Why* are you doing this?'

'Oh, Ellie. Aren't you tired? Tired of living like this? Mired in one place, subject to the will of some god-hound scrutinising our every action? Tired of doing nothing more than ministering to the sick and the stupid? Aren't you tired of the incessant *whining*?' She bares her teeth. 'Aren't you tired of living in fear? Even you, hollow thing that you are?'

That stings because of all the cousins, Audra has been the one who'd never thrown my lack at me. Was ever kind. Mostly. But, I suppose, that was all a lie; a means of getting me onside, making me loyal.

Her tone changes, becomes persuasive. 'Ellie, if the church doesn't exist, we aren't in danger. No other witch or ordinary woman ever gets burned again! Someone like my mother isn't murdered by her own father.'

And I can't say she's wrong. I can't say that the idea's not tempting. But I'm also aware that our grandmother burned her own sister. That Audra was prepared to do that to me. That not all monsters belong to the church. 'Audra, your mother was going to murder a child.' At that the howling from the circle gets louder. 'Your mother had lost any sense of right and wrong – of reality.'

'Everything demands a price, Ellie. And they're sheep.' She laughs, gestures to the milling progeny corralled in her trap. 'Look at them, my little lambs to the slaughter. All fodder for the greater good.'

'But, Audra, there will still be god-hounds. There will still be a church – they'll regroup elsewhere. And they might not know it's you at first, but they'll find out, and then they'll come.'

'Let them! This is just the first strike, Ellie!'

'Then what? Another Witches' War?'

'Yes! Only the witches will survive!'

'What about me, Audra? I'm no witch. And you're assuming that every other witch in existence would join you? You've fed off these fairy tales and fables Hebe told you, and they've turned your mind. The Three themselves – they knew they'd gone too far. Why do you think they went beneath?'

'I need you, Ellie! My general! Didn't Gisela always say that's what you were? A little general?' Her tone's wheedling now, trying to convince me, but I can also hear that note of scorn. She thinks she'll get her way in this as in all things. The moment my back is turned she'll have a knife in it.

I think of Sandor and Edgar, observing that we've grown differently, here, with the freedom to practise witchcraft without hiding it. 'You've lived in one place all your life – you've no experience of anything beyond Silverton. Nothing beyond your own wishes that are always satisfied. You just want to impose your own will on the world and pretend you're a saviour. You're a spoiled child, selfish and wilful. You're nothing new. Nothing special. A murderous brat.'

All of this has the desired effect.

Audra, enraged, steps away from her grimoire and map (both drop a little in the air as her concentration dilutes) and comes towards me. From the corner of my eye, I can see the shimmering dome waver again, the top of it seeming to melt. But I'm careful not to let Audra see me looking. I move back towards the woods so she's following me, not noticing what she's done.

However, fire's sparking at her fingertips and there's a golden aura around my beautiful cousin, leaping up into that halo once again. It's building, building, building until her fists are balls of crackling flame, and she raises them towards me – and I, hoping I've not miscalculated, run at her like a madwoman.

As I get nearer, the fire begins to splutter, but doesn't entirely extinguish. I raise the magic-dampening holly baton and swing it at her. She ducks, I miss, and she kicks me in the stomach. I'm on my arse, staring up, gasping for breath, then she's looming over me, trying to reignite her flames, but not understanding what I hold, what's happening.

Another solution is called for: Audra pulls the intricate silver knife, the one she uses each day for the red price, from her belt. And my cousin isn't beautiful anymore. Every fragment of hatred and madness inside of her is shining through the skin of her face, and she's terrifying.

The knife rises higher and higher, suspended for a second, then begins its descent.

And I think I'm done.

I'm dead and I haven't managed to fix anything, change anything, and I'm as useless and hollow as they all say.

Then: a whooshing sound.

Then: a thwack.

Then: Audra flying backwards, her knife tumbling away.

I sit up, roll to my feet, acting on instinct and fear, not much thought. My gut still aches though. I rush to her, grab the fallen dagger, pull at the tourmaline necklace around her throat and feel the chain snap. I throw it as far into the woods as I can, then tug the great ruby ring from her finger – the symbol of the

Briar Witch. I'm standing above her, brandishing the dagger, but I realise that I don't need to.

An arrow sticks out of her chest, blood welling around it, Audra coughing red. And changing: feathers, a tawny lace pattern, limned with gold that matches the eyes. A wide wingspan, stretching, shrieking, trying to rise. Then, back to her human form, golden hair, mad blue gaze, beautiful face twisted in pain. The arrow's fletchings are Nia's usual red and black, but the point has been specially crafted from Audra's own shifter feather – the feather I found clutched in Dai's dead hand. The owl that's been drifting around Silverton for as long as I can recall. Audra repeating Gisela's exact words to me that day she spoke to me about Dai – 'He's a boy, Ellie, and not fit to marry a Briar' – the library window left open, the owl circling back to eavesdrop when we were no longer paying attention. The form Audra took to get her swiftly to and from the outlier farms and the bandits' hideaway at the cottage of the Three Brothers Bear, and then back again without anyone noticing her absence. Shifters, most likely to be caught.

She glares up at me. 'You bitch, Ellie, you fucking bitch. You should have been beside me, helping me. You should have been loyal.'

'You had everything, Audra! Everything! And it still wasn't enough. You were trusted to care for our people and instead you murdered them! For what? An insane dream, a hunger for power?' I wrap a hand around her fine jaw and squeeze until she squeaks; when she makes that noise I come back to myself. Remember what I'm here to do. What I'm duty-bound and obligated to do. That I must be better than her. I let her go.

Rowella Bisbee's voice makes me turn; she's in the middle of the menhirs, soothing the children whose wails have become whimpers. Huw's just behind Eira, and Nia, who stands with her bow still raised. Frozen, as if in utter disbelief of what she's done. I have to admit, I wasn't sure she'd do it either, but presumably the distress of having Audra use briar-tongue on her was sufficient motivation. Plus the murders. And the planned murders. And Gisela.

Huw strides over, holds me gently. He touches my face, the owl scratch on my cheek, strokes my hair away from my eyes. 'Are you – alright? As alright as you can be in the circumstances?'

For a few moments I just lean against him, nodding into the crook of his neck. 'But there's more needs doing. Be a dear and take the children back to Silverton? Keep an eye on Rowella, she looks a bit frail.'

Rowella's no such thing; she looks annoyed and concerned as she checks each and every child for damage, but she doesn't look frail. Huw gives me an exasperated look. 'Really? Do you think you need to lie to me? Now?'

'Sorry. Huw, would you please be so kind as to escort Rowella and the children back to town. There's witch business to be done and it's best you and they don't see it.'

'There, was that so hard?' He plants a kiss on my lips.

'Oh. Hide this.' I return his holly baton, re-sheathing it; don't need that weakening Eira or Nia. Huw surreptitiously slips it up his sleeve, then moves off to herd the school mistress and her charges out of the stone circle. The enchanted path will spit them out in the nicest way possible, onto the sloping road down towards Silverton and safety.

When they're gone and their voices can no longer be heard, Eira and Nia join me, and we stand together, looking upon the wreck of our bright, beautiful cousin.

'All that you could have been and done…' mourns Eira.

'Oh, shut up.' Audra coughs blood again.

Nia looks at me. 'What to do with her? Should Eira heal her?'

Instead of answering, I lean down, unhook my chatelaine from Audra's waist and pocket it. Then, I call for Gisela, vaguely worried that I might be too far away from town – but if she can't hear me here, where her bones lie, then something's very wrong indeed. And our grandmother obliges, not merely appearing but boiling up from the ground like an eruption. It's impressive to say the least, and my cousins gasp, even Eira who's seen it before – and especially Audra who's got more reason to fear Gisela than anyone.

I ask Eira, 'Did you bring the book?'

She holds up the blue and silver grimoire, hands it to me.

'Grandmamma?' I call, but Gisela is staring sadly at Audra. 'Grandmamma?'

'Yes, Ellie.'

'We need three for this – can you *use* me?'

Gisela blinks, realises what I mean, then nods. I think of Sandor sitting on Lowen Jernigan's lap, trying to take control of his body, and hope this will be more successful.

I slide the Briar Witch's ring onto my finger, the ruby gleaming like blood, touch the scar on my wrist as if it might ground me. Gisela steps up to me, then into me. It's all I can do to surrender control, to not fight her, but soon she settles. Nia and Eira lift Audra, carry her to the flat altar in the centre of the stones and lie her there. She looks terrified, but I don't bother to tell her it will all be fine. She's lost a lot of blood. She might still be saved if anyone had the will to do so. But to what end? Keeping her imprisoned in the cells? All that power locked within her? As if she wouldn't use it again? And as if the folk of Silverton would let her live with all that blood on her hands and soul. Let us let her remain alive after all she's done?

No, our own survival, the survival of the Briars, depends on what we do now. So, we ignore Audra's cries and pleas, much as she did those of her victims. Much as she did the begging of the schoolchildren she'd helped nurture only to think nothing of sacrificing them when it became convenient.

We take the same positions as for Gisela's funeral, and my grandmother's presence is like a cold fire inside me. All the magic I've never felt my entire life is pent up in my veins. It's bright daylight and it feels strange – it feels as if such an act should be done by moonlight, or by blackest darkness. But no. Not today.

The chanted spell rises, Gisela/I leading. Soon the standing stones begin their shifting, shuffling dance. Whirling monoliths, spinning, the grinding noise filling the clearing and drowning out Audra's final screams.

And when all is done, when the dance has stopped, when Gisela steps out of me, when we finally stand and stare around us, the thirteen standing stones now number fourteen.

40

Three weeks later, we celebrate Eira's marriage to Sally.

It begins as a subdued affair, until the wine begins to flow and the dancing starts, then the marquees on the common are a source of noise and warmth for a wintertide wedding.

Silverton itself has been subdued and occasionally outright hostile since Huw and Rowella returned the children that day. The young ones were always going to tell what had happened to them, what Audra had done, what they'd heard, even if they didn't really understand the finer details. Eira and Nia and I didn't try to deny it.

At a town meeting, we told them, quite truthfully, that we'd judged our cousin and carried out the sentence of death, burned her in the woods. That the Briars were sworn to protect the people of Silverton. And Audra had failed in her duty. I told them, also, that we three remaining Briars understood that trust had been broken – and that we held our position purely because of the trust they'd placed in us. That, if they felt they could no longer believe in us, rely on us, have faith in us, we would step aside.

It was a gamble, and Eira and Nia and I had argued it back and forth when I practised my speech in front of them. But in the end I prevailed and I was right. The memory of everything we'd done right for Silverton was too strong, or perhaps the idea of having to make their own decisions was too unappealing. Needless to say, we still have some way to go to regain their confidence, but in time I believe it will happen.

We did not tell them what Audra had done to the outliers. We did not tell them about the deal she had done with Lowen Jernigan and his nefarious dealings. We *did* tell them about the bandits; that they were responsible for the slaughter of their kin – there was only so much truth I was prepared to risk sharing. After wintertide, the outlier farms will be resettled. Rowella Bisbee has stood staunchly by us, telling how much we risked to stop Audra, that we stood between her and the children, and we were immovable.

Huw's been extremely helpful, smoothing over the ripples and ructions, being kind and rational. He is very well-liked, a son of Silverton returning home, and I do not think matters would have gone so well without him. He still shows no interest in entering the church and preaching ('Never part of my plan!'), which endears him to me no end.

When Edgar returns, we'll have a conversation about the importance of keeping what he knows to himself, but I doubt that's necessary. And I'll ask, once again, if he wants to settle down. Lowen Jernigan's big house is vacant, and he has no family or heirs.

And we've told half-truths about the ghosts because no one needs to know what Gilly Briar did all those years ago out of jealousy. Misguided wishing and wanting. Whatever it was, a combination of all that and more. We've said that Audra broke Gilly's spell, ruined the banishment and the spectral disturbances were a result of that. But the good news is that I can send any restless spirits on to their rest, and have done so. Silverton is quiet once more, and I've not had to make up elaborate or otherwise explanations of how I've found things – if anything, it's made folk a little more respectful, a little more wary of me.

The coldness of the ghosts, the numbness in my hand and mind, has lessened since the tally of those I deal with diminished, and I laid the remainder – all but one – including Lowen Jernigan, who remained as unpleasant in death as in life. But he went on his way willingly enough, and I had Eira bring the ring from amongst his things. We opened Sandor's death-bed and slipped it inside.

All black tourmaline amongst the Briars' jewellery has been deposited in the bank vault for safekeeping. Any new ghosts must be able to find me, when they need me, and ask for their forgiveness, restoration and rest. It was pure chance that Audra wore her mother's black tourmaline necklace; it kept her safe and she didn't even know it. Didn't know what it was for – it was just her talisman, her connection to Hebe, and through it, perhaps, passed their shared madness.

I've searched all the grimoires, torn out any page bearing a briar-tongue spell and cast it into the fire. I can't remove it from the world, but I can do my best to make sure no Briar ever uses it again. With Beres's permission, we reopened Deirdre's grave, then opened her mouth. Sure as sure can be, there was a thorn in her tongue. I removed it so she might sleep easy, so she might speak freely wherever she was, if she needed to, so she might sing to her son in his sleep.

And I found, when I checked the grimoires, a letter from Maud.

Addressed to me and concealed between the pages of her own book of shadows as it lay on the lectern in her old office. Telling me about Audra because she didn't trust her sister or great-niece.

Wise as it turned out. Written before Gisela fed her the rosehip tea. Why she thought to put it in a grimoire – a book I could not use and generally wouldn't have looked at – I'll never know. Perhaps it was as simple as a matter of timing, hearing someone coming along the corridor. Or perhaps she didn't care if I found it or not. In it, she confessed to not sending the last report to Lodellan. She says it's time for the Briars to change or die. I like to think we're changing.

I think about all those souls Audra consumed in her insanity. I think about the sheer number – that only Liv's ghost somehow remained, a shred of herself, through grief or rage or a combination of both at losing her life, children, husband. It wasn't her left, not really, just an essence. An urge and a fury, and a madness. A will to do harm, a fury even greater than Audra's will.

Yet there are days, too, when I ponder Audra's plan to destroy the princes of the church, all those who threaten us. There are days when I think she wasn't wrong in her desires, only in the execution. But most days I know it's not the solution. And I also know that, if I begin to feel like a god or become forgetful of the living, then I too must go beneath.

We said goodbye to Gisela the day after Audra took her place with the Briar Witches. Eira had asked her to stay for the wedding – a sad request – but our grandmother shook her head. Said she'd already stayed beyond her span. She said she was sorry for all she'd done. At my bidding, she confessed everything to Nia and Eira. Most of it Eira knew, but I wanted to make sure Nia heard it too, straight from the horse's mouth – so neither of them might ever turn on me and say I'd made it all up. I know it hurt my cousins, but what I'm starting to see is that truth and pain are very closely related – also cousins, if you will. I wrote my grandmother's name and sins in the Book of the Dead and took her hand, and we watched her fade away.

Now, Eira's staring at Sally like she's hung the moon, and they're dancing as if they'll never let go. Nia is in a huddle with Hari Carabhille; she'd been carrying on with him but kept it a secret from Gisela and the rest of us, knowing how our grandmother felt about his brother. She didn't want to get the sort of lecture I did. The day I saw her talking to Dai, she was trying to calm him down, a sense of obligation to her lover's brother. I listen for a while to the talk – rumour and gossip, to keep my finger on the pulse – then, when folk are a drink or two away from drunk, I slip back to the Briar House.

In the library, Sandor's staring up at the woodcut of himself and his Gilly-girl. 'How was it?'

'All went well. You could have come, you know.'

'A ghost hanging around a wedding? Hardly an auspicious beginning.'

My ever-so-great grandfather has remained, to see the last of his fellows sent off to their repose, to answer questions from me and my cousins, no matter how silly they might seem, as I write everything in a new book, *A Guide to Ghosts* – it's a working title. And in these weeks, I've been struck again by how different our lives might have been if we'd had someone like him rather than Tobias. How Audra might have turned out if her mother hadn't been burned; whether Sandor's presence might have mitigated Hebe's madness after the plague, and the influence she had on her daughter.

'And you, Ellie Briar,' he asks, 'will you be well?'

I lean against the desk, look down at the ruby ring, which feels very heavy on my finger, and recall how I'd thought Audra seemed to struggle under its weight. I understand better now. This was Gisela's last decree – that I be the new Briar Witch. That no one was more fit than I. And neither Nia nor Eira complained – both looked fairly relieved, in fact.

'I think I shall be,' and I'm glad for Huw, glad for my cousins. Glad they're here for counsel and support.

'Then, I do believe it's time for me to go,' my very great-grandsire says with a sigh.

'Must you? Can't you stay a little longer?'

'I must, I must, I simply must,' he sings, then his smile fades as he drifts over to stand in front of me. 'I've been here so long, Ellie, I'm so very tired. I did what I set out to do. Haven't I earned my rest?'

'Yes, Sandor Briar, yes, you have.'

'Then, my dearest girl, where is your great book? It's time to hear my confession.'

And in truth I'd not thought of that. I'd not thought that this man who's been so helpful to myself and others would have anything to confess. Anything to keep him here beyond a sense of duty to those in need, the aimless frightened dead.

I take my seat, open the book to where the last name can be seen in my neat handwriting: *Gisela Briar (Murder – sororicide – and False Witness)*. Taking up the pen, dipping it in the ink, I write: *Sandor Briar*, then look expectantly across at him, now seated in the armchair Maud used so many times when speaking with Gisela.

'Murder.'

My stomach drops – even though recent events have shown a family proclivity for such activity. Including, I suppose, myself, having entombed Audra alive in a block of stone. I clear my throat. 'Who did you kill, Sandor?'

'My Gilly-girl. My darling wife.' He holds up a finger to forestall questions. 'When first Hilla died, I didn't know what Gilly had done. The bargain she'd made with the other witch, the price she'd paid for it. I thought Hilla had simply become depressed, unhinged by her work as a speaker. But the day came when our darling daughter Bea could no longer keep the knowledge of what her mother had done from me. She'd held Gilly's secrets, as one witch does another's, but…' He raises his hands as if in prayer, or perhaps weighing his options. 'She could no longer bear the guilt of what had happened, and she told me at last.'

'Sandor—'

'You *must* let me tell this. I had loved my Gilly-girl for so long, thought we were true to each other, united. Proud parents. Devoted spouses. I knew she still struggled with being *ordinary*. But to do what she did… to steal from Hilla the very thing that made her take breath, made the world turn for her… to do it from spite and jealousy…'

'Sandor—'

'I went to the library – here, I came here that dreadful day and I… I don't recall what I did – I don't want to – but I only know that my Gilly was dead when next I came back to myself.'

I swallow, write *Murder – uxoricide* by his name, and the date. 'You could have told me from the first, Sandor. You *should* have been honest with me.'

'Yes.' He nods. 'I should. But I didn't know you, Ellie Briar.

394

I didn't truly know enough about you, besides the times when I saw you growing up. In between the mists Gilly condemned us to. But then you were the only one to see us in hundreds of years. Our only chance. So, please forgive my overabundance of caution. My lies. And my murder.'

I think about all the things that have flowed from Gilly Briar and *her* lies. Her acts. Her murder of Hilla, intentional or not. I think about her life – and mine – without magic; I think about those long moments when Gisela's power flowed through me as the menhirs danced, and for such a brief time I knew what it was to be a true witch. Perhaps I understand her a little better than I thought.

I think of Sandor waiting three centuries and then remaining to ensure all the dead were safe at last. He's the oldest of the ghosts, has suffered the longest. He's done his penance. Again, I swallow.

'I forgive you, Sandor Briar.' And I offer my hand. He takes it, and for the slightest fraction of a second his palm against mine feels solid and warm and real.

Then he's gone, and there's a hole in me that a horse and cart might pass through.

I wonder about the future – how long we might live safely now that Huw is here, writing *his* reports and sending them back to his father.

I wonder what will happen when I'm deceased – will I or my cousins have a child to carry on this legacy? Is it likely? Possible? Or will it die out with me, leaving the dead in a terrible in-between once more? I don't know. At this moment it's too big to think about.

I wonder about the witches who went beneath, of what they might have given if I'd just had the courage to walk down those cold stone steps and take those long, grasping hands. And I wonder if, one day, I might try to find them. If I am in need. If I simply must know what they might make of me, or if I need their help to ensure the Briars survive. I reach for the scar on my wrist, then stop myself.

A knock pulls me out of head. Outside the windows, dusk has almost fallen. The door opens and a red-topped head pokes in. Huw grins.

'Come dancing.'

And for now, that is enough.

ACKNOWLEDGEMENTS

This book has had a long gestation (I mean, they all do, but this one especially). *The Briar Book of the Dead* started out as a novella way back in 2015, but I was never quite satisfied with it. I was awarded a Copyright Agency CREATE grant in 2016 to help turn it into a novel, which progressed matters, but again, it never felt quite right. It wasn't singing to me.

So, I let it lie fallow for a while (literal years). I wrote other mosaic collections in the world of Sourdough, then I wrote two full-length novels. I realised that my Briar witches were connected – how could I not have seen it in the first place?! – to the characters in my 2015 novella *Of Sorrow and Such*. That Patience Gideon, her Gilly-girl and the kindly Sandor still had parts to play, stories to finish.

I could finally hear the voices for my *Briar Book* characters. They'd changed their names, the setting was much clearer to me, the plot was bubbling like a potion in a cauldron. Ellie Briar was ready to step into the world, into the light, out of her family's shadow, and be seen and heard.

You can absolutely read and enjoy *Briar Book* on its own,

you don't need to read *Of Sorrow and Such*. But honestly, why wouldn't you want to? 😊

With gratitude as ever to my parents Betty and Peter, siblings Michelle and Roderick, housedads Ron and Stephen, my agent Meg Davis, to my wonderful editor Cath Trechman, to Hayley Shepherd for precision copyediting, to Julia Lloyd for yet another gorgeous cover, and the whole team at Titan for making me look like a far better writer than I am.

ABOUT THE AUTHOR

Angela Slatter is the author of the gothic fantasy novels *All the Murmuring Bones*, *The Path of Thorns*, *The Briar Book of the Dead* and the forthcoming *The Crimson Road* (Titan Books), and the supernatural crime novels *Vigil*, *Corpselight* and *Restoration* (Jo Fletcher Books). She's also written eleven short story collections, including *The Girl with No Hands and Other Tales*, *Sourdough and Other Stories*, *The Bitterwood Bible and Other Recountings*, and *A Feast of Sorrows: Stories*, and the novellas, *Of Sorrow and Such*, *Ripper* and *The Bone Lantern*.

Vigil was longlisted for the Dublin Literary Award in 2018, and Angela has won a World Fantasy Award, a British Fantasy Award, a Shirley Jackson Award, a Ditmar, two Australian Shadows Award and eight Aurealis Awards. *All the Murmuring Bones* was shortlisted for the Queensland Premier's Literary Awards' Book of the Year and the Shirley Jackson Award. Angela's short stories have appeared in Australian, UK and US Best Of anthologies. Her work has been translated into Bulgarian, Dutch, Chinese, Russian, Italian, Spanish, Japanese, Polish, Hungarian, Turkish, French and Romanian. Film rights have been optioned for her novelette 'Finnegan's Field'.

She has an MA and a PhD in Creative Writing, is a graduate of Clarion South 2009 and the Tin House Summer Writers Workshop 2006, and in 2013 she was awarded one of the inaugural Queensland Writers Fellowships. In 2016 Angela was the Established Writer-in-Residence at the Katharine Susannah Prichard Writers Centre in Perth. She has been awarded career development funding by Arts Queensland, the Copyright Agency and the Australia Council for the Arts.